CHARON'S CHILDREN

© ΕΥΣΤΑΘΙΑΔΗΣ GROUP 2007

ISBN: 978-960-226-619-9

EFSTATHIADIS GROUP S.A.
88 Drakontos Str.,
104 42 Athens
tel.: ++3210 5195 800,
fax: ++3210 5195 940
e-mail: info@efgroup.gr
www.efgroup.gr
GREECE

All rights reserved; no part of this publication may be
reproduced, stored in a retrieval system or transmitted,
in any form or by any means, electronic, mechanical,
photocopying, recording, orotherwise, without the prior
permission of Efstathiadis Group S.A.

Printed and bound in Greece

JACQUELINE DEMPSTER

CHARON'S CHILDREN

ΕΥΣΤΑΘΙΑΔΗΣ GROUP

NOTE

The characters referred to in 'Charon's Children' are purely fictional and are not intended to represent any real person either living or dead.

DEDICATION

I would like to dedicate "Charon's Children" to my son Graham who has accompanied me on every trip to Crete and Spinalonga and who has lived uncomplainingly with his mother's neglect during the writing of this story! Love always.

I would also like to dedicate the book to my parents, Patricia and Neil Dempster for their life long support and encouragement of both Graham and me in aspiring to greater things and making the most of our opportunities. Thank you Mum for taking the time to read the draft of this book. I hope you like the finished story and that it doesn't make you cry again!

Finally, this book is for the people who inspired it and whose presence I felt at many times during the writing - the people of Spinalonga, whose story should never be forgotten.

Jacqueline Dempster
February 2007

PROLOGUE

'She's dead! Gone. Just like that'. George Fitrakis' clammy hand shook as he took in the words that would change his life. The cockney voice on the other end became steadier, angrier, now accusing.

'You killed 'er. My Jenna's gone and it's all your fault. You sold her caustic soda mixed in with that coke you bastard. She died in fuckin' agony thanks to you. I'm gonna make sure you pay for this'. There was silence for a few moments. George didn't know how to respond. What could he say? Any attempt at regret would only be interpreted as an admission and anyway, what good was sorry now? The damage was well and truly done this time. As he held the phone to his ear, George could hear the other man sobbing brokenly, drawing thick sounding mucus up through his nostrils. Dave Hawkins' grief was all too real and raw for George to deal with, especially coming from such a rough diamond. Self preservation though was George's overriding emotion.

'She trusted you and now she's dead', Dave went on between sobs. 'Well, haven't you got anything to say?'

'I, I'm sorry mate. Look, I'll call you back in a minute. I've got to get my head round this' George replied helplessly.

'Oh you're gonna get your head round it soon enough mate. My next call is to the police and if they don't do something about you, I will'.

George thrust the receiver back on the cradle. He didn't want to listen to any more. He had to think and think quickly. His life was about to come crashing down around him and he knew he had to act now. He had collapsed on the sofa as Dave's first words resounded in his ears, the shock almost winding him as though the force of a fist had connected with his stomach. His reaction though wasn't caused by sorrow over the woman's death, despite his long acquaintance with her, but by the consequences which he knew must now follow. Sweat sprung out in beads on his forehead as panic gripped him. 'Got to think. What do I do? Where do I go? He stood up, moved towards his bedroom, turned in a circle, sat down again. Indecision and confusion competed with his attempts to think straight. Finally, he followed his instinct. Thinking would have to come later. He had to get away. Now.

And so it was, with adrenalin surging through his veins, his heart beating so hard it threatened to burst through the wall of his chest, George Fitrakis ran around his flat, gathering as many belongings as he could into a holdall. With every moment that passed, he was convinced that there would be a knock on the door demanding entry to arrest him and take away his freedom for a long time to come. That was something he could not contemplate. Finally, George was ready and he made for the door.

'Damn!' He turned back quickly, realising he would need his passport for this journey. 'Where is it?' He rifled through drawer after drawer, none of which yielded the important document which would assure his escape. 'Calm, got to stay calm', he told himself. 'In the filing cabinet. That's where it is. I remember now'. He exhaled in relief as he finally laid his shaking hands on the little red book.

The rest of that night was something of a haze. He had made no plans. He didn't know where he was going. All George knew was that he couldn't face the sorrow and disappointment of his parents when they discovered that his whole life had been a lie. His father's Greek pride would be destroyed, shame would be brought upon his parents who for all their wealth and standing in society would be vilified and ridiculed for the actions of their only son. The whole facade of their existence was about to come tumbling down and George, despite having chosen to distance himself from them in recent years, did not wish to be around to see the disappointment and the hurt which his actions would cause them.

The airport was quiet at that time of the morning. It was 3.30 a.m. and only a few passengers waited for flights now that the holiday season was over. Frantically, George surveyed the departures board and wondered where on earth he could go. It was fate that decided it for him. The first flight to leave was for Athens and he had just enough time to buy a ticket and get himself to the departure lounge. In that instant, he made up his mind. He would go from Athens to Crete where his father had been born and raised. George recalled happier days of his childhood when his father would speak of the beautiful island haven where respite and solace could always be found. He remembered the stories his father, with typical Greek exuberance, told him of all the myths and legends the island spawned. Tales of the half man, half bull which roamed the labyrinth at the Palace of Knossos and the mountains which, if looked at carefully, and at the right time of day, were shaped like the giant head of Zeus who had been born on the magnificent island of Crete.

From his father's stories, George knew that Crete would be a good place to lay low. He could travel around the island, losing himself in mountain villages until all the fuss died down. It would give him time to think. Pretty soon, no-one would remember who Jenna Hawkins was. She was just another addict. Probably wouldn't even make the news. People who died from drug abuse were ten a penny these days and there wasn't much sympathy for them. They'd close the book on her fairly quickly and maybe he could even return to England in a short time. She was probably better off now anyway, George thought to himself. She didn't have much of a life, with her run down Council house and her brute of a husband who drank away most of the housekeeping money which she hadn't blown on drugs. George comforted himself as he boarded the 737 that really, he had done the woman a favour. Calmed by that thought, he sipped a gin and tonic and settled down comfortably for the flight that would change the course of his life.

****

The wheels of the motor scooter spun as the engine, refusing to die, continued its low roar, the only noise breaking the silence so far below the mountain road from which it had flown.

The body, thrown several feet to the side of the scooter twitched and gave out the occasional low moan, meanwhile an old man no more than a kilometre away along the coastline stared in deep concentration out to sea, a satisfied, though not malicious smile playing about his lips. Moments later, flinging his head back, he stared heavenwards, searching the clouds as though seeking guidance.

As if summoned by the man, the clouds grew darker and more dense and a rare, but terrifying yet exquisite display of lightning accompanied by a fearsome crash of thunder rent the darkening skies. As though carefully orchestrated, the waves became wild and violent, lashing against the shore, soaking the oblivious old man to his knees. The pyrotechnic display moved towards the Dhikti Mountains, and simultaneously a gale sprang up from nowhere. Just a short distance away on a tiny island just off the coast of Elounda the elements gathered, creating an atmosphere so heavy and so gloomy, it seemed like another world.

The old man, in rapt attention to the elements, his arms held high above his head, palms facing upward, now bent his knees and sank to the ground as though in supplication. In his trance-like state, he mouthed a silent litany of words which appeared to cause the storm to abate. The skies, moving like a film on fast forward turned night to day in seconds.

It had been a long time, but the old man was ready once again to take on a voyage in the long forgotten, but time honoured manner. His masters had commanded him and he was ready to obey as he gathered his nets about him and waited for the moment to arrive.

"Fortress surrounded by the deep
Get thee from this ageless sleep
But whatever secrets hath thee keep
For this thirsty soil no more shall we weep"

ISLAND OF TEARS
William Ronald Hawkins

CHARON

A strange silence descended upon the landscape as the motor scooter skidded suddenly from the control of the rider who was thrown unceremoniously and violently over the rickety crash barrier contributing to, rather than saving the young man from his fate. His body, resembling a rag doll, part bounced, part rolled down the rocky abyss, his skin raked and clawed by stone and dry foliage, his bones making a sickening and audible cracking noise as they impacted against the ground.

The accident had happened so quickly that the young man had no time to contemplate the danger he had been in as he negotiated the hairpin bend on the ascending dual carriageway from Aghios Nikolaos towards the bright neon lights and playground of the rich, Elounda, on the island of Crete.

George's mind had been too occupied with his troubles and too intent on running away from them to consider that he shouldn't have stopped at the roadside taverna for a beer on an empty stomach or, with the over zealous confidence of the inebriated, to take the remainder of his journey at such speed. For the first time in a while, he experienced a real thrill, one which was not induced by a chemical substance, and he enjoyed the freedom, the exhilaration of the wind through his hair and the sun kissing his skin. For just a moment, he remembered what it was like to really live again and to find enjoyment in the simplest of pleasures which cost nothing. His speed increasing, he was able to appreciate the contrasting scenery of the menacing rocks below and the smooth glassiness of the sea, which sparkled with diamond brilliance as the sun danced about its surface. Sadly for George however, the moment didn't last for long. He glanced to his right and a momentary vertiginous sensation overcame him as the speed and height, combined with the alcohol now infusing his blood confused his senses and shattered his concentration. Losing control of the motor scooter, he tried in vain to slow down, but to no avail. The angle of the wheels became ever more acute and he found himself travelling at speed, low to the ground, fighting desperately with the machine to right himself and regain control. The fight however lost, the scooter skidded away from him and crashed into the barrier, the force throwing George and the cycle down the hillside. His mind uncomprehending and blank, he could do nothing but surrender himself to his fate. Perhaps the many shrines dotted along the roadside should have served as a reminder to him that this was a dangerous road, the little huts all dedicated to commemorate a lost loved one killed at this accident hotspot.

To George, the descent seemed to take a lifetime, everything in slow motion. Strangely, he felt no pain as his body scraped and cracked down the hillside and there was no anticipation or fear of death. His body, now in shock, seemed impervious to the violence of his fall and, if any thought did pass through his mind, it was calm and fatalistic. This was perhaps the irony of his life, the meting out of natural justice, the man made rules having been evaded thus far. His 'just desserts', 'what goes around comes around', these were the cliches which went fleetingly through his head. He was ready to accept his fate and in a way, he embraced the end. His final thought, as his body was halted by the sinewy branches of a bush, impaling themselves in his skin and scraping his eyes, was that death was just a blessed relief that would solve all of his problems. Comforted by the fact that his worries were over, George closed his eyes and the darkness enveloped him as consciousness slipped away.

For most people, to survive an accident such as George had endured, it would be regarded as nothing short of miraculous. For George however, as he slowly came to and painfully lifted himself from the tentacles of the bush and the bed of rubble on which he had come to rest, it was more a feeling of having been cheated. Initial bemusement gave way to disappointment as he realised he was still alive and suffering great pain, not just emotionally now, but also physical pain of the most excruciating kind. It took him several attempts to sit upright, gravel and stone clinging to his grazed and lacerated face, his limbs creaking and groaning as bone and muscle complained bitterly with each slight movement. Picking out pieces of the landscape from his skin and wiping his face with his ribboned shirt sleeve, George heaved in a gulp of air, straining further the ribs and muscles of his chest and let out a sob of despair. This was to be his punishment, he thought, he couldn't even achieve a fatal accident to release him from the ignominy and shame of his life. His energy depleted, the pain in his body and lack of food all now exacerbated his misery. It wasn't fair that he had lived. He had done something bad and he deserved to die, didn't he? It was even less fair that because of him, a poor, vulnerable woman had met her death and that perhaps there were others also about to meet their end. How could he go on living with that knowledge? He had come to Crete, hoping to run away, disappear, a fugitive from justice, a fugitive from his own self absorbed, selfish nature. Over the previous days he had realised however that he could never escape. He might run from the police, his family, his misanthropic life but he couldn't elude his mind, and the tricks it played on him. By day, self preservation had been his only concern, but by night, the accusing fingers of those he had harmed pointed and taunted him, wakening him with their screams, refusing to be forgotten.

With difficulty, resigning himself to life, George pulled himself together, his torrent of tears releasing in him some of the pain which had built inside. If only that pain had been more for those whose lives he had destroyed or damaged and less about his own self pity, perhaps what happened next would have been different. As it was however, his fate at the moment of his fall was sealed.

Despite the pain he was in, George was astonished that he was able to move after the battering he had endured. Strangely however, nothing appeared to be broken and he hauled himself unsteadily to his feet, intent, now that he realised he was still mobile, on continuing his journey to Elounda where he had hoped to hang out for a couple of days amongst the idle rich and experience some of the night life the town reputedly had to offer. He glanced upwards and could just see the main road above him. The world went on oblivious to the fact that he had taken a dive down the hillside and it occurred to him that had he been seriously injured, it was unlikely that anyone would have found him. Shading his eyes from the sun's glare, he gazed over the horizon. From here, he could just see the coastline and, in the distance, the silhouette of a town, the yachts in the harbour lining the skyline with tall masts and flapping sails. George reckoned he was only a couple of kilometres from Elounda and calculated that it was probably easier to follow the coastline than try to get back up the hillside and follow the main road. Either way, he wasn't sure if he had either the strength or dexterity to reach his destination at all. Stumbling along the uneven terrain, his clothes tattered and torn, the young man intermittently came upon one or other of his possessions which had been scattered along the Cretan hillside from his hastily packed bag. These he collected up and fortunately for him, he found his canvas holdall a little further along the route, still containing his passport and wallet, saving him from immediate destitution.

After what seemed like an eternity to George, his destination remained distant and elusive. Tired, and in pain, he could almost have believed it was nothing more than a mirage which would remain forever out of his reach. It was with some relief therefore when the outline of a white building, a little house, emerged from the trees ahead of him. As he approached, George saw a figure perched on a stool, hunched over something which he appeared to be working on. Drawing nearer he saw it was an old man, dressed in black shirt and trousers, his hair and beard both long, wild and unkempt. He appeared oblivious to George's approach as he neither stopped what he was doing, nor turned his attention from his work, which George could now see was mending a net. Without looking up, he barked,

"Kalimera sas", Good-day.

"Kalimera", George returned a little uncertainly. Despite his Greek roots, his Greek language was far from fluent.

"So, you have arrived at last. You took longer than I expected". The old man was brusque, angry even.

"I'm sorry Kyrie, you must be confusing me with someone else. I'm only here by chance. Are you expecting a visitor?" George looked around to see if anyone else was approaching but there was no-one as far as the eye could see. The old man did not respond however and continued silently with his work. He displayed no discomfort in his ill mannered silence and George shifted uncomfortably from one foot to the other, feeling awkward as he awaited some kind of response from the old man. Finally, the man put down his work and turned to face George, looking up at him from where he sat. He neither smiled, nor made any attempt to put George at his ease. For his part, George had the urge to turn tail and get away as quickly as he could from the shrivelled old man and yet, he felt unable to move. He was held in some sort of thrall as the man's steely, slate eyes seemed to pierce his very soul and read everything that was within. It occurred to George that through some strange, telepathic connection between the two of them the old man did indeed know exactly who he was and that somehow, he had been expecting him. It was as though the old man had the knowledge of ages coursing through his veins. Quite how George perceived this, he didn't know but it was as though pictures and voices flashed through his mind so quickly he could barely discern what was going on. As the man continued his icy regard, George felt a pain so intense rip through his head that he cried out, and fell to his knees. Flashes of bright light burst forth behind his eyes as images of his own life assaulted his senses, playing out scenes as if in a film. With each flash there was an explosion of pain.

In one moment, George was back in London, miserably departing the Stock Exchange where he had worked at his father's bidding and which had ended in his shameful dismissal. With the next flash, he was crouched in the corner of his bedroom, shivering, incoherent, helpless, his hands shaking as he arranged lines of white powder on the mirror in front of him. Then, a moment of euphoria as he pictured himself vacuuming up the powder into his nostrils and the feeling of being back in control washed over him. Next he was in a dingy pub taking small white envelopes from a man in a woolly hat. He was in control of his life and he was making a lot of money from people he despised. He had a comfortable life. Then came the darkest moments. Voices, the phone call from Dave Hawkins.

"You've killed her. You've killed Jenna".

George was fleeing from London. His broken parents were interviewed on the television. He had to get away. None of it was his fault was it? How could he have known the drugs were adulterated? That was the risk they took wasn't it?

"Stop it! In the name of God, please stop" George now cried out. He held his head in his hands. It was as though every artery in his brain was expanding and popping. As the pictures flashed through his mind, he had been riveted to the spot unable to move. He felt he had somehow been enchanted (though not in its pleasant sense) and for long moments as the scenes of his life played out, he was forced to watch, to face up to it, impotent and immobile. The old man meanwhile was implacable.

"It will stop now". The old man stated simply. "I wanted to fully acquaint myself with you and now that I have, I can see why you have been sent to me".

Gradually now, George felt the man's mental grip on him lessen and he was able to release his throbbing temples and look up from his prone and helpless position. As he did so, an involuntary shiver ran through his body as for the first time, he contemplated the possibility that this strange old man had some sort of supernatural power to read his mind and his life. The old man was a fearful sight with his dirty long beard, grey but flecked with black, his wizened features, his skin, tanned and leathery and those cold, cold eyes, the heavy lids rarely blinking.

"What did you do to me? How did you cause me so much pain in my head?" George cried breathlessly, fear and bewilderment replacing his former agony. The old man merely smiled. It was a smile without warmth.

"I caused you no pain. If you felt pain, my friend, it came from within you, from the visions you saw, from the things you have done."

"No! You did something to me. I know you did. You looked at me, no, you looked into me somehow...." George shook his head in disbelief. He sounded ridiculous even to himself. "Look, I'm sorry. I've been in an accident. I think maybe it's affected me more than I thought. Please, ignore me. Maybe I need to rest awhile. Could I have a glass of water or something?"

The old man said nothing in response but he did lay aside his nets and with some difficulty raised himself from the stool and disappeared inside the little house. When he returned, he carried a glass of water and a small shot glass filled with a clear liquid.

"Here. Drink the small glass down in one and follow it with the water", he instructed. George did as he was told and swallowed the contents of the first glass which the man held out to him. He grimaced as the liquid traced a fiery route over his tongue, down his throat and into his stomach. The burning sensation was quelled slightly as he took a gulp of the cool water.

"Better now?" the man enquired.

"Yes thank you. A little."

"Raki. It is used to heal all ills here on Crete. It has many uses." The old man settled back onto his stool and George breathed deeply, the brightness of the sun dazzling him and the heat now comforting and cosseting him in a thick blanket of warmth. The raki had at least had the desired effect of relaxing him, dulling his heightened senses once more. He felt stupid now, his earlier outburst at the old man feeling almost like an act of insanity. Looking out over the horizon, George once more felt a sense of belonging on this island where his father had been born and raised. He was glad he had come here. His father had often said that Crete had a healing and calming effect on those who visited and George felt a little of that now.

He thought back to his last few days in Aghios Nikolaos, the bustling and cosmopolitan town of his father's birth. He had enjoyed walking around in the relaxed atmosphere of the town, sitting at the lakeside tavernas enjoying a beer in the sunshine or wandering at a leisurely pace around the shops, full of tourist fripperies. He had enjoyed watching the waiters negotiate the traffic with their trays overflowing with food and their practised sales techniques used to pressurise tourists into their establishments. He had found the Cretan people to be refreshingly laid back and laisser faire, and relished the contrast between the sullen and bored staff found in British restaurants and shops and the pleasant, interested people he found here. He had been struck by the mystique of the island whilst talking to one of the waiters at his favourite taverna next to the bottomless lake in the town. The taverna had been quiet and George, buoyed up by a little alcohol and curious to know about the lakeside, resembling as it did a fairy grotto, resolved to find out more. He was charmed and intrigued by the steep, rocky incline surrounding the lake, with its strange little doors and alcoves leading inside a cliff and steps leading to more brightly lit bars and cafes set high above and overlooking the lake. As he had looked over the lake that night, coloured lights giving it an almost festive air, he imagined that the doors would lead into yet another world, unseen and untroubled by the mortal one. How he had wished he could just step through the door and begin his life again.

The waiter roused him from his reverie when he returned with yet another beer for George who was trying to drown his sorrows that night.

"Cheers", George raised his glass, a little unsteadily to the man. A wide grin spread across the waiter's face as he inclined his head and replied,

"Yammas! You are enjoying your holidays Kyrie?"

"Oh, having a wild time thanks" George responded unconvincingly. Undeterred, the waiter continued. "You were admiring the bottomless lake as I came over. Beautiful is it not?"

Nodding wistfully, George nodded, his eyes once more drawn to the fairy grotto, his imagination once more pulling him to a tempting other world.

"What do you mean, the 'bottomless lake?'" it now occurred to him to ask. The waiter folded his arms, his gaze across the lake now following George's.

"It is a name the local people gave it, 'Xepatomeni', the bottomless one. Its real name is Lake Voulismeni and its deep waters are said to contain many secrets. Whether there is any truth in them..." he shrugged, "who knows, but they say that the goddess Athena once bathed here with Britomartis, the daughter of Zeus and the Cretan goddess of hunting, fishing and the moon. Once, during the early 20th century, the local people thought that the Gods had come back when some strange and eerie fumes were seen rising from the bottom of the lake". The man let out a laugh and shook his head in mirth as he continued the story. "Do you know what caused it?" George shook his head and smiled at the man who now warmed to his theme and sat down in the wicker chair next to him. Slapping his hand down on the table in mirth, he went on, "Sulphur fumes! Many scientists believe that the Lake may be connected to an underground passage leading to the volcanic island of Santorini, which, I must tell you", he leaned over conspiratorially towards George, "many believe to be the lost island of Atlantis". George meanwhile relaxed a little in the man's company, happy to be distracted from himself and his own troubles.

"Ah yes, my friend, these are but some of the myths and legends that colour the lives of Cretans. To come back to your question though, the lake is not bottomless, despite its name. Scientists have carried out tests which have revealed the depth to be 64 metres, yet, the myth remains." He paused for a moment, lost in his own thoughts. "I think perhaps the war helped to perpetuate the story. Many of the older people here tell stories of the Germans ditching tanks and weapons in the lake during the War but, if it is true, no trace of them has been found." He raised an eyebrow quizzically as he continued. "Perhaps the stories are simply untrue or perhaps....."

"Perhaps, the lake became magically bottomless again....." George offered. The waiter laughed.

"As you say, Kyrie. Who knows?"

George was transfixed, soaking up the legends and the atmosphere of this magical grotto. It was easy to see how the mystical tales had evolved. The Lake was indeed, he thought, a suitable bathing place for the Gods.

"I hope I'm not keeping you from your work? I wouldn't want you to get in trouble for entertaining me!"

"Not at all! This is Crete! Nothing troubles us here. Besides, we are not busy now as you see. Soon, they will all come, looking to be fed, but for now, I can take a few moments break". The waiter smiled expansively and sighed in contentment. "Ah, Kyrie, you know, the whole of Crete is full of wonderful legends such as this. It is full of true stories and adventures, heart-warming and heart-breaking. For instance.." he became animated once more, "did you know that Crete is the birthplace of Zeus, King of the ancient Gods?" George shook his head. Despite his good private education in one of England's pukka schools, his ignorance in the classics was profound.

"Why yes! You can even visit the cave in the Dhikti Mountains where Zeus' mother, Rhea hid him from his father who threatened to eat him, so fearful was he that his son would usurp him! Then, when Zeus grew up and became King of the World, it was there he received his own son, Minos, and instructed him in the art of being a good King. And Minos ....
You must have heard of him?" The name was familiar to George, but alas, he was sketchy on detail and shrugged apologetically, discomfited by his own ignorance of his ancestral island.
The waiter's eyes shone in anticipation of once more displaying his superior knowledge and evident pride for the history of his homeland.

"Why Minos ruled in the magnificent Palace of Knossos where the legendary Minotaur, half man, half bull is said to have been imprisoned in the labyrinth. They say, you know, that Crete is the birthplace of European Civilisation. The Minoans prospered centuries before classical Greece and, if you visit Knossos, you will be amazed at the technology, the architecture and the art which they left behind".

George's head was by now buzzing. He couldn't tell whether it was the combined heady effect of too much sun and alcohol which was making him feel this way or whether the mystique and atmosphere which surrounded him was intoxicating. He had always prided himself on his pragmatic approach to life. Things were either black or white, but strangely, he felt an almost spiritual, for want of a better word, attachment to the island which was now making him think more about life and what it was really all about. Certainly, he felt happier, and that was a word which he hadn't applied to himself for a very long time. Of course, he had heard of Zeus and Hera and lots of the classical Gods, but they hadn't meant much to him before. Here though, on the island where they had allegedly been born and lived, their presence was somehow, almost palpable. He could believe in the superheroes of old, surrounded as he was by all the antiquity of the island.

"I doubt if I could tell you half as much about the history of England as you have told me about Crete". George was suddenly conscious of how little attention people back home paid to their own surroundings which itself was steeped in mystery, if you did but look at it. Back home of course, there just wasn't time to indulge in the luxury of knowledge. You were too busy trying to exist. Not even living, when you think about it, just existing. Go to work, earn money, travel home, go to bed and start the whole cycle off again the next day. It was so very different in Crete, he thought sadly. The waiter now rose, picking up the tray which he had laid next to his chair.

"I am a history teacher by profession, Kyrie. It is my business to know about such things."

"A history teacher!" George was astounded by the man's revelation. "What on earth are you doing serving drinks in a taverna then?" The man smiled.

"We all have many jobs on Crete. During the summer, we cater for the tourist trade. Many families have their own businesses which operate only during the tourist season. Then these business close down for the winter, the people have other jobs. Many own olive groves and so those months are spent harvesting the olives and making oil. I do not work all of the tourist season, but during the school holidays, I help out my father who owns this taverna. Now, I must go back to work and you, Kyrie, must explore our beautiful island and if you can, travel the length and breadth of Crete. You will find much more to intrigue you and to appreciate here". George stood up and shook hands with the man.

"It's been fascinating. Thank you for taking the time to tell me so much. You've really whetted my appetite". The man hesitated a moment and gazed somewhat wistfully across the lake. When he spoke, he was somehow less jovial, distant, even.

"You are right, my friend. This is a fascinating island. It would take me years to tell you all the wonderful mysteries it holds. "The waiter turned his glance back to George and their eyes locked, the man's gaze deep, intent. "All I know for sure about the island Kyrie is that for certain people, those who tune into its vibrations, they find it hard to leave. Year after year, it is as though they hear the Sirens calling them back as though they are enchanted. Crete changes lives and I believe, my friend, if I am not very much mistaken, you are one of those who will experience the true mystique of the island". He continued to regard George, his eyes piercing. For those few short moments, it felt to George as though he was reading his very soul and a slight chill passed through him. Shrugging the feeling off, George thanked the man once more and, after settling his bill, bade him farewell and set off to explore the bustling town.

****

"So, you had an accident did you?" The old man broke the silence and shattered George's few moments of reminiscence. "I wondered how they would arrange to bring you here."

George did not immediately respond but considered for a moment what a strange thing the old man had just said. What could he mean, arrange for him to be brought here? Was he suggesting that he hadn't tumbled over the hill by accident? And who were they? Deeply discomfited and somewhat apprehensively, George decided not to indulge the old man in his strange musings. Keeping his tone as neutral and unfazed as he could manage, he responded.

"Yes, stupid really. I was riding a scooter up on the mountain road on my way to Elounda. I was so taken by the scenery I lost concentration, hit a hairpin bend and came off the bike. I was thrown over the barrier and fell quite a distance. I can hardly believe I walked away without a serious injury, but, well, it was my own stupid fault. Should have been paying attention to what I was doing instead of gazing around. Wouldn't be in this state now if I had". George laughed in self derision but the old man did not share his self deprecating mirth. He looked on stonily as George shifted uncomfortably and merely shook his head.

"Oh no Kyrie, this was exactly how it was meant to be. Whether you had paid attention or not, they would have found a way to bring you to this moment. You cannot, you see change what is fated. It was your destiny to fall from your vehicle."

George's heart sank. He really wasn't up for philosophical debate just at that moment but something in the old man's tone chilled him and despite himself and his lack of desire to engage with the man on this subject, he was nevertheless unable to refrain from doing so.

"I'm sorry, but I really don't know what you're getting at. Who are they? I had an accident that's all. Nothing sinister, all my own fault, no-one else involved! What are you trying to say here?

"I am saying that you would never have reached Elounda as you planned because it was written that you should come to me now". George shook his head in exasperation. He was growing tired of the old man and his wacky pronouncements and irritation coloured his response.

"You seem to be saying that life is somehow decided for us by some higher mind. Look, I'm not much in the mood for this kind of discussion right now but I don't subscribe to that view point. We all have free will, we can make choices. How our lives pan out are down to these factors, not some supernatural force. In any case, why would I be brought here to you? I don't know you! What possible impact could you have on my life that it was so important I be led here?" George shook his head in disbelief and sighed with exasperation. The old man meanwhile remained impassive and deadly calm in his response as though he had utmost certainty in all that he said.

"You only think you have free will Kyrie, but in fact you only have free will to an extent and within the limitations which have already been mapped out for you. You may think that you make choices, but in fact, even those choices were written for you. The events of your life were decided upon long before time as you know it began. You are simply playing out the destiny which was set out for you. Think about it this way. Death is our only accepted inevitability, but in fact, the events of our life are equally inevitable. There is, set out, from the moment of our birth, a day upon which we are going to die. No question about it. It will happen. On that day, we will die of a cause, whether it is old age, an accident or an illness. It *will* happen, not *might* happen. Just because we do not at any time know the day we will die or the cause of our death, nevertheless our end will come by the chosen means at the designated time. In the same way, we will marry a particular person on a particular day if it is destined. That person is out there whether we know them or not and we will meet them if it is written that we should do so. It is all inevitable according to the laws of fate, my friend."

George listened intently and laughed incredulously, uncertainly in the face of the man's unnerving authority.

"OK, written by whom? God? Sorry, I'm not a religious person. I'm more into Darwin's theory of evolution than Adam and Eve." Disdainfully, the man laid down the net upon which he was working and following his gaze, George saw a small boat tethered at the waterside which now bobbed up and down in the gently lapping waters just a few metres away. The man's cheeks had now coloured and he bellowed in rage.

"By the Gods of course! They who have all knowledge and the responsibility for teaching their errant children! You may think you are exercising free will, but you are really following the will of the ancient and forgotten Gods who must teach you the lessons you need for eternity".

By now, George decided that the man was just deluded, loneliness and eccentricity perhaps combining to exalt his unusually pagan beliefs which were at odds with the highly Christian Greek Orthodoxy of the island. Exhausted and drained however, he felt disinclined to enter into an argument or upset the man further. Unable to support his body any longer, George lay back in the sand, his head resting upon his arm.

"Why don't you make yourself comfortable?" the old man asked, sarcasm dripping from each word. Hardly, George thought, the kindly avuncular stranger one would have hoped to meet in his current circumstances. He wasn't prepared for a challenging discourse but couldn't resist asking which gods the old man was referring to. The old salt looked at him with such contempt that he felt he would shrivel to the size of an ant under his gaze. He looked down upon George who now felt like an ignorant child. Calmer now, the old man continued.

"Where are you now?" he asked. Puzzled, George answered.

"Crete of course".

"Of course", the old man replied, nodding as though he felt he was finally getting somewhere. "And Crete is the birthplace of the King of the Gods". Recalling his classical history lesson back in Aghios, George concurred.

"Zeus! But these Gods are just myths and legends. They hold no truth, everyone knows that!" The old man grunted disdainfully and his voice raised in anger once more as he retorted.

"They are no more myth than your modern gods, of whom, I

must add, there are also many. But for their names though, and the beliefs attached to them by mortals, God, Allah, Buddah, Yahweh, Zeus - are we not speaking of the same God? And in the madness of this world of humans, do we not all fight against each other in the name of our God, whichever we choose to worship? And the reason for this is that each believer's God is self serving to his own interests. But our Gods, the ancient Greek Gods are subservient to no-one's interests but their own and in their omnipotence, they assure that the interests of mortals are best served". George was weary by now, however, he recognised that there was some truth in what the old man had to say. He had never subscribed to organised religion believing it was the interests of the organisation rather than its followers which benefited from it. Anyway, considering his exploits in recent years, no religion would want to lay claim to him. Despite himself, he listened with interest as the old man continued to wax lyrical.

"Here, in Crete, we are at the very heart of earliest modern civilisation. The Minoans worshipped the gods of Mount Olympus and thrived on the gifts of knowledge bestowed upon them. But, alas, they angered the Gods who just as easily as they once brought gifts, destroyed them with the force of nature. An exploding volcano, a tidal wave and violent weather destroyed the once great people of Greece, all orchestrated by Zeus in his infinite fury with the vicissitudes of mankind who now took his gifts for granted and forgot to offer thanks for his magnanimity and that of his many siblings and relatives. The old man was silent for a few moments, reflective as he gazed out onto the diamond sparking sea.

"But now, the ancient gods have been forgotten completely and are even reviled, replaced by new deities. This does not mean that they have ceased to exist though. They have lain quiet for centuries allowing mankind to mould their own sorry existence. But they can still wield their power if they so wish. Human ignorance alone cannot destroy the Gods of old". The man fell silent once more and resumed his work mending his net. George was unsure as to how to respond to his outburst and didn't want to incur his wrath once more. He was strangely fearsome when angry and in his weakened state, George felt unable to cope with the anger. He decided that a change of subject was probably the best course of action.

"You have a wonderful view from your house", he ventured.

"Everyone on Crete has a wonderful view. The whole island is beautiful, and", he looked out to sea, ponderously, "captivating. This place is like a woman who entrances, charms you and seduces you. She never lets you go easily".

George recalled the waiter's words which had been strangely similar to the old man's. It was almost as though a message was being imparted to him, he thought uneasily.

"Is that Elounda over there?"

"Nai", Yes. "A lucky town indeed. The inhabitants there have always known how to make money by fair means and foul. They traded off the misery of others for decades and did well out of it. Now though they make easy money thanks to modern day tourists and television cameras making their films here. George realised the old man was referring to the book and British TV serial "Who pays the Ferryman? which had been famously filmed in the town and brought tourists there by the thousands. The old man explained that people had become rich almost overnight as visiting tourists wanted to buy up the land for their holiday homes.

"Surely all of that is good for Crete though? I mean, good for everyone?

"Not for those who are so undeserving", the old man snapped.

"You mentioned something about the people trading in human misery for decades. What did you mean? George ventured.

"That is something that you should be all too familiar with isn't it my friend? Perhaps it is time that you experienced life from the other side of the coin, mm?"

Stunned, George felt unable to respond. What did the old man know of his life? How could he know anything? The man's steely blue eyes bored into his soul, just then, the flashbacks came again, pain darting mercilessly though his head. Helplessly, he stared into the man's cold eyes, but if those were indeed the windows to his soul, he could see nothing behind them. The eyes appeared glassy, dead, but George sensed that somehow the man was seeing everything inside him, absorbing every facet of his personality and every event of his life. In those eyes, George now saw pictures of his life playing out like a film.

Though less violent this time, the explosions in his head were nonetheless agonisingly painful. George wondered if his years of cocaine abuse, coupled with the effects of the accident were now resulting in some kind of stroke. It was some moments before the pain subsided and he was able to speak once more.

"Tell me why", he gasped, breathless now, "if all you say is true, would your ancient Gods be interested in me?"

The old man, unperturbed by George's distress responded.

"The answer is quite simple Kyrie, the limited choices you have been permitted to make were leading you the wrong way. You must be returned to the path of your destiny and to do that you must learn and understand certain things".

"And", George continued, becoming more bemused by the minute, "you were somehow, expecting me? I, I mean you said you have fully acquainted yourself with my life - what did you mean? How do you know me?" Barely controlled hysteria crept into George's voice, tempered only by his anger. "Who the hell are you?"

The old man hesitated a moment before responding, a slight smile now playing about his lips.

"Think of me as the guardian of your soul. You are about to embark on a journey which only a chosen few have the opportunity of taking".

George felt weak, confused. His head throbbed and all he had for comfort was an old man who spoke in riddles to compound his misery. Unable to deal with any more, he curled up, hugging his throbbing head in his hands. He couldn't decide what he found to be more disturbing, the clarity of the flashbacks, the simultaneous experience of all the emotions accompanying each recalled event, the pain that seared through his head or the nagging feeling that this was what the dying must experience when their lives were replayed just before the last breath. 'Think of me as the guardian of your soul..' that was what the old man had said wasn't it? A fearful thought struck George. Was he really dead? Perhaps he hadn't survived the fall after all? He shrugged off the thought, his rational mind refusing to contemplate such an idea. Nevertheless, he was afraid that things were distinctly weird here. Perhaps it was the certainty in his mind that the old man was actually somehow, inexplicably exploring his life, intruding into every aspect of his psyche and probing into the darkest recesses of his mind. It seemed to George that during those moments of pain and flashbacks, the man was reading him like a picture book. Despite his instincts to get away from the man, he had been strangely unable to do so, some Svengali like attraction keeping him rooted to the spot. George was certain the man was psychic. He knew things about him, of that he was in no doubt. George was not closed to such an idea having heard from his father stories about his own grandfather who was also psychic and on this very island had people travel far and wide to receive his guidance. Although George accepted such things as fact, he was nonetheless frightened by them. He was drawn back into the present by the man's voice cold and gruff. His words served only to confirm George's thoughts.

"You know all about the benefits of human misery don't you?" It was a statement more than a question. George said nothing. He was terrified by now and just wanted to take his leave.

"I don't know what you're talking about", he responded somewhat unconvincingly. The old man merely snorted disparagingly.

"Of course you do. You have profited from the dependence of others for long enough. Where there is pain, need and degradation, there is always someone waiting to exploit them. This too is ingrained in the history of Elounda. The town wasn't always the neon filled playground of the rich and famous. It has a shameful past, much like your own".

A new thought struck George now. Perhaps his life had actually caught up with him now. Perhaps the old man had seen a television or newspaper report about his exploits. A clammy hand seemed to grip his heart as he contemplated this, the only rational explanation for the old man's disdain. Beads of sweat broke out on his upper lip and forehead which he absently wiped away. Afraid that there was a manhunt out for him, George feared the old man would turn him over to the authorities.

"Look, what do you want? Money is that it? Will that stop you from any more of this talk?" George desperately hoped that perhaps blackmail was the old man's motivation. He sighed resignedly, wearily. More softly now, he continued. "I only want to get to Elounda. If you want some money, tell me how much. If I don't go now I won't find anywhere to stay tonight". The old man merely looked on as he spoke, no sign of his intentions apparent to George. His features however appeared to soften slightly.

"I am going to Elounda later, but first, I must make a trip to a nearby island. If you wish to join me, you will learn much in a very short time. Come, we will sail into the harbour at Elounda on the way back".

Slightly relieved by the old man's offer, George rose from his seated position with some difficulty and brushed down his clothes. He had no more wish to accompany the man than to give himself up, yet he found himself, despite his feelings, agreeing to go with him. If truth were known however, George made no independent decision. He was compelled as surely as if he had been hypnotised. Weak and exhausted now, George was afraid that if he didn't humour the man he would just turn him in to the authorities. In any case, the sun was still hot and on foot the journey was long. He didn't think he would make it to Elounda under his own steam. Perhaps those were the reasons he followed him to the boat, but it was more likely the powerful compulsion which he did not have the ability to resist which led him to his fate. Summoning up as much positivity as he could he smiled brightly.

"OK. Why not? The old man seemed to brighten visibly and for a second, his cold eyes glinted in the sunshine.

"But first, a little Greek tradition", he responded. "You must give me a coin in return for your transportation." 'Aha, George thought, now we're getting to the crunch'. The old man held out his dirty, calloused hand, knotted with thick, protruding blue veins. 'Might have known' George thought, 'he's just been touting for business. Must run boat trips for tourists or something'. He comforted himself in this thought and decided that his imagination had just been running wild due to the accident and his generally overwrought state. He rummaged in his pockets, but all he could find were two euro coins. The rest were notes. Reluctantly, he offered him a ten euro note. The old man shook his head, rejecting the money. 'Here we go', thought George as he drew out a hundred Euro note which to his horror, the old man also rejected.

"No, no, no. I must have a coin" the man retorted angrily, a temper tantrum threatening to spill over. Pointing to the Euro coins which George held in his outstretched hand he said, "One of those will do nicely". Amazed, George proffered the coin but the old man's actions confounded his theory. OK, so maybe he wasn't after the money, but what then?

"We go now". The man said simply, the coin having apparently satisfied him. He gathered up his nets and strode off at surprising speed, which belied his years, towards the boat moored at the shore. George followed him to the bobbing craft which he boarded with some difficulty, stiffness now impairing his movement. The engine roared into life and George felt the cool breeze through his hair as he admired the beauty of the coastline, the clarity of the blue sea below him and the vast expanse of blue sky above.

Relaxing a little with the rise and swell of the gentle waves, he spoke to his companion once more.

"You haven't told me your name", he said. A faint smile passed over the man's lips as he turned to George.

"Charon. My name is Charon". He pronounced it *Haron*.

"Pleased to meet you Charon, George responded amiably. "I am George".

"Yes", said Charon. "I know."

MANOLIS

Manolis Papadopolous squinted contentedly into the sunshine as he sat outside the Kafeneon enjoying his habitual strong Greek coffee. He was an old man now and, as was the tradition at a certain age, the Kafeneon was part of his daily routine, part of the structure of his life. Here he would sit quietly and contemplatively, watching the day to day goings on of village life, sometimes joining the other men as they drank coffee, passed comment on the state of things today and flipped their komboloi or baglieri, traditional worry beads over their knarled and work scarred hands.

It surprised Manolis that he had succumbed to such habits having sworn in his younger days never to wither away in such useless pursuits as he had seen so many of the older generation do in his time. Nevertheless, in a strange way, he was contented enough now just to pass his days waiting for the boatman to come along and ferry him to the next world.

Today, Manolis found himself alone at the Kafeneon. There was no-one to bemoan the old days, the hardships, the wartime adventures with or to discuss the village gossip. Manolis wasn't troubled by this though. He was contented, just as a cat is happy to curl up in the sunshine and let the world go by without disturbance or interference.

Manolis was an educated man. Most of his neighbours worked in their family businesses, tavernas, kafeneon, olive groves, or, as was common in the villages, practising the crafts of weaving, lace making, bootmaking and leatherwork, glass making and painting. Manolis was by birth an Athenian, however, he had journeyed to Crete over sixty five years ago with a plan to tend the sick and cure the incurable. High ideals for a young man and yet, he had never faltered from his mission. The trials of those years were etched in his now lined face, visible behind his expressively sad eyes. Manolis had known great suffering for his efforts, the loss of dear friends and the frustration that despite his superior medical knowledge and skills, he was helpless to alleviate the agony and horror of those he lived amongst. There had been joys of course, later in his career when medical research resulted in the breakthrough they had all prayed for and many of his beloved 'family' as he came to regard them were able to anticipate something of a normal life, or at worst, a vastly improved life, depending on the condition of their bodies at the time the long overdue medication had appeared.

When Manolis had seen the last of his charges return to a life of hope and after fulfilling the promises he had made to those of his charges who had died with unfinished business, he had returned to Athens to work in the hospital where he continued his research and continued to offer treatment to those few who still required it. There came a moment however, when he felt his work to be done. A realisation that his 'family' had now grown up and away from him and, though he heard from them all and met up with them now and again, he no longer had the feeling of belonging which had he known during his years in Crete. He was left with a yearning and emptiness in his heart which could only be alleviated by returning to the place he had called home and by his continued relationship with the people upon whom he had come to depend as much as they had depended upon him. And so, five years after his departure from Crete for Athens, he found himself once again disembarking on her shores at Aghios Nikolaos with the intention of finding a quieter and more useful existence in the close knit community of the islanders. Soon, he was once again using his knowledge and skills to help those who were most in need of it. Manolis had always fought on the side of the underdog and his rewards had been far greater than money. In return for his ministrations he would receive the small, but massively appreciated kindnesses of his neighbours who, in time, became his friends.

On his return to Crete, Manolis had settled in the picturesque little village of Kritsa just outside Aghios Nikolaos, a sharp contrast to the austere and unwelcoming shores of his previous Cretan home, and there, he had set up his simple little surgery. He devoted his life to the care of those around him, and, as it turned out, their animals. Most of his patients had no money, but Manolis never starved as he was treated to freshly baked bread, oranges, olives, wine, meat and vegetables from those who had gratefully received his treatment. Never a day went past when there wasn't something to tempt him left on the doorstep. He particularly enjoyed it when some sweet, freshly made 'baclava' appeared or a new pair of leather boots awaited him. Sometimes though, a live animal would appear which he knew was intended for his oven. Manolis, whilst happy to eat meat, did not have the stomach for actually killing any healthy living creature. He had been put on this earth to prolong life and stop suffering and so, more often than not, he would pass a live animal on to a neighbour who could perhaps make better use of it and in return he would receive something more suitable to his tastes. It was a system that worked well.

Of course, things changed and, as the decades went on and people became more prosperous, Manolis began to receive money in return for his care. He would never be a rich man by any standards, but, he had lived a full, useful and happy life which had been completed by the re-emergence of his beautiful Irini whom he had loved from the moment he met her. In the early days of their acquaintance, Manolis could only worship her from afar, his interest in her restrained by their circumstances at the time, the doctor/patient relationship which had to be, by its very nature detached and paternalistic and her refusal to contemplate the risk of infecting Manolis with the disease that they believed blighted her and so many others. Their distant love however had remained alive during their years of exile, but, to his delight, after his 'family' had split and scattered back to their loved ones, Irini had eventually sought him out some 15 long years later.

His heart had lurched with excitement and joy as she took his hands in hers, tossed her still thick, dark, but now greying curls over her shoulder and unselfconsciously and without guile declared her love for him.

Fifteen years earlier, Irini had believed herself to be under a death sentence, that she, like so many others would become a grotesque parody of a human being, that she was doomed to the horror of her beauty rotting and decaying as a result of the cruel disease they lived amongst. After the loss of her beloved husband from the disease, Irini felt that she could never love again. Indeed, she did not want to love again as heartache had always accompanied her short lived joy and eclipsed all that had been good in her life. She threw her heart and soul into working with Manolis to relieve him of some of his burdens on the island however and through that time, her heart, though not her head screamed out to her that she could be happy once more if only she would allow it. She reasoned however that it would have been unfair to have risked the possibility of infecting the man whom she and the others in his care regarded as nothing less than a saint. Though the disease she had mingled with had never become manifest in her, nevertheless, she was convinced that she was unclean. How could she not be so? Hadn't she loved a man who had suffered the insidious disease and hadn't she lost him to its evil grip? In truth, she probably wanted to believe that she carried the disease, for it released her from the need to engage in another relationship which she felt, rightly or wrongly, would be doomed. It was her crutch, her absolution from further emotional responsibility and she sought support from it for many years after she left the island, her belief unshakeable.

Manolis, for his part, despaired for Irini. He was certain that she did not, despite her fears, carry the evil bacillus and he tried, without success to persuade her of this fact. Her story was indeed terrible, and that she found herself stranded on an island living amongst the most hopeless of communities was in itself a crime. He knew though, as she did, that it would be impossible for her to take her place back in society in Crete, suspicion, fear and loathing of anyone in proximity of the island certain to lead to her destruction by one means or another.

To Irini's horror and delight however, taking courage to face the tests, she had discovered on leaving her home of exile many years later, after medical science had decreed that the inhabitants were no longer a threat, that she had not been a victim of the terrible disease and it was only then that she was forced to face the truth, that she had lost most of her youth and her chance of happiness for nothing.

Manolis always considered it to be his failure that he had been unable to convince her otherwise. Through the years that the pair worked together and lived on the island, a relationship so deep, sweet and meaningful developed between them that was so highly attuned that they often communicated without the need of speech. A look or a smile would pass between them and each would know the other's thoughts. The warmth which Manolis felt from Irini's presence was his reason for living and yet she could never allow him to breach the barriers which protected her equilibrium. On the day that the last of the islanders departed, they travelled in silence on the boat to Aghios together, the atmosphere pregnant with unspoken feelings, unfinished business, sorrow between them almost a palpable object and yet still, Irini could not release herself from her lonely prison or bring herself to admit that there was, within her grasp, the opportunity of real contentment with the man that was truly her soul mate. Manolis, though he desperately wanted to beg her to stay with him and never leave his side, could not find the words he needed to tell her how much he needed her and instead, they sat in silence on the short crossing, their sadness overwhelming and their fears of a new life too great. Disembarking at Aghios, the pair turned to look at each other, their few belongings by their sides and Irini held out both of her hands to Manolis which, head bent to hide the tears spilling down his cheeks, he held in his grasp, never wanting to release them. She stood for long moments, wanting to gather him in her arms, to comfort him, to tell him that she loved him and that she would stay forever yet unable to tear down the walls she had so carefully built around her heart. Instead, she pulled herself gently from his grasp and meeting her gaze, he nodded and in so doing, said everything to her without need for words. She smiled at him, love and admiration evident in her features and finally she stooped to collect her meagre belongings into her arms and slowly turned and walked from him, never looking back. His body trembled as he watched Irini, his friend, confidante and only true love walk into the distance, her head stooped, her gait uncertain. Had he thought it would make a difference he would have run after her, begged her to stay, but, he knew it would do nothing but make their parting even more terrible to bear.

On the day she finally walked back into his life, Irini explained to Manolis that after she had discovered for certain she was clear of disease, she had tried to pick up her life once again. As with many of her peers, she had become isolated, institutionalised even, by the previous years and she had retreated into a self imposed prison, unable in large part to accept that her prognosis was good or that any human could treat another in the way that her family had treated her after her husband had died. Despite the assurances of her doctors, she was now imprisoned by her mind, convinced that although she was clear now, the symptoms would show themselves any moment. She lived daily with the continued fear, self loathing and the certainty that the progress of the disease she had lived with could not be halted. It was only when a new doctor, a wonderful psychiatric specialist had picked up her case that finally he convinced her to embrace the miracle which had changed her life and finally she had come to accept and live with the awful truth, the terrible betrayal of which she had been the victim. Finally, the self imposed exile and the loneliness she had lived with was lifted and Irini dared to hope that a new life was there for the taking.

And so, the beautiful Irini, *his* beautiful Irini stood before him one magnificent day and her smile was so radiant it had lit up his heart. A warmth he had not experienced since their days on the island radiated in his home and seeped into his being. And that warmth had never left him until Irini died at the age of 60. Although she had never succumbed to the devilish disease which had been rife on her island home, nevertheless, the years of hardship, of hunger, of cold, had weakened her body which prematurely failed her, leaving Manolis alone again and grief stricken. This had not however been before she and Manolis had lived a life of such superlative happiness and joy that even at her death, he could only give thanks for the gift which had finally been bestowed on both of them. It was a gift which had been so unexpected, the riches so infinite that although he grieved every day for his lost love, he knew that Irini would have said to him, as she so often had in life,

"Manoli, I have lived the life I thought I would never have. We must thank God daily for the wonders of the gift we have been given and whatever happens in the future, good or bad, be grateful for every moment we have together. We must regret nothing, not even when we are parted by death. We must remember those whom we lived amongst, who were not so lucky, our family Manoli and take each day with joy, no matter what life now offers us". And, Manolis had to agree, she was right to feel like this.

They had shared despair, tears and even joy in the early years of their acquaintance but they, unlike many of the others, had been given a second chance and they had grasped it, held it and nurtured it, their wonderment no less than had they been parents of a new born child. Manolis harboured no bitterness that Irini was lost to him but instead marvelled at the lifetime of miracles he had witnessed, experienced, even created. He had been rewarded, though late in life, for his early sacrifice and devotion to his charges by a love that had created passion, warmth and togetherness in his once insular and dedicated life. Somehow, he just knew that forces beyond his understanding had engineered things so perfectly that he would not be parted from Irini forever. He would meet her again in the afterlife, his Orpheus to her Eurydice, only he would not be so foolish as to lose her as Orpheus had done.

And so, confident in the forces which had guided his life, Manolis reverted to his single existence again, but this time with a certainty that Irini was still with him. He could feel her around him, enveloping him with her warmth, infusing his mind with her beauty. Today was one of those days when he sensed her presence, often signified by the faint smell of her favourite scent and, had it not been for a matter which was troubling him somewhat, he would have felt contentment sitting here with the sun on his skin, the bright rays reflecting on the whitewashed houses and the exquisite woven fabrics and laceworks that hung in the shop windows and doorways of his neighbours where many of the local ladies sat in their black garb practising their skilled crafts and chatting companionably amongst themselves.

In summer, the village of Kritsa was a major tourist attraction and it bustled to life with those wishing to enjoy the sights of a traditional Cretan village and the chance to spend their holiday money on souvenirs and gifts from the many crafts on offer. Here, old Crete combined with the new. Old ladies in black widow's weeds still rode their donkeys to fill their panniers with luscious oranges whilst cars and trucks of various shapes and sizes competed with the older modes of transport, squeezing themselves up and down the narrow winding village roads. Few tourists ventured deeper into the village than the main street, adorned as it was with colourful emporia selling their vast array of goods. It became quieter as you strolled away from the main shopping area and those tourists who self consciously found themselves in the little back streets got a true taste of the spirit of Crete where wild cats roamed and the sound of cockerels crowing and goats bleating could be heard in the otherwise peaceful village.

In the heart of the village, those who lived there would happily acknowledge the tourists who smiled and greeted them, but they scowled in disdain at those who passed them by as though they were invisible or stared at them as though they were exhibits in a museum. Those who wandered to the centre of the village would stumble across the charming Orthodox Church and, if they were lucky may be invited inside where they could marvel at the Byzantine decor , the glittering gold leaf, gilt edged and colourful icons. Inside they could light a candle and offer a silent prayer for some wish to be granted.

Manolis particularly enjoyed the tourist season. He enjoyed the influx of new faces to the island, most of whom wandered peaceably and contentedly, exploring the delights that Crete had to offer. His English was good and therefore he often got talking to the visitors and from them, he learned much about life in other countries. Manolis could have told many fascinating stories of his own, but so profound were his feelings about his past, he felt unable to share those experiences with others. He could never hope to adequately articulate the myriad of emotions which accompanied the events of his life. Instead, he extended the typical Cretan geniality and spoke of nothing more than the mundane, the attractions and the history of Crete, of Kritsa and all that it offered. Few would guess or enquire about him, his education or his astounding personal history and that suited him well. He did not seek validation or admiration for the events of his past. He did not wish to dilute or cheapen the lives of those he had known and loved by using them to tell a good story, nor did he wish to be known simply for his association with a place which was now nothing more than a macabre tourist attraction. He felt that its current status served only to diminish the true sorrow of the place, the degradation, yet courage and fortitude of its inhabitants and the human misery which was absorbed into every surface and stone of the island.

In recent years, since their evacuation, Manolis had ventured to his old home only once and the emotions which the tourist trip had engendered in him were something he did not wish to experience again. On that day, as he stood in the doorway of his former quarters, surrounded by tourists eager for as many of the gory and sickening details as possible, he felt that he and his 'family's' lives were reduced to nothing more than a freak show, only to be discussed in terms of folklore for public delectation and entertainment. Manolis alone here knew the truth of the tears, the horror, the hardship, the corruption and yes, even the joys which his charges, his many brothers, sisters, parents, grandparents and children had endured. His family had been the biggest in the country and he had loved each and every member as though they had been blood relatives. He wept uncontrollably when he had lost any one of them, unable to fight the battle to save them. Manolis vowed he would never venture there again.

On his last visit, he had seen shadows, familiar faces, long gone, yet moving in and out of the now partially restored historical village. All the renovations served to sanitise and somehow make the shocking truth of the place more palatable for fee paying visitors. He had wanted to shout at the guide who selectively told the story of the place. He wanted to shout that this had been hell, the Hades of the living. But instead, he said nothing. He wept silently inside, a sob threatening to rise from the pit of his stomach and overwhelm him. Unable to listen to the guide any longer or watch the enthralled faces of the sanguinary crowd he separated himself from his companions and made his way up the steep hill to the graveyard which was nothing more than a series of deep holes in the Cliffside separated by a grid system into a number of rectangular chambers where the multiple bodies of the dead had lain, one on top of the other until their bones were removed to make way for the most recent casualties.

From this vantage point, Manolis looked out to sea and in silent remembrance paid his own tribute to the courage, the love and laughter which had rung out in the face of the most appalling adversity and suffering. He would have liked to have spent some time alone here, staying on after the crowds had left but that was no longer a possibility. The place was a carefully guarded tourist attraction and money had to be paid for entry. No boats other than those on scheduled trips were permitted access to the island. The reality therefore was reduced to the banal, the trivial and the history, as told by the guides, so unsophisticated as to simply detract from the truth. Manolis was relieved to get away from his former home, now desecrated by those who tramped on its hallowed grounds. Since that day, he had never returned to witness the dishonour he perceived was now paid to his family.

Sitting, alone in the sunshine that day, Manolis was preoccupied, thinking and remembering the details of those long ago days. They had now ceased to occupy his thoughts in every waking moment as once they had done, but today was different. For now the past had come back to haunt him and a mystery which had lived with him all his life had re-emerged suddenly and quite unexpectedly in the last 24 hours when he had, for a fleeting moment seen the face of his rival in love, yet his closest friend and confidante from those days.

Manolis had believed that his dear friend, in seeking his freedom that fateful night in 1941, braving the seas which surrounded their little island home, had lost his life in the most brutal fashion.

Although his death was to some extent unconfirmed, he had never turned up again on the mainland or in the intervening years and Manolis could only believe that he had perished as his companions had done in their attempt to escape the confinement they endured. His sorrow at his friend's loss had been deep, yet he had never given up hope of finding him once again.

Today, uncannily, it appeared he had somehow risen from the dead and the sight of him had shocked Manolis. Unlike himself, now an old and frail man, his beloved friend looked exactly as he had done when he had appeared on the island, not a day older and not changed one iota. How could this be? Manolis struggled to rationalise it. It had to be someone else, someone who looked exactly as his old friend had done in those days. A relative perhaps? Yes, that must be it surely! This must be the grandson of the man who had worked with him and helped him throughout the difficult days of the war and before. It had to be. More troubling still however, was the fact that the man's face was plastered all over the television news and the newspapers. He was apparently missing and the authorities had launched a full scale search for him, believing him to be in Crete. An appeal for his whereabouts had been launched. The sight of Georgios had reawakened so many memories in Manolis, but more than that his fiercely loyal streak was aroused as he realised that the man was in trouble and that he needed his help. He could not pretend to understand what was unfolding in front of him but he was excited and intrigued and determined to unravel the mystery of what had happened to his old friend.

Manolis drained his cup and set off purposefully to his home. He needed to know more about the young man and he felt somehow in his bones, he was about to enter a very strange phase of his life and, yet, Manolis embraced it.

SPINALONGA

The waters lapped gently around the side of the boat and George was lulled and soothed by the rhythmic movement and rippling sounds which felt like the rocking of a crib. His eyes were heavy and he closed them against the sunlight as he recovered from the pounding headaches which had assaulted him earlier and now dulled his ability to think clearly or attempt conversation with his strange and taciturn companion. Despite his torpor and the heaviness of his limbs however, George could not relax in the man's company and he fought the urge to close his eyes lest he should sleep. Pulling himself upward from his now slouched position in the little boat, he forced himself to attempt conversation with the socially inept Charon who gazed impassively into the distance. In uncharacteristic acknowledgement of George's presence in the boat, Charon now wordlessly pointed towards a mass of land now rising in the distance from the waters and George beheld those steely eyes as they bore once more into his own. Lifting a hand to his forehead to shield his eyes from the sun, he squinted into the distance.

"This is our first stop before Elounda, I take it?" No reply came from the Skipper. 'It's like travelling with Captain Nemo', George thought wryly. 'Captain No-one, can't get much more apt than that!" He tried again.

"Doesn't look too inviting really does it? What is this place?" He didn't expect an answer really, but talking made him feel better, particularly now as the little boat continued into the shadow of the dark and brooding mass which dominated the horizon and cast a shadow over George's soul, a feeling of dread now creeping through him as they grew closer to the island. He could now make out that the island was dominated by a huge circular fortress and imagined that soldiers of days gone by hid behind its walls and were waiting to attack as the little boat breached the surrounding waters. He felt instinctively that the island to which they were now headed was God forsaken and unwelcoming. Despite Charon's refusal to engage in conversation, George felt impelled to keep talking.

"Looks like a place full of history anyway", George ventured, competing with the outboard motor which roared and spluttered. Charon kept his gaze fixed on the horizon, but, to George's surprise, after a few moments more, he killed the engine, slowing the boat's progress. He turned to look at George, his face never breaking into anything remotely describable as congeniality to put his companion at ease.

"We are approaching the island of Spinalonga, a place with a dark history, misery ingrained on its shores and within its walls. A place where the dead live on and the living may as well be dead".

'Sounds a blast', thought George, his inward flippancy failing to dispel his growing uneasiness. He shivered involuntarily as something passed into his mind and made his body tingle, the hairs on his body stand on end; a premonition? Deja vu perhaps? He wasn't entirely sure, but gazing at the island, he felt a familiarity with the place. But that was impossible. He hadn't been to Crete before, nevertheless, the feeling was strong and a deep and inexplicable sadness overwhelmed him which he knew was somehow connected with the island. 'This is ridiculous, I'm letting Lurch here spook me, that's all. Get a grip'. George sensed that Charon was enjoying his discomfort and resolved not to give him any more satisfaction.

'Unusual name, Spinalonga', George commented absently, unsure if he really now did wish to hear more about the island.

'It's a Venetian word. It means 'the long arm'. The island of Crete has long been regarded by pirates and plunderers throughout the centuries as a golden treasure. Its people have been subject to attack from all corners by those wishing to subjugate them and possess its treasures'. Charon was warming to his story.

"Crete traded with many lands, Africa, Europe and Asia and imported new ideas from these distant but accessible places. Many of these lands saw the jewel of Crete and the benefits of its location and so it came under attack throughout the centuries on a regular basis'.

"I read something of its history while I was in Aghios. It's been turbulent hasn't it?', George was keen to encourage the old man to keep talking. Somehow, it felt more comfortable than the awkward silence which had persisted between them.

The old man nodded. 'Nai', Yes, Crete had been home to the Romans after they conquered its shores in 66 BC and it became part of the Byzantine Empire. It has been the home of pirates when the Arab Saracens took the island in 824 AD and then, later, in 1210 the Venetians came to rest here and, as you see, they were influential, building many of the fortifications which you see to this day across the island. The Turks came here for the second time in 1669 and the island to which we are now going, Spinalonga resisted them until 1715 when the citizens there were besieged. From then, Turkish forces remained on Spinalonga, relocating their families and reconstructing the remains of the Venetian Fort and the houses on the island for their own use. Eventually, over 1000 Turkish families lived on Spinalonga. When Crete finally regained its autonomy in 1898, most of the Turks left the main island. Those who resided on Spinalonga however, refused to leave. They had homes and an established trade in smuggling you see". The old man pondered a few moments before continuing. 'Yes, turbulent times indeed'. He shook his head thoughtfully; almost, George thought to himself, as though he were remembering those times himself - as though he had lived through them. But that was impossible! George decided his mind was overwrought with the events of the day.

Charon, whose gaze had fallen upon the fortress which loomed ahead of them now regarded George once more, his eyes resting impassively upon him.

"The Cretan people did not want to share their land with these invaders - well - who could blame them? They were glad when the Turks departed their island. Those on Spinalonga though, they were stubborn! They remained there until 1903 when the Cretans played their cleverest card and the Turks fled Spinalonga as fast as their thieving pirate vessels could carry them". Charon gave a self satisfied laugh and George detected a glint of amusement in the old man's flint eyes.

"What made them leave in such a hurry?" Despite himself, George was eager to hear what it was that the Cretans could have done to strike such fear in the hearts of the Turks. Ignoring him however, Charon, to George's extreme frustration, chose this moment to re-start the engine. George sensed that the most interesting part of the story was yet to come but he knew the old man was playing with him, teasing him and that he would have to wait until he was ready to continue.

As they drew nearer to Spinalonga, the semi circular walls of the gloomy fortress loomed above them, dwarfing the little boat and its occupants. The gun emplacements and look out points reminded George of empty eye sockets staring blindly, unseeing, yet aware of their unwelcome approach. 'Yet more intruders on this Godforsaken place' thought George, apprehension now causing him to tense his body and clench his jaw. He couldn't imagine why anyone would want to live on the island. It had a distinctly unwelcoming aura about it. Something overpowering emanated from those walls and he sensed a feeling of despair as they approached. It was a feeling which belied the belligerence of the island's history as told by Charon. George had never been what you could call a sensitive person, and yet puzzlingly, he was overcome by what he felt as he stared at those cold grey walls.

Whilst they were unwelcoming, even forbidding, at the same time they seemed to beckon him to the island's shores like a Siren. He felt, in some peculiar way that was more disturbing than comforting, that he was returning home.

George's reverie was broken as, within moments, they reached the jetty and disembarked on the sandy bay punctuated here and there with the leafy greenery of a few trees. The place was deserted and George wondered what Charon's business could be here. As though reading his thoughts, Charon spoke.

"It is late in the season now, but this island is a popular tourist attraction these days. People come to gawp in mawkish curiosity and revel in the gory details of the island's less romantic period during the 20th century". I come here when they have all gone so that I can comb the beach for items they have so carelessly lost or discarded". Charon made a 'Pah' sound of disdain before working up to a tirade.

"Most of these people value nothing. I can make a good living on the things they leave behind. If they knew how it was the last settlers on this island survived they would not be so careless with their possessions. They would be shamed by their actions".

George was tempted to ask Charon about the 20th century settlers. He found it hard to believe how anyone in modern day history could have lived here on the remains of a Venetian fortress but Charon had already turned his attention to tying up the boat and was now disembarking. George tentatively followed him, still unsteady on his feet from the after effects of the accident and even more so having spent a short period on the sea. Nevertheless, he accepted Charon's beachcombing pursuits as a likely explanation for the eccentric old sea dog's visits here.

Stepping onto dry land, George was exhausted, the sun making him feel heavy and disorientated. It had been a long day and despite his customary lack of concern about what had led him to Crete, somewhere in the recesses of his mind, either conscience or, more likely the fear that his past may catch up with him, reminded him that problems were not far behind. It had been an eventful few days. He had almost killed himself this morning, he was on the run from the authorities, he was probably responsible for the death of at least one person, maybe more, and here he was going on a sightseeing trip! Ludicrous! Still, his travels were keeping him out of the main towns and villages and the longer he could do that, the longer he could keep his head down and evade the police, Interpol or whoever else might be on the lookout for him.

Charon looked up as though remembering he had company once more. He pointed ahead towards a flight of steps.

"Go! Look around. I will call you when I am ready to leave" Charon ordered, as though dismissing George. The old man clearly wanted his solitude. Perhaps he thinks I'd want a share of his spoils, though George disdainfully. It seemed to him that Charon wasn't above carrying on the age old tradition of plundering that Spinalonga was so familiar with. Glad to get away from the oppressive presence of the old man for a short while, George bade him farewell and upon eliciting his assurances that Charon would call him when he was ready to return to Crete, he set off reluctantly to explore.

Alone for the first time in some hours, relief flooded through George. It felt to him as though Charon was draining the very life from him and he felt his spirits lift just a little as he moved away from his dark and miserable aura. Strange how another person could affect one's own moods, thought George as he mounted the short flight of steps which led him into a long, dark and gloomy tunnel supported by arches. Far from feeling uneasy in the darkness which enveloped him, George found it to be a welcome relief from the heat of the late afternoon sun. Within moments however, he emerged from the tunnel back into the heat of the day and, as his eyes re-adjusted to the bright light, there appeared before him the outskirts of a village, much like many a Cretan village he had seen, except this was dilapidated. Shielding his forehead with his hand, he scanned the area around him and decided that with imagination, the place could actually be quite charming. Now he could see that behind the medieval fortress lay the remains of a once habitable little town. To his right, there was a two storey house and ahead of him a concrete path which he followed as it widened out into a small square. An old drinking fountain was set behind the tunnel entrance and, to his left, George saw another house. He was fascinated by what he saw. Although the houses had stood from ancient times, they appeared to George to have a recently vacated air of modernity about them. A sudden breeze caught a weather beaten and sun swollen door which lay half open at the first house causing it to creak. George pushed it slightly further ajar, just enough to allow him to squeeze through the opening. Inside, a room overgrown by weeds lay, still partially furnished with a rotting chair and a few plant pots lying in a corner. Debris of bricks and wood were strewn across the floor, no doubt the result of wintry gales and rain storms. Moving on, George explored other houses, one sporting arched windows, once brightened up with a lick of bright red paint, the remnants of which were visible in patches on either side of an arched doorway. A tree burst forth through the balcony which ran the width of the facade, splitting into two parts. Excited and intrigued now, George continued along the pathway to the next building which appeared to house a number of shop fronts with shuttered double doors, others yawning emptily into the sunshine. On each side of the pathway there were houses in various states of decay but which eerily still revealed the signs of occupancy and domesticity. George's curiosity spurred him to closer investigation into some of the buildings. Warily, he stepped across their thresholds, fearing that any moment debris could come tumbling down upon him. To his amazement, he found cupboards lying open, baskets sat in corners as though waiting for the homeowner to fetch them in readiness for some daily chore. Clambering over bricks and wood, George explored buildings where supports sagged and timbers rotted. In one house, the stairs leaned almost drunkenly to one side and the colours of the decor were still in evidence. One or two of the buildings revealed large rooms with wide arches and huge fireplaces which George deduced were probably tavernas judging by the remnants of a few tables and chairs.

On and on he went, unable to pass any building he could enter and which might give him some clue as to the community who had lived here in the recent past. In one of the tavernas, he found the year 1940 etched into the wall beside pictures of small ships carved into the plaster. On occasions, George heard a rustle or a creak which caused him to jump. Strangely, he felt as though he were not completely alone as he conducted his solo tour of the island. So many of the houses looked almost as though they awaited the imminent return of their inhabitants. Several times George turned abruptly as he thought he heard a whisper in his ear or the brush of a limb next to his. 'You're being ridiculous - there's no-one here!' he told himself over and over, trying to re-assure himself that there was nothing to fear. 'Imagination, that's all!

Stepping out of the 'taverna' back into the warmth of the day, George proceeded along the path. At the end of the rows of buildings he came upon an area where there were heaps of stone of varying sizes, blocks and chippings, all discarded. Further in still, he came to a small neat building, well kept, which was clearly a church. The area around it was neat and he had the impression that the little building was probably well maintained. George was at once bewildered and enchanted by the little island. It held so many secrets from him. What were the 24 concrete basins built into the walls of a large purpose built building and interspersed with several fireplaces used for? Why was there such a contrast in the design of the buildings, many of which seemed built more recently of concrete, others of the oldest Venetian style. On and on he went, forgetting about time, exploring former homes with wild gardens offering splashes of bright colour as geraniums, roses and daisies sprung from the untended grounds backed by a profusion of green trees of varying types. Here and there, George stopped as some new enigma caught his attention. What, for example, was the building he now looked down upon, built well below the ground level on which he now stood? So many questions, yet no answers forthcoming from his companion. A poor tour guide he had turned out to be! George decided to follow the steps built next to the 'basement' building. It led him out through an archway to the beach from which he could look out once again to the sea and the towns and villages which overlooked the island in the distance. His eye was caught by a white lion carved into the archway together with an inscription he could barely make out. Every so often he started, the silence and eeriness of the place broken by a rustling somewhere, like someone hiding in the bushes trying not to be heard or seen, or the occasional breeze like a breath on his shoulder. George shivered. Were they the ghosts of a forgotten time or perhaps, the ghost of Jenna, following him wherever he went, destined to taunt him forever more?

Turning on his heels, George returned to the town. He was becoming more uneasy by the minute. There was an atmosphere about the place which was palpably ingrained within the walls of each building. He could easily be convinced that eyes watched him from behind the shuttered windows, that life continued on this otherwise seemingly deserted and derelict island. It was as though the place had been abandoned abruptly, so many clues as to former domesticity just left in situ. It reminded George of the story of the Marie Celeste, the ship which was found abandoned, meals still on the table, as though the sailors had been spirited away. The air of melancholy on the island pervaded his senses, making him deeply uneasy and agitated. There was evidence of extreme modernity, electrical fittings, tiles and, amongst all the antiquity a tall concrete building which appeared to be a block of flats. Another building nearby declared itself to be a hospital. But why would there be a hospital on such a small island when Crete was so nearby with its own medical facilities? Surely the community would just have travelled to the mainland for treatment?

Questions occupied George's mind as almost absently he approached a set of stairs which he followed off to the seaward side of the island and which climbed some distance. At the summit, yet another puzzle greeted George. A massive grid of 44 separate rectangular holes was set into the ground. As George ventured toward them, he could see they ran to a considerable depth but could not imagine for a moment what they would have been used for.

Suddenly, a cloud passed before the sun, and, just for a moment, goose pimples rose on George's skin as the hairs on his arms reacted to the sudden, yet inexplicable drop in temperature. He shivered. 'Time to go, I think', George decided. He looked at his watch. He had been here nearly two hours! Where was Charon? Why hadn't he called? Surely he couldn't still be beachcombing? George felt a chill deep in his bones now, and yet, he had never felt cold before since arriving in Crete. Even at 9 or 10 in the evening, it had remained warm. It was something to do with this place, he was sure of it. As he looked back at the grid, a dawning realisation of what they were crept over him like a shroud. As he understood, Charon's voice broke the chilling silence and confirmed his worst fears.

"Yes, you are quite right Georgios. They are graves of course and you are disturbing the dead of this island, of whom, I can assure you, there are many. They still walk the streets here, many trying to find a way out of their living hell. But you know that don't you? You've felt them. You've heard them. Alas, they can never succeed. They are my children you see. I brought them here, just as I brought you here. And now, you must stay here and join them.'

Horrified, George whirled around, expecting to find the wizened face of the old man directly behind him, for that, as sure as anything, was where his voice came from.

"Charon?" George called, uncertainly, belying the anger he felt at the man's childish pranks. "Where are you? Come out here and show yourself".

To his horror and disbelief however, George found he was alone and there was no-where Charon could easily have hidden. Besides, his voice had been right beside him. A sudden burst of terror and adrenalin coursed through George's veins. His heart thumped so hard that he could hear it beating in his ears. At that moment, he realised all was not well. All was not as it seemed. Charon had spoken to him, but he wasn't here. There was no doubt about it. Telepathy? Wild imagination? Either way, George had seen enough. He didn't want to be here any longer.

'Time to go, let's find Charon and get the hell out of here' he thought, trying to keep rational. He'd imagined the voice, that was all. It was just his imagination speaking to him. A place like this, well it wasn't unusual was it? Maybe he had a touch of sunstroke. That would be why he felt shivery. That combined with his accident of course. Anyone would be the same after the traumas he had suffered that day.

Turning on his heels, George quickly made his way back down the steps, half running, half stumbling, his heightened senses convincing him that urgency was required. In descending however, he felt a wave of dizziness overcome him and he found it difficult to focus his eyes on the route ahead of him. The steps melted into one sandy slope and he could no longer differentiate between them. There was sand, stones and bits of rubble littering the already crumbling steps and George felt his foot slip from under him. In a moment of panic, he knew he couldn't stop himself from falling. Surrendering to his inevitable fate, he tumbled downwards, stones and grit piercing and scraping his face and arms. Reaching the bottom finally, George lay there, his energy sapped, unable to cope any longer with the confusion of the day. All he wanted now was to sleep. He could no longer fight it as he allowed the familiar blackness to engulf him as for the second time that day, he lost consciousness and fell into a deep and blissfully untroubled sleep.

Stand, stay for just a moment
Hidden from the glare,
Feel the hideous strife and torment
That ever lingers here.
ISLAND OF TEARS William Ronald Hawkins

THE AWAKENING

George slowly regained consciousness some hours later, his eyes, as he did so, rebelling against the sunlight which was searing and harsh sending darts of pain through his skull. Unaware of his surroundings or his predicament, George's eyes fluttered rapidly, struggling to focus as he held them open for a few short moments. He lay still then, incapable of any further attempt at movement and caring nothing for whether he lived or died. The thudding agony in his head dulled his senses and he was completely unaware of the danger he now faced, lying as he did, under the unrelenting rays of the sun.

George had been troubled in his fitful slumbers by dreams, nightmares really, which took him back to his home in London and the events leading up to his arrival in Crete. In those nightmares, he had relived the first telephone call from Dave Hawkins on that fateful night when Jenna had died; when George had killed her. He had been out doing the rounds, delivering his customers' orders. It had been a fairly lucrative night for him and he felt good. He'd taken a couple of hits himself that night and he was buzzing. George had returned home after an evening out with his old friend Charlie Graham at one of London's more exclusive nightclubs. He felt he had earned a some time off. Returning to his flat he saw the answering machine flashing. It showed there were two messages. This was fairly unusual as most people tended to contact him on his mobile, however, that had been switched off most of the night. Only a couple of his older and most trusted customers had his home telephone number. His parents also preferred to use the house number for some reason, even though they knew they would rarely reach him on it. The advance of technology didn't suit them so well, he thought. Although he had been tempted to go straight to bed, curiosity won out and, almost despite himself, George had pressed the play button. The first caller had left no message and he heard, after a few moments of hesitation, the receiver clicking down. The machine beeped and the second message played.

"George, Dave Hawkins here". George was slightly taken aback; the Hawkins' didn't usually contact him at home and Dave's usually abrupt and aggressive tone sounded somehow breathless, urgent.

"Listen mate, I dunno what you sold me tonight but Jenna collapsed only seconds after taking it. I've had to give it over to the hospital. The poisons unit are checking it in case there's something not right with it. I've gotta go now. Call you back later".

On hearing Dave's message, George's heart sank to the bottom of his 'Jones the Bootmaker' designer shoes and a slight shiver of fear ran through him. This was something he hadn't anticipated. There could be questions over this and a direct link to him. Surely, he thought, this was just a case of Jenna's over indulgence catching up on her? George tried to reassure himself. Dave wouldn't want to give the police details of his dealer, surely? There was a code of honour between users and their dealers. The trust and confidence which was long established and necessary to that very special relationship would be destroyed. If word got out that Dave had snitched, well, no self respecting dealer would deal with them again and that just wasn't an option for chronic addicts such as he and his wife Jenna.

Just as George had lulled himself into a sense of security, it was then that the phone rang and Dave made his dramatic announcement, made all the more disturbing as he imparted his devastating news sobbing intermittently, his grief all too real and raw for George to acknowledge as possible from this usually unemotional rough diamond.

Throwing his belongings hurriedly into a bag, George tried to think. How many contaminated wraps had he sold that day?

What the hell was Amjit playing at? Was he some kind of amateur? George derided himself for having trusted his new supplier so quickly. At the end of the day, the trade was all about money and who knew what shit people would do to make a fast buck, get the next fix, or more likely, pay off some heavyweight somewhere higher in the chain.

Disembarking at Athens first and Heraklion later, it was with immense relief that George exited the airport. On arrival at Athens, he had been convinced that he would reach Passport Control and be immediately arrested and frog-marched unceremoniously to some God-forsaken prison like the one in Midnight Express. Trembling, he handed over his passport to the young officer whose inscrutable face regarded him with a look of either indifference or contempt. He held on to George's passport for what felt to him like an eternity, looking first at the photograph and then raising his dark brown eyes to scrutinise him. Up and down he looked, until finally, satisfied, he muttered dismissively, "Endaxi" and waved him on. George's heart was threatening to burst through his ribcage and, as he passed through, he released his breath, which he only now realised he had been holding. In utter relief, he exhaled every last ounce of air, deflating his lungs which, he felt had been close to exploding. One stiff drink later and George relaxed knowing that he would not have to repeat the tension of Passport Control at Heraklion as this was a domestic flight he was about to board. With a bit of luck, he thought, he could just disappear in Crete for a while. He hoped no-one would trace him there, although, he supposed, it wouldn't be too difficult if the flight records were checked. By that time though, he hoped he would have slipped into peaceful anonymity.

The flight from Athens proved to be a less than comfortable one for George, who hated flying at the best of times. It was an old 737 that shuddered, creaked and roared its way skywards. George's nerves, already raw, jangled with every new dip and turn that the aircraft took. In an attempt to distract himself from the flight he studied his fellow passengers who were mostly Greek citizens, obviously used to commuting between Crete and the mainland of Greece. The mix of people and contrasting styles of attire, which ranged from immaculately dressed women, chic and full of the mystique and poise lacking in most British women, business men in lightweight beige suits to wizened old men and women dressed in traditional working garb or widows' weeds, both astonished and absorbed George. The mix of people and contrasting styles brought together both the old and new world rarely apparent in many other European countries and non existent in Britain. The guttural and complex language, though familiar to George, still sounded foreign and exotic as it echoed around the cabin in the snatched conversations of the passengers. Everyone spoke animatedly, excitedly and, very loudly. Even the simplest of conversations, to the uninitiated could sound aggressive, as though an argument were ensuing. George thought it was like being in the middle of a busy market place with the stallholders competing against each other to be heard. It would not have surprised him had there been a cargo of livestock, chickens in crates and the like tucked under the seats of some of the more rustic travellers.

Gazing out at the dazzling blue sky and the few fluffy white clouds drifting by, George could almost have believed he was close to Heaven. Not, he guessed, that he would be going there in the event of a sudden demise. Thus far, the events of the last 24 hours had really hit home. Everything was surreal. He felt like an outsider watching the soap opera of his life. Perhaps it was the enormity of what had happened that made it so unreal. It was, he supposed, almost like watching the news and seeing images of some war torn region where the horrors are part of everyday life to the people involved, but because of the scale and remoteness of the thing, other people couldn't relate to it. So it was with George. He couldn't quite grasp that Jenna was gone, or how she could have suffered. She had just died, end of story. Perhaps the truth was though, that George didn't really care. The people whom he had affected (and those others who might also be affected) were distant, too far removed from him to worry about. It wasn't the done thing to develop relationships with customers and George felt no remorse for the lifestyle he had chosen or the goods he supplied; quite the contrary in fact - he despised the people he dealt with, especially those who were dependent on him for their drugs. They could be a real pain in the ass, especially when they didn't have the money to pay him and they wanted credit. Many of them, George knew, wanted to get off the treadmill they were on, but they were too weak. George, who had reduced, but never fully kicked his own habit prided himself on his strength and willpower in maintaining control over the drugs and never again letting them gain control over him. He had been there once and, if nothing else, many of his customers reminded him that it was a place he never wanted to go again. George had no sympathy for the weak. Everyone, he reasoned, had freedom of choice. No-one forced drugs down their throats, although the self righteous would have it that people like George did exactly that. No, George comforted himself and salved any conscience he might have had with the thought that he was merely a facilitator. After all, if he stopped dealing tomorrow, that wouldn't stop the drug trade would it? Someone else would be ready to fill his shoes. In any case, the more desperate his clients were, the more money he made, so he wasn't about to encourage any of his clients to stop buying was he? Their need was his security and they funded a very comfortable lifestyle for George. So what if one or two were lost along the way through their own excess? It would probably come as a blessed relief to them anyway. And so, in his way, George managed to rationalise and condone his conduct, easily persuading himself that he provided a valuable to service to a certain sector of the community. He was often indignant at the bad press dealers received.

George's reverie was interrupted by the captain's announcement, first in Greek, then in English, announcing the final descent into Heraklion. He breathed a sigh of relief although just for a moment, he wondered whether there would be any flashing blue lights on the tarmac waiting to pick him up as he landed. Alighting however from the aircraft George saw nothing untoward and as the heat washed over him and pervaded his bones and muscles he relaxed, feeling instantly lighter and happier.

On the bus journey to his father's birthplace, Aghios Nikolaos, George was struck by the vastness of the island and the contrasts in the landscape. Travelling on the main road which was the artery across Crete the bus passed through the rugged mountains of green and brown on either side. Glancing from the window George saw that the roadside bordered an abyss. One false move by the driver and they would fall into the ample valleys below which appeared to descend into the depths of the earth. Somewhat discomfited and vertiginous by the sight, George settled back into his seat and closed his eyes. He was so used to the grime and bustle of London and he rarely saw the countryside back home so he was taken by the beauty of the island with its strange configuration of high and majestic mountain peaks and wide open valleys. The colours were vibrant as the bus passed by towns and villages built high on the hillsides, startling white buildings contrasting against the darkness of the hills. Houses sprung up from the mountains with no apparent means of reaching them let alone building them. George, almost despite himself was intrigued by the mix of new towns and quaint traditional villages which time and modernity seemed to have passed by. His eye was caught by an old woman riding along the road on a donkey as though from a parallel existence to the technological advances of the 21st century. The panniers on the donkey were filled with brightly glowing orange globes picked from one of the nearby groves. The old woman was untroubled by the bus speeding past her and she continued, apparently unconcerned with removing herself from a bygone age, yet accepting that modernity and antiquity could co-exist without conflict on this beautiful island. And so it was that George, a man previously without sentimentality or appreciation for art or beauty, fell under the spell of Crete and found himself longing to be absorbed by the island, its tranquillity and beauty.At last, exhausted, George arrived at the bus station in Aghios Nikolaos and made his way down the hill into the bustling and cosmopolitan town, yet another contrast with the rustic villages through which he had just passed. He crossed the little bridge in the centre of town and reached the tourist office which he hoped would direct him to a nearby hotel. Stopping on the bridge for a moment, George looked at the many boats which were moored nearby. There were little fishing boats, probably belonging to the locals, others were yachts, perhaps owned by the wealthier holidaymakers, residents of the town, many of whom he guessed would be ex-pats. Other boats were clearly used for daytrippers as they boasted tours to various destinations, but mostly to a place which was to have the most profound effect on George's life, Spinalonga. He was so taken up with the whole atmosphere of Aghios Nikolaos in those few moments that George almost forgot why he was there. He chastised himself when reality once again struck. He was a fugitive; he was in Crete to save his skin, not to enjoy a carefree holiday like most of the other people here. Now wasn't the moment to get in the holiday mood. The most urgent thing now was to find somewhere to stay and try to find out whether or not the shit had yet hit the fan at home. With a renewed sense of purpose and a cloud of doom once again descending upon him, he crossed the bridge and entered the tourist office where a smartly dressed, attractive looking woman sat behind the desk.

"Kalispera", 'Good Evening', the woman greeted George.

Although polite, he found her rather dour and intimidating, coldly businesslike. Speaking Greek, he returned the woman's greeting.

"Can you tell me where I might find a hotel with a vacancy?"

"Do you wish to be in town or outside?" the woman asked.

"In town if possible". Although an out of town hotel might have protected him better from the outside world, George felt it was better to stay central for the time being, at least until he found his bearings. Besides, he was exhausted and longed to collapse into a deep, if not untroubled sleep.

The woman directed him to a couple of hotels nearby and he followed her directions towards the harbour where they were situated. He chose the nearest of the two and approached the concierge, a genial enough man who chatted about the extreme heat for the time of year as he unhurriedly completed the administrative details.

"May I see your passport please?" he asked George whose look of shock followed by a momentary delay compelled the man to explain further. "It's just a formality - nothing to worry about. I need it for our records you see".

Pulling himself together, realising how suspicious his behaviour must have appeared to the man, George responded quickly.

"Of course", he stuttered. "Sorry, I've had a long journey and I'm rather exhausted. Guess I was miles away for a minute". The man smiled and inclined his head in empathy as George pulled his passport from his inside pocket and crossed his fingers that the man didn't have a list of passport numbers circulated for fugitives from justice. He need not have worried though. The concierge didn't bat an eyelid or check any lists. He noted the number on his registration form and the business done, he picked up a key and led George to the apartment whilst chatting about the town, the best places to eat and visit. George was grateful to the man who made him feel more at ease and less alien in his new, albeit temporary abode.

After showing George how to work the air conditioning unit and the television, the concierge took his leave and George swung open the balcony doors to take in the view. It took his breath away. A slight breeze cooled him as he stared out at the sea which was the deepest shades of clear blue and green he had ever seen. The setting sun burned red and orange reflecting into the clear waters revealing a scene which George had only read about in books. Gazing across the harbour and the stretch of beach in front of him, George thought how fortunate the Cretans were to belong to such a jewel of the Aegean and wondered how on earth his father could have exchanged such a place for the grimy, gloomy streets of London.

****

George slept surprisingly well that night, strangely detached from his life back in London and all that had occurred recently. Since arriving on Crete, he had felt as though he were living in a parallel universe, a completely different world from anything which he had known previously. He felt far removed from reality and somehow invincible, protected and comforted as he was by the calming atmosphere of the island he now inhabited.

He rose just after 8.00 a.m., refreshed and clear headed. The room was cool from the air conditioning and George eagerly greeted the day as he threw back the curtains and the doors leading to the balcony. The brightness of the sun dazzled him and the heat cosseted him as through wrapping him in a thick blanket of warmth. His mood was lifted by the sunshine as it cast its sheen of optimism over the bleakest of situations. He realised, as his stomach grumbled that he was ravenous and quickly threw on a T-shirt and lightweight trousers. In his hasty departure from London he realised he had packed clothes which were totally unsuitable for the climate here in Crete. He resolved to find some new clothes after breakfast which he ate heartily and eagerly in the restaurant downstairs.

Aghios Nikolaos, even at this hour was already bustling with early morning shoppers, mostly locals, the tourists not yet having surfaced. George spent a carefree day wandering up and down the two shady and tree lined avenues, Koundourou Roussou and 28 Octovriou, which were the main shopping streets of the town and admired the many jewellery shops selling their unique and exquisite pieces. In and out the tourist shops he went, picking up shorts, t-shirts and cheap but quality leather belts. He delighted in the colours, the atmosphere and the friendly, laid back people. He liked the fact that time seemed to have little meaning in Crete, people weren't weighed down by the same self imposed constraints and pressures that burdened Western Europeans, perhaps the climate and family values here contributing to the more laisser-faire, less time starved lifestyles. George felt he could fit in with this way of life. The mystique and sheer breathtaking beauty of the island entranced him.

All thoughts of home and the traumatic events of the previous days had left George as he meandered contentedly along the streets of Aghios. That was until he passed the newspaper rack containing papers from all over Europe, including Britain. The familiar red tops taunted him, the gravitas of the broadsheets, The Telegraph, The Times, and The Independent threatened him. His heart raced and although he wanted - desperately wanted to resist, nevertheless he was compelled to stretch out his hand which shook with trepidation to grasp a copy of the nearest paper which happened to be the Daily Mail. He looked at the date expecting it to be a couple of days old but was surprised to see it bore today's date. It was printed in Greece. Obviously since his last holidays abroad computer and e-mail technology had advanced to allow same day production of newspapers from abroad. He glanced at the headline between half closed lids, afraid that if he opened his eyes fully, he might see something which he would rather avoid. George breathed an audible sigh of relief when he saw that the front page was taken up with the disappearance of two children in Cambridge. Taking courage from this, he decided to buy the paper. After all, he thought, if there was anything in there about him, he ought to know about it. Reluctant to possibly ruin an otherwise perfect day by checking it then, he placed it in a carrier bag along with his other purchases and continued his leisurely exploration of the town, the harbour and the small beach, occasionally stopping at one of the many cafes for a cool drink. All the time though, it was as though the newspaper in his bag were taunting him, "Read me! Read me!" a small voice in his head kept urging. George knew that the newspaper could tell him which way his life was heading but determinedly, he resisted the nagging urge to rip it from the bag, so intent was he that day not to allow anything to interfere with his sense of wellbeing. As he sat in the sunshine, overlooking the calm, translucent sea, George almost gave in however, believing, just for a moment that there would be no gathering storm to deal with back home. He almost persuaded himself that in this haven of peace where trauma and drama seemed anathema, that nothing could touch him.

Finally, after a solitary meal, he anaesthetised himself with a good few drinks on top of the half carafe of local wine he had polished off with dinner and headed back to the apartments. Although it was only just after nine, he was pleasantly tired. Meandering somewhat unsteadily through the reception area, the concierge nodded a friendly 'kalenichta', 'Goodnight' which George returned with a wave as he doggedly tackled the polished marble stairs to his room. Through his mildly drunken haze and his previous feeling of well being, his nerves once again gripped him causing a sudden urge to run to the bathroom. The newspaper still beckoned him, haunted him, and he knew he couldn't put off the moment much longer. Still though, he delayed just long enough to switch on the television which offered a limited number of SKY channels. To his horror as he pressed the remote control flicking from one channel to another, the BBC World News burst forth and, like a rabbit in the headlights, George was transfixed by the words and images which assaulted his eyes and ears. For there, emblazoned for all to see, was his face between a photograph of his father and another of Jenna Hawkins linking them all in a macabre triptych as the story back home unfolded. George's blood ran cold and he collapsed onto the chair to watch in horror as the newsreader impassively reported the details of Jenna's death, single-handedly destroying all hope that things would die down quietly.

"It is believed that George Fitrakis, son of Dmitri Fitrakis, Head of the Aegean Bank in London was responsible for the distribution of the contaminated cocaine which has now killed three people, Jenna Hawkins, Kevin Mahoney and Edward Bleasdale. Two others, Sarah Barnett and Terry Maynard are both critically ill in hospital". All were known heavy users of cocaine and all are linked by the one common denominator, George Fitrakis who regularly supplied them all. Police are searching for Fitrakis who has not been seen at his home in the last 24 hours and an appeal has been launched for information as to his whereabouts..."

The camera switched from the studio to an outside broadcast showing a house which was all too familiar to the now trembling George. It was surrounded by reporters who clamoured around a man trying to fight his way through the crowd, maintaining a quiet dignity. It took only a few moments for the true horror of the scene to sink in, for there was George's father, microphone thrust in his face, questions being fired at him from all angles.

"Do you have any comment to make about your son's alleged involvement in the death of these people, Mr Fitrakis?"

"Were you aware that your son was a principal dealer in cocaine, Mr Fitrakis?"

"Do you know where your son is at this time?"

George, though never close to his father felt the first pangs of guilt and shame as he watched the assassination of his family's reputation so proudly held by his parents. George wished that by just switching off the television, he could switch off the reality of what was happening. Though he didn't want to see or hear any more, he was captivated, unable to move from the screen.

Behind his father were two policemen who fended off the reporters and escorted him to a waiting vehicle as though he, and not his son, were the criminal. George felt an unusual pang of compassion for the man who had been such a distant, yet constant part of his life. Dmitri Fitrakis looked pale, drawn and utterly defeated. He hung his head in shame, taking on the mantle of guilt which his son had failed to display thus far. Despite the barrage of questions, he made no comment as he passed through the crowd, the shame and degradation he obviously felt evident in his posture, his Greek pride dealt a fatal blow. The camera switched again to the reporter.

"Mr Fitrakis has declined to comment about the allegations concerning his son but he is being questioned as to the possible whereabouts of George Fitrakis. To date, no clue has been given as to where he may be but police are now checking ports and airports as they suspect he may have left the country. For a man so frequently in the public eye, this must be a devastating blow to Dmitri Fitrakis. Now, back to the studio...."

George could watch no more. He had broken out in a cold sweat and nausea welled up inside him. He rushed to the bathroom where he was violently sick, the alcohol making his head spin. Staggering back to the bedroom, he slumped miserably on the bed, his head clutched in his hands he wept uncontrollably. He hadn't thought of the consequences to his mother and father. He had only thought of himself. Maybe he should end it all now?

How could he possibly go on after this? How could he face his family and friends ever again?

"Oh God, he groaned, what will I face when I'm caught? Years in prison for murder, at best manslaughter". His mind worked on - he would be subject to all sorts of horrors and indignities from his fellow inmates. He shivered, despite the heat of the room. He thought of his poor parents weighed down, ruined by the shame he had brought upon them. Unable to sit still as reality and panic sank in over the ruins of his life, George paced up and down the room for what seemed like hours, turning the latest events over in his mind, trying to find a way around them. Maybe he could give himself up, deny it was anything to do with him. After all, it was really all Amjit's fault wasn't it? George hadn't adulterated the cocaine. He knew better than to use lethal chemicals as a mix. The odd caffeine tablet sometimes, but that was harmless. He could take the rap as the supplier but maybe he could divert the real blame elsewhere. It wouldn't be good, but maybe things would be better for him that way.

If George had almost come to a moral decision at that moment, it quickly passed. He knew he couldn't face the music. He felt bad, really bad for his folks but going back wasn't going to help them or him. No. He had to disappear. He would have to get out of town. With so many Brits around he knew he was on borrowed time. Any minute there could be a knock on his door. He had to go somewhere off the beaten track, some quiet village where maybe he could just hide away. He would change his look, get his hair cut very short, shaved maybe. There was a barber in town he could visit first thing next morning. George's mind reeled, replaying every past scenario and every future plan like a video tape on constant loop until finally he gave way to exhaustion. He didn't have the energy to go anywhere right now and he drifted off into a troubled sleep, his plan to head into some remote place where he would re-invent himself and create a simple, hermetic life, at least until the heat was off.

George awoke at around six the following morning, bathed in sweat after an uneasy sleep which had been haunted by images of Jenna Hawkins and others, their faces contorted with pain, accusing him, chastening him for killing them. His subconscious acknowledged that which he had refused to contemplate in his waking hours. He was a murderer.

Flinging his few belongings into a holdall, George slipped an envelope under the Concierge's door which contained enough euros to pay his bill. He followed the route out of Aghios towards Elounda. There was little happening at that time, just a few shops and street traders beginning to set out their stalls for the day and the cafes setting up tables and parasols in readiness for the early birds who would be seeking breakfast. The barber had been open early and George had followed through on his plan for a drastic haircut. He hardly recognised himself as he had looked at the mirror, his foppish dark hair now lying in a heap on the floor.

On the road out of town, George had passed a shop which hired out scooters. Several were lined up on the street outside. Hesitating a moment, George decided to take the plunge on some transport. He crossed his fingers and toes as he completed the hire paperwork and handed over his licence. Luckily for him, the guy behind the desk could not have been less interested as he gave the licence a cursory glance and noted the details on the form. George handed over enough cash to cover a week's hire, but, as he did so, he knew he would not be back in town to return it. He could take no chances now and he had no compunction about abandoning the bike if necessary.

Speeding along the carriageway towards Elounda, George climbed higher and higher into the hillside above the dazzling sea and the menacing rocks below him. He was grateful for the breeze as he sped along, his confidence growing as climbed ever higher, bending at ever more acute angles as he negotiated the hairpin bends. Despite his troubles, George was exhilarated by the freedom of the journey and breathtaking scenery around and below him. Reaching the summit of the climb, he stopped at the roadside for a moment, the sun's reflection sparkling like diamonds in a sea of deepest blue. The mountains around the island rose majestically as though to protect the delicate villages inside their sentinel walls.

Next came the moment when George's life took on a whole new dimension following his fateful decision to stop for a drink at the cafe. His thirst quenched, he had sped off as the rear wheel of the scooter spun and slipped on the dusty road. He was momentarily overcome by vertigo as the speed and the height at which he was travelling confused his senses. Dizzy now, and light headed, his earlier confidence ebbed away and instinctively he tried to slow down. For one sickening moment, which was to change his life forever, he lost control of the bike as it slipped out from under him, the angle of the wheels becoming ever more acute so that he was travelling, at speed, low to the ground, desperately trying to right himself and regain control. It was no use though. The bike finally skidded away from him and he was thrown over the crash barrier, part bouncing, part rolling down into the rocky abyss below. His body took a severe battering, his clothes and skin were torn as he made his ungainly descent. George could do nothing except surrender himself to his fate, which was surely death.

****

Except of course, George didn't die. He'd met Charon who had abandoned him on this God forsaken deserted island and here he lay, jumbled thoughts flooding through his mind. Charon's face with its strange knowing smile haunted his mental meandering and as he came to, he could not be sure whether the man was real or whether he had simply been a product of his imagination. In his mind, he heard Charon's voice, uttering words which though they resounded in his memory, he could not recollect as having come from the man himself.

"Soon you will understand a great deal more about your life and purpose Kyrie. You will have cause and time now to contemplate the ills and joys of your existence and you will face choices which only a considered man can make wisely. Celebrate this, for through the suffering you will experience the mysteries that the ancient Gods can manifest and receive the knowledge you are lacking to guide you through your life."

The fog in George's mind was gradually clearing and it struck him how strange the man's words were and how odd that they were so clearly remembered. It was almost as though a voice had spoken them in his ear. Questions ran through George's mind. "Where the hell is Charon now? He can't have left me on this deserted island, can he? The island was hardly big enough for George to have become lost or hidden from view of the old sailor and surely the old man couldn't have just forgotten his erstwhile passenger and left him here?

Braving the sunlight to open his eyes fully, George sat up and despite his fear and confusion his soul was cheered and his spirit warmed as he gazed upwards into the brilliant azure sky. He relished the kiss of the sun's rays which again gave him comfort. He was amazed once more by the colour and magnificence that only the sunshine could paint on the dreariest of landscapes. His moment of pleasure was short lived however as he was distracted by the sound of something shuffling nearby and a moment of fear gripped him. Seconds later, the sun was covered by a rare cloud and his surroundings became gloomy and alien once more. George remained very still, his hearing strained for any further signs of movement. He tried to tell himself the movement had merely been something blowing in the breeze - a door or a window from one of the derelict buildings brushing into an overhanging tree perhaps. His senses however were telling him otherwise. He felt that there was a presence near, a living thing, as yet unidentified, its shape and form indistinguishable merely by the sounds it made. George felt wired. His heart was thudding as every instinct alerted him to the proximity of something unnerving. Perhaps there was some sort of wild animal indigenous to the island? There were thousands of wild cats in Greece. What if there were big overgrown wildcats just lurking in the surrounding foliage? George doubted he had the strength to fend off any creatures which might prey on him right now. Hardly daring to breathe, let alone move, he listened intently. After what felt like an eternity, he relaxed a little, relieved that there had been no repetition of the sound. He was tempted to call out. Perhaps it was Charon. But, what if it hadn't been the old sailor? What if it was something else entirely? Strangely, George perceived a discernible change in the atmosphere of his surroundings. In contrast to the cheery brilliance which the sun, only moments ago had created, there was a distinct feeling of, well, what he could only describe as, sadness, oppression even. Within moments, he felt as though every human emotion was mixing and compressing into one suffocating space, threatening to tear his senses apart. What was going on here? George wanted to run, get as far away from here as possible but a kind of paralysis accompanied his fear and despite the heat, a chill filled his bones. In any case, where would he run to? He was on a small island for God's sake! He wouldn't exactly be difficult to find here, would he? Short of jumping into the sea, an equally terrifying prospect as George did not swim well, there was nowhere to go.

Again, there was that shuffling sound. George jerked his head to the right and squinted into the foliage. This time he was certain that something, or someone was lurking out of sight, somewhere just on the periphery of his vision. His heart thumped against his rib cage as a shadow fell over him and, as it approached, the umbrous shape assaulted his olfactory and auditory senses with a strange, inhuman 'snuffling' noise accompanied by an indescribable smell of decay and putrefaction.

Not yet having moved from his resting place, George now attempted to get up, intending to flee. His body, stiff and dehydrated complained bitterly at the disturbance however and, his head thumping to a crescendo, he fell back down and eased himself up more slowly this time, aches and stiffness inhibiting every move. The shadow had retreated into its hiding place, perhaps more afraid of George than he was of it. Seizing the moment, George stumbled along a few metres and gasped as he surveyed the surroundings. Although the place was vaguely familiar from his first encounter yesterday, there was a difference both in the look of the place and indeed, in the atmosphere. George recognised the intrinsic detail of the place, but what now confronted him both mystified and terrified him. The houses, though not in pristine condition by modern standards, had become, well, habitable! Gone were the crumbling artefacts, sad, but somehow majestic in their ancient dereliction. In their place were whole buildings, imbued with colour and life, the doors and windows painted in bright, cheerful hues of blue, green and red. The place looked no different to any other traditional Cretan village.

George rubbed his eyes, as if by doing so, the scene before him would revert to that which he remembered on his arrival. How on earth, he thought, was this possible? Who had come here overnight and given the entire island a makeover? Surely he was concussed? Or worse? Perhaps, he thought, he was hallucinating, going mad even? Or perhaps the more rational explanation was that his memory wasn't serving him well and he had simply stumbled to a different, and as yet, unseen part of the island? Perhaps he was suffering from amnesia, unable to recall what he had actually seen yesterday. His mind worked on rapidly, trying to find some sort of explanation for this. Maybe, he thought, this was just some chimera devised by his own imagination. A lucid dream, perhaps, induced and intensified by the injury he had sustained in the accident? He closed his eyes, convinced he had seen a mirage and truly wanting to believe it. When he re-opened them however, all was as it had been only moments before.

George was bemused and the first stirrings of terror gripped him. The chill in his bones intensified, the hairs on his arms standing to attention belying the intense heat emanating from the morning sun.

He thought back to his arrival on Spinalonga. There was no doubt about it, the island had definitely been deserted and in ruins when he arrived. He recalled his exploration as he waited for Charon. He had passed through the gloomy tunnel which formed the entrance to the fortress and the town. It had felt eerie, the shadows and claustrophobic walls closing around him like a vice for the few moments it had taken him to reach the end. Walking through that structure he had become instinctively aware that it held many ancient secrets and history he could only guess at. He recalled walking into the derelict houses, the abandoned detritus of the last inhabitants leaving the mark of a long forgotten community, the trees growing through the foundations and roofs of the houses. There was nothing of this here now though.

George's thoughts were interrupted once more by the same snuffling sound behind him. It felt nearer this time, as though gathering courage from his obvious debility and weakness. George felt as though some kind of primordial sixth sense was awakening within him, alertness and awareness tingling through his body like an electric current. Like a dog with hackles raised, he took courage and turned to face whatever creature had made him his quarry. George felt the blood drain from his face and his bowels loosening as his eyes fell on the creature before him which could only have been conjured in his worst nightmares. What confronted him was beyond imagination. Accompanying the creature's hideous appearance was a stench, vile, indescribable and asphyxiating. It was the odour of death worsened by the fact that the creature from which it emanated was still alive, its living flesh in the process of putrefaction and decay. George's empty stomach lurched in violent retaliation at the sight and smell which confronted him. Whoever or whatever this was would not, George thought somewhat hysterically, be out of place in Michael Jackson's "Thriller" video. George was overwrought and this latest shock had overwhelmed him so that his imagination was running wild. It was only a moment later that he properly focused on his companion and it became clear from the shape and build that this was a human male. From the ravaged features however, it was difficult to tell. In truth, George found this revelation to be more horrifying - the fact that a person's body could suffer such corruption and still continue to live. It seemed like the cruellest of tortures. Forcing himself to look, George scrutinised the man whose face, neck and arms were covered with nodules and suppurating sores, the skin peculiarly whitened in parts. The nose was partially eaten away and George was glad he was far enough away not to be able to look beyond into the dark gleaming cavern beyond. One of the man's eyes was ulcerated and sightless, a mixture of milky white and a painful red, visceral mess. Both of his feet, encased in bandages and some kind of protective sock were misshapen resembling a pair of stumps at the end of his legs rather than feet. Both hands were whitened and drawn into claws, much as one might see on an arthritis sufferer only this was much, much worse; George could now see that the fingers were actually worn away. He must have studied every detail of the man in those few short moments, horror giving way to disgust and then, a rare moment of compassion as George looked into his companion's good eye and saw the spark of humanity trapped in that pitiful body. In that one moment, George perceived that through the man's most terrible suffering, there was huge spirit and determination that despite his condition, the will to live was undoubtedly the strongest and most powerful driving force.

As George gaped, the man barely moved. It occurred to him then that in his own able-bodied state, he was probably more frightening and more of a potential threat to this poor ravaged creature than he was to George. He found his tongue and spoke in Greek.

"Yassas", 'hello', he ventured with what he hoped was a friendly smile.

The man returned the greeting and his mouth stretched a little across his cracked and knobbled face in an attempt to return the warmth of a smile.

"Mi lene George", he said, then, "Georgio" remembering to give his name the Greek emphasis. The man inclined his head in acknowledgement he understood and said that his name was Niko. Small talk was difficult from that moment on. George didn't want to launch into a tirade of questions as to what was ailing the man, nor did he feel he could question him about the island which seemed to have its own dynamic in overnight regeneration. Despite his growing empathy for the man, George was unable to dispel his earlier revulsion at his repugnant appearance. At that moment, perhaps through hunger, shock or just the after effects of his own accident, dizziness and weakness overcame George and he stumbled forward. As he did so, the two clawed hands extended towards him solicitously posed to prevent him from falling. Although he appreciated the gesture, nevertheless, George could not bear the thought of those hands touching his flesh and he retreated involuntarily from the possibility of those grossly disfigured limbs making contact with his own. Niko took a step backwards, as though used to such reaction, in reassurance that he understood George's reluctance to engage in physical contact. He held his hands up in a signal that he would advance no further nor attempt to touch George again. In that moment,

George felt a rare connection with another human being and he felt ashamed at his rejection of the man's offer of help. Though he was discomfited by it, he could not help but shun Niko's help, not least because the closer he came to George, the stronger the stench which emanated from became in the enveloping and strengthening heat of the day.

"Sit down. I will bring help. You are unwell. There are people here who can tend to you", Niko gestured for George to sit on a grassy mound. Once satisfied that he was comfortable, he turned in the direction of the town calling back to say "You wait there. Everything will be fine." Niko shuffled painfully away, his centre of balance clearly impaired by the loss of at least part of one or both of his feet.

George felt exhausted; emotionally drained. There had been no sign of life when he arrived on the island, so where had these people been yesterday? George's instinct was to run, hide, find a boat, anything - just get away from this madness. His body however was not co-operating and he could do no more than sit and wonder about his fate. As he waited for the others whom Niko had gone off to find, his mind conjured up wild images. Was he about to be surrounded by visual horrors worthy of a Goya painting? He tried to calm himself and guiltily remembered that the man had meant him no harm. And yet, what foul disease had caused such physical degradation and, more to the point, was it infectious? The sound of approaching footfalls interrupted George's increasingly colourful imaginings and, from the pathway, he could see a man hurrying towards him. To his immense relief, George saw that this man's features were unmarred and his movement unhampered by any physical defect. In fact, this was a handsome man, typically Greek in his looks, dark in both his hair and skin. He wore black trousers and a cool white shirt. He approached George and smiled, almost deferentially and with kindness. He extended his hand in greeting.

"Ti kanis?" 'How are you', he asked.

"A little confused, tired. I had a bad accident yesterday you see. I took a bit of a battering. I think the effects are taking their toll on me".

"Your Greek is fluent Kyrie, but, I hear a slight accent. Where are you from?"

"From London. I'm visiting Crete".

"Ah - Anglika! We do not often have new residents from other countries!"

"New resident?" George laughed uncertainly. "No, you don't understand. I haven't come to stay here. I was just brought over to Spinalonga as a tourist. I understood a lot of English and other Europeans came over here regularly". The man looked puzzled, but he merely smiled and nodded politely as George continued. "A boatman from Elounda brought me over yesterday. Silly really, but I must have fallen asleep and he left without me. He was an old man. Perhaps he forgot he had a passenger with him or maybe he just couldn't find me ... who knows?" George shook his head in wonder. It sounded a strange tale even to himself. What this man must be thinking, he really couldn't tell.

The other man's handsome features creased in consternation as he replied, a note of incredulity in his voice, "Kyrie, no-one comes to Spinalonga as a tourist. No-one chooses to come to Spinalonga. I think your accident and exhaustion must be playing tricks with your mind".

"No. That's what happened - really. The funny thing is though, that when I arrived, everything was different".

The man knelt down next to George, a look of concern on his face.

"What do you mean, different, Kyrie?"

"Well, it sounds strange, I know, but perhaps I came in at a different part of the island. The place was deserted apart from me and the old sailor. The house, they were, well, falling down;

derelict. I must have walked further than I thought and somehow missed the inhabited part of the island".

The other man scrutinised George as though trying to read from his face whether he was joking, lying or just plain mad.

"No Kyrie. The whole island is inhabited. It is not very big. You could not have missed the community here. As for the houses, well they are not in the greatest of repair but we have been working to make them more habitable for some time. There are no derelict buildings here now".

"That's impossible" George retorted with some indignation at the man's clear disbelief and worse, pity. The man chose not to inflame the situation further by pursuing the matter and quickly changed the subject.

"Well, now, let me tell you first, my name. I am Manolis Papadopolous and you are...?

"George" he responded for the second time that day and once again, remembering he was in Greece, he corrected himself, "Georgio Fitrakis".

"Well Georgio. I am pleased to make your acquaintance. Now, may I look at your injuries? I see you have a bad cut to your head and some bruising. I think it is important we get you to the sanatorium quickly to check if they have caused any complications to your condition".

George gave an uncertain but polite laugh.

"Oh, I don't think my injury is any more complicated than a bad cut, a rather bad headache and possibly a bit of concussion, but I'd certainly appreciate it if you could help me get cleaned up. Perhaps then you could help me to make arrangements to get off this damned island and back to some normality".

Manolis frowned but said nothing. George felt a little irritation at the man's somehow concerned acquiescence. He felt he was being humoured. Manolis stood up and grasping George's arm he steadied him as George struggled to stand up. He felt the blood drain from his head as he rose once more and the two men remained still for a few moments until George felt able to move.

"Ready now?" Manolis asked kindly. George lifted his head and took a deep breath.

"Yes, I think so. I think I've been lying in the sun too long and I'm dehydrated. I feel sick and my head is thumping". Manolis inclined his head acknowledging George's explanation.

"Come", he said. "We must get you to the sanatorium at once. It is important to make sure open wounds are treated properly, especially here", he finished, somewhat enigmatically.

George's heart soared. Surely there isn't a sanatorium here on this little island? They must be going back to the mainland. He smiled at Manolis in relief.

"You have a boat?" he asked hopefully. "To get us to the mainland? Where is the sanatorium? Elounda or Aghios?" Manolis merely shook his head.

"No Kyrie, we have our own medical facilities here on Spinalonga"

"Here?" George exclaimed. "But how can that be? Yesterday this island was nothing but a ghost town! There was nothing here except a pile of ruins! How could I have missed a Sanatorium?"

Manolis, unable to supply the answer to this strange, confused man's questions merely shook his head, helplessly.

"I think, Kyrie, your health is in a more serious state than you think". With Manolis' help, George followed the pathway he had walked along only yesterday.

"I'm beginning to think you might be right Manolis. The man who found me, Nikos, he seemed to be rotting away. He frightened the living daylights out of me. I even thought there might be more who would come for me and take me away to some living hell".

Manolis stopped for a moment and turned to George.

"Nikos is a good man, but, as you saw, he is seriously ill. He came and told me that he had found you and you were in need of help. It was dark when you ran off last night and we felt it better to wait until this morning to look for you. We could not afford injury to anyone else in the darkness". Manolis scrutinised George's face for any sign that he recognised the truth of his words. George however looked bemused. He didn't know what the man was talking about. He had no recollection of any events of the previous night as he described them.

"What are you talking about? I didn't run off. Didn't you hear me earlier? There was no-one to run from when I arrived as well you must know". Exasperation and just a little fear were manifesting itself as aggression towards George's companion.

Patiently Manolis persisted with his version of events.

"Georgio, you are mistaken", he said gently. "You have come here because you are the same as the other poor souls on this island. You are a very sick man and sometimes that can make a man behave strangely, become delusional temporarily. Maybe you are even in denial about what is happening to you. It would be understandable my friend. Try not to get yourself so distressed. You must stay calm and not deplete your energy. I am here to help you. Things will be better soon now you are here".

George was incredulous at what he was hearing. He wasn't sick. He hadn't run off from anyone into the night. And yet, this man, Manolis seemed to genuinely believe the tale he was telling. The two men carried on walking, all the time George wondering if he was going mad. He was too exhausted to protest or think any more about it for now though. Time would sort out the obvious misunderstanding and what George needed now was food, water and some rest. Once that was sorted, he could work out what the hell was going on here.

As they passed through the little town though, one thing was for sure and this terrified George. His recollection of the streets they passed through was entirely different to that which he now saw. To his extreme dismay, George recognised the town he had passed through the day before except the row of derelict buildings had now been completely transformed into well kept houses and shops on either side. Bursts of colour shone out from the open shutters like flags flown in pride. Glorious flowers in huge earthenware pots adorned the doorways and steps of the houses. Though he saw no-one, it was clear the village was inhabited, signs of life all around. Washing hung out on the balconies, gardens were lovingly tended. Chairs sat outside the houses, beautiful pieces of gleaming white lace and colourful embroidered linen in the process of hand manufacture lay on them. Manolis explained that it was siesta time and that most people remained in the shade for a few hours whilst the sun was at its hottest. As they passed one house however, a man of indeterminate age sat on a chair outside and with the familiar mixture of revulsion and pity he had felt for Nikos, George glanced at what could only be described as the living remains of this poor individual whose face and ears had been eaten away by his pernicious affliction. Worse though, both of his arms and one of his legs had, George presumed, been amputated to slow the progress of what must be a horrific and excruciating death.

The rising horror George felt was building to hysteria and he asked Manolis about the man they had passed and what it was that afflicted him and Nikos. Manolis stopped and turned to George, raising his gaze to look him in the eye.

"My friend, you really do not remember why you are here?" George, frowning deeply, shook his head.

"No - I've already told you. Charon told me..."

"Charon?!" Manolis cut George off in mid sentence.

"Yes. He's the man who brought me here on his boat yesterday".

Manolis said nothing but simply looked at George for a long moment, deep sorrow reflecting in his eyes.

"Georgio, I suppose, in a way, you are right about Charon bringing you here, but, I think you are mixing reality with fantasy. It is an understandable delusion, a metaphor for your situation perhaps. You did not cross the water alone yesterday though Kyrie. You came on the weekly boat with the new intake. Now, let us hurry. I fear you may have a bad infection which is causing your to be delirious".

George didn't know what to say. How could he continue to have a conversation with this man whose version of events were so at odds with his own? It was pointless but, unable to bear it any longer he could not help but ask more.

"Forgive me if I'm being slow, but what intake? What are you talking about? George looked into Manolis' earnest gaze, laughter lines creasing his eyes, but no laughter there now.

"The new intake of patients, Georgio. Lepers. Like you. You are a leper Georgio and now you are a patient on the colony, the community of Spinalonga".

It was all too much for George. His mind was overloaded. The man was a fantasist clearly. He could not understand why he was being lied to in such a fashion. This was an elaborate set up. It had to be. What other explanation could there be? Panic, fear, and confusion all led to George's mind closing down as Manolis' words sank in. Once again, he felt the sweet relief as blackness enveloped him.

"So this is Spinalonga
A fortress protected from all foe
But who would want to live here
Amidst a Leper's woe?
ISLAND OF TEARS
William Ronald Hawkins

ISLE OF THE DAMNED

George awoke to find himself lying on a bed in a small room. Recollection of the events a few hours earlier hit him like a blow and he sat bolt upright in the bed taking in the details of the room, dazed and confused. He could only hope that he had hallucinated or dreamt up the whole thing, that all would be back to normal and soon he would find himself back in Crete.

The room was unfamiliar, but it was clear to George that he had been well cared for. He was wearing a white clinical gown and he presumed that he had been brought to the sanatorium. Absently touching his head, George found a dressing had been applied to the injury he had sustained in the scooter accident.

If nothing else, George felt more rested on this awakening, clearer in his thoughts now that he was out of the sun and had spent some time in relative comfort. He was resolute. Unable to accept any alternative explanation, George decided that everything that had happened to him prior to waking up now, in this room, had to have been either the product of wildly imaginative dreaming or simply the result of his head injury. He thought back to Manolis' last words to him. Leprosy indeed! Whilst George's knowledge of the disease was limited, he didn't think the disease was common in the modern world. It was a disease from Biblical times wasn't it? Maybe still around a bit in darkest Africa. How on earth could Manolis have believed he had leprosy? But then, how could he explain away Nikos and the other man he had seen on his way to the sanatorium? Surely though, if it was a big problem in Greece, the authorities would make it a big thing for tourists to know about. It was crazy. Ridiculous! It had to be an overactive imagination. It was obviously linked to the accident. He must have been more injured than he knew but George was mystified as to where on earth his mind could have dredged up such obscure imaginings. The mind, he thought was a fascinating but very frightening organ if it could do all this to a person. Having rationalised the situation in his own mind, he felt confident now that things would get sorted out and a simple explanation would be offered for all this.

Stretching luxuriously, George yawned, feeling more secure and comforted by his conclusion. Of course, he hadn't had any cocaine for days. That could be contributing very heavily to his delusions. Contemplating the events of the previous hours, George concluded that they must have indeed brought him back to Elounda. Maybe Charon had never really taken him to Spinalonga. Maybe the whole thing was just a dream, none of it real.

Swinging his legs off the bed, George treated himself to another long stretch as he stood up. He noticed a little window which was shuttered and closed, no doubt to darken and cool the room. Throwing back the shutters, convinced that he would see the bustling town of Elounda with its host of neon lit tavernas and cafes or its impressive harbour teeming with the mix of small work boats and rich man's yachts. He was to be disappointed however as he looked out at the view. Instead of the tourist haven he had convinced himself awaited him he looked out upon the pathway, the same one which he had walked along with Manolis - when? Was it today or yesterday? Perhaps it was even longer. George had no way of knowing how long in fact he had lain in this room. His spirits plummeted. He still refused to believe that any of this was real. How long though could a lucid dream or nightmare go on? He slumped miserably back onto the bed and rested his head in his hands, the familiar feelings of despair and utter confusion descending once more. Things just seemed to go from bad to worse. How could he be sitting in a hospital on an island that had been nothing more than a derelict ghost town when he arrived? It made no sense, but then, nothing did any more. Lifting his head, George looked around the room for any clues. It was small and sparsely furnished. The walls were typically whitewashed and a couple of cheerful scenic pictures, all whitewashed buildings with blue domes, bright flowers and deep blue sea adorned them. On the wall directly in front of the bed hung a crucifix and one of the brightly coloured, silver and gold gilded icons of Jesus Christ, typical of Greek Orthodoxy, took pride of place. He was not generally a religious man (he would have been drummed out of any Church years ago, he thought) but nevertheless, he found himself looking at the icon and praying that if there was a God or a Jesus Christ out there that they please help him to find his senses again and get him out of this. Despairing, he felt he could take no more.

In truth, George had never experienced such fear as he now felt. Is this what true madness was like? Being trapped in a mind that could play tricks and place you in unimaginable situations? Was this what they meant by eternal damnation? At least when you could understand the thing that you most feared, you could deal with it but how could you do so when even reality appeared to have deserted you? George felt he was well and truly caught in an episode of the "Twilight Zone", or a Stephen King horror. If only he had the talent to write, he thought, this would make a great novel.

Perhaps the worst thing about all this was that the only rational explanation could be that there was something seriously wrong with him. Either, George thought now, he was brain damaged after the accident or he was so befuddled that he was descending into insanity. Everything here now had to be the creation of an entirely broken mind. Thinking back on his life, perhaps it was not so extraordinary. In some ways it was probably highly likely that he should end up like this. After all, it's a known fact that years of drug abuse has an effect on the mind. Sudden withdrawal wouldn't help. He remembered the days after his dismissal from the

Stock Exchange in London when he had come close to a nervous breakdown, fearing yet again the disdain of his father in whose eyes he had always been an utter failure. Add to all of that the pressure of the days following Jenna's death. Well, it was hardly surprising he was now having some sort of mental breakdown. Whilst not a comforting thought, at least it was an explanation he could understand. What was terrifying though was the thought that he could be trapped in this frightening, self created world forever. Condemned for eternity, never knowing what was real or imaginary but nevertheless having to live it and endure it. And here was a question; had he made up his past or was it the present that was just the figment of his imagination? How would he ever know? All George could do, he decided, was go with it all and see what happened.

Searching the room for any clues to the mystery, George noted that there was another bed, made up with crisp white sheets. No blankets or duvets here, he noticed. Between his own bed and the window was a water stand, and beside that a chair on which his clothes lay, now washed and neatly folded. A jug of water and a glass were on the stand. Pouring himself a glass, George drank deeply, gratefully relishing every mouthful. Feeling a little more revived now and working hard to control his rising panic, he resolved to go and find Manolis and get some explanation for all this. He would tell him to get him off this island immediately. After all, they must have some means of transport to the mainland. But, could he trust Manolis? He knew nothing about the man after all. Maybe it would be more sensible to just slip away quietly, make his way to the harbour without alerting anyone and find a way off the island. If there was no boat immediately available, he would just find a place to hide and wait until one came ashore.

His mind made up, George could wait no longer. Time for action. Sitting around ruminating all day wasn't going to provide him with any answers and it certainly wasn't going to hasten his return to normal life, whatever that may be. Grabbing his clothes from the chair, he quickly slipped on his jeans and T-Shirt. Tentatively, he approached the wooden door and put his ear against it. Somewhere, not so far away, he could hear the murmur of voices. Damn! His chances of making a furtive departure were probably thwarted. Gripping the handle, George carefully turned it. To his great dismay, he found that it was locked from the outside.

"They're holding me prisoner!", George thought in horror. Turning quickly back to the window, hoping to find an escape route there, he stumbled, knocking over the water stand and the glass jug. As it fell, there was a loud clatter on the stone floor as glass and the remaining water splattered everywhere. Cursing himself, George considered any other means of egress, frantically searching around the room in the vain hope of discovering another door or ceiling hatch. Of course, there was nothing.

Glancing at the window again, it was clear this would provide him with no opportunity of escape either. For one thing, it was far too small for his rather bulky frame to get through; for another, the significance of which had eluded him earlier, the window was barred. Defeated, yet enraged, George thumped the wall in frustration and slumped to the floor, clasping his head forlornly in his hands.

Moments later, he was roused by a commotion outside the door followed by the jingle of keys in the lock and voices, urgent and foreign. The door opened and Manolis warily entered the room, flanked by another, heavier set man, his unkempt curly hair framing bronze Mediterranean features.

"Ah Georgio, my friend! Good! You are awake and feeling a little better than yesterday, yes?"

George did not respond immediately, but merely returned Manolis' genial greeting with a look of what he hoped was open hostility. When he did finally speak, it was in anger.

"Friend?" Do you keep your friends locked up in here, a prisoner? What are you playing at?" Manolis looked perplexed, hurt even.

"No Kyrie! You have it all wrong. Of course you are not a prisoner here. We were just concerned that you might get up in the middle of the night and get yourself lost or hurt again. There was no other reason for locking the door. You must realise Georgio, you were so confused and disoriented yesterday, we could not be sure of your safety unless we kept control over you. You seem to be very erratic in your behaviour. We have no wish to restrain you here. That is not what Spinaloga is about. This island is to give people such as you freedom to live as normal a life as possible!" The man was deeply apologetic and it seemed to George that he was genuine. Manolis stretched out an arm in an apparently conciliatory gesture and invited George to walk with him.

"Come". "We shall go to the surgery and I can check you over. Later, we will take a walk on this beautiful island and I will show you where you will live once you are discharged from here".

"LIVE?", George exclaimed. "What the hell are you talking about? Live here? You've got to be joking! Manoli, you can check me over, certainly, but after that, I want you to arrange for me to get out of this hell hole. I'm certainly not planning an extended stay in a 'des-res' on Spinalonga!" At George's outburst, Manolis and his companion exchanged a worried glance.

"Excuse me?" What is this word, 'des-res'?" George had inadvertently used the English buzz word in his frustration.

"Desirable Residence. I was being sarcastic. Oh! Never mind! I'm not staying, that's all you need to worry about!". Manolis shook his head, clearly at a loss with George, his new and enigmatic charge.

Refusing to rise to George's anger, Manolis turned towards the door.

"Come, we will talk. Come through to the surgery. He turned and left the room, George following meekly behind. Quite honestly, he was in no mood for any more of Manolis' platitudes. It was time for a showdown. He entered the room containing a desk, chair and an examination table. There were cupboards on the walls and down below which contained bottles of pills and potions. In the corner stood a trolley containing a rather disconcerting array of medical instruments. The whole room appeared rather primitive and the instruments reminiscent of a mediaeval torture chamber. If this was the sanatorium, it was a far cry from the technological wonders of even the worst NHS hospital back in London.

Manolis stood at his desk and motioned for George to come in and sit in the chair next to his.

"You don't seem very well equipped for a hospital", George sullenly remarked.

"As you say, Georgio". Manolis sighed regretfully. "And yet, we do everything here, from the treatment of minor cuts and burns to major amputation in this very room although, as you say, we are very poorly resourced. Things are slowly getting better thanks to our Governor however. We are optimistic for the future".

George couldn't believe what he was hearing. They did amputations in here? Without proper equipment? He shuddered. It didn't bear thinking about. But then, when he did think about it, it couldn't possibly be real anyway, could it? Nothing was adding up here. How could a modern Government refuse necessary medical equipment and supplies to people so clearly in need? It made no sense. Greece was no hard line or inhumane country. It wasn't a poor third world country, and yet, if anything about Manolis's story were true, then this island was being treated as such. Perhaps it was all lies? Perhaps this was an elaborate set up intended just for him? Now there was a conspiracy theory! But why would anyone go to that much trouble just to play a joke on him? And how could it have been done? Perhaps George had been drugged long enough for them to create a whole new town around him? No, that was ridiculous!

Discounting the conspiracy theory, George considered that maybe he had just inadvertently stumbled on a bargaining tool to hasten his departure from 'Nightmare Island' as he had now begun to think of it. If resources here were tight, he could offer to do something to help when he left the island. He, after all, could afford it with the fruits of his ill gotten gains. The more he thought about it, the more the idea appealed to him. It would be like putting something back into the community. One thing was for sure. He had learned his lesson and he had no intention of returning to his criminal life again. He had enough money to live in comfort and he was getting too old for the adrenalin rushes these days. Maybe now, he could re-train, do something useful when he got back. He decided to try his new tack with Manolis.

"Look Manoli", he began, "It's been very good of you to care for me and treat my injuries, but I really do have to get back to the mainland now. I have business I must attend to. I need to contact the UK. I have family there who have no idea where I am. Help me now to get off the island and I promise you, I'll make sure you get financial help to get supplies and equipment. What do you say?"

Manolis looked sorrowful, his deep brown eyes, it seemed to George, penetrating him through to his soul. His very bad soul. Manolis, for his part, was concerned that this young man was unable to accept what had happened to him. He didn't know how to deal with someone whose denial of the truth was so deeply constructed that the young man seemed genuinely bewildered as to where he was or why he was here. How could he deal with someone who was so deluded? He tried again, determined to make George accept his situation by responding only with the truth. No platitudes; no acceptance of George's delusions in order to humour him.

"Georgio, apart from the medical staff and the mainland helpers and traders, no-one ever leaves this island". Manolis sat thoughtfully before continuing, trying to find the right words to impress upon George the sheer impossibility of his request.

"You have referred to this place as 'this damned island'. All who know of it however, call it 'Island of the Damned'. So, you were not far wrong. Once you come here as a patient my friend, you must live here until the end of your days. Sadly all who reside here will, sooner or later, die here. It is not so bad Georgio. You will see. We have a house ready for you in the town and..."

"But I'm not a bloody leper!", George yelled, interrupting Manolis who looked visibly shaken by his fervour. "Don't you understand that Manoli? *I - am - not - a - leper!!*" George shot up from his chair, knocking it over behind him with a loud clatter. Calmer now, he bent over the desk and, his face, close to Manolis', said quietly and menacingly, "I want to speak to someone. The British Consulate. A lawyer. I trust I have some rights here surely?"

Manolis was becoming uncharacteristically impatient now. Whatever he said though, nothing was going to deter George in his quest to return to the mainland.

"Sit down!", he commanded. "No! You have no real rights when you come here. You must understand this. To the outside world, you are an outcast. Unclean. No-one will come to visit you for fear of the disease. If you try to go back to the mainland you will be picked up and sent back here. Or worse! You might end up in a hospital in Athens where they will lock you away like an animal and even forget to treat or feed you! The Government will pay you a pension to help you live here, but that is all the help you will receive. We do our best for you with the resources we have, but that is it! Believe me, you at least have a chance of a life here, much more so than you would anywhere else. Now, as for your condition, hold out your left arm."

Shocked into silence by Manolis' unusually firm response, George sighed and decided to go along with him for now. He held his arm out in front of him as Manolis had requested.

"Good. Now, straighten your arm and the fingers out in front of you". George complied. Straightening his arm, he splayed his fingers, all except one, which was slightly bent due to an accident with broken glass which had severed a nerve in childhood. George stared at Manolis defiantly, daring him to find any sign of leprosy on his body.

"Now Georgio, look at this finger". He pointed to the crooked index finger. He took George's wrist and quickly jabbed a needle into the finger. "Did you feel anything?" George almost laughed out loud in relief. Was this what all the fuss was about? Was this the only sign upon which Manolis was basing his diagnosis?

"No, Manoli. I didn't feel a thing and if you look closely, you'll see why. I severed a nerve with a broken glass years ago and my index finger has been numb ever since. Look more closely and you'll see the scar tissue".

Manolis obliged, examining the area around George's index finger carefully. When he had finished, he looked up. "Nothing Georgio. No scar tissue, no sign of any previous trauma".

"What?" George exclaimed, snatching back his hand to inspect the finger. Sure enough, the familiar patch of keloid scarring wasn't there. Turning his hand back and forwards as if by doing so, the scar would magically reappear, George frantically searched in vain for the raised skin which had been there for almost as long as he could remember. He just couldn't believe it, much less explain it.

"Hold out your arm again. There is more I'm afraid. Look here". Manolis pointed to the area of skin on the inside of George's arm which revealed a dark spot, just smaller than a one penny piece. Turning his arm once more, he pointed to another area on George's wrist.

"And here" Manolis continued as he pushed the leg of George's jeans just above the ankle. Again, a small, dark spot was plainly visible. His arms and legs were naturally hirsute, but the area around and on the dark spot appeared to have lost hair. There was also a slight blanching of the skin surrounding the area.

Again, Manolis produced a needle. This time, George expected to feel pain and winced as Manolis plunged the needle into the affected spot. To George's amazement however, he felt nothing at all, either when the skin was punctured or as Manolis drew out the needle.

"You felt nothing, did you?" asked Manolis. George, subdued now, shook his head.

"No. Nothing. But that doesn't mean I have leprosy does it? It could be any number of things. Perhaps I damaged nerves in the accident".

Manolis, his tone now softened once more, replied gently. He had made his point.

"It means that you have the first stages of leprosy my friend". Manolis could see that with each new revelation, the young man before him was sinking into an ever deepening sense of despair. He could not have known though the extent of the quagmire which George was in, nor all of the reasons for George's fragile mental state. George, with each minute that passed here on the island, was faced with the possibility that he had gone completely insane or, equally, if not more horrifying, that he had stepped into a parallel world where nothing was as it seemed. He just didn't know any more and he did not want to confront it.

Manolis held out a glass of water which George gratefully accepted.

"Before you arrived here, the Medical Commission in Crete carried out tests on you Georgio. They positively identified the leprosy bacilli".

George was stunned into silence as Manolis held out an official document from the Medical Commission. It contained his name and the results of a number of tests which had apparently and unbeknown to him been carried out. All the tests were conclusive. He had leprosy. If any of this was true, all George could expect was a slow, painful degeneration. A horrific death during which he would lose his face and gradually all his limbs as the evil disease ate its way through his body.

"Manoli, I don't know whether this is some sophisticated, but very sick practical joke, or whether somewhere along the line I've lost part of my life, but all I do know is this; two days ago, I was holidaying in Crete. I was healthy and normal. I met a man near Elounda; Charon, he said his name was. He told me I should not leave Crete without visiting Spinalonga. On the way, he told me little about the place except to say it had historical significance. He brought me over in his boat. I went for a walk and stupidly fell and knocked myself out as I waited for him to take me back to the mainland. The next thing I know is I'm waking up to a horror movie and apparently, I've contracted leprosy. How can that be? I can't have invented my life, surely?"

Manolis listened intently to George's story. The strange thing about the young man was his utter conviction. He had never studied psychiatry in detail, but Manolis did know that the mind, the brain, could be a powerful instrument. In cases of severe traumatic shock, it could create all sorts of barriers to save the person from having to face the most dreadful of truths. Perhaps that is what had happened to this young man.

"I can only tell you what was told to me when you arrived Georgio. Perhaps it will help. You were found lying on a hillside not far from Elounda. You were sick and weak. Indeed, you had taken a bad tumble and, as you say, many of your injuries, the cuts and bruises are consistent with such an accident. You had some documentation which bore your name on it. It was presumed that, as is common with lepers, you had been cast out from your village and were seeking shelter when you slipped and fell. You were reported to the Medical Commission who diagnosed your condition and you were brought here on the last incoming boat two nights ago. When you arrived here you were, well, shall we say somewhat difficult? I thought you were delirious. You refused examination and became violent and difficult to handle. There was a fracas and you ran from the sanatorium into the darkness. We tried to find you, but, for a small island, there are many hiding places. There are dangerous areas, particularly near the fortress walls and on the steeper parts. I was not prepared to risk anyone else's health in an attempt to find you that night. The next morning, as you know, Nikos found you and came to fetch me. I have to admit Georgio, I find your delusions incredible, particularly as there appears to be no delirium or infection present. There may be other explanations. Perhaps your head injury, combined with over exposure to the sun may be responsible for it, or perhaps your mind is protecting you from the truth by creating delusions. I am not an expert on the mind, but I have heard of such situations".

George sat quietly as he listened to Manolis. He absorbed the information with utter astonishment. 'That's it then. I've gone crazy. It's official', he thought. 'I've gone insane and I'm going to descend into an abyss of my own wild creation. So now what? I have leprosy? My body as well as my mind is about to betray me and become useless.' George was by now overwhelmed. Too much to think about, unable to process more information or formulate the questions now bombarding his overworked mind.

"Look", Manolis said brightly. "I think you should stop thinking so hard for a while. If you allow your mind to relax a little, perhaps things will start to fall into place a little easier. Why don't I tell you more about where you are and what we do here? It isn't so bad you know. It will help I think".

George appreciated the sense in what Manolis was suggesting. It was pointless to fight against this any more right now.

"Perhaps you're right Manoli. I need to know about this disease you say I have first. I thought it had mostly died out with the Biblical times, or at least that it was confined only to primitive countries these days".

"Of course", replied Manolis. "We will start with an explanation of leprosy. It is always easier to deal with the known than the unknown".

George listened intently to Manolis as he told him all he needed to know about leprosy. He caught himself however, involuntarily regressing into his own thoughts, his own confusion and struggled at times to keep up with the information he was being given. It was, in those moments as though he dissociated himself and hid behind a protective barrier against the world and the horrors which he now faced. He thought of 'Alice in Wonderland' and almost laughed out loud as he imagined the white rabbit or the Mad Hatter popping out from under the desk or shadowed corner. He was reminded, in those moments, of what dark stories, so-called fairy tales often were.

"First" Manolis began, "I should explain that I am one of the Doctors on the island. I specialised in skin diseases in Athens before coming here. I trained partly in Greece and also in London, so I am familiar with many parts of your home country. I was approached two years ago by the governor of the island to work with the lepers to help make their lives more bearable. They have had other doctors of course. Good people who have tried to make a difference. I am the first to actually become resident on the island. In the past the doctors came here once or twice a week but I found it easier just to stay". He laughed a little. "As you might imagine, one doesn't make too many friends on the mainland when they hear that you work on Spinalonga. My real friends are here now.

You and I shall work closely together Georgio and I will do my utmost to alleviate your distress in any way I can. I must however ask for your co-operation. It helps no-one if I have to spend my time restraining and fighting with you". Manolis looked at George and was gratified to see that the young man nodded in quiet acquiescence.

"As to the disease itself, it is commonly known as leprosy, but the medical name for it is Hansen's Disease after Doctor Armauer Hansen of Norway. He first identified that the disease is caused by a germ, Microbacterium Leprae. Until he discovered this, many myths about the disease abounded. It was thought to be a hereditary condition. More ridiculous explanations were that it was the result of a curse, or a sin against God". Manolis paused for a moment allowing George a moment to absorb the information.

"Leprosy affects the skin and, more particularly, the nerves of the extremities, hands and feet. It also causes problems with the eyes and nose". George visibly shrank as he recalled the visions of horror from the previous day.

"But how could I have caught the disease? I thought it was rare, almost eradicated nowadays". Manolis shook his head.

"Unfortunately no, you are mistaken Georgio. There is no cure or effective medication for the disease at present. Naturally, scientists are trying to develop treatment, but, it takes time. I try to contribute as much from my own research as possible to finding a cure but it is a slow process. As for how you contracted the disease, I cannot say. Most commonly, it is developed by contact through an open wound with an untreated sufferer. Other theories suggest it is airborne and thus transmittable. If you had a cut and came into direct contact with an infected person, perhaps you contracted it by this means".

"And the symptoms? What are they? Am I likely to end up like Nikos or that other man we saw?

"Georgio, the good news is that many people do not develop

the most pernicious symptoms. When I take you to meet the community, you will find that most are not in the same condition as Nikos. You would hardly know with most of the residents here that they had such a terrible disease. Essentially, leprosy is a skin disease which has many of the same qualities as the cancer bacterium. There are three types of the disease. As yet, I cannot tell you which you are suffering from. This will take anything up to seven years for us to know.

First of all, you will experience only mild symptoms and then the disease will develop into one of the three variants. The first stage is what you see now. The earliest signs are spots on the skin which may be slightly red. They can be darker as yours are, or indeed lighter than normal skin. In contrast with skin cancer, the spots, which appear at the site of nerves, may become numb and hair growth will be arrested. As the disease progresses, the spots may increase in size and spread to other parts of your body including your arms, legs and back.

Other sufferers may never develop a spot in the early stages and will only experience some numbness in a finger or toe. You are exhibiting both of the symptoms now. If you remain this way, you can count yourself as one of the lucky ones as you will have Variant One of the disease, Tubercular Leprosy. Your main difficulty will be the loss of feeling in your extremities and you will be vulnerable to accidents such as burning or deep cuts. Because you will be unaware of the damage your are doing to yourself, you will become prone to serious infections". Manolis stopped for a few moments, allowing George a moment to take in the information. His expression as he looked at George, was sympathetic, knowing that his words passed a death sentence over him.

The young man stood up and strode over to the window. Looking out onto the gloriously sunny day, in the distance he could see the glinting sapphire blue of the sea and all around the deep reds, yellows, pinks and greens of the glorious flora and fauna which covered the island. 'So much vibrancy of life amidst the decay of death', he thought. It was ironic really. He took a deep breath and spoke with mock cheer.

"So, that's the good news! At best I may be able to do nothing because I'll have no feeling or because I'll be in danger of chopping or burning my own limbs off by accident? For God's sake man! I want a second opinion from a proper hospital. I want to get back to the UK. At least there I'll have access to proper medicines and treatment!" George was now working himself into a rage. How dare this man dictate he should stay here on a backward under resourced island? He had never heard anything so crazy! And he expected him to actually live here?

Manolis said nothing and remained seated at his desk. He knew that convincing this young man of the truth was becoming an increasingly difficult task. As ever though, he chose not to engage in a heated debate and made no response to George's impossible demands.

"Are you listening to me? Did you hear what I said? I want a second opinion. I have medical insurance; I want to go to a British hospital!"

Manolis shook his head apologetically.

"I am sorry Georgio. You are quarantined here by the Greek Government and for very good reason. We cannot arrange your transportation overseas and put other citizens in danger. It would be weeks by sea and I..."

"By Sea!?" George was incredulous. "It's four hours by air! What are you talking about, by sea?"

Manolis looked perplexed, as though George had said something so extraordinary he could not comprehend it.

"Why, you would have to go by sea if you want to return to the UK. I do not understand what you mean about going by air. You would need to travel from Crete to Piraeus and then get a passage on a voyage to England. You may be able to find an alternative passage by land and across Europe, but not in your condition. You would be a great danger to anyone you came into contact with and the authorities would never grant you passage".

"This is madness Manoli. You spin me this incredible story and now you try to tell me I can't get a flight to Britain? What games are you playing? Has someone set me up to be involved in some sick mind game here? Trying to make me think I've gone crazy? Well it won't work, I tell you!"

George, exhausted after this latest outburst slumped back into the chair, his anger spent. Manolis stood and began to tidy the surgery as he spoke, this time with a firmness and finality he had been trying to avoid up until now.

"I am not prepared to indulge your delusions further Georgio. We have more pressing things to attend to right now and there are others here that need me far more than you do. Let me assure you that you will be well cared for here and will receive the best treatment we can offer for your condition. However, if you continue with this obstructive behaviour we shall have no alternative than to restrict your freedom here and keep you sedated and in isolation until you agree to co-operate with us". Manolis returned to his seat next to George, his tone now more placatory.

"Truly, we have your best interests at heart Georgio but you must be prepared to work with us, not against us. Now, do I have to call Alexis to assist me in isolating you for everyone's safety, or shall we continue like reasonable people?"

Taking a deep breath which he exhaled, resignedly, George nodded. He was getting nowhere fast with this tack. It was obvious he would have to play along until he could work out what was going on and formulate a plan to get out of here. If he was sedated and locked up, he had no chance of getting away.

Somewhat ungraciously, George replied.

"OK doc. Have it your way. Now, tell me the bad news so I can appreciate how lucky I am right now".

He oozed caustic sarcasm which Manolis ignored.

"You saw Nikos. He suffers from the second variant of the disease. Lepromatodis. This is the cruel strain. It begins to rot the extremities following the appearance of large wounds". Pausing for a moment, Manolis looked sad as he explained the progress of variant two. "This is an extremely painful process of decay, and, just as you saw with Nikos, it eats the nose, ears, eyes, lips and continues with the toes, arms and legs. When it reaches the limbs, we have no alternative than to amputate, one by one. Usually by the fourth limb, the sufferer is unable to withstand more and will die".

"Why bother to treat the disease in this way then? Surely it must be better to die sooner than later, before all the limbs are lost? Why would anyone want to go on knowing that their fate is to be slowly butchered until the end? Quality of life must be non-existent".

"Ah but you underestimate the power of the human spirit Georgio. You may not understand this unless you are unfortunate enough to have to face it. The will to live is powerful, despite the odds. As for quality of life, when you settle into the community here, you will be amazed at the quality and the joy of living that exists here. For many, their lives here have brought an autonomy and sense of belonging previously denied to them. You will learn more of this later".

Silently, George absorbed Manolis' words and yet found them impossible to believe. If indeed he had leprosy, then he was sure, he would end it all before it really took a hold. There was no way he would just sit around waiting to be eaten away and chopped to pieces. Despite everything however, he could not truly believe that any of this was relevant to him.

"So that's variants one and two. What about the third? How much worse can it get?"

"Not so much worse Georgio. Variant here 'Form Indeterme'

combines the symptoms of both the others.

"What must I do to protect myself?" George now asked.

"Good Georgio. Now you are asking the right questions. What you must not do is lose hope. Medical research is being carried out every day to find medicine for this disease. The longer you can avoid infection, the greater your chances of survival are. You must take great care of your limbs. Any repeated injury of the fingers and toes will cause the bones and the tissues surrounding them to shorten. We will ensure you have suitable footwear. We even have our leather shop and cobbler here on the island who will make sure things are right for you" Manolis smiled and his eyes twinkled. He was proud of the facilities on the island.

"I will check you over every few days here at the hospital. If you experience any changes, further numbness for example, you must let me know. If you are worried, come here at any time between appointments. You must take care of your eyes.If you cannot feel anything in them the greater the chance of damage. If you suffer any redness, you must regard this as an emergency and come to me immediately or you could lose your vision. I will provide you with eye drops. Use them regularly to keep the eyes moist. Be careful when cooking, using knives, or even washing to avoid cuts and burns".

George quietly accepted the advice, his head now reeling. Surely if this was a joke or a set up, Manolis would not be going through this with such precision? George believed however that Manolis had lied about the availability of drugs. He was certain that leprosy had more or less been eradicated, just like smallpox, bubonic plague and diphtheria. There were so many things he could not understand here. And what was all that business about not being able to get flights back to England? Where had Manolis been all this time?

"So", George continued. "Is there any treatment available for the disease?"

"Alas, nothing curative or preventive right now. All we can offer is morphine for the pain I'm afraid. But do not worry so much my friend. You are indeed lucky. You are in the very early stages. If you develop the second variant at all, you have anywhere between seven and thirty years before you fully start to exhibit the virulent symptoms. Hopefully, by then, discoveries will be made".

'Great' George thought. 'A thirty year cliff-hanger and the potential of staying on a primitive island for the rest of my miserable life? What more could I want?'

"Now, I'll check you over and then arrange for you to be taken to your accommodation. After that, you can meet some of our community here who will help you settle into the way of life". Manolis smiled reassuringly. "Try to be calm Georgio. Things are not so bad as you will see very soon".

"Fourteen steps to the door
I would there were eleven
For I swear that these three steps more
Might be three steps to Heaven".
ISLAND OF TEARS
William Ronald Hawkins

1940

Manolis

At the time of the strange young man's arrival on the island, it was July 1940 and Manolis Papadopolous had lived on Spinalonga for the last three years. Europe was at war but so far the effects had not touched Spinalonga or its residents. Indeed, the islanders waged daily battles against a foe which was far more deadly and unrelenting than any human enemy. That foe was leprosy and Spinalonga was a colony established by the Greek Government for those sufferers exiled from the mainland and islands. Manolis had come here after studying medicine in Athens where he had specialised in contagious diseases and dermatology. During his final year he had conducted research into leprosy and, as such had become known as a specialist in leprology. Wishing to continue his studies and use his knowledge, Manolis had applied to work and carry out research at the colony. He had arrived on the island full of hope and optimism of a breakthrough in the treatment of the disease, but, to date, he had been disappointed and all he could do for the island's diseased community was tend to their ravaged bodies as best he could, prevent the spread of infection and operate when required to stave off for as long as possible the spread of the disease, usually by removal of limbs, reducing a person, piece by piece into nothing more than a thinking, feeling slab of butcher's meat.

Manolis despaired at his impotence in the face of such adversity, but his heart swelled with pride and joy at the bravery of this little community, which, despite their trials, managed to overcome terrible adversity to live useful, fulfilling lives, to love, spread joy and rarely allow the cruelty of their existence to bring them down. Manolis had an island full of friends and he regarded each and every one of the people here to be his family. Manolis felt that he belonged here more than he had done anywhere else in his life. He was loved and needed here and he returned that love to his people, his dependents, in equal measure.

Manolis' own childhood and adolescence had been difficult. His parents had died when he was ten years old, victims of a storm whilst at sea. They had, ironically, been returning from a trip to Crete when the yacht they had been travelling on with friends had capsized and dragged them down into the not so benevolent Aegean waters. His uncle and aunt had taken him in and though nothing was ever said to his face, or even within earshot, he knew he was a burden to the family. Nevertheless he had a stable upbringing if lacking in warmth. He studied hard at school and his imagination was captured by science lessons and the stories of great scientists making incredible discoveries to help alleviate human suffering. Manolis felt that although his suffering was not so easy to cure, he could help others in some practical way if only he could continue his studies. His joy was immeasurable when, on his 18th birthday, his aunt and uncle called him to the sitting room where a strange man in a dark suit was sitting at the table, a black briefcase open in front of him. The man was introduced as a lawyer, whom, it transpired had news for him of an inheritance from his parents. Apparently, a trust fund had been set up for him which allowed his aunt and uncle an income during his minority. Now that he had attained 18, he was a man and the trust settled on him. Manolis was stunned. His parents had been comfortable but insurance policies had matured on their death and left a considerable sum for his benefit. He knew exactly what he would do now. He had sufficient money to see him through university and beyond. He would pursue his dreams of studying medicine. He had the capability and he had the desire. And so, he continued his studies with great aplomb and academic success. He was driven, although, he wasn't entirely certain why, and eventually, he had come here, to Spinalonga. His true home and his true family.

This morning, Manolis was tired. A boat had come from the mainland yesterday bringing a new intake for the island. It was always difficult when new residents arrived. For a while afterwards, the dynamics of the island altered as new people struggled to accept their fate or the fact they had the disease or to deal with enforced separation from their lives and freedoms. With them, came news of the outside world which often unsettled the other inhabitants who would also pine anew for their old lives.

Settling in for the newcomers took longer for some than for others, depending on their previous circumstances, personality and attitudes. For many, it had to be said, arriving on the island was a joy in comparison to the life they had been forced to lead previously.

Whilst Manolis never referred to his charges as 'lepers', nevertheless, this was how they were known elsewhere, carrying with them the stigma of the cursed, the unclean and the inhuman. Many of those who lived on the island had suffered terribly at the hands of not only villagers but even close family and friends who banished them from their homes and cast them out of their villages at the onset of the disease. They were ostracised by those communities who, understandably feared the disease and seeking to protect themselves forced the lepers to live solitary lives in mountain caves, never permitted to enter the city, town or village boundaries again. These poor souls had no access to medical treatment or indeed to the kind words or gentle touch of another human being. They scavenged for food like wild animals and, if they were lucky, family would leave supplies close to their dwelling, though not too close lest they should be banished from their homes too. The lepers would collect their food packages only once a safe distance had been put between the relative and the sufferer.

Many who came to the island however were resentful at their

exile, feeling they had been confined to a prison, punished for their illness, condemned to die, forgotten and unloved in a place far from home.

Those from Iraklion were not allowed to enter the town or even to beg on the outskirts. Anyone leaving food for the lepers were required to maintain a certain distance. Families were split and the disease created devastation. Yesterday, a young girl was brought to the island because she had ventured too far into the cave in which her infected father was living. One of her fingers had become crooked and the villagers, fearing she had contracted the disease, banished her. Both she and her father had arrived on the island together. Manolis doubted she had contracted the disease, but time would tell. Nevertheless, a normal life was now denied to this girl who would carry the stigma of a leper forever more, irrespective of whether she had truly caught the disease.

Manolis had carried out an initial assessment of his new intake last night and a full day awaited him. First though, he had to deal with their new problem resident, Georgio, who had taken off the night before. Georgio had been disorientated and confused when he arrived off the boat. He had barely known his name let alone anything else. At first Manolis suspected delirium and he and a couple of the other islanders had supported him as they walked him up from the beach into the town. Georgio had been taken straight to the sanatorium while the others went to assist with other newcomers. When Manolis returned however, Georgio had disappeared. By this time, darkness had fallen and a perfunctory search of the island had been organised. Manolis however called off the search, fearing that someone would sustain injury in the darkness. On Spinalonga, even the slightest injury and resultant infection could lead to fatality. Manolis knew the man couldn't go far on the island, although there were dangers if he climbed up towards the fortifications. It was a risk Manolis was forced to take however, for the greater good.

That morning, Manolis was about to launch a new search party with the more able bodied islanders when a disturbance from outside the sanatorium caught his attention. A clamour of excited voices gathered in volume and intensity as a gaggle of the island's men responded to Nikos who was shuffling hurriedly towards them, calling out instructions. Manolis approached the door just as Nikos reached the others and amid much discussion and interrogation, Manolis gleaned the fact that the missing patient had been found.

The scene before him amused Manolis. No matter the trials which this community faced, the spirit and goodness of the people remained typical. The Greek trait of inquisitiveness (some might say nosiness if they were not Greek), one upmanship and the need to give unsolicited advice or opinion to anyone in any situation still prevailed here as much as in any other Greek village.

Nikos, having imparted all he knew of the missing man's location, demeanour, condition and appearance speculated with the others as to where he came from what he did for a living, whether he was married/rich/foreign and on every other personal detail possible. The ritual completed, he finally shuffled his way into the sanatorium where Manolis was waiting.

"You've found him then Niko, well done!" Manolis gripped the other man's shoulder warmly. A little praise went a long way in a place where there was little else to make a person feel good. Nikos beamed with pleasure, at least as much as his poor, deformed features would allow him.

"Near the church, Manoli. He was barely moving. I thought he was dead, but then he spoke to me. I think you need to come now". Nikos beckoned urgently with his poor, clawed hand.

And so it was Manolis had his first enigmatic encounter with Georgio. The man was deeply afraid on their first meeting, convinced in some strange delusional world that he was not from this time or place. Manolis put his delusions down to a fever at first, convinced that he had contracted an infection leading to delirium. It was not long into their first conversation that Manolis came to realise there was indeed something strange and different about Georgio. His style of dress for example was a little odd. Some of the expressions he used Manolis was not familiar with. Most puzzling was his version of how he had got here. What could have made him believe he had come to the island as a tourist? Tourists would put an ocean between themselves and this island, not that there were many tourists to Crete in any case. The part which perplexed Manolis most however was Georgio's conviction he had been transported by Charon. A light chill ran through him. The man's delusion would not be so far out of place, he thought, but still, very odd. He would have to explore this further at some later time. He was clearly suffering from some secondary problem, and yet...,

For now though, apart from the delusions, the man's symptoms displayed nothing unusual and Manolis was concerned to welcome him to his fold and to treat him as a friend and equal. He had helped him walk from his overnight resting place near the Church to the sanatorium where Manolis tended to him as though he were his child.

Now, some days, later, Georgio had recovered sufficiently to demand answers from Manolis. The answers that were sought however, despite his experience and knowledge, Manolis still felt unqualified to give. He took no pleasure in informing any of these vulnerable people that their likely fate was simply to rot, wither, decay, slowly fall to pieces and ultimately die. Instead, Manolis concentrated on the preventive aspects. He told the man how to take care of his limbs, explained the possible progression of the illness and emphasised that in Georgio's case it was not advanced. He highlighted, as was his practice, the positives; that it may be years before Georgio would really see deterioration. Perhaps never, if the cure, which was being actively sought as they spoke could be found.

No matter what Manolis told Georgio however, there was a feeling that the young man believed nothing of what he was hearing, that while Manolis dealt in euphemism, the young man dealt in scepticism. Even as Georgio listened, Manolis had the feeling that he was simply being humoured and that the young man had another agenda.

Perhaps it was the only way he could deal with the horror of his certain death by the slowest and most painful means imaginable. He could not blame him. Denial was a powerful antidote sometimes.

Manolis felt it necessary to keep a close eye on Georgio for some time after his recovery. He felt that he was always a danger to himself, if not by suicide then by accidental death. This one wasn't just going to lie down and accept his fate. He was a fighter and something else, something indefinable. There was an air of the ethereal about him. Manolis couldn't yet put his finger on it, but it was almost as though the stranger wasn't quite of this world.

George

Almost in spite of himself, George instantly warmed to Manolis whom he quickly decided was a kind, genuine, yet resolute man. Notwithstanding the mysteries to which he felt sure Manolis held the key, George felt that compassion oozed from every pore in the man's body. In the following days, he was extremely solicitous, ensuring that he did everything possible to protect himself from the disease which he believed George carried.

George was punch drunk following his talk with Manolis. He took the doctor's advice however but continued to ponder the mystery of his residence here. As far as personal information was concerned, George imparted nothing of any consequence, for nothing he could tell Manolis matched up with anything that was known about him on the island. He felt therefore, until he could delve deeper into the circumstances of his arrival here and the strange transformation of the island, it was better to keep his own counsel, discretion being the better part of valour for now.

Whilst the diagnosis of leprosy was a new horror for him to deal with, it was the least of his problems for now. It was the remainder of George's life which caused him angst. Everything had a quality of unreality and absurdity. Extreme fatigue also gripped him and all he really wanted to do was sleep. Each time he did so, he hoped on every waking that this time he would find himself back in his own world, unpalatable as even that might be. Disappointment greeted him however, when each day he awoke back on the island in this strange, diseased world. In between his sleeping hours, Manolis dutifully visited him, checking his vital signs for any change or deterioration and trying unsuccessfully to establish more information about him.

Eventually, on what he understood to be his fifth day on the Island, George felt stronger and more ready than ever to take his leave from the Sanatorium. Despite himself, he felt compelled to find out more about this place and the man who had shown him more kindness and compassion than he could remember in recent times.

It had occurred to George that perhaps staying on the island a while would not be such a bad thing. After all, if the authorities caught up with him and believed him to have leprosy, they were hardly likely to pursue him over the Jenna Hawkins fiasco. Every cloud had a silver lining indeed, George thought. If he could just put aside the weirdness of the situation then perhaps it was preferable after all to stay here for now and forget what he had left behind in the past and indeed, what awaited him in the future. He could just play along here, let everyone continue thinking he was a leper and live peacefully for now in his exile. Wasn't that what he had planned anyway? To disappear and start again somewhere else. He could certainly lose himself here for a while. Weren't these people really the forgotten ones? Who would care about a leper? The downside of course was that if he didn't already have the disease as Manolis believed, he might well end up with it after spending time here. Staying here would probably seal his fate. George's head hurt from going around in ever decreasing circles. He couldn't understand anything of what was going on, so how could he even begin to work out a logical solution?

If an island could completely transform itself overnight, what was to say that the outside world hadn't in some way metamorphosed into something alien as well? The more he thought about it, the more sick with fear and confusion he felt. There was no-one he could talk to about it. Anyone listening to him thought he was delusional. George felt in his bones that really, there was only one person who held the key to this mystery and that was Charon, the elusive boatman.

Though Manolis seemed convinced that George had leprosy, he could not believe it, despite apparently displaying classic symptoms. George needed to know more, much more about what was happening to him before he could even begin to make an informed decision.

Manolis visited George daily. This morning, the sun shone through the open shutters and George felt strong, almost optimistic once more. So far, George had been reserved and withdrawn, wishing not to engage in much conversation or form any kind of relationship with Manolis. After several days of this quiet contemplation however, George was becoming bored. This coupled with the realisation that he wasn't going to wake up one morning and find this had all been a horrible dream had led him to resolve that a change in approach was necessary.

Dressing quickly, George left his room and sat down on the blue wooden chair outside the sanatorium and allowed the warmth of the sun to seep through his body and give him the comfort of a hot bath after a tiring day. Presently, Manolis returned from his daily round of home visits and pulled up a seat next to him. He appeared genuinely delighted to see his charge apparently rejoining the world and his genial face lit up with a smile as he greeted George. Despite himself, George felt an extraordinary sense of belonging.

"Well good morning Georgio!" he greeted him. "And how are you this fine morning".

"I'm good, thanks Manolis. Ready to join the human race again, I think".

"I am pleased to hear it. Tell me, do you speak Greek when you are back in London?"

"Not so much. My father is Greek and was born on Crete. My mother is English and doesn't really speak much of the language. Dad was always keen that I should learn his mother tongue so he spoke to me from an early age in Greek. It doesn't come as easily to me as English though, I'm afraid".

For a few minutes there was a companionable silence between the two men, George thinking of his family back home, wondering what on earth they were going through and whether they were OK after everything he had done. Finally, it was George who broke the silence once more. He cut to the chase.

"I have questions", he blurted out. "Manoli, I can't pretend that I understand what any of this is about. I think we both know that there is something not right about my arrival here. Will you help me to find out? I'm afraid you see. I feel locked in a world where nothing can be trusted. I don't know where reality starts. I fear I may be going insane".

Manolis regarded the troubled young man for a few long moments, his deep brown compassionate eyes penetrating him, trying to read, George thought, the mysteries which he must present to him. He smiled.

"Of course, I will help you Georgio. What is it that you want to know in particular?"

What did George want to know? What could he really ask or tell Manolis that wasn't going to make him look as though he was suffering hallucinations or delusions?

"Well, for a start, I have a different recollection about my arrival on the island and I can't reconcile myself to the fact that I have no recollection of the events you described. I cannot, however hard I try, find any rational explanation for the transformation of the island from deserted ghost town to inhabited community."

Manolis shook his head in bewilderment. "Unless you had a vision of the past or indeed, the future of the island, I cannot explain it either my friend. The obvious answer is that you have been delusional. That is the only explanation I can offer." Manolis pondered for a few moments. "Tell me again what you recall about your arrival here".

Once again, George explained about the accident on his way to Elounda and his meeting with Charon. Manolis asked George to describe Charon which he did in some detail.

"The strange thing about him was that I thought he was touting for business to take me on the boat trip but when I offered him a 10 Euro note, he insisted he could only take a one Euro coin". Manolis looked agitated on hearing this information and with some consternation, stopped George, mid story.

"Wait, wait, what is this Euro you speak of?" Manolis looked genuinely perplexed. George was even more so and looked at him in disbelief. Here was an educated man who didn't know about the Euro! He went over to Crete on a weekly basis, how could he not know that? Incredulity written on George's face, he addressed Manolis' odd question.

"It's the currency of many of the Member States of the European Union of course! Manolis, how could you not know this? You must deal in Euros whenever you go to Crete!" Manolis looked puzzled and uncomprehending.

"We use the drachma here Georgio. I have never heard of the

'Euro' that you speak of. And what is this European Union?"

Stunned, George was barely able to speak. He could not believe that Manolis displayed such ignorance of world affairs, let alone the local currency. Nevertheless, feeling Manolis might just be having a joke at his expense, George explained about the alliance, the economic arrangements of the EU and listed as many of the countries as he could recall were part of the union. He explained that since the second World War the countries of Europe had felt safer as part of a joint community to ensure that no country could ever again rise to claim power over the others as Germany had done. He did not add that in his own view, the dissemination of power to Europe had merely given away the autonomy which had been so hard fought for during World War II.

Manolis looked sick and paled visibly by the time George had finished. Quietly, he asked what George thought was the strangest of questions. He wanted to know what was the outcome of World War II. George thought now this man had to be joking. Either that or he was the one who was crazy. There was no way he couldn't know that.

"Oh come on Manolis! What are you playing at? Crete was at the centre of a German invasion in 1941 and the war ended with Germany defeated in 1945! You're a doctor for God's sake, how can you not know these things?"

Manolis simply stared at George, open mouthed.

"Georgio, how can this be? How can you know these things?" Manolis stood up, shaking his head. He didn't know what to say or do next. Finally, he turned to George and spoke quietly. "Georgio, Europe is now at war There is no alliance between the countries. Germany is bombing its neighbours and we fear that we shall be next. And now you tell me that we shall be invaded! Are you a German spy? Do you have some intelligence that my people should know about?"

It was George's turn to gape, open mouthed.

"Of course I'm not a German Spy!" 'Oh God', he thought, could things get any worse? What madness was this? Then, a dreadful, horrible thought struck him.

"Manoli, what year is this?"

"1940 of course".

Suddenly and with the feeling that the whole world was collapsing in on him, it all started to make sense. No flights to Britain; Manolis' ignorance of the Euro or the EU; the lack of medical technology on the island, the transformation of the town. Of course, George thought wryly. How did I not realise it? He was stunned by this new information. He felt his mouth fall open in utter disbelief. He tried to speak several times but found himself succeeding only in opening and closing his mouth like a ventriloquist's dummy. His thoughts, one after the other arranged themselves to formulate one unbelievable but wholly logical answer to this whole enigma. He was reeling. This couldn't be happening. George looked helplessly at Manolis, unsure whether to explain the revelation. As Manolis returned his gaze, George could see the cogs turning in his own mind as he tried to decide if he had a German Spy, a madman or indeed something entirely different in front of him. He didn't look hostile, just as flummoxed as George surely was. Now all sorts of possibilities presented themselves to George. Was he mad? Was he ill? Or, impossibly, had he somehow travelled back through time to find himself on a wartime Spinalonga? He could barely contemplate it, nor, it seemed could Manolis. Gathering himself, it was Manolis who broke the silence. He was erring on the clinical explanation, clearly reluctant to contemplate anything less rational.

"Georgio. I think you are very ill", he said firmly but gently. "Perhaps you have been affected by a fever. I think we need to run more tests on you". In a way, George was happy to go along with Manolis' suggestion. How could either of them contemplate anything else? George felt in his heart that although Manolis was avoiding thoughts of any less rational explanation, it had nevertheless crossed his mind that he was dealing with something beyond his knowledge here. If both of them simply acknowledged that George must be delusional however, it made life easier at least until George could get his own head around this.

"Do you know Manolis. I finally think you are right. I must be very sick. I can't think where all this information could have come from. I can't remember anything about my life. I only have recollection of the things I have just described". George felt it better to lie and feign amnesia. It would make Manolis feel better and reduce any questions about his past.

"Tell me a little more about leprosy Manolis. Does it often result in amnesia or delusions?" George sensed that with his question, Manolis felt more comfortable on familiar ground. He was happy to move on to his pet subject.

"These are not usual symptoms unless of course there has been infection and fever accompanied by delirium. But, we do have to remember that you had a nasty fall which could have left you with some minor damage to the brain. We will keep an eye on you and see if it improves. As to the leprosy, well, it is the cruellest of illnesses, both in the medical and social context. Let me tell you a little of the history. I think that way, you may actually appreciate what you will find here to help you".

Somehow, George doubted that, but nevertheless he wanted to know more. What Manolis told him was as fascinating as it was horrific.

"You will find many references to leprosy in the Bible and I think it is correct to say that this was where the terrible stigma of the disease becomes apparent. It was in the Bible that leprosy was first associated with punishment for sins". Manolis looked at George sadly. "In those days it was believed that the corruption of the person's soul was matched by the corruption of the body. Sufferers were being punished by God for their sins. In the book of Leviticus, from the English translation, it says:-

'And the leper in whom the plague is, his clothes shall be rent and the hair of his head shall go loose, and he shall cover his upper lip and shall cry, unclean! Unclean! He shall dwell alone; without the camp shall his dwelling be.'

"And that, my friend, to this day is how it remains. Lepers are reviled and cast out, recorded as unclean and forced to live apart. The people you will meet here, they have all suffered, they have all been, what is the word? Dehumanised. Leprosy sufferers were classed in 314 AD by the Church as heretics, morally and bodily unclean, corrupt. The Mediaeval church attributed to the lepers many sins, branding them a threat, not just because of their infection, but also because it was believed that only their evil behaviour was the cause of the disease. They were forbidden to enter the church or houses, prevented from washing in streams, from touching things, from talking to people or socialising. It was decreed that the lepers must wear a grey or black mantle and carry a bell or horn to warn of their presence. They were regarded as shameful and were degraded and rejected. Nothing has changed to this day, sadly, enlightened as we are".

Manolis was sombre now. George had detected anger in him as he told his story.

"How can you live here, amongst all this disease? Aren't you likely to catch it yourself? Aren't you afraid?"

"It is possible of course, yes. But in fact, most people are naturally immune to leprosy, even when exposed to the bacteria. I have made it my life's work to care for these people. They have no-one but me and each other. If I and my few colleagues didn't care for them, they would perish alone and without anyone to ease their suffering or give them comfort. Don't misunderstand me. It isn't always easy".

Manolis fell silent for a few moments and George was struck by the peacefulness of this place. It was a different quietude from that which he had experienced on his arrival here. This time, there was the distinct presence of human and animal life. George could hear goats bleating, chickens squawking, cockerels crowing and the odd cat mewling. Now, there was a living breathing village, where only days ago there had been dereliction and silence. The island itself had taken on vibrant colour, flowers and fruit growing around him. Where the houses had been crumbling, they were now intact and well kept. Gardens bloomed, washing hung on lines from balconies, cats roamed free and the smell of cooking wafted from the houses. No matter how hard he tried, George could come up with no logical explanation except perhaps that Manolis was lying. Somehow though, he didn't think this was the case. Yet, how could he be sitting here in 1940? It was ridiculous, crazy and above all, impossible. George had listened intently to all that Manolis had said. He had scrutinised him but could find nothing disingenuous about him. He was a fairly young man, in his thirties George guessed. A little older than himself. Manolis had done so much more with his life than he had. At least he was making a difference to the world. So was George he supposed, only where Manolis preserved life, George destroyed it. He experienced the feeling of shame, of inadequacy once more. He supposed he had never really had time to think about what he was doing in his life or the consequences of his actions. Manolis had a gentleness about him; a kindness, compassion and generosity of spirit. Qualities which George did not recognise in himself.

Despite the strangeness of the situation, George believed all that Manolis had told him. Somehow, incredibly, he had to accept that he had travelled to the Spinalonga of the 1940s. Whether it was real or imagined, George could not tell. All he did know was that he wanted to return to normality, even the strange and frightening normality which had been the last few days of his life. George was drawn back to the present reality of the situation by Manolis who now rose from his chair.

"Georgio, I must now visit some of my patients. You should come with me and I will introduce you to your neighbours who will soon become your friends".

George rose, eager in some ways to discover as much as possible about what and who else was here. Maybe some more of the mystery would be unlocked. Manolis went into the sanatorium and picked up his medical bag. Locking the door behind him, the two men walked slowly through the village, now buzzing with life. Manolis stopped for a moment, something clearly troubling him.

"Georgio, you spoke of Charon, the man who brought you here".

"Yes, that's right. He was a miserable son of a bitch", he replied somewhat bitterly. 'Miserable enough to abandon me here, to goodness knows what fate', George thought, but did not say.

"I have only heard of one person by that name Georgio".

"You know him?"

"I know of him. I have not yet met him my friend. I would neither expect, nor hope to meet him for a long time, if indeed he exists at all".

"What do you mean? Of course he exists! Who is he? What is he?" George was beginning to feel alarmed. Manolis turned to look at him.

"Georgio, Charon is the Ferryman. In Greek mythology, he transported the dead on their last journey over the Styx to Hades, the Underworld". As if to emphasise the significance, Manolis repeated, "He transports dead people my friend. He is known to be a surly, avaricious old man who demands a coin from the dead person. If he receives it, he ferries them to either the Elysian Fields if they have been heroic or virtuous in life, or to Tartarus, condemned to walk forever more as a dull shadow, a tortured wraith, if they were a wrongdoer".

On hearing Manolis' description of Charon, George almost

fainted. Surely, his logical brain told him, he hadn't met some mythological character as well as travelled back in time! He couldn't have made him up, that much George knew. He had never taken any interest in myths and legends and he had certainly never come across Charon before. What did strike him though were the circumstances of his arrival here. Charon had transported him in return for a coin following a terrible accident which by rights ought to have killed him. George's mind reeled once more. Was it possible that he was in fact dead? What greater vision of hell could there be than this place. He was now living on the island of the dead, for nothing was more certain than the fate of these people. Everyone who came here was headed for the grave and if hell was a place, this was certainly it.

So was this the answer George was seeking, he wondered. Perhaps he was being punished in Tartarus for his sins, brought here by Charon, the strange, mysterious old man who now, it appeared, was part of the supernatural world. It all added up in a strange kind of way. George recalled the power the man seemed to yield over his mind. The painful visions he had been forced to endure under Charon's gaze. Were these the visions of a dying man? Didn't they say that a dying person saw flashbacks of his life played out before him? It all made a terrible kind of sense. If this was death, thought George, it didn't really feel any different to being alive. He was continuing to exist in some form or another, yet in a terrible, other world. Of course, he could talk to no-one about his fears. He didn't want to be condemned as a madman as well as a leper.

Manolis scrutinised George, trying to determine the effect his words were having upon the young man. They sat in silence as George considered how to explain the inexplicable. He shook his head.

"Manoli, I can't tell you any more. Perhaps he was just an old boatman with the same name as a mythical character. Perhaps he was playing a game with me. Unless we try to find him, I don't know if I'll ever solve the mystery. Perhaps my accident caused me to conjure Charon up as a figment of my imagination or perhaps I did have some knowledge of the story buried deep in my memory which the accident brought to the fore. I just don't know. I wish I could explain it."

Manolis merely nodded, staring reflectively out to sea.

"Yes my friend, of course." Manolis smiled in reassurance.The brain is a complex organ and any one of your explanations is possible. One of them is sure to be the answer, although I have to say, I do not know of any man who is named after the Ferryman. It would be an inauspicious name to give to any child".

The two men walked companionably through the town, Manolis stopping every so often to speak to one resident or another and to introduce George to his new neighbours. Though Manolis said nothing, he was uneasy with all that George had told him about the encounter with Charon. He wasn't a superstitious man or one who held much store by tales of the ancient gods, the myths or legends but this, combined with the strange things which George had said about Europe and in particular his conviction that Crete had been invaded by the Germans were enough to trouble him. Something felt very wrong about the young man and the circumstances of his arrival on Spinalonga. Manolis knew that George was holding back and that if he wanted to find out more, he must be patient and gain his trust. He could tell that George was deep in his own thoughts now and that to pursue matters further would lead nowhere.

"I think perhaps you need to take some time for yourself now. It is overwhelming to meet so many new people all at once. Now, I must go and dress this patient's wounds. I will be some time. Why don't you go and rest in the sun for a while. I will come and find you once I have finished here". Manolis, pushing open the door of this last house they reached disappeared inside and

George gratefully made his way down to the beach. Gazing out upon the sparking waters before him he pondered the conversation he had just had with Manolis. The conundrum seemed to become ever more complex, the answers ever more elusive. It was hardly surprising he was becoming more withdrawn by the minute, unable to turn to anyone for answers. Was he descending into total madness, he wondered, or was he really about to be plunged in the middle of World War II? How absurd would he sound if he even voiced any of this thoughts to anyone? How could he pretend by day that everything was normal when it was so far from the truth? Whatever was happening to him, George thought now, was either supernatural or a creation of his own mind which had caught him in a seemingly inextricable and unrelenting dream state. If it was the latter though, this was unlike any dream he had ever experienced before. In this dream, there was a logical progression of events. Day passed to night and night to day. He fell asleep at night and awoke in the morning to find that his life went on in one continuous, fluid existence. Each night he prayed (although to whom he prayed, he was unsure) that he would awaken back in his old life and in his own time, despite what he had left behind. Then, there was the strange tale about Charon. George had known nothing of Greek mythology, despite his ancestry, yet the symbolism of Charon's appearance was not lost on him. Perhaps, he thought, the accident did kill me. Perhaps I'm in some kind of limbo after death. Was this, he wondered to be his waiting place or was it to be his final, eternal hell?

Of course, there was one final possibility; he really had travelled back through time; caught somehow in a time slip. The scientists acknowledge it is, at least in theory a possibility, don't they? He remembered, years ago, when he was still at school, his father had bought him a book called "The Unexplained". It had fascinated him and he had thumbed through its pages time and again until the stitches of the binding frayed and the pages became dog eared. Now, in a moment of sudden recollection the details of one of those stories which had gripped his imagination came flooding back.

The tale concerned two English women who were visiting the gardens created by Marie Antoinette at The Petit Trianon near Versailles in France. George could even remember their names; Eleanor Jourdain and her friend, Anne Moberley who were academics from Oxford University. Whilst holidaying in France in 1901, the two women visited the Palace of Versailles and became lost whilst searching for the Petit Trianon. By their own account, a heavy mood which oppressed their spirits descended upon them. Hadn't George experienced that very feeling? Continuing through the grounds, they came upon a deserted farmhouse, an old fashioned plough next to the road and, perhaps most curious, two men in long coats and three cornered hats to whom they spoke, asking directions. According to the womens' account, the men obligingly directed them to a path which led them to a gazebo shaded by trees. There, they met a man whom they described as having an evil look about him. His face was pitted by smallpox and he stared at them belligerently. At this point, the dark mood they had experienced earlier became even more intense.

The women were saved from the man by another man who rushed up to them and in urgent tones told them they were going the wrong way and directed them to a bridge which he instructed them to cross. They obeyed the man, fearful of what might transpire if they did not and, on reaching the other side, they happened upon a woman sitting on a stool, sketching. She wore an extremely elaborate, very old fashioned dress and a white powdered wig. As her eyes met the startled gaze of the two women, both felt the pervasive sense of gloom descend upon them once more. The woman did not speak to Eleanor or Anne and the two women merely nodded their acquaintance and passed on, neither of them speaking to the other as they did so. Eventually, it was a footman who directed the women back to normality. He told them they would find the entrance to the Petit Trianon on the other side of the building. Following his directions, they came around the other side of the building where they met a wedding party waiting to tour the rooms of the Palace. The party were dressed normally for their own time and their mood simultaneously lifted once more.

Like George, the women did not, for a very long time afterwards, discuss the events of that day, perhaps even more inexplicably not even between themselves. Finally, they did confess to each other their perceptions of that day and discovered their experiences to have been essentially the same. They later discovered that the day they visited Versailles was the anniversary of the day in 1792 when Louis XVI and Antoinette had witnessed the massacre of their Swiss Guards and they were imprisoned

George shivered as he compared his own experience with that of those women he had read about so long ago. Explanations, he recalled now, had ranged from a ghostly sighting, to a mutual telepathic 'tapping-in' to memories which were indelibly impressed into the location itself. Years later, the women published a book and further investigation revealed that there were several other pieces of corroborative evidence to suggest that the women had actually somehow stumbled backwards in time.

George recalled the atmosphere he had felt as he stepped off Charon's boat and emerged from the tunnel into the derelict town. Hadn't he felt a gloom descend upon him then? Hadn't he felt he was being watched by unseen eyes? Could he have tapped into memories, trapped within the stone walls which were now replaying like a video tape around him? Was he living some past leper's life? Was it possible moreover that he had somehow met up with a man previously only believed to be the stuff of Greek Mythology? George's rational mind discounted the whole idea as preposterous, yet how else could he possibly explain the situation. It was even more preposterous to think that someone had created this whole scenario, renovated an entire island and populated it with lepers as he slept. For one thing, how could they have done it? For another, why would they have bothered? It made no sense; but then, nothing did any more.

The best he could hope for, George thought hopelessly, was that someone would come rushing up to him, just as the footman in the Jourdain and Moberley story, to point him in the right direction and show him the way home.

****

Finishing up at his patient's house, Manolis exited sadly. It would not be long before another of his 'family' was lost to him. He had known this old man since he had arrived at the island and regarded him as a favourite uncle. He recalled how the man had joked with him, when he had first visited the surgery, his face a mass of lumps and sores, about how, if Manolis didn't get his finger out and cure him the girls would stop chasing him. They had laughed together and the young, handsome Manolis had responded that if he had half as much success as his patient, he would be a happy man. It never ceased to amaze Manolis how accepting his patients could be of their situation and how their humour and determination carried them through the most horrific indignities.

Manolis headed off towards the beach, his calls now complete for the day. He resolved to keep a close eye on Georgio. He feared that the young man's mind was damaged and that he could be a danger, not only to himself, but to others here. He could not afford to take chances. It was important though, he felt, that he helped Georgio to try and integrate into the community and introduce him to his fellow islanders.

The island itself was in one of its transitional periods. A few souls had recently died and some newcomers had arrived to take their places among the beleaguered, but stoic community. These days were always difficult for Manolis. With the new residents came news from the outside world. This always created a feeling of restlessness amongst the community who would become unsettled, longing for the freedom they had lost and the love and contact with the families they were so cruelly denied. The incomers meanwhile, were disoriented, many in denial about the disease they suffered and horrified as they were forced to confront their neighbours, many of whom were in the advanced stages of illness and served as a sobering and terrifying reminder of what was to come. Manolis often had his work cut out just preventing anarchy on the island during these times. With skilful counselling however, Manolis and some of his most trusted helpers, soothed the physical and emotional pains carried by these poor, damaged people and soon, daily life returned to normality, the status quo redressed. Manolis wondered how the strange young man would integrate into his beloved community and what ripples of unrest he would create.

During George's stay in the sanatorium, Manolis had visited the Governor of the island and his committee in order to go through the usual ritual of placing the newcomers into their accommodations. This often depended on the advancement of their illnesses and the particular attributes of available housing. It had been decided that George would live in one of the smaller Venetian houses which had, until recently, housed a young woman, now tragically deceased. Reaching the beach, Manolis called out to George and beckoned him over.

"Now, Georgio", he began, "I am going to take you to your new home". His eyes twinkled. Most of those who arrived here had not had the luxury of a decent home for months, even years and it always gave him pleasure when he was able to offer them one of life's simplest pleasures, a sense of belonging. Leading George into the centre of the village, Manolis stole a glance at the young man whose spirit seemed broken as he walked compliantly next to him, a distant, poor bewildered soul. Manolis' heart went out to him as he thought what a terrifying thing it must be to be locked in an alien and unfamiliar world, particularly one which was haunted by strange imaginings. No matter, Manolis thought, what a person may have done in his life, good or bad, to find himself a victim of this evil and pernicious disease was indeed a tragedy.

Manolis actually regarded himself as a lucky man and it was the simple pleasures in life which gave him joy. He never considered the risks he undertook to live here amongst the diseased, on the contrary, he was grateful for the abiding love and friendship of the wonderful people whom he felt privileged to serve in this community. To sit in the sunshine on this beautiful island, to share a joke over an ouzo or a glass of wine whilst chatting happily to his friends here, surrounded by the colours of Greece or sometimes dancing the night away to the sound of a bouzouki was all he wished for in life. If he asked for one thing more, it would be to find a cure for the evil disease which killed and maimed those whom he loved and cared for. Manolis hoped that as George grew to know the people here he would come to appreciate the many advantages which the island offered to those in the young man's position and that he would count himself amongst the fortunate few who had not been forced to suffer the indignity of surviving alone in a cave, shunned by his community.

In the square, Athena and Maria, two of the village's most vociferous and eager gossips sat weaving their exquisite lace cloths, their hands still nimble and useful but with early signs of the decay beginning to affect their fingers. Soon, they would be unable to weave their beauty. Athena, the older of the two women, somewhere in her forties, put down her weaving for a moment as Manolis and Georgio approached. She waved, a smile lighting her face.

"Manoli, my dearest man!" she cried in delight. "Come, sit with us". Looking at George as she spoke, taking in every detail of the man, she asked, "And who have we to greet on the island this week?"

"Athena, you are looking wonderful as ever", Manolis took the woman's slowly withering hands in his. "You never cease to amaze me with the beauty of the cloth you weave and the beauty of your smile". Athena stood up painfully and unsteadily, her feet bandaged and clawed within the carefully constructed leather sandals she wore. Pain was etched upon her face, ageing her prematurely, but determinedly, she rose to greet both Manolis and George.

"This is Georgio, Athena. I know you will welcome him to our island. I'm relying on you to help him settle in". Eager to extend a welcome, to Manolis' great amusement, Athena immediately bombarded Georgio with all manner of personal questions.

"Yassou, Georgio", she greeted George, immediately followed by, How old are you? And where have you come from? Do you have a wife? Children? How did you come to be here? What did you do for a living?

George was utterly bemused as the woman addressed him, the questions left hanging in the air for some moments as he thought how to answer them without arousing suspicion of his apparent madness.

Watching, Manolis sensed George's discomfort and intervened.

"Now Athena, give him time. Don't overwhelm the poor man". And to George he said quietly, in his ear, "Don't be offended by her questions my friend. As you know, it is their way of being friendly. Athena means no harm and doesn't intend to pry. She is genuinely interested".

George smiled at the woman and, not wishing to offend, or draw attention to himself, he responded warmly and confidently telling her that he was 31 years of age, that he was not married, had no children and that he had come from London. He gave only the basics however, preferring to keep his own counsel and discouraging, by the lack of information he gave any further questioning. Athena's companion, he noticed, had remained quiet during their meeting and kept her eyes averted from him in shyness. She looked up at him from under a veil of shining dark hair, her deep brown eyes like warm pools, warm and welcoming, yet expressive in their sadness. She was, he guessed, about his age, her beauty marred by some signs of diseased flesh on her cheek which she tried in vain to hide from his view. Whilst she may have wished to join in the conversation, she was clearly self conscious, wishing not to draw his eyes upon her.

The pleasantries over, Manolis and George bid their farewells to the women and they went on their way.

"May you live long", Athena called out to George, accompanied by a dry spit. George looked questioningly at Manolis, wondering why he had elicited such a response from the woman.

"She is warding off the evil eye from you Georgio, nothing more", Manolis laughed. "I suppose you do not see this custom so much in London eh?" If only, George thought, such a simple action could really protect him. But hey! He had already met a mythical ferryman of the dead, arrived on a deserted island which had become mysteriously populated overnight, contracted leprosy and discovered he was living in 1940! Hell! he thought, with some amusement, anything is possible! Despite the oddity of his very existence at this time though, George felt strangely and inexplicably at home on the island the longer he stayed and the more of the people he met. How it was that he could feel almost a sense of normality, he really could not fathom.

Approaching the row of buildings which George recalled had been in the process of historical restoration on the day he had arrived, he was astounded at the difference now. Whereas the road had been deserted that fateful day, it was now a bustling thoroughfare, full of people in varying degrees of illness, making their purchases in the avenue of little shops which were laden with fresh meat, fruit, vegetables, cheeses, leather boots, belts, shoes, olive oil, woven cloths, wines and ouzo. George was stunned at the transformation. The ghost island had become a vibrant mercantile town. Many of those who shopped here displayed little in the way of disease. They looked just like any other Greek villager, the only difference being that they mingled unconcernedly with others who, like Nikos, were rotting away, almost beyond recognition as human. Ashamedly, George found it difficult to see those in such advanced stages of disease as anything proximate to human, and yet, as he passed through the avenue, he perceived the kindness within them and the determination that fuelled them to enjoy life to the fullest extent possible.

Stopping at the leather and cobbler's shop, Manolis introduced George to Yiannis and explained to the man that he would be in need of good protective shoes. George, as ever, stood transfixed, staring at the horrific vision before him. The skin on the man's face was so tightened and cracked by sores and blisters that each effort of speech clearly pained him. The man wept, not from his eyes with each painful exertion, but from a thousand suppurating lesions. A foul smell emanated from him, causing George to heave inwardly, not wishing to offend. In spite of the man's affliction, his hands worked deftly to produce a magnificent pair of boots at his block. As George watched in fascination, the man drew a painful rictus of a smile across his ravaged features.

"Ah! You like my boots, I see! I'll make you a magnificent pair of Cretan boots for the winter. But - how much will you pay me for them my friend?" George didn't know what to say. He had no money. How could he pay for anything here. He looked helplessly at Manolis, unsure how to respond to the man's question.

"Don't look so worried" Manolis smiled. You'll receive about 30 drachmas a month which is a benefit paid to the lepers here by the Cretan Government. It is, I suppose, an incentive for them to stay here and it eases the Government's conscience that they make life a little easier here for the exiles. Indeed, it is some consolation for those who live here George". Manolis paused, thinking a moment, pondering how little consolation or comfort there was for any of the community on Spinalonga. If they could swap the money for their health, they would have no hesitation. Continuing to explain the financial benefits of the lepers, he shook his head sadly. "Alas, Kyrie, many Cretans resent the allowance paid to these people. They earn less by working from sunrise to sunset, they say, so why should an island of lepers gain money for nothing? Can you believe that? That anyone should be jealous of such sick people? " Manolis' voice had risen in anger. That anyone should denigrate his people for receiving just a little comfort in their lives incensed him. He continued, the disgust and disdain evident in his voice.

"Unfortunately Georgio, the people here, because of the little money they receive are ripe for piracy by their own people. It is human nature sadly, to exploit the weak and the defenceless. Every luxury here is at a premium and every luxury on Spinalonga is just an ordinary, commonplace item elsewhere on Crete." A look of anger flickered in Manolis' otherwise placid and friendly features. He could not help but feel fury at the injustice and inequity afforded to these already downtrodden and unfortunate people. They asked for so little, yet the tiny comforts which made their lives bearable were lining the pockets of those who could afford to be generous of spirit. Manolis went on to explain that because of their physical condition, many of the community of Spinalonga were unable to maintain their homes or undertake simple tasks such as washing their clothes. Food preparation presented a huge danger to them. Deformed and painful hands, often shrivelled into nothing more than claws meant that cooking over flames was a major danger because of the risk of fire.

Because of this, it was necessary to recruit domestic help from Crete. Fear and prejudice kept most people away, but there were a few of course who unselfishly gave of themselves to help out, reassured by the many precautions in place to protect them. The chances of catching the disease were kept to a minimum, but, there was always a risk. For the most part however, only the promise of money would attract help to the island. Knowing that their services were at a premium, there was plenty of scope for exploitation of the community. Greeks were renowned for their bargaining skills and they knew only too well they could seek danger money for coming to the 'Island of the Damned' as it was popularly known. Although things had slowly improved, many Cretans cashed in on the lepers' financial benefits and their helplessness by demanding high wages in return for their help.

"Ah, Georgio, I suppose, in many ways, these people cannot be blamed for their reluctance to come here and their high demands for doing so but it means that money for food for the community to nourish themselves and for medical supplies is rapidly diminished".

George shuffled restlessly from side to side as Manolis spoke of the islanders' exploitation. For the first time in his life, he now began to appreciate what dependency was and the repugnance of those who would benefit so grossly and without conscience from the weak and vulnerable. He saw, for the first time, how he too had lived a parasitic existence at the expense of those less fortunate than himself and he felt disgust. He could say nothing of his thoughts to the two men who stood before him however so he tried to disguise his self-loathing by enquiring as to how and when supplies came to the island. Manolis explained that each week, amongst great excitement and anticipation from the residents, a boat arrived, loaded with food and other goods for the islanders to purchase. The boatman ventured no further than the harbour and left the goods, much of which had been ordered the previous week by the residents on the beach. Manolis would meet him and hand over the money which had been through the disinfection room. The prices charged for these wares, Manolis explained, were so high that the community could barely afford the essentials, let alone the occasional luxury to buy a small pleasure in a life barely worth the effort of living.

George, chastened and sombre, lost once more in his own thoughts was silent as Manolis bade farewell to Yiannis.

"I will see you again soon, Kyrie", he called after George. "And you will shortly have your new dancing boots my friend", he teased, a twinkle in his eye. "We shall give them a display they will never forget at the welcome party this week Huh?"

Embarrassed, George grinned self consciously. "I am sure, Yianni that I shall be lighter than air in these boots." In truth though, George felt he would never feel light hearted again as the grim realisation of self-discovery weighed heavily upon him.

"This street that God hides
from the sun
Protected many an
innocent one
Listen for they are not
gone
Their Ghosts forever
linger on"
ISLAND OF TEARS
William Ronald Hawkins

A LIFE LESS ORDINARY

George was left reeling with the discovery that he was living in a time and place over 30 years before his birth. What was there to say about that? And to whom? Had there been an elaborate joke played on him? It was about as unlikely as the other option; that he had tumbled into a time slip and was now living the life of a leper, exiled from the rest of the world. Over the following days, George battled with the possibilities and, he thought finally, if he wasn't mad already, he soon would be as his mind was torn between one answer and the next. His decision therefore was to make no decisions at all. The answer wasn't going to come easily, not at the moment anyway and his mind was becoming so tortured that sheer exhaustion persuaded him that he should stop struggling against whatever situation he was in and simply accept it for the time being. Everything was just so bizarre that there really wasn't any point in trying to fathom it out. George reasoned that everything may become evident if he just relaxed a little. If his mind was the culprit for creating all of this then he needed time to heal it. If someone was playing a joke, then time would tell because whoever was responsible would slip up, make a little mistake when they became complacent and the answer would be clear. If neither of these were the case, well, George shuddered, he was in a truly terrifying situation, the outcome of which he couldn't even begin to speculate about. He reminded himself of his reason for coming to Crete in the first place. To disappear, start a new life, retain his freedom. At least, he thought, he had his wish. The old saying was true, he thought, dejectedly, 'Be careful what you wish for - you just might get it'. It was a favourite saying of his mother's and it had never seemed truer that it did right now.

George had met, during the afternoon with Manolis, a great

many of the townsfolk, all of whom had greeted him with geniality and warmth. He, however, had found it difficult to overcome his revulsion as he greeted one diseased person after another, some decidedly worse in their condition than others. He recoiled from the touch of anyone who came close, terrified, not only by the appearance, but the smell which emanated from the worst affected, making him want to vomit in horror and disgust.

"How do you cope with these people each day?" he now asked Manolis as they returned to the surgery, the afternoon's business complete. "I mean, I know it sounds cruel, but they are hideous; and that smell! I want to be sick whenever someone comes too close. How do you do it?"

To George's surprise, Manolis seemed unperturbed by the question. He made no protest about George's confession of disgust. Shrugging his shoulders, he was pragmatic.

"It is neither easy, nor pleasant to work and live amongst such a disease, my friend, but if I did not do it, then there are few of us who would be around to help these people. Besides, I care for the people I tend to and after a while, well, you see just people, not their disease. It takes time, you will see".

George somehow doubted that he would ever become accepting, or used to the sight and smell of the disease. If he really thought that he had leprosy (a matter which, despite remaining open minded on other aspects, he refused to believe) he would, he thought, just end it all now. He couldn't contemplate the slow, painful process of rotting away.

Reaching for a book on the shelf above his desk, Manolis flicked through the pages and, finding the passage he had searched for, he handed the book to George.

"Here, read this. You will see that even the most dedicated of us have our difficulties in dealing with leprosy sufferers. You are not alone in this George, and I do not want you to feel bad about your feelings. I understand them and, you will find, so do the sufferers themselves. No-one will blame you for feeling revulsion or disgust. Such is the cross these people must bear. They know that they would have felt no different towards a leper when they were healthy". Passing the book to George, Manolis explained, "This was written by a missionary who once cared for the lepers on an island called Molokai in Hawaii. It is from his diary which he kept throughout his stay. You will see that even the most philanthropic and Christian minded of people also express revulsion". George looked down at the passage to which Manolis pointed and read,

"The flesh decays and yields an infectious odour. The breath of the lepers poisons the air... I sometimes experience a feeling of repugnance. I am quite puzzled how to administer extreme unction when the hands and feet are but one sore. It is the sign of approaching death".

George found it difficult to imagine why anyone would choose to work with lepers, considering the risks and the sheer vileness of the disease. He was filled with admiration for the man to whom he now, in many ways looked up. He had known him for such a short time, but George felt certain that Manolis' kindness and compassion was genuine.

"I doubt, Manoli, that I could ever have your compassion or magnanimity in working amongst these people. I just hope that I can control my urge to recoil every time someone says 'Good Morning' to me.'

"George, believe me, eventually you will get used to the way things are here and eventually you too will stop noticing the scars and deformity. It will be commonplace".

"And, if you are right about my own condition Manoli, I suppose I would do well to remember this when some healthy person vomits when they see me or turns away in disgust".

Manolis said nothing but simply smiled sympathetically in quiet of acknowledgement of George's words.

Amazingly, during the following days and weeks of George's time on the island, he came to learn the truth of Manolis' words. He kept to himself initially, fearing the inevitable questions and the difficult answers, but boredom soon gave way to a desire to find out more about the people here and incredibly, George gradually found himself settling into the life of the island. This was due in large part, to the efforts of the people around him who refused to allow anyone to feel alone or excluded.

In the first weeks however, George took time in quiet contemplation and reflection of all that had gone before in his life, something which he had never really had the opportunity to do before. Here, on the island, normal life was suspended for him and his main purpose now was really just to exist. He had no work to go to, no customers to visit, no traffic or shops around him. The whole pulse of his life had calmed, become steady and peaceful. It was then that the ridiculousness of 21st century living struck him. Before, in London, he hardly noticed anything or anyone around him, so consumed was he with rushing around, fighting the traffic to do his business, to earn a living, to buy a house and spend his money on some frippery or other that lost its charm almost the moment it was bought. Sitting by the sea, watching the sun rise in the morning on this island, George awoke to appreciate the simple joy of a glorious morning on an Aegean idyll where he could savour the peace, and appreciate the beauty and joy of a picture book sunrise and feel the warmth of the sun soaking through his skin.

George had moved into his little Venetian House in the village which was situated near the hospital. It was basic, but serviceable and he soon came to regard it as his home, his own little haven from the world. He had nothing except the clothes he had stood in when he moved into the house and therefore, he had nothing to mark the place as his own.

Inside, there was one main room containing a table and

chairs, a little cooking area with a wash basin and, through an archway lay a very small bedroom with a stone based Cretan bed inside. The obligatory icon of Christ with the Virgin Mary hung on the wall. An outhouse contained a less than desirable lavatory. The house was whitewashed inside, in keeping with the interiors of most of the buildings George had come across in Crete, but outside retained the original brown stone of the Venetian style. Shutters blocked out the sunlight and during the day, kept the house at an almost bearable temperature. As soon as he entered the house, George instantly felt at home and, following a cursory exploration, exhausted, he collapsed gratefully onto the mattress which lay bare, for a much needed rest. He did not however, lay for long as his rest was disturbed by the first of the many visitors he entertained on that day.

****

Irini Xanthis looked on in quiet amusement the day that George Fitrakis entered her life. Georgio was to be her new neighbour and, from what Manolis had told her, he presented the community with something of an enigma. Of course, a little intrigue didn't go wrong when there was little else of note happening in the lives of the community. Irini's house was opposite George's new home and she was tending to her vegetable garden as Manolis and the young man stepped over the threshold. George barely registered her presence, but Manolis, who had spoken to her at some length about the new arrival, grinned and waved before turning to follow George into the house. The two men had left a short while later, with George returning alone once Manolis had completed his home visits. Now, fifteen minutes after the young man had shut the door behind him began the stream of welcome visits from the other locals. It was Nikos who shuffled up to his front door first followed by Athena, Maria and Yiannis. As each one left, with perfect timing, another approached the door, none of the visitors wanting to share their first meeting with George with any of the others. Irini would introduce herself, but, all in good time. For now, she wanted to observe her neighbour from a distance after the little information her dearest friend and confidante Manolis had imparted to her on his recent visit to her home. He had asked her to keep an eye on George and had arranged, via the committee that he should be housed next to Irini. Manolis was a little concerned for the young man's welfare after their first inauspicious few days and explained to Irini that he feared he was unstable, haunted, as he was, by strange delusions and wild imaginings.

Naturally, Irini was a little perturbed by Manolis' request, not only by the responsibility which he was placing upon her shoulders, but also fearful that George could be dangerous. Manolis had allayed her fears though.

"Irini, it is a strange thing, but, although George has confided some very odd things to me, the conviction with which he spoke almost convinced me that the things he said, which go far beyond anything that you or I could understand, were based on some sort of truth."

"What do you mean Manoli? When you say it goes far beyond anything we can understand - what do you mean?"

"Irini, I do not want to say too much about Georgio just now. Just do one thing for me. Befriend him if you can. Gain his trust and see if he will confide more in you. Make your own mind up about him but let us discuss it further. Don't worry. I don't think he presents danger to anyone else. I fear for his own safety though. He is troubled and confused."

"Then of course, my dearest Manoli, I shall do as you ask. But I have to say, I am intrigued. Can you not give me a clue as to the mystery which surrounds my new neighbour?"

Manolis shook his head slowly.

"I'm not sure I would know where to begin Irini. All I will say to you is this; it struck me that, if you believe in such things, he may be a seer or a prophet of some kind. Some of the things he said; it was almost as though he had certain knowledge of things which may yet come to pass." Manolis laughed, a little embarrassed.

"Oh, ignore me. I am talking nonsense. Forget what I say! He is a sick, troubled young man and we must take care of him that's all there is to it."

Irini had spent enough time with Manolis to know that, for all his protestations, something had unnerved him about George and she was determined to discover what it was for herself. Raising her eyebrow inquisitively, signalling to Manolis that she knew he was withholding something from her, he dropped his gaze to the floor and smiled.

"You know me far to well, my lovely Irini. Now, don't push me for more information. You will have me saying the same ridiculous things that he does and then it is I who will be thought of as mad." They both laughed companionably and Irini disappeared into her little pantry returning moments later with a carafe of local wine.

As was their habit, Manolis and Irini spent the rest of the evening, contented just to be in each other's company. The silences between them were comfortable, the unspoken sentiments palpable yet the voicing of them unnecessary. The relationship which had grown between the couple was solid, unbreakable, yet incapable of the binding which each might have wished for had circumstances been different. Despite their unspoken longings, the boundary which existed between them could never be broken. Now, here in Manolis' company, Irini, though grateful for the small moments of happiness which she shared with him at these times, felt the vacuum of her emptiness and the hopelessness which had accompanied her since she first stepped off the boat to Spinalonga, alone and abandoned by those whom she had trusted.

Irini recalled now, some years ago when she had sat with her husband on just such a night, sipping wine and making plans for the life they would spend together. And what plans they had made! They would travel and see a little of the world beyond Crete, they would work the olive grove and build their own press to make the finest and world renowned olive oil! People would come from everywhere just to see how the oil was made and to take away bottles and canisters by the dozen! They were young then, and full of hope. The only blight on their happiness was the bitter opposition she and Spiros had encountered from his family when they had told them of their wish to marry. Irini was the daughter of one of the family's workers and Spiros was the son of a wealthy and respected Cretan dynasty. It was unheard of for two people of such social diversity to contemplate marriage. Irini had known the family all her life. Indeed, she and her family had always been treated well by them and she was often permitted to play in the grounds of their home and would run to the kitchens whenever she smelt the sweet aroma of baklava and the other delicious pastries that Aleka, the cook would produce for the lavish dinner parties held in the big house. Aleka would always wrap some of her delicious sweetmeats in a cloth for Irini, who would disappear into the olive grove to savour the treats she had been given.

Irini met Spiros when they were both only ten. He was running in and out of the olive trees, the sun adding highlights of golden brown to his otherwise thick, dark hair. Irini had watched him from her hiding place close by and, gathering courage, she slipped out shyly to greet the lively lad in the hope that perhaps they could run together, play hide and seek and find some new adventures. From that moment on, Spiros and Irini became inseparable, until, one day, shortly following his 18th birthday, he broke the news to her that he was leaving to study in Athens. Irini was distraught by the news and the depth of her sorrow surprised both of them. The more Spiros thought about it, the more he too realised that his life would not be the same without Irini, but it was not until he found himself alone in his student rooms in Athens that the loneliness and despair threatened to suffocate him. Only weeks after his departure, he returned and asked Irini to be his wife. Overjoyed, Irini had no hesitation in accepting his proposal but on one condition; that he complete his studies in Athens first.

No announcement as to their matrimonial intentions was made at this time. Spiros knew that his mother, in particular had designs upon the daughters of other influential families in the area and would not take kindly to Irini as his intended future wife. His parents had tolerated their friendship throughout childhood and were relieved when he moved to Athens lest their closeness develop into something stronger. Spiros mother, Calista meanwhile visited the families of Crete's most eligible women during his absence and laid on extravagant dinners whenever he came home to orchestrate meetings with those whom she hoped might entrance him. To Calista's great disappointment however, Spiros would barely exchange a sentence with any of these women, preferring to bid them an early goodnight and, unbeknown to his mother, escape into the evening warmth to find Irini. Spiros was only too well aware of the problems they would encounter when they finally announced their intention to marry and whilst he was commuting between Crete and Athens, the couple felt it wiser to remain silent and secretive about their continuing relationship until Spiros could return and become a permanent buffer against his parents' and in particular, Calista's inevitable wrath. His mother was not one to accept things quietly. In the meantime, Irini kept her head low and continued to work in the olive grove, helping her father to harvest the olives whilst also working in the nearby town of Rethymno serving tables in one of the tavernas there. It would have horrified Calista to think that her future daughter in law was one of such low social standing.

Finally, the day came when Spiros returned to Crete for good. Irini ran to the door as he tapped out their own secret code and flung her arms around him, eager to shower him with kisses and all the love she could muster. They saw no reason to delay their marriage any longer and so, that very evening, Spiros sat down with his parents to break the news that he wished to spend his life with Irini.

"Are you insane?" Calista spat out, the venom tingeing each and every syllable. "Of course you cannot marry Irini! They are our employees; little better than servants! What could make you suggest such a thing to us? Do you care so little for our family name or reputation? There are plenty of beautiful young women out there who can provide you with the support you need and your future children with the right upbringing. What can an olive picker's daughter offer you? Why, she isn't even educated! I will never allow it, do you hear? Never!"

Spiros knew that it was pointless arguing with Calista when she was in such a mood. His father meanwhile, always the mild mannered parent tried in vain to reason with his wife. After all, hadn't they known Irini and her family all these years? Hadn't they been good and faithful workers? Irini had gone to school, she was educated. All she lacked was wealth and the trappings that went with it. She could be trained to become a worthy wife for Spiros surely?

Calista merely flew from the room in hysteria, unable to believe that both the men in her life were willing to contemplate accepting someone into their family who was nothing more than a servant girl.

The initial storm subsided eventually however and though Calista would never accept Irini into her family, she knew there was little could be done to prevent it if Spiros was determined to marry the little slut and his spineless father refused to intervene and forbid it. She could not bear the thought of her wealth falling into the hands of such guttersnipes.

Despite Calista's bitterness, which ran high on the day of the wedding, nevertheless it was, for everyone else who attended, a most joyous occasion. Spiros' father, Andreus, presented the couple with a cottage built upon their extensive lands and made Spiros the manager of the olive business. He for one, was glad to be able to step back and give the responsibility to his son. Andreus welcomed Irini into the family with open arms. He had always liked the girl, her sunny disposition and her devotion to Spiros far outweighing the objections of his wife. Andreus joked with Spiros and Irini:

"Spiros, take a look at your mother! I think she has found a wasp's nest to chew judging by the expression on her face!"

"I wish she did not feel like this father. My happiness is spoiled only by her unhappiness".

"She is a difficult woman Spiros, but mark my words, she will come round eventually when she sees what an asset you have in Irini and you present her with some beautiful grandchildren. She will be unable to resist, you wait and see!"

And so, Spiros and Irini had started their married life full of optimism and plans for a great future. They were financially secure and they both wanted to work hard to preserve the family business and assets. Irini's family would also be well taken care of due to her good marriage.

For the first months of their marriage, the couple were ecstatically happy. It was not to be for long though as tragedy struck and cast all of their lives into turmoil, despair and disarray.

Spiros was working one afternoon with Irini's father, Kosmo, when the latter stood on a knife and cut his foot badly as it pierced the exposed part of the skin in his leather sandal. Kosmo had not noticed as the knife lacerated his flesh and it was Spiros who called to him as he saw the wound bleeding copiously. Spiros rushed over to the other man and quickly tore up the cloth which contained their lunch in order to dress the wound and stave the bleeding.

"There, that's better. Did you not feel the knife go into you Kosmo? The cut is deep and you will need medical treatment".

"Why no, I felt nothing. It is strange, but I seem to have lost the feeling in certain parts of my hands and feet. If you hadn't noticed the blood, I doubt I would have known anything about it until later".

"Kosmo, I think you need to see the Doctor. I will call him as soon as we get back to the house".

Spiros, as good as his word, had called the family doctor out to take a look at Kosmo that very afternoon but the news that was imparted hit the entire family as though a bomb had exploded in their midst. A simple cut had led to the appalling discovery that Kosmo had contracted the most horrific and feared of diseases, leprosy. The family reeled at the news, stultified in the immediate aftermath into inaction, no-one really knowing what they should do next. Irini comforted her mother as her father lay alone and bemused in the back room while a family conference was called back at the big house with Calista presiding.

"We have to get him off our land! No-one will come near us again! Spiros - now do you see what you have done by marrying into this family? You have brought the greatest shame possible to us! Our business will be ruined - we are finished!"

Angrily, Spiros responded to his mother, whose histrionics were now beginning pall with him.

"Mother! Whether I was married to Irini or not, Kosmo would still have contracted leprosy! Do you think the disease discriminates against people because of those whom they choose to marry? You really are a stupid woman sometimes!"

"How dare you speak to me in this way? After all I have done for you? Don't you understand, it is because he mixes with the wrong company that he has this disease! People of our standing aren't exposed to the great unwashed unless of course, you choose to marry into it!" Calista spat out the last words before descending into a wail of misery and tears.

Spiros could endure no more of his mother's vitriol and strode from the room, his anger propelling him from the house in search of his distraught wife and mother in law.

As news spread of Kosmo's illness, workers and visitors to the family's grove and home diminished rapidly and the family found themselves alone and shunned. Something, Calista determined, had to be done - and quickly. She instructed the family's doctor to make enquiries and two options presented themselves; either Kosmo must go to Athens where the hospital was used to dealing with lepers, or he must be exiled to the island of Spinalonga which was off the North Eastern coast of Crete. Irini and her mother were devastated when officials from the Medical Commission arrived at the house with papers authorising the removal of Kosmo to Spinalonga. It was a sad day for Irini and her mother as they waved goodbye to poor Kosmo, his bewilderment clear for all to see. An uncertain future now faced them all.

If Irini's sorrow was profound when Kosmo left for Spinalonga, her life, as she had known it was about to come to an end when Spiros discovered the telltale reddened patches on his arms and feet signifying that he too had contracted leprosy. When the diagnosis was confirmed, she fell to the floor, a wail of "No!" emitting from her amongst the sounds reminiscent of a mortally wounded animal. She knew at that moment, that the second of the men whom she loved was about to be torn from her.

This time however, it was Calista who refused to allow Spiros to be taken from the family. He was isolated in the little house on the family grounds and only Irini was permitted to visit him from anything other than a distance. In her perverse way, Calista felt it a fitting punishment for Irini, who had wanted her son so badly. Well - now she is welcome to him, Calista thought cruelly, now that no-one else will have him. The news of Spiros' illness was suppressed amongst the villagers who were told that he was working away in Athens for some months. The panic over Kosmo's illness had subsided after his removal from Crete and the last thing the family wanted was further disruption to their lives.

Irini was forced to witness the rapid deterioration of her husband as she nursed him and sat by his bedside throughout the day and as a vigil by night. There were complications due to the disease having not been detected sooner and the onset of infection in open wounds. His demise was speedy as blood poisoning blackened his feet and toes and gangrene spread through his body at an alarming rate. Although the doctor had been frantically making arrangements to transport Spiros to Athens (his mother insisting that anywhere in Crete could result in the community finding out about his infection), he was not fast enough to prevent his death only days following the diagnosis.

Irini was a broken woman. She had lost her husband and, if her bereavement were not bad enough, news had reached them that her father too had developed similar complications and was not expected to last the night. Irini and her mother supported each other as Spiros' funeral was quickly dispensed with and they were ostracised from the gathering inside the house where the story went that he had died from blood poisoning following a bite from a wild cat. Irini knew that her days as part of Spiros' family, such as they had been were now at an end. She could not, however, in her wildest imaginings have guessed what would happen next.

Calista had good contacts in Crete and there was always someone in authority willing to take a few risks for a generous reward. She had decided that it was all Irini's doing that her family had come to this. Kosmo's continued mingling with the pauper villagers at the local tavernas had brought this upon them. Now that her beloved son Spiros was cruelly torn from her, a kind of madness had gripped her mind and her focus for revenge became Irini. Calista would never allow Irini and her scum family to inherit Spiros' fortune. She had to do something to remove her permanently from their lives.

Irini was summoned to the big house only days later, her mourning still evident for all to see as she had grown thinner by the day, her pallor due to heartache and sleepless nights.

"Irini, I have asked you here so that the Doctor may check you over for any signs of leprosy. You must realise that you are at extreme risk of contracting the disease having been so close to it".

"Calista, I care nothing for whether I have leprosy or not. I would surely embrace death now that I have lost the love of my life and my dear father."

Calista was cold, impassive.

"Nevertheless, it is my wish that you are examined. I do not wish to have any more lepers on my doorstep and you must think of others now".

Nodding in acquiescence, Irini was led away to another room by the Doctor who apparently had travelled from Aghios Nikolaos to take blood and skin samples from her. Once finished, she was ordered to remain in her own home until the results came through.

Days later, two officials came from the Medical Commission carrying papers which stated they had found the bacteria which signified leprosy present in Irini and she was sentenced to exile on Spinalonga. Only Calista knew the truth but she could not resist the final cruel cut as Irini was led away, compliantly and without fuss to the waiting van which would transport her daughter in law to the Spinalonga boat.

"Well, I suppose you thought you would live a comfortable life by marrying Spiros. I told you and him, that nothing good would ever come of such a match. But now, I've made sure that you never get your filthy, grasping little hands on Spiros' fortune. Enjoy your new life Irini. I'm sure you'll be more at home where you're going now".

And so it was that Irini arrived on Spinalonga, lost, alone, bereaved and in despair. It was only months later, as her emotions began to heal that Calista's words came back to her. Try as she might though, she could not work out what she could have meant when she said that she'd made sure Irini would not inherit Spiros' money. In many ways, there seemed little point in dwelling on it. It would make no difference. Her medical papers diagnosed leprosy didn't they?

In his usual way, Manolis had cared for Irini, as he did with the others who arrived on the island. However, the pair had found themselves to be kindred spirits, both kind and compassionate, wanting only to help those around them and indeed, each other. Irini's presence on the island baffled Manolis to a great extent because although the medical results categorically diagnosed leprosy, there seemed to be no physical emanation of the disease as yet. He presumed that it simply lay dormant now but with the onset of time, its symptoms would become manifest. All the same, he was troubled by her exile to the island. She was a beautiful, vibrant woman, touched by goodness and humanity. Her life was wasting here and yet, for purely selfish reasons, he was so glad that she had come to Spinalonga. She had become the one person he could confide in; express his sadness and frustration at his inability to help the islanders; she was the one person who could comfort him with her wise words. He longed for her to comfort him in her arms, but Irini would touch no-one. She blamed herself for bringing death to her husband, for having brought him down to the social level in which he could contract leprosy. She refused to believe that paupers and Kings alike could contract the disease but, all the same, she would never be responsible for passing her curse to any other person, especially not to someone she loved and cared for now. She could not bear the burden of another death at her hands. Manolis, for his own part knew that he must be restrained in his love for Irini. He was her doctor after all and their relationship must never be compromised if he was to care for her properly. Besides, if he did contract leprosy, what good would he be to everyone else here? No, he had to remain distant whatever their feelings for each other might be. And so, over the years, the pair had developed a close and loving though entirely proper relationship, each happy in the knowledge that they could spend time together in their estranged little world.

****

George's rest was disturbed first of all by a feeble tap on his door. Upon opening it, he was confronted by the very same vision of horror which had confronted him as he awoke from his slumber by the Church. It was Nikos, smiling his painful, rictus grin, barely recognisable as a smile.

"Yassou Georgio" he greeted George brightly. George, trying to disguise his revulsion, returned the greeting as Nikos proudly held out a shopping bag in his poor, painfully deformed hands. Wishing he didn't have to hold the bag, George nevertheless accepted it graciously and looked inside. It contained oranges which Nikos told him were grown in his own garden which he lovingly tended when his pain wasn't too bad. Also there was bread, some feta cheese, olives and tomatoes inside the bag. George looked up from the bag at the man who now stood eagerly before him as he inspected the contents. He felt unutterable shame at his reaction to Nikos and was genuinely touched by his kindness. Here, after all, was a man who had virtually nothing, yet was willing to share the little he did have with a complete stranger. Looking into those rheumy, clouded eyes once again, George could see the person behind the grotesque mask, his joys and his sadness all compounded into those expressive orbs.

"Efharisto poli, Niko" 'Thank you very much', George smiled, nodding his gratitude and wishing he had more he could say to the man or something he could offer in return.

"Parakalo", 'You are welcome' responded the man who was clearly unused to simple acceptance or geniality from strangers as he kept his head bent in humility and no doubt, shame. He spoke no more and gesturing a wave of goodbye, his business done, Nikos turned and shuffled laboriously away, looking back only once more to wave farewell.

Nikos, as Irini had observed, wasn't George's last visitor that day. In fact, he was the first of many and George's induction into the community of lepers was swift, leaving him no time to worry about how he should deal with them. A procession of people knocked upon his door, each bearing a gift.

Athena was next to arrive and presented George with a beautiful white tablecloth, woven by her own hands. A little later, Maria arrived, clearly struck by the handsome young man who had come to the island and caused such a stir. Her beautiful face was curtained by the shining dark brown hair which she re-arranged constantly to cover the unsightly blemishes which were attacking her lovely features. She brought him baklava, a traditional pastry, drenched in syrup.

Word about George's arrival in the village must have spread like wildfire as more complete strangers arrived bearing something useful or designed to provide him with some small comfort. He received some white cotton shirts, a pair of black trousers, and, when Yiannis arrived, it was to present George with the most exquisite hand made leather shoes.

"I will make you a fine pair of Cretan boots for the winter. You must take care of your feet and they will take care of you my friend", he laughed.

"Yianni, these are beautiful", George said delightedly, marvelling at the stitching and admiring the crafting of the shoes. "Poli Kala, Yianni", he grinned.

Yiannis, looking around the room, observed the piles of

George's newly acquired possessions.

"I see I am not the first to bring you welcome gifts"

"Everyone here has been so kind."

"Of course, it is the way here Kyrie. We must look out for each other on the island because believe me, no-one else will. We all have something we can give whether it is an item or our time. We know you won't have received your money yet. These things will help you until you receive your allowances". Yiannis lowered himself into one of the chairs next to George's little table. He was a large man, powerfully built and he sported a thick, black beard, flecked through with grey. He reminded George of the actor, Topol from the film, 'Fiddler on the Roof'. It would not have been inappropriate had he burst into a rendition of 'If I were a rich man' and George had to stifle a laugh at this thought. But then something else struck him. How could he know of such a film, such an actor and this song when it came from 1963 if he had not travelled backwards in time? Another paradox, he thought.

Yiannis shifted uncomfortably in his seat, pain obviously causing him distress which he tried not to show.

"I was thinking you know", he continued. "There are few people here who speak any English. Maybe you should have a class to teach English? We are always glad of something new to interest us here; something to take our minds off approaching death".

George thought for a few moments, considering Yiannis' proposition.

"You know Yianni, that's not such a bad idea. I'd be happy to give English lessons. It will help me to give something back here".

"Of course! Then that is settled then. You can use the back room in my shop if you wish". Now, I must go, but tonight, we have a gathering at the taverna. We will eat, drink the finest ouzo and raki - maybe even dance a little eh?" Rising stiffly from the chair, Yiannis made his way painfully to the door.

"You must come. 8.30. See you there". With that, Yiannis was gone. George sat down to inspect all the gifts he had received that day and strangely, they felt like the most precious gifts he ever had.

Finally, the tide of visitors abated and George was able to sleep for a while during the hottest part of the day, awakening some hours later, refreshed and feeling pretty good. He washed and changed into one of the cool, white handmade shirts, his new black trousers and superbly crafted shoes. He rolled up the sleeves of the shirt which was open at the collar and inspected himself in the mirror over the sink. He still looked tired, he thought, but, if he did say so himself, he thought he cut something of a dash in his new outfit. His skin was lightly tanned and his own Greek features, the slightly large nose and black hair were flatteringly accentuated. He threw open the shutters and almost immediately, a waft of deliciously roasting meat invaded his nostrils and he could hear someone softly singing. He guessed it was the woman across the way to whom Manolis had briefly referred. Irini, he thought her name was. The delicious smells emanating from her house made him realise that he was famished. He actually couldn't recall when he had last eaten. As there were a couple of hours before he was due to meet Yiannis and the others, George cut himself some of the soft white bread, the crumbly, tangy and brilliantly white feta cheese and the deliciously juicy, firm tomatoes. All of this he consumed with relish. He couldn't remember the last time bread and cheese tasted so good. Sated, George ventured out of the house and glanced over at the house opposite. There, he saw Irini watering the colourful hanging baskets which adorned her doorway. She looks perfect, George thought to himself, no sign of any infirmity or deformity. He wondered how one such as she found herself on this island. At the same time, he felt an instant attraction to the woman who, though a little older than he, was stunningly beautiful. She glanced up and smiled, shyly, a little uncertainly, he thought.

"Yassas", George ventured. Wiping her hands on her apron, she returned the greeting and came towards him. She held out her right hand to shake his own.

"Isn't this the preferred greeting of the British?" she asked, a twinkle of amusement in her eye.

"Indeed, it is" George smiled, grasping her hand in a firm shake with his own. Hers was smooth, delicate, like a flower, he thought.

"I am Irini, and you are George", she smiled. Welcome to Spinalonga. How are you settling in to your new home?"

"Well, I've had so many visitors bringing me all sorts of wonderful things. I think I shall be very comfortable here. Under the circumstances, that is", he added as an afterthought.

"Ah, yes, the circumstances. Better not to think about them too much. We are the forgotten ones here on Spinalonga and it is probably for the best. If we tried to return to a normal life in Crete, or anywhere else for that matter, we would be treated with disdain and hatred. People do not like our kind. Even our families prefer to believe we no longer exist. Such is their shame". Irini looked sad and reflective. She shook off her fleeting sadness.

"So Georgio, shall we see you at the taverna this evening? The welcome evenings are always a lively affair. I am preparing some food now take along with me".

"Well, how can I refuse when such a glorious smell is wafting past my window? I wouldn't miss it for anything. I'm looking forward to seeing some of the friends I've made here already".

"You will make many more here Georgio, you may depend upon it. I think you have a good heart. You will help many people here, I am sure".

If only she knew what he was really like, George thought. She wouldn't want to know me at all. Still, he accepted Irini's compliment without protest and waved her farewell as he meandered through the village a while before heading off to the welcome evening. Appreciating once more, the Mediterranean heat, George thought how perfect this place would be in different circumstances. Passing the little church, he noticed the door was ajar, so he stepped inside. It felt peaceful, safe and cool in there. In contrast with the stark austerity and forbidding atmosphere of the few churches he had entered back home (which was generally only to attend the obligatory wedding, funeral or christening), the Orthodox Church was friendly and cheerful. It felt like a place of celebration, hope and joyful worship with its burst of colour in the form of Byzantine icons, gold ornaments and flickering candles. George supposed there could be few celebrations as such at this particular church, but, if nothing else, the visitor could gain a sense of comfort and wellbeing. At home, in the unwelcoming, cold stone walls of the churches there, George had never had any sense of the alleged benevolent presence of God and yet, here, despite the curse of this island, he could envisage God. Why though, any God should have behaved so cruelly to those in exile on this island, he really could not imagine. George lit a candle and, for the first time since his childhood, uttered a prayer, asking God for help to get him out of here and to set his life straight again. If, thought George, he could believe in the world he now found himself in, he couldn't possibly deny the possible existence of a God. After all, he now found himself in a situation where, it appeared both the Christian God and the ancient pagan Gods co-existed. At that moment, if someone were to tell him the Easter Bunny, the Tooth Fairy and Santa Clause were on Spinalonga, he would surely have believed it.

After a short period of quiet contemplation in the church, George continued with his constitutional. As he passed various townsfolk, he greeted them with a "Yassas" every so often. Retracing his steps of the first day, George ascended the steps to grid area once more. He was startled when a voice interrupted his thoughts.It was Manolis who had appeared suddenly and without warning at his side. George jumped out of his skin as Manolis spoke.

"They are graves, Georgio. I am sorry", he now laughed. "I didn't mean to startle you".

"I was taking a break down there by the fortress walls when you passed me", he explained. "You didn't see me. Too engrossed in your own thoughts, I think".

"So, these are graves, are they? I wondered what they could possibly be".

"These are, I'm afraid, the paupers' graves. Those who either have relatives willing to help them, or who choose to save their money for a decent burial will have a fine wooden coffin and a wooden cross for an individual grave made for them by Aristotle, our carpenter here on the island. Sadly, those with fewer resources are simply discarded in these anonymous, mass graves and every four years, they are joined by those from the individual graves to make room for the newly dead. Alas, it is the only way we have of dealing effectively with the disposal of remains on the island".

George supposed it was a practical solution. How else could they dispose of the bodies on such a small island? Nevertheless, it was sad, so impersonal, with nothing remaining to mark the existence of someone who had once been vital, a person who would have loved and been loved, erased from existence. To end up as nothing more than refuse was the final degradation. George shook his head in sorrow. The two men then walked slowly down from the graveyard, the silence between them palpable, each of them lost in their own thoughts. It was George who broke the silence, seeking to satisfy his curiosity about Irini.

"I met a woman called Irini today", George began conversationally. "Why is she here? She looks perfectly healthy"

"I have wondered that myself, many times, Georgio. I do not have the facilities here for diagnosis, only for treatment of the disease. But, she has the papers from the Medical Commission to say that she has leprosy and therefore I must accept what I am told by them and treat her accordingly. You are right though. I have long suspected a mistake but I have been unable to get the Commission to review her case. I have my suspicions Georgio as to why she is here, but I cannot prove them".

"Manoli, what are you suggesting? What suspicions do you have?"

"Simply that it is not the first time that a healthy person has been sent to Spinalonga for political or other reasons, my friend. Money is more powerful than justice and I am afraid there is little I can do alone to fight the authorities when this happens."

George was stunned by Manolis' revelation. If this was true, then wasn't it possible that he had been sent here for some ulterior motive too?

"Do not trouble yourself over Irini too much, Georgio. In her way, she is happy here. She is part of the family. It saddens me, but in truth, she is safer here and is accepted. If she went back to Crete now, whether she had the all clear or not, she would be ostracised for her time on the island. No-one wants contact with anyone who has been near leprosy. She helps me with those who are unable to care for themselves. Sometimes, I wonder how we would cope without her". He paused for just a moment and all at once, George understood as he finished, wistfully, "Or how I would cope without her". He realised then that Irini's choice to remain on the island was perhaps just as much about being with Manolis as her fear of returning to the mainland. George felt just a little disappointed as he realised that there was obviously depth of feeling between the two people.

That evening heralded the beginning of George's integration into the little community on Spinalonga and, in some strange way, he felt proud to identify himself with the lepers. This was quite something from a man who had never given a thought to anyone than himself for at least the last twenty five years.

As the two men approached the centre of town once more, the sound of the bouzouki plucking out its jaunty rhythm could be heard from one of the village tavernas. George guessed that most Greek parties would sound much the same and his spirits rose as he listened to the part Mediterranean, part eastern cadences of the joyous, yet haunting sound. Arriving at the largest of the four tavernas, George saw that it was filled with the island residents. A cursory look from an observer would have led him to conclude there was little difference between this and any other traditional Greek social gathering. On closer inspection though, the varying degrees of physical disability would have soon become evident. Many appeared largely unscathed, perhaps the odd spot or two signifying the beginning of the disabling and painful sores. Others had the milky film of sightless, ulcerated eyes, whilst many suffered the numbing, crippling deformity of the extremities which would hamper and disable them from carrying out the simplest of activities. Then of course, there were the most horrific of sights, people with their entire bodies covered by a mass of cracked, weeping skin, their faces tightened, resembling some ancient leathery mask, barely recognisable as human skin. Ears, noses and lips were eaten away to reveal a few rotten teeth, hands and feet were clawed inwards, crumbling bones leaving nothing but stumps. The worst affected were missing entire limbs, some of them with two and three parts of them missing. Nothing could prepare the observer for the sight of these poor, damned souls.

Notwithstanding a visit to this taverna was not for the faint hearted, almost from the moment he entered, George was caught up in the atmosphere of bon viveur, the conviviality which pervaded the place. Within moments he had identified some of the people whose kindness, warmth and welcome he would never forget. Amongst the crowd, there were a few brave souls whose condition was so plainly advanced, yet who refused to have their spirit broken. George's own saviour and new best friend Nikos, to his astonishment and admiration was, despite his obvious pain, the centre of attention as he moved his afflicted limbs with grace and rhythm to the music of a traditional Greek dance, losing momentarily the shuffling gait as he lost himself in the movement. He was dressed in traditional Cretan garb, a black woven and beaded bandana tied around his head, black shirt and trousers tucked into long black leather boots. Several others were similarly dressed and some of the women wore colourful complementary dress; full skirts in black, cream aprons, embroidered with colourful motifs, their hair covered with embroidered head scarves. Amongst clapping and whooping, they performed the dances with style and dignity, clearly enjoying the atmosphere of the evening. George clapped along and tapped his foot, enjoying the warmth and feeling of belonging which was growing within him. But for the obvious differences, he could almost have believed he was holidaying in an authentic Greek village, enjoying the hospitality for which the Cretan people were renowned. George marvelled at the courage and determination of these people.

Every so often, George was caught by hands pulling him out from the table, hurling him into the centre of things, the dancers embracing him into their ranks, eager to teach him the steps so that he too could fully participate in the festivities.

A short while later, the most delectable smells of roasting meat wafted through the room and George's mouth watered as succulent chicken and pork souvlaki were brought out on large plates together with tender kleftico, lamb baked in the stone ovens in its own juices in foil and paper together with potato, vegetables and feta cheese. George could not resist the kleftico and, tasting it for the first time, the meat literally melted onto his tongue with a burst of delicious flavour. He tried a selection of mezethes, appetisers which included dolmathes, juicy vine leaves, stuffed with brown rice and flavoured with mint, vinegar and olive oil; tzatziki, Greek yoghurt with cucumber and garlic; olives, taramasalata, mashed potatoes, huge butter beans in tomato sauce and delicious aubergine pate. Finally, baklava and a selection of pastries and sweetmeats were produced to complete the feast. George felt he had never eaten so much or so well.

The dancing and the meal over, the gathering mingled, their exuberance and excitement infectious, their chatter loud and animated. As the ouzo and fire water raki circulated, many of the women took their leave as the men sat swapping stories.

Nikos chose this moment to appear at the table where George sat with Manolis and Yiannis. He sat down and, as the proceedings became more sedate, George took the opportunity to find out a little more about the men who had befriended him.

"How long have you been here on the island Yiannis?", he asked.

"Too long", he answered abruptly. "But", he now winked mischievously at Manolis, "my old friend Nikos and I relive our freedom every once in a while by escaping for a short time!" He chuckled as he imbibed yet another glass of ouzo, his large, defective frame bouncing as he laughed heartily, his enjoyment of the good, yet simple things in life evident. As he uttered the words 'escape' George's ears pricked up and, eager to hear more of their escapades, he pushed the men for more information. Yiannis however, was in a reflective mood and before he could steer the conversation into the mechanics of their escape attempts, he learned more of life on the island from those who had been there longest.

"Ah Kyrie, this island was not as it is now when I first arrived. There were far fewer of us of course, but we were a broken and dispirited bunch in those days. Nikos and I are amongst the very few remaining from the early days", Nikos nodded in quiet acknowledgement of the things which Yiannis related. He delved deep into his pockets and drew out a battered, but clearly precious sepia photograph. It showed a family, the man, dark haired with a wiry frame and handsome, if somewhat simian features, a stunning woman smiling by his side, looking down at the baby she held in her arms. A small girl of perhaps four or five stood between them completing the family group, They looked contented and loving. Nikos proudly held the photograph out to George and, as he looked from the picture to the unrecognisable creature now holding it, he realised, with horror, that this once handsome man now sat next to him, a ruined life, plain for all to see. The man that Nikos had once been had all but disappeared behind the mask of sores, ulcerated eyes and that ever present smell of decay. He had once had everything which was important in life and now, he had nothing. The tragedy of the disease was evident in these terrible before and after pictures.

"Your wife and children?" asked George. Nikos gazed at the picture longingly as he nodded his head absently in the affirmative. Yiannis took up Nikos' story.

"Poor Nikos. He lost everything to this disease. He ran a successful little kafeneon with his wife over in Elounda. When he fell to the grasp of leprosy, his was a familiar story. He was shunned by the community and no-one wanted to go near him or his family again. His business failed of course and Nikos was banished to the island. His wife was left with nothing but debts and a business she could not sell. She was ostracised from the community. She lost her friends, her customers, even her closest family, all afraid they would catch leprosy from her. She felt dirty and ashamed. Finally", he stole at glance at Nikos, "she took her own life, unable to bear the loss of her husband and the degradation and shame which his disease had brought upon the family".

"What of the children?" George asked.

"They were taken to an orphanage in Athens. No-one wanted to take them in for fear of contamination. Nikos did not find out about his wife's death until three months later. He has neither seen, nor heard anything of his children from that day to this. I remember the night poor Nikos finally got word about the fate of his family. All over the island, wherever you went, you could hear the keening, wailing despair of a broken man. It was horrifying for all to hear, none of us able to bring him any comfort. He withdrew into himself for a long while after that, but when he did finally emerge from his solitary existence some months later, he swore he would find his children again and somehow find a way to have them cared for".

"And did he?" George was anxious to know whether this poor man had managed to triumph over adversity in some small measure.

"Alas, not yet. Nikos is our greatest escapee", Yiannis grinned mischievously, "followed only by myself. Of course, it is becoming more difficult for us to go on our little adventures these days. We are watched more carefully and our condition worsens by the day. Quite aside from this, our bath tubs have been confiscated".

"Your bath tubs? What on earth have they got to do with anything?" George enquired, somewhat confusedly.

"They are what we use to drift to mainland of course! But alas, we are less inclined to wander now, our adventurous spirits dampened by pain. Nikos swears he will never give up though and I think his determination will ensure that he succeeds in finding his children one of these days. Manolis has done his best to find information but records were not so well kept back then".

Yiannis leaned over conspiratorially as Manolis' attention was distracted for a few moments by another islander. In a whisper, he continued.

"We are planning a mission to escape soon - maybe you want to join us, yes?"

Did he! At last, a glimmer of hope on the horizon that he could get away from here and discover what was really going on.

George lifted his glass of raki in toast to his companions.

"I'm with you. Let me know when!" Yiannis glanced at Nikos and laughing, they raised their glasses, the three of them downing the fiery liquid. As the music started up again, Nikos, now a little the worse for wear stood up abruptly, his chair pushed back, his arms raised, outstretched and lost in reverie as he swayed to the rhythm once more. With some impressive footwork, particularly for one so physically disadvantaged, he lost himself completely in the mood and spirit of the music. Moments later, he was pulling George up with him, trying to teach him some of the steps. Soon, several of the men were up, spinning joyfully and skilfully, jumping and bending their limbs in such a way, even with full mobility, George could never, he thought, hope to achieve. He joined in as best he could, but never having mastered the co-ordination necessary to move in any form of choreographed movement, he feared his career as a Greek dancer would be limited. He thoroughly enjoyed the attempt however, the mix of alcohol and bonhomie providing an outlet for pent up physical and emotional energy and a much needed powerful release. He felt relaxed and comfortable soaking up the atmosphere on the island that night. George felt nothing but admiration for Nikos, the once handsome, agile and adept man who refused to succumb to the miserable hand which life had dealt him. He reminded George of Zorba in Kazatzakis' novel, "Zorba the Greek". He had the same exuberant, hedonistic yet sensitive and philosophical nature of the character who was the film's namesake.

How easy it was, George thought, to fall in love with Greece and its proud, courageous and determined people.

Presently, as is often the way when celebrations die down, a quieter, more reflective mood descended on the party as the alcohol hit those gathered. George caught a glimpse of Irini in the far corner clearing away the dishes from the tables. He excused himself for a few moments and made his way over to talk to her.

Yiannis, now slumped over the table, stretched his arm out and gestured around the room for all those present in the taverna to gather round.

"Don't be long Georgio. I am about to tell you all you need to know about life on Spinalonga".

"Don't worry Yianni. I'll be back shortly", he called as he made his way across the room to speak with Irini.

"Built by those who came
Using every limb
A house of leper pain
With leper pain within".
ISLAND OF TEARS
William Ronald Hawkins

"Houses never built to last
For leper perished in the past
Had but a few bricks to cast
Had but a few years to waste"
ISLAND OF TEARS
William Ronald Hawkins

YIANNIS' STORY

George, returning to his place at the table listened intently as Yiannis began to recount his own story.

"Things were not always this way you know Georgio. We have had to work hard and suffer great hardship to reach this level of independence. When I first came here, mine had been a miserable existence for many months. The same for Nikos. In those days, if you had leprosy, you were on your own. You had to fend for yourself, living like a wild animal and respected even less. When it was discovered we carried this curse, no-one, not even our most cherished families wanted to come near us. Can you even begin to know what that is like? To have no-one to turn to, no-one to rely upon? We were sick. Terribly sick and instead of giving comfort, our families could only look on helplessly as the news got out and the villagers demanded that we take our leave to God only knew where. As soon as the disease showed itself, we were no longer treated as people. No-one would come near us. We were hounded. Anything we touched was burnt, aggression and hatred poured from those we had known all our lives, fear fuelling their venom. We were made to feel as though we were dirty, vile creatures who had somehow brought this terrible thing upon ourselves and we were forced to hang our heads in shame. Nikos here has known great tragedy and he lives with it every day. He cannot rest and every day, his mind is working on a new and probably impossible plan to find his children, at the very least to know what became of them and that they are safe. He asks for little, but generally that which he does ask, particularly of the Government and authorities, he is denied. He is a non-person, barely worthy of a second thought. We are paid money to keep us quiet and out of the way so we do not trouble anyone again.

My story is similar, but perhaps, in many ways, I have been more fortunate. I at least know that my family are well and that they still love me because now they are able to visit me here.

I came from a large family and lived high on the hillside in the village of Elos near the Acrotiri peninsula. I had lived there all my life as my parents before me and our family was large and happy. We were by no means wealthy and we worked day and night tending the olive groves, picking the olives and making them into oil just to be able to live a modest life. What we lacked in money, we made up for in just enjoying everything that life had to offer. I have three sisters and two brothers.

When we were children my parents made sacrifices so that we could eat, go to school to get an education and have shoes on our feet. As we grew older, my eldest brother went to Athens where he studied to become a lawyer. We are all so proud of him. My younger brother and I learned a trade and became bootmakers. Our business was successful with visitors coming from all over the island to have their boots fashioned by us.

We lived, of course in a small, close knit community, surrounded by many villages, much like our own. Everyone looked out for each other and we would often gather together with the other communities to celebrate their joyous occasions and to support them in their sadness. These occasions were also opportunities for the young people to mingle and dance together and hopefully to meet a good match to settle down and have families of their own. I met my wife, Elpida on just such an occasion. It was October and we were celebrating our traditional festival amongst the chestnut groves. Everyone was dancing and laughing and suddenly, I was aware of an angel, a vision of such perfection as she laughed and clapped to the music, revelling in the atmosphere and radiating joy. My heart soared and I knew at that moment I had found the love of my life. It is strange, I think that when you meet a person who is to be important in your life, it is almost as though you both know it from the moment that your eyes meet. It was this way for us as I caught Elpida's eye and, holding out my hand to her, I led her to dance with me. We were inseparable from that moment and as the evening ended and we strolled together amongst the chestnut groves, holding hands, I told her I loved her. The first time I had ever uttered those words to anyone, "S'agapo, Elpida" I whispered. To my great joy, she told me that felt the same. You might think it was very quick Georgio, but I knew. I knew she was the one I wanted to spend my life with. I am happy to say that we married only a few short months later and we have been married for twenty five years.

Elpida gave me three strapping sons and a wonderful life. If I were to die tomorrow Georgio, my memory of the life I had with Elpida and the boys would be enough for me to say that everything had been worthwhile. My only sorrow is that I have left them to fend for themselves so much earlier than I would have wished to, but such is life".

Yiannis was silent for a few moments and it was clear that he was reliving some of his memories. It must have been devastating for the poor man to have been ripped away from the heart of his family in such a cruel manner, thought George. Gathering his thoughts together, Yiannis continued.

"One morning, I awoke to find a couple of strange spots on my arms and on my body but thought little about it. My brother Michalis and I were working hard at the shop, fulfilling orders in time for winter when I noticed that I had no feeling in the area where the spots had appeared and that just occasionally, depending on what I was doing, it hampered my work a little.

Over the next few months the spots increased in size in some places and one day, I slipped with the knife I was using to cut a sheet of leather, slicing into my arm. The strange thing was, that although it was a bad cut, going deep into my flesh, I barely felt it. Because of this, I tended to the wound and forgot about it. Two days later however, I developed a fever which was so serious I became delirious and hardly knew where I was. Elpida called the doctor who found that the cut on my arm had become badly infected, so neglectful of it had I been. He was astonished that I was not in terrible pain and Elpida explained to him that I had been suffering from areas of numbness. I learned later from my beloved wife that the moment the doctor heard of my symptoms, his face displayed every emotion a human is designed to feel. In the matter of a few seconds she saw, horror, pity, revulsion and, perhaps most of all, fear.

"What is it?" She asked, becoming fearful herself. "Why do you look at Yiannis like this? Will he recover? What shall I do?" She told me that the doctor had visibly recoiled from me, and from her as though he had been attacked by a snake or some such creature. He took out a kerchief and held it to his face. He was eager to leave our house, but first, he told Elpida that there was nothing he could do for me. My wound had been tended and the fever would probably pass, but she was shocked when he added that it would be better for me if it did not. Elpida became distraught and as the doctor made for the door, she took him by the shoulders and screamed, "What is wrong with him? What should I do?"

"Kyria Fourakis", he replied gravely, "your husband has all the signs of a terrible disease, leprosy. You should stay as distant as you can from him and wait to see if his fever breaks and clears. If it does, steps will have to be taken to isolate him from the village lest he spreads his disease to others" Elpida felt as though the doctor had struck her and she doubled over in shock and pain as his words sank in. Moments later, the doctor was gone and Elpida was alone. She was not about to leave me to die and she did not heed the doctor's words to do so. She bathed and dressed my wound and sat with me until the crisis of my fever approached. I survived, as you see and from that moment on, my life changed course and I would never again be able to enjoy the simple pleasures of my old life.

Elpida told me of the doctor's diagnosis when I was well enough to comprehend her words and I have to admit that my first reaction was to laugh out loud, denying the possibility that I had leprosy. I had seen lepers close to the outskirts of the village! They weren't like me! They were barely human! How could the stupid man believe that I could possibly have such a terrible disease. It only happened to bad people, heretics and the like! Isn't that what they said? You see, Kyrie, I was as ignorant about leprosy sufferers as most other people in those days.

As soon as I was strong enough, I made my way to see Dr Arvanitoyannis. I wanted to give him a piece of my mind, show him how strong and healthy I was and to ask him why he had alarmed my poor Elpida so. When I arrived at his little surgery, he looked shocked and fearful. Once again, he took a cloth to his face, clearly not wishing to breathe the same air as I. He was not however unsympathetic and leading me outside, he sat me down on a log while he sat several feet away and questioned me about the spots and the numbness I felt round about them. I conceded that the nodules had grown in size and that there was some whitening of the skin around them. Yes, I had also lost a little feeling in the areas affected. Dr Arvanitoyannis shook his head.

"I am sorry Yianni, but I am certain that you have leprosy. If you are lucky your symptoms may not worsen for many years. If you are not so lucky.." he shrugged and shook his head, "well you know what will happen. You have seen them for yourself". Indeed, I had. They carried cow bells to announce their presence outside the village and to beg for food. Some had limbs which were being eaten away in front of our eyes. I shivered in horror. If I was not amongst the 'fortunate' ones, I had this degradation to look forward to, condemned to live my life with gradual corruption of my flesh until I was so rotten my very life would be eaten away. I closed my eyes. Surely this was a nightmare. Perhaps my fever was causing my mind to behave in strange ways. But I knew, of course this was not so. With growing horror I contemplated my fate, life without my family and the terror of this disease. Refusing to accept it so easily, I grew angry with the doctor, trying to convince myself he was incompetent. I drew myself up to my full size and challenged him. He looked fearful as I looked down upon him and demanded,

"How can I have leprosy? I have never been near anyone with the disease? I stay as clear as everyone else when the beggars arrive outside the village!" In truth, I often left food for these people who came down from the mountains. Although I had never known anyone from this village who had succumbed to the disease, I knew of some from neighbouring villages.

Indignantly the doctor replied, "How does anyone get the disease? I don't know - you meet many people in your line of business. You probably breathed in the germs of someone with the disease when you made boots for them. Perhaps you touched an infected part. As you can see yourself, it is not always easy to identify that someone has the illness unless you are aware of the symptoms".

Of course, in those days, there was little known about leprosy or how it was spread, especially in the remote villages such as ours. It is only in recent years that Manolis has been able to explain to me that it is passed by direct contact with a leper's open wound to a fresh wound of a healthy person. To this day, I do not know how I caught leprosy. As the doctor said himself, people came from all over to buy my boots. I often nicked and cut myself with the instruments I used, so perhaps, unbeknown to me, I did catch it by this means.

I was already in shock, but there was worse to come.

Dr Arvanitoyannis told me that on no account should I return to my home or even into the village. He would send word to Elpida. I must remove myself as far as possible from any human contact. How could I refuse? I may have already harmed my family and friends unwittingly. I was in despair - so many things I should have said, so many of my affairs I would have liked to deal with first. If I had not been so stubborn in my denial of the disease, perhaps I would have done things differently. So much went through my mind in those minutes. Where would I go? How would I live? Try as I might, I could not equate myself with those lepers I had seen. Had they been quiet, family men, perhaps with businesses just like me once upon a time? I had always thought of them as paupers, never having had lives outside the mountain caves where they lived. It was unthinkable that I would not return to my home, my wife, my children. And yet, at that very moment when I had been forced to recognise the truth of my situation, everything had changed. If I did not do as I was asked, I would be hounded out of the village. Better to go quietly, of my own accord and with some remaining dignity. My mind made up, I bade the Doctor farewell and headed out of the village, determined to accept my fate whatever that may be and to spare my family any further sorrow and humiliation.

I headed into the mountains where I had heard other outcasts lived and found shelter in a cave, high above the village. I cannot tell you the loneliness I suffered in those first days. The feeling that I was now less than human and that through no fault of my own I had brought bad fortune to my family was more than I could bear. I thought about ending my life then and there but it was not something I found would be so easy. I worried about my family, how they would manage now that I was gone and how they would feel about me knowing that I carried this terrible disease. I wondered if I would ever see them again. I felt that the God I had so dutifully and sincerely worshipped had, for no apparent reason, turned his back on me and left me to wither and die alone. Two days and two miserable nights passed. I had no food and only some water from a nearby stream. I was running a fever again and so, on the third night of my isolation, I thought I was delusional when I heard voices calling my name. I made my way to the mouth of my cave home and saw lanterns bobbing in the near distance.

"Yianni, can you hear us? Yianni if you hear us, shout and let us know where you are!" So weakened from hunger was I that my first attempt to articulate a response came out as a croak. I was determined however to respond.

"I am here. Up here in the cave!" I finally managed , though the effort left me near to collapse. I heard a murmur of excitement amongst those in the search party and I saw the lanterns move quickly upwards in my direction, their light finally illuminating the cave where I now propped myself up. I could just make out my brother, Michalis who had stopped just 15 feet ahead of me and the familiar faces of some of my neighbours and friends.

"Yianni, Elpida is going out of her mind with grief. We could not bear it that you had to abandon your home and family in this way. Whatever you may think, we will always be here to help you. I cannot come closer my beloved brother, but we have brought you food and drink. I will leave it here for you and I will bring you more next week and every week after that. Now we have found you, Elpida will come too. We will not leave you to suffer alone, my beloved brother. Whatever you need, just tell us. You have many friends here Yianni. We will all look after you".

Hearing his words Kyrie, I do not mind telling you that I broke down and wept. My tears were of despair for all I had lost; of joy, as my faith in humanity was restored; of gratitude for the small kindnesses which meant so much; and of grief, for I was now bereft of all that I held dear.

For a time after that I embarked on a life of endless loneliness and cavernous emptiness. There were no home pleasures and never a pair of loving arms to sink into for comfort. My days were endless, with nothing to do other than look at the dark, damp walls of my cave, shading myself by day from the intrusion of the sunlight which hurt my eyes. Some days, I would wander the hillside, finding wild berries and collecting water from the stream. Occasionally, I came upon a mountain goat, or a kid which I would kill and roast on a fire. On dark nights, when no-one could see me and with only the stars and the moonlight to guide my way, I would descend from my mountain exile to the outskirts of my home village. I would sit, just slightly above the village staring at the lights of all the familiar houses, beckoning their welcome to all but me. I hoped on those visits that I may catch a glimpse of Elpida at the window and dreamt of a day when by some miracle we may be reunited once more. I had to keep hope alive, you see. How else can anyone survive such a terrible thing? As the days turned to weeks and months, I became like a wild animal, deprived of everything that makes us human. My appearance deteriorated and slowly, I could detect a worsening of my health. Before long, the spots on my skin spread to other parts of my body and I developed huge lumps and swelling, which, though unpleasant to the eye, were relatively painless due to the numbing effect which accompanied them.

At that time, I did not of course know how to look after myself properly or how to best care for any wounds I sustained, which often I failed completely to notice. I continued to hunt for food and water and take occasional excursions to the village outskirts, but my skin, tightening with the swelling, often bruised and cracked and I was soon covered in the ulcers and open wounds which I had no means of treating.

I lived for the weekly visits from the members of my family whom I could only see and speak to from a safe distance. Elpida now came regularly on the long and arduous trek upwards from our village, accompanied by my sons and always my loyal brother. She left not only food and drink for me, but small comforts to try to ease my suffering. It broke my heart not to be able to go to them and hear in detail news of their lives. As my appearance degenerated, I retreated more and more into my twilight world and even when my family came on their weekly visits, I no longer ventured far enough out to let them see what I was becoming. How could my lovely Elpida continue to love the monster that I was turning into? I could not face their revulsion and pity when they saw me. When they arrived on their visits therefore, I only shouted my acknowledgement to them, despite their pleading for me to show myself. Gradually, unable to bear my decline to hermit and my rejection of their pleas to come out of my cave, Elpida and my boys came less regularly leaving it to Michalis to make the deliveries of food and comforts. I now carried the burden of shame and self loathing with me.

Finally, just as I believed and indeed hoped that death was only a few heartbeats away, I awoke one morning to the sound of my name being called. It was Michalis. Such was the urgency in my brother's voice that for once, forgetting my appearance, I rushed to the entrance of the cave. A chill went through my heart that day, fearing that something terrible had happened to someone in my family. My fears were unfounded though. Michalis was excited about something. I could just make out his words, "...island - others just like you.....people to live with..... medical help". I went a little closer, as close as I dared and saw as Michalis tried to hide the horror he felt as he saw me properly for the first time in months. Quickly, he told me that he had heard on a visit to Heraklion that a colony for lepers had been established for some years on the little island of Spinalonga, off the North East coast of Crete near Elounda. He had also heard that treatment was available there. He had enquired of the Medical Commission who confirmed that this was the case and they had more or less insisted that I should be taken there for my own good and for the good of public health. Apparently, they were themselves rounding up as many of the lepers as they could locate in the surrounding mountains. They had wanted to come for me, but Michalis had asked for time to speak with me personally so that he could explain himself what he had discovered.

In truth, I did not want to go. How could I hear of my family and have those few precious glimpses of my brother. I would not be able to hear anything of them if I went to Spinalonga. I was afraid I would never see them again, abandoned on an island of lepers, tucked away safely and forgotten by everyone. On the other hand however, I was now in a sorry state with my wounds untended, infected and worsening by the day. The eyesight in one of my eyes was failing as an ulcer grew and robbed me of the chance to see all that was still beautiful in the world in contrast with my own terrible ugliness. Michalis told me they had doctors who visited this island, which I knew had been the last bastion of the Turks. He told me they could treat me, ease my suffering, and who knew, perhaps one day, even find a cure. It was these words that I focused on. Perhaps there was one small glimmer of hope shining in my abyss. Perhaps one day, if I went to this island, I might be cured and able to return to my family. What, after all, was the alternative? To remain here and die a lonely, miserable death? Or go to a place where there were others like me and I could at least mingle freely, perhaps even be cured. What choice was there to make? I had less than nothing now. It could not be worse.

"How do I get there?" I asked Michalis.

"I must take you to Aghios Nikolaos where a boat leaves regularly for Spinalonga. You will be met first by the Medical Commissioner who will examine you to ensure that the diagnosis of leprosy is correct".

"But it is a long way to Aghios Nikolaos. I cannot travel there alone" I objected.

"Brother, I have a cart and a donkey ready. If you can get yourself down to the road, I will drive you there in a matter of days. All you will have to do is lie in the cart". I had walked many times down the mountainside to look at the lights of the village but now I was weak and unsure. Nevertheless, my determination won out and I told my brother I could make it. Michalis went ahead, unable to turn back and help me down. I was Eurydice to his Orpheus as he led me from my underworld, back, we believed into some sort of light.

On the way, I lost sight of my brother but knew that he was hurrying to reach the village where he could gather Elpida and the boys to wish me farewell. I dreaded them seeing me in this state, but, I knew it may be my last chance ever to see them again for who knew how close to death I now was? I stumbled on down the rough terrain, falling many times on the way. As I reached the rough track road below, I saw the large cart harnessed up to the donkey which would take me to Aghios with Michalis' help. I sat on the hillside, waiting for Michalis to return. A short while later he arrived and, with difficulty, hoisted myself up into the cart and settled myself gratefully for the journey. I could tell that Michalis had to restrain himself from running to my aid as I struggled with the effort of lifting myself. I was indeed a pitiful, helpless sight and I felt ashamed at what I had become.

After a short distance, descending on the road, we reached my home village and, as I saw the familiar little houses on either side come into view, and the kafeneon where I had spent many a leisurely hour with my friends and acquaintances, flicking my komboloi, my worry beads, whilst enjoying good strong coffee, I felt a boulder suddenly grow in the pit of my stomach. It was only when we came out at the other end of the village that the weight I carried there found release as I saw the little crowd gathered. My beautiful Elpida cried out my name in despair and pity as she beheld the monster which had been her husband. Her hands flew to her face in horror as she tried not to let me see her tears. She ran towards the cart, her arms held out.

"Come no closer" I commanded her, fearing as she approached the cart that she would try to touch me. I detested the rebuke but above all, I had to protect her.

"Yianni", she wailed, "Yianni, my love. I cannot bear for you to leave. My poor Yianni, I will always love you". Michalis' wife Melina restrained Elpida from venturing further towards me. As the cart moved on slowly through the village, voices shouted their farewells and their good wishes and parcels were thrown into the cart next to me. Fruit, cakes, bread, a bottle of ouzo, a bottle of raki, feta, olives, tomatoes, some shirts, handmade in the village, all landed with much love into the cart. As we ambled on, the crowd gradually grew smaller in the distance. Elpida did not move from her spot and our eyes locked until finally she was nothing but a dot on the horizon.

I had tried to be strong for Elpida, but now all the torrent of emotion I had been holding inside was released and the boulder in my stomach finally gave way to emptiness and the deepest, indescribable sorrow.

We reached Aghios Nikolaos in the early hours of the morning. We had travelled without stopping. What would have been the point? We sat at the harbour waiting for the Spinalonga boat to leave. A short while before we were due to embark, the Medical Governor met us and, looking me over, much as you would inspect a horse before purchase, he confirmed that I had leprosy. Some official paperwork was completed before a truck arrived carrying others destined for the island, amongst them, Nikos. We clambered aboard the little boat which would take me to my final destination and as we sailed out, the harbour in Aghios diminishing in the distance, I saw my earnest and caring little brother waving me off. I raised my arm, somewhat painfully and signalled my farewell. I saw that he was crying and I struggled to keep my own emotions in check.

Of the several people who travelled with us that day to Spinalonga, I am sorry to say that most have not survived as long as Nikos and me. We were all in a sorry state, but it was only then that I came to realise the true horror of my future. So far, I had only experienced the lumps the sores and the ulcers but I had not yet contemplated how truly dreadful things could yet become.

Two of our companions were indeed a hideous sight. They had suffered this torture for ten or eleven years and the decay had become so virulent that they had no faces to speak of. Their noses had been eaten away, much as ourselves now and the flesh of their ears had virtually disappeared. Their lips were gone, revealing only a few bad teeth in their heads to show where their mouths should be.. One, the woman, had no fingers left on either hand and her eyes were sightless, milky white ulcers covering the surfaces. I am ashamed to say that I could not look at them or sit near the putrid smelling creatures that sailed out with me, although in truth, I was little better.

Nikos was at a similar stage of the disease to me having only been diagnosed a year or so previously. Had it not been for him, I think I would have thrown myself overboard at that moment, or at least found a way to end my suffering a short time later. Despite Nikos' illness and the hardships he suffered, he never let it get him down, or at least he never let on to others how it affected him. He had lived in the beautiful town of Elounda. He was confident that he did not have leprosy and was angry that he was now being forced to go to the island. Whilst at home, he had a thriving business, a beautiful wife and two wonderful children. His story you have already heard. Suffice to say that after he arrived at the island and he heard of his wife's death, he was crushed for a time, but his determination to live for the sake of his children was an inspiration to us all.

So, we arrived on the island, a bedraggled and pathetic bunch. As I stepped off the boat, I felt the historic atmosphere of my new home. The island as we approached, looked austere, frightening and frankly unwelcoming, the great circular fortress looming above us as though hiding something evil lying in wait behind its walls. I shivered as I saw it and could not imagine how we were to make a home here. As we stepped onto the shore I saw the Venetian Lion at the archway entrance to the fort, a symbol of the power which the current inhabitants could never hope to achieve. However, I took this as a good omen and decided that perhaps, after all, my move here would symbolise my own empowerment once again. I later learned that we, the lepers, had in fact been used by the Cretan republic under Prince George as a means of scaring the Turks off the island in 1913. They had been a constant thorn in the Cretan Government's side and the last remaining Turks here lived on Spinalonga. By sending us here, the Government ensured a speedy departure!

There were a number of people already resident on Spinalonga and one glance at them confirmed that they were a dispirited community. Far from that first vision of empowerment which I had on disembarking from our boat, I quickly discovered that we would have to fend for ourselves in much the same way as we had previously. My hopes of good medical treatment and the possibility of a cure evaporated as quickly as a rain shower.

The houses, the majority of them at least, were in poor condition and there were no facilities such as we have now, either for medical care or necessary hygiene. The residents at that time had to treat themselves in the old hospital building and we relied on the kindness of a few friends and relatives who would bring food and water for us. There was no regularity to this though and often we would be thirsty and starving for days if the supplies grew short between visits. Our lives were worth nothing. We felt helpless and hopeless. Even Nikos' exuberance was dampened by the soul destroying barrenness of our lives.

I grew quickly restless and discontented, resentful of my living death. Life was intolerable. The houses were nothing short of ruins for the most part and they became more dilapidated as time went on, so incapable were we of even the most basic maintenance. My first winter on Spinalonga was cold and bleak. Many people perished and it is a surprise to me that so many of us did survive. The will to live was diminishing rapidly.

One fateful day in February, a boat moored on the island bringing supplies of food and water. There was always great excitement when a supply boat arrived. Communication with our families was difficult and we relied therefore on the messenger to call out messages and to take messages back to the mainland. Many could not read or write, either because of lack of learning or because physically they were no longer able to. Those who could write and whose family members were also able to do so sent and received letters.

We all clamoured at the Lion Gate on these days, watching as the boatman unloaded his booty, unable to approach him to help or speak to him. On this day, his consignment unloaded, he stood, hands on hips and called out to us,

"Is there a Nikos Spiridakis here?" Nikos called out,

"I am here. Do you have news of my family?" He looked eagerly towards the boatman. The man's response however was shocking and Nikos recoiled as though he had been punched in the stomach as the news came that his wife had thrown herself over a cliff and had dashed herself to pieces on the rocks below. Bankrupt and poverty stricken, shamed and despairing, herself an outcast in her community since Nikos' illness, she found herself unwilling to go on. This once proud and respected woman had been reduced to begging in order to feed her children, reliant on the charity of others. Aside from those indignities, she had lost her beloved husband. Nikos, disbelieving and shocked, managed to stumble out with the words, "My children? What of them?" The boatman who had delivered his news with relative disinterest, as though denying that the islanders should still experience human misery, merely shrugged his shoulders. He was unsure, he told Nikos, but he had heard maybe they had gone to the orphanage in Athens.

Nikos was a different man after that. The light of hope no longer burned within him. He retreated to his house and for days he refused to come out at all. All we could hear was a keening sound from within that would have made your blood run cold. His suffering was there for all to hear and Nikos was trapped and powerless to do anything which could ease his pain. He knew his children would be frightened and distraught and orphanages in those days were sorry places. After a few days of mourning, finally, Nikos opened his door and stepped back out once more. I had kept watch day and night since he closed his door as I was afraid for his safety.

"Niko!" I cried, delighted to see him. "You have come back to us?" He stared at me, but I knew he was not really seeing. Nikos had been replaced with an automaton. Nevertheless, as he spoke, there was a chilling determination in his words.

"I cannot stay here, not while my children are uncared for. I must go to them. When night falls, I shall take my leave". I thought he had lost his senses at that moment and I tried to talk him round, bring him back to the real world. It was useless however. It was as though the Nikos I had known had been taken over by another person I could not recognise. That night however, he came to me with his plan. I nearly laughed out loud when he began explaining that he intended to make his escape in one of the wooden bath tubs! He was deadly serious however and as I listened I became intrigued and impressed with his audacity and tenacity. In fact, the more I thought about it, the more it occurred to me I should follow his example. Why should I stay here just to be forgotten? Treated as though I had never existed! I wanted to exert my independence, just, if nothing else to prove that I could take my life into my own hands once again and make my own decisions. With that thought, I responded positively to Nikos' idea.

"If you're going, then I'm coming too!" At that moment, the old Nikos returned. My small sign of empathy and support had reached him and for the first time in days, I caught a glimpse of the old Nikos behind the mask of pain. This time the fire was fuelled by determination rather than hope, but all the same, the fire was there and that was the important thing. With that, his eyes creased with the old mischief I had known and, as we looked at each other, we were conspirators, ready to buck the system.

We couldn't actually go that night as Nikos had originally wanted. Our plan had not yet been properly worked out. The sea was too choppy and we had to know between us what our plan would be. Hastily, we made the decision to go the next night, subject to a calm sea. As soon as the island was asleep, and using roughly fashioned oars, we would sail to the mainland using our wooden tubs. It seemed ridiculous and despite Nikos' pain, we laughed at the incongruity of our plan.

Nevertheless, the next evening we were ready and each put to sea in our baths. They were not well designed for sailing and my heart sank as they keeled over from one side to the other, threatening to cast us into the dark waters below. It was an adventure, but terrifying nonetheless. The sea lapped up towards us and it was difficult to manoeuvre our tubs, but we followed the lights on the mainland. Quite what we would do when we reached Elounda, neither of us knew. We had thought no further than the journey itself. There were many moments on that strange voyage when I doubted I would live to tell the tale. I hardly cared any more though. I was exhilarated by the fact I was taking control of something in my life again. We battled against the current, Nikos determined to discover the fate of his children.

Just as dawn was breaking, we washed up on the shore of Elounda and abandoned our tubs. In honesty, I was amazed we had survived the voyage but we had stayed close to each other and, disembarking, we tried to make our way up the beach as nonchalantly as possible. I suppose it was a crazy idea, but we really thought we could get away with it. We reached the town, but, then what? Perhaps neither of us really believed we would get this far, but we hadn't worked out what we would actually do once we reached Elounda. I was still miles from home and even if I could get there, I wasn't going to be welcomed by most. For Nikos, this was his home town, but the reaction would be the same. Anyone who saw us in the meantime would know instantly where we had come from. We had no means of disguising our condition.

Wordlessly, we made our way up to Elounda and, as we reached the town, we looked at each other and knew what the other was thinking. Despite the tragedy and the reasons for our journey, our eyes met and both of us collapsed in laughter. Whatever happened next, we had achieved a small but significant victory. We had successfully escaped the confines of our island and made a break for freedom. In hindsight, the result was inevitable and our euphoria short lived. We headed off to Nikos' home. In Elounda, it was impossible to be inconspicuous in our condition, though we covered our heads as best we could with cloths. Those we passed however recoiled in horror at what they saw, covered as we were in the sores that distorted our features and bowed our limbs. Even Nikos' neighbour did not recognise him as we approached. He fled into his house the moment he saw us. Nikos rapped on his door.

"It's me, Nikos", he called.

"Please Niko, leave us. We cannot help you. You must go back to the island or you will infect us all".

Nikos persisted however, pleading with the man to give him

news of his children. The very little he did know he imparted to us quickly from behind his closed door, eager that we should be on our way. He confirmed that as far as he knew the children had indeed been taken to Athens but suggested that the local Doctor might know more. Nikos was determined to get the information he needed and he therefore approached Dr Eliopolous. His eyes widened with horror as he saw us. Even he shunned our approach. Refusing us entry and demanding that we keep a distance from him so that we should not be sharing the same air, he confirmed that the two girls had gone to Athens but only the Government Offices would be able to give him more information. Nikos was in despair by now. He was separated by miles of sea from his last remaining family and he feared for them. He was defeated. He had no means of travelling, nor did he know anyone who would be willing to take him across the water. Even if he got that far, no-one would want to deal with him.

"Nikos", the Doctor spoke appeasingly, "you put everyone at risk here. Let me arrange to have you taken back to Spinalonga and I give you my word I will make enquiries to find your children". Nikos knew this was his best hope and so, our spirits dampened, our freedom curtailed, such as it was, we returned to the quay and waited for a medical commission boat to take us back to Spinalonga. We knew there was no future for us there, but all the same, we revelled in our small victory.

Yiannis stopped speaking and reflected for a few moments. A familiar twinkle was in his eye as he looked up again.

"It hasn't, of course stopped us from escaping every once in a while - just to remind ourselves we still can! Now, another round of ouzo, I think before we continue.

"Did Nikos get the news he needed", George now asked Yiannis.

"Oh, the Doctor was as good as his word and an address for the orphanage was obtained. Nikos wrote letters but he has never received a reply. We do not know if the letters are sent or whether they are simply ignored. He continues to write though, in the hope that one day his prayers will be answered." Yiannis shook his head as if in wonderment. "Somehow, our break for freedom helped Nikos to regain his strength and determination, despite the lack of welcome!" Yiannis sighed and raised his glass in toast.

"Yammas!"

"We did not try to escape again though for a very long time after that. Island life left us dispirited and hopeless. You cannot imagine how very different things were here during the earlier years. We had no comforts, nothing to ease our misery. The promised medical treatment was rare and basic. Eventually, a doctor began to visit the island once or sometimes twice a week. He did his best, but he had few resources to help him. We witnessed some horrific events at this time.

During the week, whilst we awaited the Doctor's visit, Marilena was taken with a terrible fever. She had been working in the laundry and had scalded herself that day. Alas, due to the deadening of her nerves she did not feel any pain and so she took no precautions to tend and cover her injury. Infection spreads so quickly through our bodies that a simple injury is a serious matter for us. By nightfall, her arm was badly swollen and she was unable to move it properly. By morning, fever had gripped her. We knew she was dangerously ill, but, as her arm began to blacken it was clear she would die soon without proper medical help.

Thankfully, some supplies were brought over the following day by one of the islanders' relatives and an urgent message was sent back with him to Crete that medical treatment was urgently required. I feared the worst for Marilena. I had seen this infection before. I knew it to be gangrene with its blackness and rotten smell. I also knew there was only one treatment which would stay the progress. Removal of the limb. I sat myself with Marilena, delirious as she was, waiting for the Doctor to arrive. We did not know whether he would make an unscheduled visit. After all, we were dying anyway - why hurry if it was simply to delay the process for one unfortunate? Marilena, poor soul, had no family who cared about her. They had cruelly cast her out as 'unclean', accused her of atheism and declared she was suffering a punishment from God. Only those on the island here were her family now. She had treated me like a son with kindness and care and I was determined to stay with her to provide some meagre comfort. I was determined she would not die without a fight. To my great joy, there was a banging on the door some while later and some of the islanders clamoured to announce the arrival of the doctor from Crete.

Nothing could have prepared me for the next few hours. The doctor examined Marilena's arm and, as I had suspected, he diagnosed gangrene. He told me that he would have to amputate. Several of the village men were called in to help move poor Marilena onto her kitchen table. The Doctor told me he would need the help of a strong person to assist with the operation. I told him I would be happy to help in any way I could. He warned this would be deeply unpleasant but I assured him I would be strong for Marilena. She was conscious, though still delirious as the Doctor produced his instruments from his bag.

"Hold her other arm and keep her steady now", he said to me as he picked up a knife and a metal saw.

"Surely you will give her something for the pain?" I asked, horrified.

"I am sorry, I have nothing but Raki and I don't think she will be able to take that. We must do what we can with the resources I have. Be brave for her. The faster I can work, the sooner this ordeal will be over for her".

And so, holding Marilena still, I spoke softly to her and stroked her dear forehead as metal clashed with bone in screaming rhythm. Her body writhed in agony, arching and threatening to leave the table as the Doctor continued his grisly treatment.

"Keep her still!" he barked angrily as I struggled with difficulty to prevent her movement. "I will cause more damage if you do not!" Fortunately, at that moment, Mitsos, hearing the terrible screams came into the little house, saw the difficulty we were in and moved to Marilena's other side. With both of us pinning Marilena down, the Doctor continued. By this time, a cold sweat had broken out on my forehead and I thought I would pass out. Still, I persevered, holding Marilena's good arm, speaking softly to her in reassurance and stroking her forehead. I prayed for the ordeal to be over for all of us, but it seemed to go on forever. Marilena, delirious though she was, screamed out in agony and despite our efforts to keep her still, she writhed and pulled with the strength of ten men in her attempt to escape the torture to which she was now exposed. I wept for her, feeling every moment of pain, sickness and horror with her and I longed for this vision of hell to end.

After what seemed like an eternity, the ordeal did end and the Doctor cauterised the wound with an iron he had laid on the fire. Old rags were all that were available to dress the wound and there had been nothing to disinfect the table. These factors, combined with the shock which her body had just endured, I was not optimistic that Marilena would survive. I regretted in many ways having allowed her to be put through this. It may have been kinder to allow her to die in peace.

No-one was more amazed however and thankful when, over the next few days, Marilena began to show signs of recovery. She was in terrible pain of course, but soon her old personality began to flood back and she was soon impatient to be moving about and adapting to her disabled state.

The will to live, even on Spinalonga is strong, despite the overwhelming odds stacked against us. We suffer constant pain and indignity and yet, even we realise how precious life is and grasp onto it with every breath in our bodies. When one of us dies, we do not just accept it merely as a blessed release from a tortured existence but mourn it deeply as the loss of a friend, a member of our family, a soul who brought something valuable to the lives of those they touched.

When one dies young, it is a greater tragedy. All that potential, snuffed out to soon, never having the opportunity to make a mark on the world. I remember many years ago, a young girl, oh, only about eighteen years of age was brought here. She was stunningly beautiful and showed no outward signs of having leprosy. For her, being brought to the island must have been horrific, her life over before she had even begun to taste of its fruits.

Anyway, there was no accommodation ready for her and, as was the custom back then, she stayed with another islander, this time Athena. It turned out that the girl, Ismene, had leprosy of the throat and was therefore in great pain and discomfort. She spoke little, partly because of the physical pain she suffered in the effort of speech, but also because, I think, of the overwhelming sorrow, sense of abandonment and betrayal that she felt. Whilst the older people suffer the same sentiments, we are at least more able to rationalise our thoughts about these things. She was locked tight within herself, withdrawn and unable to come to terms, at least for now, with the injustice that God had visited upon her. We tried, of course, to bring her out of herself Everyone is welcomed into our community and no-one shall be lonely if we can give comfort. This is a place where community spirit is strong, where we each give strength and encouragement to others.

On the evening following her arrival, a dance was arranged in this very taverna. As now, whenever we have new people arrive on the island, we celebrate their acquaintance by having a party where everyone can meet and get to know each other. Ismene was told of the evening's festivities and Athena and I spoke excitedly of the party, hoping to rouse the girl from her torpor. We told her that just because she has leprosy, it wasn't necessarily the end of the world. We explained that there were many other young people on the island, some of them handsome men of around her age or just a little older who had not been entirely ravaged by the illness. We tried to give her hope by telling her of the many couples who had even found love on the island, despite the odds and who had gone on to marry and yes, even had beautiful healthy babies. I did not add however that those beautiful, miraculously perfect children were not permitted to remain on the island with their ailing parents but were sent to the Crete to be cared for in hospital. I did not mention how the air on those occasions were rent with the howling and pleading of a grief stricken mother as her beloved child was torn from her arms, perhaps never to be seen again. No, I did not tell her this, for there were many good things that, God willing, life may still hold for her. I wanted to give her a little hope for a future that may not just offer pain and misery. As I spoke to her, the girl sat across from me looking so small and helpless that my heart went out to her. She reminded me of my own daughter and my instincts were to protect her as a father would. I took her hands, one in each of mine and tried to sound jovial.

"So, will you do me the honour of coming to our dance tonight?" She looked up at me, her dark hair falling about her shoulders, curtaining her perfectly formed face, her skin so clear and gave me an almost beatific smile. I looked into her eyes and although she returned my gaze, it was as though she did not really see me. There was nothing behind her eyes to suggest that she was really with us. Slowly, she shook her head in refusal.

"I m tired tonight and feel a little unwell" she said. "Forgive me if I appear rude to refuse your kind invitation, but I would sooner stay her and rest", she whispered. And with that, I knew the matter was closed. I took my leave and bade her farewell, leaving her to settle in with Athena, adding as I left, that should she change her mind, I would be delighted to see her and take care of her at the taverna where I would command the first dance. I arranged to call for Athena later that evening.

Something though, was troubling me. It nagged and tormented me for the rest of the day, yet it was nothing I could articulate or describe. Perhaps it was just the aura of tragedy that I picked up from that young girl, a presentiment if you will. Whatever, I struggled with unease as I went about my business that day. I was eager to see how Ismene was getting along when I finally called for Athena that night. I have to say, by way of digression, that I had never seen Athena look so radiant as she did on that evening. It is a difficult world we live in here Kyrie. In our other world, exists a host of people we love dearly, my wife included. But my wife was now denied to me probably forever. Athena too was married and, unlike my wife, her husband neither visited, nor enquired after her. I think it is fair to say therefore that in our separate world relationships develop through shared experience, suffering and kindnesses. Situations develop which, in our normal lives would never otherwise occur. I confess to you now that I had and still have feelings for Athena and had I been a single man, I would have wished to marry her. I know that she has similar feelings for me, but would never betray her husband despite his failings. That night however, I tell you, I loved this woman and vowed that I would always take care of her. She opened the door and I beheld a vision of beauty. I no longer saw the badges of her disease. To me, Athena was beautiful and I told her so. Despite her radiance and her pleasure at my compliments, Athena was also troubled.

"How is the girl", I asked.

"She is quiet and withdrawn still" Athena replied. "I haven't managed to get her to eat a thing since she arrived. She would take only an apple from me tonight but hasn't eaten it yet".

"I'm sure in no time at all she will settle down. Come, let us go to the dance and see who we might introduce her to when she is feeling better".

"Georgio, from that day to this, I wish I had heeded the nagging voice in my head and stayed behind that night, for what happened next has haunted me since. You would think, wouldn't you that to have been dealt the cruelty of leprosy that you would be spared from further catastrophe? Well, in the way of things, it is not so. I escorted Athena to her door after an evening of joy and conviviality. We are not a pretty bunch Kyrie, but our spirit is warm and warmer still as the raki and ouzo flows. Underneath our lizard skins live people who still want to enjoy life to the fullest extent possible. All of us have more worries and sorrows to deal with than most people. When the opportunity presents itself to have a little fun, we all grasp it with both hands.

As we returned home, this was what I hoped to impart to Ismene; to tell her that she must not despair. Alas however, it was not to be. As Athena opened her door and called out Ismene's name, I knew that something terrible had happened when we were greeted with nothing but silence. There was a quietness to the house which felt unnatural. A sixth sense perhaps, but I felt a sudden chill in my bones. We hurried inside and found poor Ismene slumped over the kitchen table, the apple next to her on the floor beneath her arm which hung limply downwards. As I rushed over to her, I took her head in my hands and realised what must have happened. Her lips were blue and there was no pulse or breath in her body. The poor child had tried to eat the apple she had taken from Athena but her diseased throat had been unable to cope with it. She had, quite simply, choked.

If I were to tell you this was the worst of it, I'm afraid I would be lying.

Already, I was consumed with guilt. I should have stayed with her to make sure she was alright. That night, I wept like a baby, unable to forgive myself for the girl's death. I had been thoughtless and stupid. We had no doctor on the island to officially confirm her death or the cause of it, but Christos who had some medical training gave the girl a cursory examination and concluded she had indeed choked to death on the apple.

With the heat and risk of infection, it was important that we buried the dead quickly. The girl had no money and we had no way of contacting her family to see if they wanted her to have her own grave, but such was my own grief that I could not bear for this tragic girl to be thrown into a mass grave. I spent my own burial savings organising an individual grave for her. I asked the island carpenter to fashion her a coffin and a cross as quickly as possible and many of the islanders turned out in our little Church which we use for burial and interment on the east of the island. One of our most deeply held rules had been broken, that no person should die alone here. In compensation for that fact, the village turned out en masse to ensure she was not buried alone.

At last, she was lowered into the ground and laid to rest. Or so I thought.

To explain what happened next, you must understand how we bury our dead here. Those who have saved money or whose family wish to pay for a good burial with an individual grave may do so. Those who are not so fortunate are buried in the mass graves and the bodies are disposed of 12 feet under the concrete tower on the hill. However, the island is small and there are many deaths, so we cannot accommodate many individual graves. It is therefore the practice to exhume the individual graves every four years and the bodies from within are laid to rest in the mass grave.

Eventually, it came time, four years later for Ismene to be exhumed in this way and I wanted to be there to make sure that once again she was not alone. On the appointed day of the exhumation, I climbed up the steps with the gravediggers. Over the years, the girl's death had continued to haunt me and I still blamed myself. Standing by the side of the grave, it was all brought back to me. I stood to the side as the grave was opened to recover her body, lost in remembrance of the day she died, when suddenly, there was a gasp of horror from one of the men charged with opening her tomb. I ran over to where he was standing and I think every drop of blood drained from me as I looked down. For there, in the darkness, it was clear she had moved from her burial position with a hand now raised above her head where she had struggled to escape. She had not died on that night after all! We had actually killed her, burying her alive! She must have been merely unconscious or perhaps in a coma when we found her. Not having any proper medical diagnosis, a terrible mistake had been made. Georgio, I will never forget the shock and horror of that moment. I have punished myself daily for this since. The girl will haunt me for the rest of my life.

So you see, life is hard on Spinalonga, but more so for some than for others. When we first came here, we had only the old hospital building, but no doctor to treat us. Food and water arrived from the mainland on an irregular basis and often we were starving for days, particularly if the weather for a sea crossing had been difficult.

We endured many years of great hardship and it was only as more people were sent here, mainly from Athens, that our lives began to improve. The lepers in Athens were hospitalised for the most part and were not confined to caves and shacks as we had been. Many were well educated. Lawyers, teachers, engineers and skilled craftsmen succumbed to the curse. Leprosy is not discerning. It doesn't just take the poor and uneducated.

Due to the arrival of these newcomers, the community gradually became more organised. Working parties were formed to renovate the buildings and the facilities on the island. We worked hard repairing these houses which were less damaged by taking materials, stones, timber and such like from the dilapidated buildings. Our water supplies were enhanced by the construction of water sheds from the roofs or our houses in which we placed pots and buckets to collect the rainwater. When they were filled, we transported them to tanks built on the far end of the island. This was the start of a new period of independence and autonomy for us. You see, many of these newcomers were rebels from Athens. Their education and standing in society meant that they did not just accept things in the way that those without such a voice had been forced to. These people had spoken out, refusing to be condemned as unclean or to simply accept that their rights should be taken away from them. Consequently, they became a thorn in the side of the Government and the only way to silence these rebels was to isolate them on Spinalonga. Their exile was our gain however and they brought a new fighting spirit back into the community and taught us that we were still worth something.

Slowly, but surely, our self esteem and pride began to return to us as we saw all that we could achieve. The Athenians, having received hospital treatment and having asked questions about the disease of their doctors were able to teach the rest of us something about the care of our wounds. We made sure that soap was always requested from the mainland. A small detail, but one which is so important for us in fighting the spread of infection.

You have probably seen the room containing many sinks. During our 'renaissance' period, we opened up what had previously been the Turkish Laundry where we used the open fireplaces to heat up the water to clean our clothes and bandages. For the first time in many years, a new hope came to Spinalonga. We were fired up with enthusiasm. At last we were not just sitting back and accepting the island as a graveyard. We no longer sat around waiting to die. Instead, we began to live useful lives, adopting the island as our home, not just a place of enforced exile or abandonment.

Of course, for many of the incomers, particularly the more educated or those who had been used to prosperity, it was hard to accept this new life. Many could not accept their fate and sadly, committed suicide. But, happily, the majority retained the will to live and the hope of a cure, so they ploughed their skills into improving the life of the community. Of course, it was not only the manual work that was important to us but also, we had plenty of time on our hands to learn new things. I, for example, learned to speak English from one of the teachers who came here. All of these achievements restored our pride and our lives". Yiannis smiled in satisfaction as he recalled with evident pride the events which had restored self esteem to him and his friends.

"Now, Georgio, the hour is growing late and I am growing tired and a little drunk with this fine ouzo, but I have one more tale to tell which I hope will amuse you before we retire to bed. I have told you much of the sadness ingrained on this island but this story continues to make me laugh even now, years after it happened.

I explained to you that we keep our water in tanks on the hill at the far end of the island. We noticed however that our supplies appeared to be dwindling rapidly. We checked the tanks for leaks and even put new seals along the bottom, just in case there were tiny holes allowing seepage which we could not detect. The quantity of water that was disappearing each night was significant though and the leaks would have had to be large to allow loss on such a scale. We were baffled and becoming concerned because everyone had a daily ration and it was becoming increasingly difficult to meet these.

A meeting was called to discuss the crisis and, following a heated debate, for there were many theories, we determined that the most likely explanation was that someone was stealing the water. But who? None of us wanted to believe this theory as it would mean that someone was knowingly denying others of their essential supplies. Surely, we thought, no-one in our midst would be so selfish? Still though, we had to investigate and after dark on that very night, two of us, Dmitris and I, hid behind the tanks and waited. We had resolved to keep a vigil over the next few nights to find out what was going on.

We didn't have to wait long though, for just past midnight, we heard the scuffling of approaching feet, some whispering and the stifled giggles of a group of women. We stayed where we were and watched as they each helped themselves to a bucket of our precious water. I was shocked to discover that my dear friend Athena was amongst the group of six. Dmitris and I looked at each other, shocked. In silent agreement, we nodded and came out from our hiding place to challenge the women.

"What, in the name of God do you think you are doing?" I shouted, my anger evident. "you have your rations each day! How selfish can you be to deprive others! This could mean the difference between life and death to someone. And you Athene, I am so disappointed in you that you are a party to this deception". Athena broke down in tears, the other women's faces a picture of shock and shame.

"Yianni, we didn't mean to do any harm. Sometimes there just isn't enough water to last the day. We get so very thirsty and we thought a little more wouldn't harm. Please forgive us". The others looked on, nodding their heads in agreement.

"Be off with you now and don't let us catch you doing this again or there will be sanctions next time". The women turned and fled, but not before I had removed the buckets from them and returned the water to the tanks. Whilst I was confident that Athena had learned her lesson, I was less sure about the others. It was decided therefore that from now on, a guard should be posted at the tanks during the hours of darkness. For a time there was no further trouble but eventually, the guards grew bored with their nightly ritual of climbing the hill and staying there until after sunrise. They believed the women would not return, but, just before they left their post, they ensured that on one night, an effective safeguard was put in place.

Nikolaos, the youngest and fittest of the guards came rushing into the taverna one night, where several of the women were gathered for an evening meal and a gossip. His face had a look of terror on it and his playacting that night was worthy of the best Greek drama. He panted and shook and stuttered out his story. He had been sitting atop the hill next to the tanks when he heard a wailing noise accompanied by a very cold breeze which had reached, so he said, to his bones. Nikolaos had called out, "Who's there" but there was no response. All of a sudden though, from nowhere, there appeared before him the tallest, darkest skinned man he had ever seen. His features, he said, were a most fearsome sight and the apparition brandished a sword in one hand. Nikolaos shrank back as the terrible creature raised his sword, bringing it down to his neck as though to decapitate him. As if that horror was not enough, the sword sailed straight through Nikolaos without harming him. With that, the evil looking man let out a mighty roar of laughter and disappeared before Nikolaos' eyes. Well, if I had not known the truth, that this was all part of a plan we had devised to scare the women, I would have believed Nikolaos' story and I would have been terrified, such was his dishevelled and petrified appearance.

As part of the plan, a team of men were despatched to search the area, but of course, nothing was found. As the days went on, the rumour mill worked and the man was described as an ancient Greek warrior, an angry ancient God, a Turkish or Venetian Smuggler and finally, he became a negro slave. Whatever the ghost was, it worked. The women would hardly go up to the tanks at all now unless in twos and threes in daylight. They would never venture up there after dark. Time passes however and, as is the way with such things, the story passed into the annals of time and, as new, sometimes bolder people came to the island, the stories were discussed until eventually fear gave way to greed once more.

One night, after a particularly hot day, we were roused from our beds by squealing and shouting. I went to my window and, on opening the shutters, I was surprised to see three of the women clinging on to each other, their hysteria making them almost unintelligible. I quickly pulled on some clothes and went down into the street where a small crowd was gathering. As the women calmed down, they confessed, somewhat shamefacedly, that they had ventured once more up to the tanks. It was a beautiful clear night and the moon shone brightly. The women described how, as they approached the tank, a huge dark skinned man had suddenly appeared to them and waved at them whilst speaking in tongues. They described a terrible, fearsome face, which, they believed incanted curses upon them.

"It was the ghost we saw. How could we have been so stupid?" they wailed. "We did not think the stories were true, but he's real! What if he comes back to haunt us at night? We dare not be alone".

Well, of course, as the women told their story, those of the men gathered there looked at each other in bewilderment. We knew that we had invented the ghost and whilst we were faintly amused, we also wondered what the women could have seen. I myself took charge of the situation and asked Athena, roused by the noise from her own bed to take the women inside and calm them down.

Nikos, Dmitris, myself and a couple of the old guards went off to investigate, speculating that it was probably just a case of mass hallucination and hysteria sparked by the old stories. You can imagine our astonishment then when we reached the hill, bathed in watery moonlight, exposing in its backdrop the silhouette of a tall man, his arms full of bulky boxes and sacks! Immediately however, we could tell he was no ghost. He was as real as you and I. Quietly, we hid ourselves at a vantage point where we could observe. The man made his way down the hill and down to the bay where a boat was moored and three other men stood in a line as they passed the boxes and sacks down the line to the last man who loaded the boats. Finally, it dawned on us, the men were smugglers! The island had been used by smugglers throughout the centuries although, we had never experienced it first hand. In our condition, we did not want to be confronted, so as quietly as we had arrived, we turned and made our way back to the village. Everyone clamoured around us as we returned. What had we seen? Was the ghost still there? Was it as dreadful as the women made out?

Well, let me tell you my friend, if that 'ghost' had seen any one of us up close, I assure you he would have been far more terrified of us than those women had been of him. But, did we say anything to comfort the women? Hah! Of course not! We told them we had seen a strange figure moving around in the moonlight, a wraith perhaps from the Venetian or Turkish invasions, left here to wander the earth forever more. We told them as soon as we saw the figure, like them, we had fled, not wishing to disturb it or attract it to us.

From that day onwards, Kyrie, the water levels have remained steady. The following morning, we discovered a discarded sack which told us the smugglers had been Italian. The man must have seen the women approach and waved to them in the belief they were his colleagues. How we have laughed over the ghost of 'Water Hill' Kyrie. It could not have shown itself more perfectly had we arranged it.

Raising his glass to his lips, Yiannis downed the remains of the ouzo and, having done so, he gazed warmly around the table at each of his companions, content to be amongst good friends

And now, my friends, I must bid you goodnight. I hope you have enjoyed our evening of welcome Georgio and I look forward to seeing you in the morning.

DAY BY DAY

Yiannis ended his story and rising slowly and painfully to his feet, his infirmity exacerbated by the copious quantities of ouzo and raki consumed that night, he bade his friends goodnight.

"Kalenichta" he called, making his way to the door of the taverna. Moving slowly, his shoulders stooped as though carrying a heavier burden than usual, George wondered if revisiting such painful memories was the cause. The evening had drawn to a close and everyone dispersed to their homes. Strangely, in the midst of this crowd of misfits, George felt very much at home and, as Manolis had predicted, as the evening had progressed, he saw less of their disfigurement and infirmity than their warmth and colourful personalities, determined as they were to make the best of the very worst situation. Once again, it struck George what a selfish, shallow and worthless creature he had been in his former life. These people were vulnerable and either forgotten completely or unashamedly exploited by those looking to make a fast buck from their desperation. For the first time, George appreciated how wrong it was to prey on the need of others and how he, in his drug dealing days had been no better than those who preyed on the lepers. It was uncomfortable for him to confront his own shortcomings and he felt deeply ashamed of his former conduct.

George had found Nikos and Yiannis to be entertaining company, the sparkle in the eyes behind those dreadful masks showing that the spark of life could not be extinguished, no matter what the circumstances. Yiannis' story had evoked great emotion as he described the many terrible experiences he had endured, but he clearly relished equally, if not more so, the humorous stories, his mirth barely contained as he had related the tale of the island 'ghost'. Nikos, whose conversation was limited due to the severity of his condition, nevertheless danced the evening away, showing a remarkable skill, despite the pain he clearly endured in his legs.

George had spent a few moments with Irini as she busied herself clearing away the plates and cleaning tables after the meal.

"The food was wonderful. Was it you who baked the kleftico?" he enquired.

Irini blushed in pleasure.

"Yes, it was! How did you guess that?"

"I could smell it this afternoon. It wafted through my windows. I can't tell you how difficult it was to restrain myself from jumping through your kitchen window and grabbing every piece of it to eat right there and then!"

"Why, you should have said! Irini responded. I could have given you some had I known". George smiled and reassured her that he had eaten that afternoon and he would not have wished to spoil the delight of the evening's meal by partaking of her delicious cooking too early.

"And have you enjoyed the company here tonight? You seem to have been having fun", Irini observed.

"Have you been watching me then? Have you found it difficult to tear your eyes away from my good looks?" George teased as Irini visibly reddened.

"Of course not! she replied with mock indignation. "I watch everybody so don't flatter yourself!" she laughed. "I am always fascinated by people. I like to see how they react to each other. There is much you can tell you know by people's movements".

"Oh really? And what could you tell from mine then?" George wanted to know.

"I could tell you were very comfortable; that you were enjoying yourself and happy to be here, strange as that may sound"

George nodded. "I think, Irini, your reading was correct. I do feel at home here, although, goodness knows why! It's hardly a place I would have chosen to come to!"

"I think perhaps you could do some good work here Georgio" Irini hesitated a moment before continuing, uncertain of George's reaction. "I wondered, would you like to help out with some of the less able bodied here? I mean, it would be a help to Manolis". Irini glanced at George, trying to read his face which appeared to blanch a little at her suggestion. "I assist Manolis in the actual care of the people, but we need someone who can do practical things for them; you know, lower shelves when they can no longer reach, help me to take them outside, make ramps for their wheelchairs, that sort of thing".

"I'd be glad to help you and Manolis, Irini", George found himself saying. He liked the idea of spending time in this woman's company and wondered whether she and Manolis were more than just good friends. In so many ways, he hoped not.

George bade Irini goodnight after arranging to meet with her in the village the following afternoon and rejoined Yiannis and the others.

Back in his own home, George thought about the conversation that night and his mind returned to the idea of escape, a prospect which had initially intrigued him. Now, though, recalling his conversation with Irini and the friendly atmosphere of the island, strangely, he felt no urgency to leave. In fact, in many ways, he felt he wanted to stay and experience more of island life, but his reluctance was also founded on the fear of what he may discover away from Spinalonga if they did escape back to the mainland. What were the possibilities? Either, he would be escaping straight into the arms of the police for his 21st century crimes or, he would be returning to Crete of the 1940s, which he knew from his scant knowledge, was due for a turbulent time at the hands of the Germans. Of course, his rational mind refused to accept that he was actually in the Spinalonga of 1940, but, he felt the answer to the enigma lay on this island rather than in Crete and he wanted to wait a little to find out what would transpire.

George's evening in the taverna had left him feeling mellow, but he could never shake off the feeling of unease arising from the continuing mystery of his presence on Spinalonga. There were moments in his new life where he could actually forget that he was in some sort of 'Alice in Wonderland', dark parallel universe, but then the bizarre nature of his existence would strike him once more and he would pinch himself, hoping to wake up from the living nightmare he must be in.

On the following morning however, and for days, weeks and months more, George continued to wake up in Spinalonga and he had little choice other than to immerse himself as best he could in the life of the island. To while away his days, he held classes in English, just as Yiannis had suggested and found, for the first time in his life a sense of achievement as his students studied enthusiastically and gradually began to form sentences in their newly acquired language. It was clear to George that these small, stumbling successes made his students swell with pride as he offered praise for their progress. George's Greek language became more fluent during this time so that after a few short weeks, one way or another, he was communicating well with his fellow islanders and became an accepted and well liked member of the community. It was a sudden revelation to George just how rewarding the acts of giving and receiving knowledge could be. He felt as though he was discovering a whole treasure trove of rare and precious jewels.

One day, as George accompanied Irini on her rounds to the sickest of the islanders, another little routine which he had come to enjoy, partly because he enjoyed the work and partly because he loved being in her company, he found himself extolling the contentment he had found from his work with the islanders and how he had so much more pleasure from this than he had when he was making easy money back home.

"You were wealthy back in England then, I take it?" Irini asked as they strolled companionably through the town, stopping to gaze in at the shop windows as they went.

"I had money yes, but Irini, I would never have believed it but I feel I am a richer man here", he said wistfully.

"Tell me about your life before Spinalonga. What did you do? Doctor? A lawyer perhaps?"

George laughed, just a hint of bitterness in his mirth.

"Nothing so grand I'm sorry to say. Oh, I could have been, but - Irini I am afraid that if I tell you about my life you will hate me. I couldn't blame you, or anyone else for that. I've done some very bad things in my time, possibly the worst of things. You will never speak to me again if I tell you".

"I do not judge people so easily, George. We all have good and bad in us. None of us are saints. It is what we do about it that matters. Here, why don't we stop awhile and have some strong coffee and baklava and you can tell me all about it. It will help, I think to talk about things a little. Perhaps it will even help you to remember things a little better."

And so it was that George confided in Irini all that had led up to the death of Jenna Hawkins. She was so easy to talk to, such a good listener that he unburdened himself to her, almost without thinking. He told her of his privileged childhood in Kensington, his private education which had proved him to be an average student. He had, largely to keep his parents happy, gone on to university where again, he had failed to set the world alight but had come out the other side with an average degree in the Arts & Humanities but very little in the way of life skills or career plans. In truth, he had no real ambition and nothing that he had studied really gave him a natural progression in terms of a future career.

"My father was hugely impatient with me". George smiled, remembering the fights they used to have. "The Mediterranean temperament always came out when I failed so spectacularly to show any aptitude for business. Can't really blame him, I guess - especially not after the money he spent on my education." George recalled how, in contrast, his mother maintained her cool and well groomed indifference towards his indecision and tried to calm his father down whenever a new argument erupted by suggesting that he just 'hadn't found his niche yet'.

"Dad had come to London to head up one of the major Greek banks which had opened in London. Mum was from good banking stock herself, my great grandfather having established a merchant bank in the city which of course, became a family affair. I guess, I'm more like her. She wasn't at all academic like others in her family but she attended finishing school where grooming, deportment and the art of entertaining made her an adept socialite and debutante. My father wooed her, and although I think her family were a little disappointed she hadn't married into the British aristocracy, his credentials were approved and they married".

Irini listened intently.

"It all sounds very romantic. How nice it must be to find someone and settle down to a happy life with them", she went on wistfully.

"I'm not sure the romance lasted long", George laughed. "To dad's credit, he kept my mother in the life to which she was accustomed, and she, despite his often abrupt and dismissive attitude, provided him with a son and heir - me - and great respectability within the business circles and London society. Sometimes, I think it was more of a business transaction between them than a marriage".

George related how he had inherited his mother's rather laid back, laisser faire attitude to life and like her, he had taken it for granted that most things would just land in his lap without the need for great effort. He showed no aptitude for anything much and his father's disappointment was profound. They had frequent arguments when his father would bluster a tirade of questions;

"What are you going to do with your life? How will you make money?" To his father's fury, George generally responded with a shrug of the shoulders. His view of things were that his father made enough money to keep them all, so why worry? Until he found his 'niche', well, his family would keep him, wouldn't they? What George hadn't bargained for was his father withdrawing his allowance and demanding that he prove himself. Instead of taking the planned year out after university, much to his mother's chagrin and George's profound horror, his father presented him with an ultimatum. Either he agreed to take up a job he had secured for him on the London Stock Exchange or, he would withdraw permanently any financial assistance.

"George!" Irini exclaimed. "You sound as though you were a terribly spoilt young man! I think your father was entirely right in his decision", she laughed.

"Oh Irini, don't laugh! Of course, I know you're right, but really, this is the tip of the iceberg. Wait until you hear the rest of my shameful story". He continued. "Well, Dad was exercising 'tough love' on me. He wanted to make a man of me he said. He had pulled strings to get me the job, but in truth, I knew nothing about, nor had any interest in banking or the financial markets. After a crash course in the basics, which only emphasised my ineptitude, I found myself on the trading floor, trying to understand invisible sales of things like pork bellies, oil, stocks and shares. The whole thing just perplexed and defeated me. I was desperately unhappy and totally out of my depth in this world. Every day going into the mayhem of the trading floor, I'm ashamed to say, I began to fall apart. I wasn't like the others there who loved the cut and thrust of the day, the thrill of the gamble. I couldn't think fast enough on my feet, my concentration was shot to pieces. I hated every moment of the pressure and stress. Where my colleagues thrived, I dreaded the break of each new day. Misery and fatigue plagued me, adrenalin and fear bringing me close to breaking point".

George stopped for a moment, tasting the bitterness of the strong coffee which Irini had brought him. He shuddered, not just with the taste but with the recollection of those horrific days. Irini, sensing the rawness of George's memories took his hand in hers. The electricity of her touch reminded him of her presence and as their eyes met, he longed to take her face in his hands and draw him to her to kiss her full and inviting lips. Irini however, withdrew her hand quickly not wishing to encourage such intimacy.

"Go on", she said softly. "Tell me what happened next".

Disappointed that the moment between them had passed, nevertheless George continued with his story.

"I began to feel inadequate, I suppose. I just couldn't cope with daily life. I was making mistakes by the dozen and my job was only secure, at least for now, because of my familial connections. Even so, my father received reports of my errors and failures and his disdain for me reached an all time high; or perhaps I should say, an all time low."

"But, I do not understand Georgio. Why did you take it all to heart so much? A job after all, is just to earn you some money. It is not your whole life. How could it have affected you so badly?"

"It's the nature of that kind of work, Irini. You are using clients' money to gamble with. Life on the Stock Exchange is stressful even for those who know what they are doing. A bad judgement can bankrupt a client. It's even been known to bankrupt an entire bank. The responsibility is immense and I was terrified of letting my father down as well as the possibility of doing some real damage to a client. Anyway, I suppose that's why, if I can make excuses for myself, things went way downhill from there".

George explained to Irini how the traders work hard, but played even harder. He told her that as soon as the working day was over, they would all head for Covent Garden or some other gathering place where drink would flow freely into the night.

"We were paid well, Irini, but it was a high price in terms of our mental health. It was at this time that I experienced my first flirtation with drugs".

"Drugs! What, you mean medicines? This was to help your nerves I suppose?"

George laughed at Irini's naivety which also charmed him.

"No, I don't think you quite understand me. I mean I was taking drugs that I had bought rather than those prescribed by a doctor to treat a specific illness. They make you feel good, put you on a high." He wasn't quite sure whether Irini understood him but as he looked at her, understanding spread across her face.

"Oh, Georgio, I've read all about your Lord Byron, our hero. He fought for the Greeks against the Turks in the War of Independence. He died from taking drugs and too much alcohol".

"Yes! I think you're right. It was that sort of thing only instead of laudanum and morphine, I smoked cannabis which was common around London. It helped me to relax and wind down after a hard day on the trading floor. I would look forwarded to the nightly gathering of my friends for the ritual rolling of a joint. It's funny really, I'd always thought in my naivety that drugs were the province of either the really adventurous or the lower class Council Estates but, I couldn't have been more wrong. It was a common recreational activity amongst all social classes. The trouble is, it rarely stops with just cannabis. Once you get used to one thing, you look for another. Something which will give you even more of a kick".

George paused, unsure whether to tell Irini any more, yet finding it strangely cathartic to confide in someone after such a long time of bottling it up.

"One day, I had a particularly bad time at work. One of my trades had been a major disaster and I knew I would be up before the boss next day for a roasting. One of my colleagues, Charlie Graham had invited me to a dinner party that night. I was reticent about going at all really, depression having really gripped me. I didn't much feel like making the effort to be sociable. I knew there would be cannabis passed around but I had felt recently that this was actually exacerbating my fears and depression. The thought of my own miserable company for a long evening ahead was a less appealing option so I livened myself up with a shower and decided to forget about what lay ahead for me at work the next day and just try to enjoy the night.

The party was in full swing when I arrived at Charlie's. He was cheerier than usual that night and almost swamped me in a welcome embrace as he flung the door open. 'Great to see you!', he grinned, slapping my shoulders and bear hugging me in his delight. I couldn't understand it. He had only seen me a few short hours ago, but you would think it had been years the way he greeted me. Charlie and I were great buddies though and he had taken me under his wing at the Exchange. He bailed me out of trouble so many times and I felt indebted to him and grateful for his friendship. He's really successful as a trader and a real party animal. He lives life to the full. I so often wished I had his effervescence, popularity and his confidence. I envied him in many ways; he was a rising star, he had the money, the charisma, the flat and the girls to prove it. In contrast, I was yet again the failure, the albatross, a hanger on, hoping that some of his success might rub off on me".

"Georgio! You are so hard on yourself you know. You are not a failure! How could you ever believe this?"

"Because the sad fact is that it was true Irini! Maybe I'm changing a little now, but I was a complete waster in those days, believe me". Irini shook her head, refusing to acknowledge George's summation of himself. "Shall I go on?" Irini nodded her assent.

"Dinner was great that night. Charlie's latest girlfriend had set out to impress him, probably hoping that she might be asked to stick around for a while, and had provided a magnificent meal for us all. The wine, as usual, flowed copiously. We were all laughing and joking as coffee arrived and I expected the usual joint to be circulated. Charlie, though, had quite another idea up his sleeve. 'Feel like joining in with a new experience then Georgie boy?' he asked me. 'It'll put hairs on your chest and buck you up!' he promised. As ever, I wanted to keep up with the others. 'Sure thing, Charlie', I said, 'bring it on'. If only I'd known better. If only I hadn't been so stupid".

George stopped speaking for a moment, shaking his head miserably at his own stupidity; his weakness in being unable to refuse. Softly, Irini spoke.

"What was it George? What did you do?"

"Well, I was expecting a different kind of cannabis. There are lots of different types and strengths on the market you see. How wrong I was though. Charlie produced a small envelope of blotting paper. As he opened it out, he displayed a small amount of white powder. He asked everyone whether they were up for it. Sue Morgan, one of the girls from bank asked what it was. It was coke of course, cocaine, that is.

"I've never heard of such a drug. Why do you take it?" Irini asked.

"It's an amphetamine which has the effect of giving you extreme energy and a great feeling of well being. You feel invincible, like nothing can ever bother you again. I have to confess though, I was wary. The people who sell it mix it up with all sorts of things so that it makes them more money. Chalk, cleaning powders, that kind of thing. It can be very harmful if taken when adulterated like that". If only George had remembered his own caution when he had sold on cocaine to his customers. Perhaps he wouldn't be in this state now, he thought. "Anyway, I asked Charlie if he had taken any of it yet. He told me that he had and that it was great. He seemed OK so I decided to give it a go. It's sort of fashionable where I come from and idiotic though it may sound, I didn't want the others to think I was scared or anything. That's how immature I was", George added sadly. He recalled how Charlie coaxed him seductively, 'Come on Georgie, it'll make your troubles go away for a while, believe me'. George had always regarded coke as the preserve of the criminal fraternity or sad no-hopers but now it seemed that his impression was wrong. Drug taking was a party treat in the middle class circles of London it seemed. Looking back on it now, he realised how weak and easily influenced he had been in those days, ready to embrace anything which might gain him acceptance and, more importantly, make him feel good about himself. George had watched in awe as Charlie produced a mirror, deftly poured some of the white powder onto it and began, what appeared to be a well rehearsed ritual to divide the grains up into four equal lines with his credit card. Finally, when satisfied, he produced a five pound note and rolled it up into a thin tube. Bending over the mirror he inserted the tube into one nostril while holding the other closed and inhaled deeply, vacuuming up the entire line of powder. He had leant back, smiling and passed the tube to Sue, her boyfriend Mike and then finally on to George. As he bent over to take his first line, Sue had begun to giggle uncontrollably. 'Come on George, hurry up! It won't make you sneeze you know!' Sue had shouted. For some reason, all three of them seemed to find his discomfort hilarious and they convulsed with laughter. Determined to join their club, George replicated the actions of inhaling the powder, and so began his disastrous love affair with cocaine. The effects had been almost immediate. He had a bitter taste in his mouth followed by a rush of excitement. Where he had felt tired and flagging, he was now infused with energy. Despite his earlier depression, he now felt on top of the world.

"I felt confident, invincible and, do you know, Irini, for the first time since childhood, I felt happy after that first line of coke. I was euphorically happy. I felt like the person I'd always wanted to be;

happy, confident, in control. I was completely alert and my senses were so completely heightened that I appreciated the beauty in everything I saw, touched and tasted for the rest of the night. It seemed that colours were spectacularly beautiful, textiles felt sumptuous and comforting, even sensual. I didn't just like my friends at that moment. I loved them all. I wanted to draw them near and tell them how much they meant to me.

Anyway, the initial euphoria lessened after about thirty minutes and Charlie prepared another line for each of us. I felt excited at the new world which had been revealed to me and I waited in eager anticipation for my next turn with the rolled up note. I think, from that first moment, I was hooked Irini".

Irini who was listening intently to George's story shook her head in disbelief.

"This is such a strange thing that you tell me George. The only reason people take drugs here is to make them better when they are sick or to relieve their pain. I cannot imagine taking them when healthy".

"But that's just it! Don't you see? I was in pain. I was sick. Not physically, but mentally. I was in the throes of a breakdown and I thought the drugs were my saviour. That's why it was so wonderful. It gave me a lifeline to grip onto where everything had previously seemed to so hopeless. It's hard to explain, but I can only describe the effect of the drug as being almost like a spiritual experience. It was as though I was seeing and feeling all that the world truly had to offer. I felt spiritually connected. All that was bad in life was stripped away and everything shone with an aura that was bright, I was struck by a sense of awe. That's what it does to you. It heightens your senses. I felt that the drug was giving me the knowledge to change my life. All the secrets were contained in that line of powder. We talked incessantly for the rest of that night, all thoughts of sleep now gone. Our intellectual grasp of all subjects seemed immense and I remember feeling that our discussions were the deepest and most meaningful I had ever had. It was an epiphany. Life changing". George recalled how Charlie had been absorbed and astounded by his new found lease of life and his erudite pronouncements. No doubt, he had been talking rubbish all night, but it had sounded great. All night the party talked, laughed and enthused, until finally, as dawn broke, they decided they had best call it a day. Sue, Mike and George had decided to share a cab to their respective homes. George recalled how he had hugged Charlie, thanking him for introducing him to this new world. He was almost looking forward to work on Monday. He could cope with it now. He would really make a go of it and get rich by the time he was 35. He had been raring to go that night.

London was just in the process of waking up as George had turned the key in his front door that morning. Still buzzing and unable to sleep, he had whizzed around his house doing all the jobs he had been putting off for weeks. He was enervated and it wasn't until later that evening that George finally felt the first stirrings of fatigue. How he had resented that feeling. He just wanted to go on and on achieving. His bubble however, was about to burst.

Having slept the clock around until early the next morning, George had awoken to find his euphoria subsided, the big black cloud back over his head, his depression returned. Now, as he sat relating his story to Irini, he considered how his whole existence had become Kafkaesque, but that morning, he had never felt more as though he were a beetle stuck on its back, its legs flailing wildly, trying to find its feet and the right way to go. Things had only worsened for the remainder of the weekend and on Monday, back at the Stock Exchange, George's senses had felt dulled, his enthusiasm and confidence quashed, extinguished like a flame between fingertips. Unable to concentrate, his mood black, he made yet another serious error of judgement and his boss suspended him pending investigation and disciplinary proceedings. Back at home, George knew he had reached the end of the road with his job and probably, with his father. He explained to Irini how his only hope had been to get hold of more of the magic dust which he knew would restore his thinking. He had contacted Charlie in desperation, blurted out the disasters of the day and begged him to help him get some more coke.

'Hey, hold your horses, slow down George', Charlie had said. 'You don't want to be taking this stuff regularly, especially when you're down. That's how you get hooked and it's downhill from there, believe me'. George had only laughed dismissively, determined not to be fobbed off.

'It can't go much further downhill can it Charlie?' he had asked. 'Come on!' he had cajoled, 'what do you take me for? I just need a pick me up, something to help me through the day. It helps me think more clearly, that's all.'

'George', Charlie had warned, 'cocaine is powerfully addictive. You have to control it, not the other way around. Look at yourself! You're already restless and anxious'

'That's because I've had a shit day and I'm about to be sacked. Wouldn't you be just a bit restless and anxious if that was your day?' George had snapped back. The last thing he had wanted to hear was a lecture on drug abuse. Finally, Charlie had given in and promised him a hit later that night. Not satisfied at that though, George had asked for the number of the dealer. He didn't want to have to go through Charlie every time and face his disapproval like an errant school pupil.

'He won't deal with you direct without a personal introduction from me. Look, I'll see what I can do OK?' Go easy man', he had cautioned. 'You should treat this in the same way as a good bottle of champagne. It's an occasional treat, not a daily fix'.

"Of course", George continued with his story, "I didn't heed anything Charlie said. I couldn't see anything beyond getting the drug and though I appreciated his concern, I felt I could control things. I wasn't an addict and there was no way I'd become one. Later that night, true to his word, Charlie brought me a gram of coke. I settled up with him and couldn't wait until he went so that I could get to that little envelope in peace. Finally, when I was alone I could hardly contain my excitement as I prepared that first line and inhaled. Although I experienced the instant high once more, I had already developed a tolerance to the drug and needed to take another line soon afterwards to maintain the euphoria. Well, it doesn't take much to predict how things went from there. Soon I was in a cycle of drug abuse, needing more and more just to stand still. As my dependence increased I was soon spending more on coke than I was earning in a month and of course, the negative effects of my addiction intensified. I became erratic. I would experience tremors, muscle twitching, vertigo at even low levels and, worst of all, paranoia. My interpersonal skills, never great , deteriorated as I became more irritable and irascible. The physical effects weren't pretty either; palpitations, headaches, nosebleeds and a constant runny nose were the minor ones. I lost two stone in weight as my appetite decreased and my metabolic rate increased. My old friend Charlie tried hard to get through to me, make me understand what was happening, but, I was too far gone by then. I know he felt guilty for introducing me to the drug, but, to be fair, he couldn't have known what a mess I was in before I started taking it. Finally, inevitably, I completely lost my grip on reality. I was dismissed from my job and became a penniless drug addict, with no way of getting my next hit. It was only a matter of time, I knew, before my father would find out but my priority was to find some way of earning money just to feed my habit. It was then that I made my final descent into the abyss, I'm ashamed to say."

Irini listened with growing horror at the terrible experiences of this young man. How things could have got any worse than this, she could not imagine. She felt angry on his behalf that such a troubled soul had been introduced by his so called friend to such an evil habit. Looking at George now, his vulnerability more evident than on any previous occasion, she realised that what he had lacked in parental support, he had sought in this terrible drug. She felt like weeping for him. Standing up, she moved silently to his side and placed a hand upon his shoulder. As she did so, he turned and burying his face in her apron, he wept, inconsolably, for the first time in many years.

It took George some time before he was recovered sufficiently to continue with his story. Pent up emotion had built within him for so long that he thought the release, though welcome, would never end. It was like a dam breaking, he thought. He took comfort however in the warm concern he received from Irini. It felt good to lay his head on her shoulder as she held him close. Eventually, the racking sobs subsided and Irini produced a glass of raki with a cool glass of water.

"Here", she held the raki glass. "Swallow this quickly. It cures everything you know, even sorrow". George did as he was instructed. The liquid burned his throat as it slipped down into his stomach. It certainly had the effect of reviving you, he thought. He pulled himself together and suggested that they leave the taverna and walk down to the beach.

"Yes, it is a little dark in here, perhaps the sunlight will help you to feel better."

They walked together in comfortable silence, George, his head hung low, disconsolate as his memories burdened him once more. It was only when he felt Irini's hand reach for his that a grateful smile lit his face momentarily. The two of them continued, hand in hand and sat for a while staring out to sea, each of them lost in their own thoughts as to what the life beyond could ever hold for them again.

Unbeknown to George and Irini, as they had passed through

the village, their hands locked in mutual support and comfort, someone had been watching them. Manolis now sat, his head in his hands, tears coursing down his cheeks as he now contemplated the loss of Irini to another man. What could he do though? Even if it were possible for them to be together, Irini would never agree to be with him lest she pass on the disease. What right had he to be anything other than happy if she had found comfort in another man who shared her condition? Manolis wasn't bitter. He wished Irini nothing but happiness. It was just that he wished she could have found it with him. He feared though, that their special friendship would inevitably have to end if Irini and George were to become close. In the meantime however, he wondered if he could bear to watch the two people he was closest to develop their own special relationship which would naturally exclude him.

It was Irini who finally broke the silence, anxious for George to continue with his story.

"Over those next few days, I had to keep my head low. My parents, thank God, had just embarked on a cruise for six weeks so they wouldn't find out I'd been dismissed for a while. My first priority was to find a way of making money both to feed my cocaine habit and to lessen my father's wrath when he discovered what had happened. I thought if I could at least support myself financially and not be reliant on him, he couldn't really say or do much that would affect me. The trouble was, I was by then caught up in a vicious circle. Without coke, I couldn't function properly to find a job and without money, I couldn't buy the coke I needed so badly. Fortunately for me though, Charlie had kept his word and introduced me direct to the dealer, Gaz.

At first, I thought it would be better to just get myself clean. I figured that although it would be painful for a few days, maybe I could just sleep through it. It isn't that simple though. Just hours after ingesting my last line, and without another one available to me, I was climbing the walls. It felt as though the whole world was closing in on me. I sank into the deepest despair and desolation stretched before me. I suffered from mood swings ranging from irritable to murderous and then suicidal. I paced the floorboards as the mother of all headaches took over and I crouched in a corner unable to do more than hold my head and moan in agony with each thud. I had reached the Nadir of my existence. Finally, I either fell unconscious or asleep; I'm not really sure which. Anyway, I was out cold and didn't come to until nearly fourteen hours later. I awoke, cold, stiff and ill in the corner of the living room where I had lain clutching my head. Within minutes of awakening, I craved another fix. Somehow I managed to boil some water and made myself a cup of strong coffee but the caffeine was a very inferior substitute for the coke hit I so badly needed".

George recalled the events as they then unfolded that day, relating them somewhat dispassionately to Irini.

Sitting in his kitchen, he had what he thought was a brainwave. Why hadn't he thought of it before? It was perfect! He had lurched into the shower, and stood, palms against the glass, the blissfully warm, comforting spray of water falling on his sweat drenched and failing body. Slightly revived, he went to the meeting he had arranged half an hour earlier. He entered a dark pub, the loud music assaulting his ears, his eyes blinded momentarily as they adjusted to the dim lighting. It was the middle of the afternoon and yet, as soon as he entered the pub, it could well have been any hour of the day. He spotted Gaz almost immediately, perched on a tall bar stool, chatting to the barman, his trademark woollen cap pulled low over his forehead covering his No.1 close shaved head. In other circumstances, he was a man George would have avoided. As he approached, Gaz looked round, a wry smile flickering at the corners of his mouth. He enjoyed control and George's obvious demise was no doubt a source of great satisfaction to him. He was about to lay himself on his mercy, and Gaz knew it.

"George, my main man! How ya doin'? George had shuddered inwardly at his rap culture, pseudo black patois. Now, however, was not the time to be superior. George needed him far more than he needed him. George bought the man a drink, ordered a large gin for himself and they retired to a private booth in the corner. George came straight to the point.

"Gaz, I've lost my job and I have no money. I haven't had a fix since yesterday and I think I'm going crazy. Will you help me?" Gaz had regarded him with his hooded eyes, the knowing smile fixed on his otherwise inscrutable face. You could tell he was no soft touch.

"Sure man, but nuthin's fo' nuthin in 'dis world, ya get me? You want me to he'p you, but I'm gonna assist you in he'pin yo'-self bruvva". He sat back, folding his arms. "You got no money right, so you need to earn, am I right?" George couldn't argue with that premise, but what was coming next? Gaz chuckled at his obvious confusion. 'Da ansa, is simple man!' He leaned forward conspiratorially and George leaned forward to hear what he was going to say. 'I need to expand my network, right, but I don't like to meet up with users'. George nodded, listening intently. 'My customer base needs to expand. It's simple. Can you sell coke George? Good profits in it if you can!'

George had been flabbergasted. He had planned to ask Gaz for a buy now pay later deal on a supply of coke for himself, so this was an idea which came completely out of the blue, and one which he had never considered.

It's a great business proposition, George; a franchise, if you like". George had almost laughed out loud at his analogy with a bona fide business structure.

'But how can I afford enough stock to sell?' George had asked, somewhat naively. Gaz laughed once more.

'Man' he exhaled in mock exasperation, 'You know nuthin'!

Here's how it works, right? You get your first ounce on tick, the never never, whatevvfa you like to call it - on account. No investment required. You sell it on with your mark-up. You charge enough to pay for your original supply and to give you a profit. Then you pay me and I give you another supply. Simple!" Gaz's manner changed then. He became sinister, his voice taking on a more threatening cadence. "What you cannot do, though, friend, is use it all yourself. Remember that. You do so and you get a little visit from a couple of friends of mine, understand?" George understood OK, but what Gaz was offering seemed like the ideal solution. His head was spinning with the relief of his next fix and the profit margins which would be coming his way.

"So you see, Irini, I started a life of crime just to feed my bad habits. I was willing to feed off the vulnerable just to make sure I could get through each day".

Irini looked disappointed, he thought, but she passed no judgement upon him. She asked him to continue to the end of his story.

"One thing I had learned over the previous days was that it was essential I reduce my own dependency on coke if I was going to succeed. At that time, I felt like shit but, I have to say, I was comforted by the knowledge I had that whole ounce of coke nestling in my pocket. I was excited as well. If I could do this, I thought, it would be such an easy existence. I was focused and determined. I would cut down my own consumption and sell this lot as fast as possible. I had already been without coke for some hours and I resolved just to take enough of it to kick start my brain again and keep myself going. I hadn't enjoyed the cold turkey and I vowed never to get that bad again. To my own amazement, I didn't rush back to my flat to prepare a line. Instead, I went for a walk on the common and for once, I appreciated the feeling of natural, rather than drug induced pleasure. I knew I had a long way to go though and I still had a lot of problems to resolve, but I realised that being sacked from the Stock Exchange had actually lifted a huge weight from my shoulders which had been a contributory factor in my speedy decline into drug dependency. It was important though that I now made some serious money. I was determined to support myself so that I didn't have to go back, cap in hand, to ask for my father's help.

In the following days, I was pleased that I maintained control over the cocaine, instead of the other way around, but it was a struggle. I took a modest quantity but worked hard on weaning myself off it. In the meantime, I had no difficulty in making my sales, mainly to friends and acquaintances whom I knew indulged and in turn to friends of friends. On Gaz's advice, part of my on the job training and induction course, I began to frequent clubs where there was always a new and expanding market. My first ounce was quickly and easily paid for with plenty of profit over and I was up and running. I decided that I was going to make a business of this game and I approached it with the cynicism of a businessman. I did my research and learned as much as I could about the market. The facts and figures were amazing. In the UK, the drugs market was worth in excess of £8 billion per annum and one in five people use recreational drugs in London alone. My eyes were opened as I discovered more and more about my new, and highly lucrative vocation. I discovered that drugs were just like a tall latte - you could get them anywhere and many people simply perceived them in much the same light. The consumer society, I want it, so I'll buy it. To my delight, I found there was a ready market in all areas of society. One day I would find myself delivering to a posh London W1 address, the next to a hideous slum in East London. I was so pragmatic and methodical with my research, I even prepared a customer profile and a long term business plan".

Irini shook her head, silent disapproval written upon her face.

"And your customers, Georgio, what sort of people would get themselves into this position? How could you have got yourself in this position?"

"I've asked myself the same questions, time and again, Irini. Probably more so since I've been here. It's a different world here in Greece, Irini, particularly at this time. There are things where I come from that you could not possibly comprehend". George did not elaborate on his observation, but merely went on;

"There were common life themes amongst my clients, all of which, of course were familiar to me. Although it is easy to dismiss many drug users as either fuckwits or as simply hedonistic in the pursuit of constant pleasure, this isn't the end of the story. Sure, the pursuit of pleasure is probably one of our most basic human instincts, but why do people resort to drugs in order to find it? I guess most people aspire to find something more in their lives. They get restless. Some people want material things, others want more satisfying emotional or spiritual understandings and experiences. Others, like me, want to escape from something, to find contentment and feel adequate. Most of the people who depend on drugs for these feelings have no idea how to even start looking for it naturally. Many don't even realise they are missing anything, but they take their first hit and, hey presto! A whole new, unimagined world opens up to them when just for a while, life looks brighter or they develop more confidence.

Then, of course, there are the restless types; fuelled by the hope of something better, but which always just manages to elude them; is always just beyond their grasp. Depression dogs these types whose lives feel purposeless; their spirits crushed. These, I have to say were my most lucrative customers, because once hope dies, addiction is likely. These customers don't seek the drugs out for hedonistic experience or a temporary boost of confidence. For them, escapism is the only answer to their problems, the anaesthetic properties of the chemicals colluding with them to make another day bearable. These were the customers I wanted most of all. They were faithful. They were dependent on me and, in a terrible, perverse way, I liked the power over them. Most of these customers came from the poorest areas, where hope, if it ever existed is in short supply. Here were people with little, or no education, no career prospects and, on the whole, devoid of the possibility of any personal happiness or contentment.

I became something of an amateur psychologist. I could read my potential clients well. Within a couple of minutes of speaking to them, I could tell who would be the five minute wonders, the hooray Henry brigade with too much money to burn in pursuit of mindless pleasure and whatever was fashionable at the moment and those who were the needy ones. The ones who would beg me for drugs and would be calling me every other day.

I was cynical in my approach to my clients. I didn't try to psychoanalyse the effects the drugs may be having on their lives, or the part that I was playing in their inevitable downfall, even destruction. This was just a job to me.

"Well, Georgio, if these people had any idea of how lucky they are, they would not take their lives so lightly. We on Spinalonga would give anything just to be having a bad day; in fact, we would be grateful if that was all we ever had".

"I know Irini. Don't you think I haven't realised that now? I am ashamed of the life I led, but, I need you to know the truth, so will you hear me out?".

"Oh, of course, Georgio. Don't mind me. I shouldn't judge. None of us has entirely clean hands. I'm sorry. Tell me though, what happened when your father discovered you had lost your job? Was he angry?"

"Well, not that it's anything to be proud of, but I became an accomplished liar. Naturally, there were questions from my parents whose shame and disappointment in my Stock Exchange embarrassment had been profound. I managed to blag a tale about working for a friend with a successful city estate agency business, and, as I appeared to be doing very well financially, which indeed I was, my father took very little interest in the mechanics of how I attained my wealth. He wasn't much interested in me really, just as long as I didn't let the side down or cause him any problems.

I did very well for a number of years in my new trade. I was, of course, just part of a pyramid and even at the lowest level, I could be making anything between £1500 and £2000 per week. The rewards were great and, contrary to popular belief, the risks relatively few. I worked for myself as my own boss and the operation is set up so that no-one knows anyone else in the business except your own supplier. Of course, I soon saw the benefits of cutting the coke supplies I received with other, harmless substances such as caffeine pills which gave the user a kick and tasted similar to cocaine. I could increase my supplies this way for very little money, although, I couldn't go overboard on this as it wouldn't have been wise to risk losing customers with over diluted supplies. Even the drugs chain was consumer orientated. Clients would complain if they received a bad batch in the same way as they would complain about a bad meal. If that happened, you would lose your client to another dealer. If anyone was unhappy therefore, I always made it my business to give them a replacement free of charge. That's good business. Mostly however, no-one really noticed my adulterated supplies.

My own life during this period was good. Without the pressure on me to succeed in a career that didn't suit me, I no longer felt the same imperative to take drugs myself. It isn't the case that once you are addicted to drugs you will always be addicted. At first, I just cut down and, as my head became clearer and my income potential became evident, I knew I had to get clean otherwise I would never make money. I was so happy to be free and doing my own thing at last that I no longer needed to take cocaine to feel optimistic about my life.

It was difficult, at times, to keep up the fiction of my life. I didn't reveal to any of my friends, even the ones to whom I supplied drugs, or family, the true nature of my work. The friends I supplied thought I just got it on a social basis as a favour and my family of course never knew anything about it at all. I had to create whole scenarios about my estate agency career and the mysterious friend, Tom Harker, who had given me a second chance in life. Charlie, on one or two occasions, had suggested he meet me for lunch or after work and I always had to make sure that we met somewhere after a 'meeting' which had taken place away from the office. I was always vague about the exact location of my 'City' office. Mostly however, it wasn't difficult to maintain my fantasy life. I became adept at lying and deception. Of course, it didn't help much when it came to forming relationships with girls. I was so much in demand at my peak, having to respond quickly to calls seeking my services that I was an extremely unreliable date and my secretiveness about work proved largely unattractive to those females who did stick around long enough to find out more. In many ways therefore, although financially I was fine, I did have my regrets over my disastrous personal life. I promised myself I don't know how many times, that I would get out of this game in the next few months, which became years, and find myself a proper job. Trouble was, there was nothing I could do in the real world that would provide me with anything near the income I was getting now. Still though, I promised myself, the time would come when I had enough money to give me breathing space to get training or have a go again at a legitimate job. I knew that I had to be living on borrowed time. My secret would out, one way or another, and the proverbial shit would hit the fan.

I'd got away with the story for a number of years and I had all the trappings of wealth to go with it. I'd progressed into Commercial Property with 'Tom' as my story went, and I'd made fortune. I now worked from home as remote working saved on the huge cost of office rental in the City (a brainwave that saved any more awkward questions about my work location).

Over the years, I had in fact developed a continually growing and diversifying clientele and my supplies had varied from cocaine to occasional heroin and with the dawn of the Dance Culture, crack cocaine and another popular drug, ecstasy. Over the years, I had witnessed the paradoxical increase in wealth and disposable income, particularly in young people, but also, in direct correlation, there was an undeniable increase in misery, dissatisfaction, stress related problems and depression. Divorce rates were at an all time high and so, therefore was the desire for both recreational and dependency drugs. My business was booming".

The two were silent for a while, both lost in their own thoughts. What George did not tell Irini though was anything about Jenna Hawkins who had been one of his regulars for years and who barely existed without several hits throughout the day. She was on a slippery slope. Generally, George had dealt direct with her, but sometimes, her husband Dave met him if she was just too out of it. On that last occasion, it had been Dave who collected the final gram from him.

Gaz had recently changed to pastures new, largely serving the drugs market in Ibiza and a new supplier had arrived on the block. He supplied the coke ready cut and in their envelopes instead of in the crumbling white lump Gaz had supplied. George now knew he should have questioned the practice, but, at the time, he didn't. He was too unconcerned. For a time, he sold the wraps, ready made, and without problem. That day though was to be different. George recalled how he had asked Dave how Jenna was as he hadn't seen her in a while. He quite liked her really. She had always been a cheerful type, though clearly beaten by her miserable, non aspirational existence. She was married to Dave who was, in George's opinion, little more than a single cell amoeba.

He was a dysfunctional and perpetual reprobate whose visits in and out of jail had ensured a life of constant debt and struggle for Jenna. It was little wonder the poor woman sought solace in cocaine. Jenna had always engaged in a chat and idle banter on the frequent occasions when she and George had met. According to Dave however, Jenna had lost so much weight over recent weeks, he barely recognised her. He even seemed concerned about her depleting health and energy. Nevertheless, both Dave and George knew she wouldn't survive simply by coming off the cocaine. More likely such a radical move would undoubtedly be the death of her. George spent little time that day concerning himself with Jenna however and merely sold the wrap to Dave. Little did he know what the consequences of that transaction would be.

George lived an almost vampiric existence during this time. Most of his clientele surfaced in the evenings, and, by the very nature of the drug, he would receive calls at odd hours of the early morning from one or other of his very distinct market sectors; the rich kids who were busy partying or the desperate no hopers who had run out and needed their next fix urgently. The rich checked in to places like The Priory to get clean but the working classes had no such haven and, even if they had, what was there on the other side for them? Getting clean didn't remove the misery and grind of their daily lives. George believed he was providing a social service to such people.

Now, on a strange island in Greece, in a strange time and in the strangest of circumstances, George had time to consider everything that had passed before and the disaster he must have wrought on so many ordinary people.

"You must think me a terrible person, Irini. I don't even know why you would want to talk to me after hearing this. I wouldn't blame you if you hated me".

"I won't pretend that your story is one to be proud of Georgio, but, you were young. I think that your parents failed you in many ways. These things have an effect on a person I think. Remember Lord Byron Georgio, he is one of our greatest national heroes, fighting so valiantly against the Turks in our War of Independence. Drugs did not make him a bad person did they?" 'But I'm no hero', George thought, but did not say. If only Irini knew how much worse his story became. He could not tell her however.

"Thank you Irini, for being so understanding. I can hardly compare myself to Lord Byron though. I think his story is a little different don't you?"

"Perhaps for now, but you can make yourself a hero too George. You only have to help in the little battles to make a mark in Spinalonga you know. I think you are already doing that". Irini smiled, her face immediately transforming to that of a beautiful angel, thought George. They held each other's gaze for a few moments until Irini, aware of an intensity which had become evident in George's eyes, turned away quickly. Flustered, she stood up and dusted the sand from her dress.

"Oh, but I must go. We have been here too long and there are things to be done. Manolis must be wondering what has become of us!"

"Irini?", George asked hesitantly

"Yes?" she responded warily, afraid to hear what he would ask.

"I, I'm very fond of you, you know. I wondered, that is, I thought, perhaps we could be close friends? You know, very close friends".

Irini looked confused, crestfallen even. Trying to keep her tone light, she responded.

"But we are very close friends, Georgio. I am sure we always shall be". She had feared such a moment occurring between them and now sought to steer the conversation back to business.

"Come, let's return to the village". She held out her hand to help George to his feet. He grasped it and pulling himself up, he held on to it, unwilling to let the moment pass. Irini did not attempt to pull away, for in truth, she was unsure of her own feelings. She needed to think before she risked hurting anyone. Squeezing George's hand, she told him, "I am very fond of you too Georgio, but there are many reasons why I cannot at this time tell you what I think you would like to hear. I cannot make any promises Georgio, but please, give me time. For now, can't we just stay as we are?"

"Of course we can Irini. I understand. Please, forgive me if I have spoken out of turn or misread the situation", George responded quietly.

"There is nothing to forgive, Georgio, nothing at all. Now, let's get on. We still have to tend to Kyria Maniadakis' gardens and it will be getting dark soon. The two of them headed off in the direction of the village, each lost in their own thoughts, unaware of the events which were soon to overtake them and take any decisions which they might have made about the future completely out of their hands.

LIFE, LOVE AND DEATH ON A SMALL ISLAND

George was disappointed by Irini's hesitation to become more involved with him but he did not pursue things further for fear that she would distance herself from him completely. He knew that she and Manolis had a very close relationship but when he had asked Manolis about this, he had been circumspect in his reply indicating that their friendship was based on a number of years' acquaintance and mutual hardship. He had seemed reluctant to talk about it further, except that unusually for Manolis, he was a little short with George on the day that they spoke about Irini. With uncharacteristic brusqueness, which indicated he had little more he wished to contribute to the conversation, he said,

"What Irini does of course is her affair. I can see that you are fond of each other and, if you can both find happiness in each other's company then of course, I wish you well". His words though, George could see, belied something else which told him that Manolis had very different feelings than those which he voiced.

"Manoli, I would not wish to see you or Irini hurt, nor would I wish to interfere in any relationship that you two may have either now or in the future. Tell me to back off and I surely will".

Manolis merely shook his head. "There is no future for Irini and me as a couple Georgio. It can never be. Yes, I cannot deny that it will hurt me to see her with someone else, but, I have grown to like you as a good friend and if it must be so, I would rather it were you. Besides, I think she needs someone. Her life has been difficult, her story tragic. Look after her well Georgio and I will never think badly of you".

To Manolis' relief however, nothing further had so far developed between his two friends and, though he tried not to hope this would remain the situation, he was only human after all.

George meanwhile continued to settle into island life and it occurred to him what a waste his life had been up until this point. If he could turn the clock back, he would take an entirely different approach to life. He would have made the most of his opportunities, maybe even travelled to Greece anyway to work in this beautiful country and amongst its hospitable people.

In Spinalonga, the people had nothing in comparison to all that George had owned in his privileged life and yet, he was so much more contented here than he had ever been previously. In addition to the handywork which he had undertaken, George had begun to help out in other ways too. Having worked so closely with Irini in the community, Manolis had begun to train him in the care of the lepers. Whilst he had not been keen initially, once he got used to the sights and smells which he encountered each day, gradually George was able to clean and dress open wounds or the stumps of amputated limbs. With Manolis' help and encouragement, George learned to look at the lepers, even the worst affected, with new eyes as he administered drops, oils and unctions to ease their pitiful suffering.

George's admiration for the people of Spinalonga was profound. They refused to allow the disease to defeat them and following his arrival, the community grew quickly. Unbeknown to George, he had come at a time when development on the island was to be at its most active and he was privileged to witness the gradual improvement of life on Spinalonga. Those with land around their houses laid out beautiful little gardens where they grew the most succulent vegetables or reared livestock which would be roasted to provide a feast for all. In some ways, Spinalonga had been a more thriving micro-economy than mainland Crete, a fact which had caused not inconsiderable consternation amongst the Cretan people. George learned from Manolis during one of their many days together that the Medical Governor for the island had been responsible for the large concrete basins being built in the laundry area. Medical treatment had improved tenfold when in 1937 a new hospital had been built and the building of a laboratory commenced shortly afterwards. The laboratory was still in progress but would, it was hoped, be finished in the coming months. Until Manolis' arrival on the island, medical and laboratory help had had to commute from Crete, but all too often, bad weather or other circumstances had prevented their arrival.

One day, soon after George had arrived on the island, Manolis came to tell him that his first allowance of 30 drachmas had arrived. The decision to pay the lepers, he learned, had been made by the Socialist Government of Crete. The drachma carried strong buying power and he experienced first hand now, just how much the community was at the mercy of some unscrupulous people, eager to divest the people of the few comforts the money could buy them. Many on the mainland disapproved of the social security those on Spinalonga received, even knowing the miserable existence they had to endure. The attitude prevailed that the lepers must have been bad people to receive such a terrible punishment from God. Why therefore should the Cretan Government give them such rewards for their sins when they, the ordinary Cretans, had to work from sunrise to sunset to receive much less? George was stunned by the small mindeness of those who were unashamedly jealous of the islanders. Looking at these poor people, he wondered how anyone fortunate enough to have their health and ability could ever be jealous of, or begrudge the doomed people on this island the little assistance they had.

Domestic help was recruited and transported to the island on a daily basis to undertake those tasks which were too dangerous for the lepers. Laundrymen and women, maintenance people and cooks, all came to the island, but few of them arrived for altruistic reasons. Most begrudged the work, many complained, and it was during these times that the lepers' self esteem shrank once more in the face of open disgust and disdain from the domestic help. Those who came to the island demanded danger money, very high wages for their services, knowing that the lepers received social security money. Knowing also the difficulties for the islanders in communication with the outside world, they would extort even more from people desperate to hear news of their families or relay messages home. It was difficult for the community to know how many messages got to the families as the islanders were wholly at the mercy of some unscrupulous characters. Poor Nikos paid fortunes of his money to various domestics to make enquiries of his children. His face beamed occasionally when someone assured him they had heard from a friend of a friend in Athens that his children had been seen and were happy and well. Unfortunately, this was the extent of the information he ever received and although it was impossible to tell, George doubted whether there had been any genuine enquiry. Deep down, he suspected Nikos knew this too, but he chose to accept the messages as truth and gained some temporary comfort from them until he heard him weeping quietly in his room, determined not to let his emotions show.

There was always great excitement when the merchant boat arrived from Crete brining with it an array of wares including bread, cakes, fruit and meats, material for clothes, ready made clothes, leather, newspapers and various other sundries. There was no regulation by the Government of the prices which could be charged and once again, full advantage was taken by the visiting merchants who charged the highest prices for their tempting wares. In a society denied so few pleasures, it was not uncommon for the women to blow an entire month's money on some frippery which would, for a short time at least, restore their feeling of femininity or self worth. Of course, when this happened, it was up to the rest of the islanders to support her for the remainder of the month. Still, no-one really criticised these occasional human weaknesses. Everyone on the island understood they could each be guilty of recklessness once in a while and as long as they didn't succumb to temptations at the same time, what harm? They suspected that those in governing office may be conspiring with the merchants to increase prices so that they could get their cut of the lepers' money. Manolis was greatly concerned about such rumours which abounded but he never had sufficient hard evidence to do anything about it.

One of the most appreciated developments in recent years on the island was the ability of friends and relatives to visit their loved ones on Spinalonga. Of course, it wasn't without its difficulties, not least of which was the disinfection process which had to be endured before leaving the island. Anyone who visited Spinalonga, or anything which was taken from the island had to go through the disinfection room where carbolic and disinfectant washes were doused over them to eliminate any possibility of taking infection back to Crete. Even money had to be disinfected before it could leave the island.

The community elected a President of the Colony periodically and, during this time, it was a schoolteacher, banished to the island some years before. He had become something of a legend. According to the islanders, under his governance, things had never looked better for the island with concrete roads under construction, plans being drawn up for new modern housing and the building of a new Church, Agio Pandelemonas. In recent times, the much admired President was responsible for bringing a sense of order and purpose to the little community, helped along by the many forward looking entrepreneurs who brought a vision to the lepers of leading a useful and even prosperous life. George continued to play his own small part in broadening the horizons of his fellow islanders. He would leave his little schoolroom at the back of Yiannis' shop to find everyone working hard converting the derelict buildings in the main street into kafeneon, workshops, other tavernas, bakers, butches and grocers' shops. The doors and shutters were painted in gloriously bright colours and a cheerful little picture book town began to emerge from the previously desolate and dilapidated ghost town of George's first recollection.

During all of this activity, it amazed George how he actually forgot about his own bizarre presence on Spinalonga. He had come merely to accept that he now existed as part of this little world, this island microcosm and he barely thought about the bewildering set of circumstances which had conspired to bring him here. Perhaps, he thought, it is the mind's way of protecting him from insanity, because undoubtedly, had he really considered the enormity of the experience which had trapped him in an alien world, so far divorced from anything he had ever known, he could only have concluded that he was deranged. It was only in the occasional unguarded conversation with Manolis or Irini when George inadvertently made reference to something from the 20th or 21st century that he was reminded by their bewilderment that he was not from their time.

George recalled now the most spectacular of these errors which he had made whilst relaxing with Manolis and Irini at the taverna one evening. One glass of wine too many and George, glancing up at the clearest of skies, had marvelled at the shooting stars and the brilliance of the full moon. He found himself waxing lyrical about the beauty of the moon when he forgot himself and expressed his desire to follow in the steps of Aldron and Armstrong to land upon it and explore its secrets. Manolis and Irini had exchanged a look of utter astonishment and then shrugged as though they thought George was just having one of his crazy moments. Humouring him, Manolis joked,

"You will have to sprout wings like Icharus and Daedalus my friend, but take heed from their story - don't be too ambitious, or your wings will melt and you will return to the earth with a bump." George laughed.

"It takes a bit more than wings to get to the moon, Manolis, but I think I would prefer to wait until they get the technology a little better. I don't want to fry like Challenger when it flew back into the earth's atmosphere. Still, they're talking about package tours to the moon now, so maybe I'll get there one of these days!" Of course, George had completely forgotten himself and where he now was. Space travel was the stuff of science fiction in 1940s Europe. During these last few moments, Manolis had gaped at him as though he should be constrained and locked away for his own safety.

"You have quite an imagination, my friend, quite an imagination", Manolis laughed, though less heartily this time. It was only then that George realised his error. He laughed it off as best he could.

"Yes, always given to flights of fantasy I'm afraid. Just ahead of my time, Manolis, I think". Though Manolis smiled as George tried to cover his tracks, there was something in the young man's tone, which again, made him uneasy.

George and Irini maintained their easy friendship, laughing, joking and teasing each other but never crossing the line which would cement their flirtation into a serious relationship. Manolis had avoided speaking with Irini about it, afraid perhaps of what she might tell him. He knew however that their relationship was cemented by years of shared endurance and Manolis was comforted by the fact that Irini had not changed in any way towards him, nor had their deep affection been diminished by her friendship with George. Still, on many an evening, it was he she would choose to visit, their conversation animated, based on knowledge of each other which could not be usurped by any newcomer to their friendship.

For Irini's part, she had been confused for a while, charmed by

George and protective of his vulnerability. At first, she had thought that perhaps there could be something more between them, something which she would not dare to have hoped for with Manolis. Perhaps, she thought, she could have a normal relationship with someone else now. Wasn't George, after all, a leper like herself? Many people on the island had relationships, some even had children together. Why shouldn't it happen to her? Something however deterred her from encouraging George's affections in such a way. She couldn't put her finger on it, but his strangeness, for one thing, made her wary. The way he spoke of the most peculiar things as though they were fact. Like tonight and his nonsense about flying to the moon! In truth, he frightened her a little when he talked of these things. Also, she realised, her affection for George was based on more maternal feelings than anything else. He was only a little younger than she, but he seemed in many ways childlike. A boy still entrenched in childhood, grown up too soon perhaps. More importantly however, there was Manolis. Try as she might, and no matter how much she told herself it was an impossible dream, she could not entirely dismiss the hope that one day they might find a cure for leprosy and that her life might take an altogether different turn.

As for George, whilst he held out hope of wooing Irini, in his heart, he knew the truth. There was no doubt in his mind that although he felt sure he loved her, her heart belonged completely to Manolis. Although, she had been adamant there could never be anything between them because of her disease and her determination never to put him at risk, nevertheless, she would not, could not embark on a relationship with another man. She had never voiced these things to George, but he knew the two of them well enough now to be able to interpret every small look, each intimate smile between the two of them and to know that they had such a strong bond that words to communicate were almost unnecessary. Even if Irini now chose him, he would always know he was second best in her eyes and he could not bear that. Besides, how could he, in all conscience embark on a relationship with someone so good and kind as she when he didn't even know how he came to be on the island or whether he was destined to stay? It was all so overwhelmingly complicated. George had spent a great deal of time going over and over the possibilities in his head until finally he had decided that irrespective of their difficulties, Manolis and Irini were soulmates. He would not try to come between them, deciding that he would rather have both of them as his closest friends.

Over the following months, more and more reforms took place under the eye of the President and, with the population on the island growing, it was clear that some method of law enforcement was needed. Prosperity was also beginning to grow for many on the island and there were those, even on Spinalonga, who felt they could take without permission or otherwise live outside the unwritten rules of the previously law abiding community. There were occasional fights of course, which in a community such as that of Spinalonga, could mean the difference between life and death, even in a relatively minor confrontation. Officers were appointed therefore to keep law and order.

Work continued on the new hospital and on the new laboratory, where, it was hoped, perhaps some research and advances in treatment could be made. The little island took on a new vibrancy as the lepers regained their self worth and new things sprang up. Appearance could be improved for example, by a visit to the barber or the hairdresser. A former journalist set up an island newspaper called the 'Satire' which contained news about the people, snippets obtained from the mainland and the ever increasing events which were now taking place on the island. Entertainment was also plentiful with weekly dances where everyone on the island met to exchange gossip, eat, drink and for some, luckier than George, embarked on romance. Unlikely as it may have seemed to outsiders, a number of romances blossomed on Spinalonga between couples young and old. George was fortunate enough to watch just such a relationship develop between two of his younger English class pupils, Alexander and Sofia.

Alexander was a handsome young man in his twenties who resembled pictures of his namesake Alexander the Great with his classical features and fairer colouring. Alexander had arrived from the Athens hospital and had been denied a promising career as a lawyer when the first ugly symptoms of leprosy had shown themselves. Although he had not yet succumbed to the aggressive development of the wounds, Alexander's hands were painfully crooked with the swellings which grew upon them. In recent months his gait became laboured and painful as the disease spread to his feet and toes. Alexander however, in much the same spirit as Nikos, refused to be beaten by his misfortune. He enjoyed a good joke and flirted mercilessly with the women, young and old, all of whom he could wrap around his little finger. This often resulted in him taking away little extras from the shops as some pink faced lady, her face shining with the flattery she had long since forgotten rewarded him for his welcomed impertinence.

"Why, you are looking more beautiful than ever today Athena - what have you done to your hair that makes you like the Goddess herself?"

Athena, though secretly delighted by his attention would respond, "Get away with you! Your eyes are obviously failing. Here! Have some fruit to make you healthy!"

"My goodness, Maria, how your eyes shine brighter than the stars today. What has put such a twinkle in them?" Maria, hiding her mouth shyly behind her hand, her gaze lowered, merely giggled self consciously.

Alexander amused George immensely with his cheek. Everyone had instantly taken to the lad. How he got away with the things he said, particularly to the older and more proper of the ladies, George would never know, but they fell for his charms without exception and each of them, irrespective of age, were a little in love with the bright, charming young man.

George was standing chatting with Yiannis in his workshop on one occasion when Alexander limped into the main street, stopping to exchange compliments with all the ladies he passed. Yiannis looked up, his dark eyes scowling under his thick brow, scratching his increasingly patchy beard where his skin had begun to crack.

Pah! Who does he think he is and how do they fall for his pretty words so easily? They won't give him a second look when his looks start to crack like the rest of us." George smiled at Yiannis' surly comments, knowing that he wished he too could get some of the attention which Alexander commanded so easily.

"Now now, Yianni, leave him alone. He brings a little sunshine into their day. Surely you don't begrudge them that? A positive attitude can go a long way you know".

"Hah, well I'm positive he annoys me. He should take his pleasantries elsewhere".

George realised that his dear friend, for he had become such, was in a great deal of discomfort these days and his work was becoming more difficult for him. Yiannis' hands were deteriorating rapidly and he was forced to keep a dressing on his left which George changed daily for him. He worried how Yiannis would cope when he could no longer practice the trade he loved, a day which he feared would not be far off. Yiannis wasn't usually so mean spirited and George understood it was due to his pain.

For George's part, he enjoyed Alexander's company. He was a breath of fresh air. They were close in age and their conversations were lively and stimulating, though sometimes difficult since George's life experiences were of a different time and place to Alexander's. They would sit together sometimes in the kafeneon or tavern, watching their little world go by, combining the grotesque with the beautiful. There were a few very stunning young women on the island, whose illness had not progressed to be disfiguring. For those people, men and women alike, they must have questioned every day the injustice of their being on Spinalonga. How easy it must be to deny the disease, George thought, when there are few visible signs that you have it and how soul destroying the future, black as it must seem.

George noticed that Alexander became unusually tongue tied whenever a certain young lady, Sofia, was around. His compliments were not so freely or confidently showered upon her. George knew the young woman slightly, having met her at the hospital whilst assisting Manolis but beyond the odd 'Kalimera' or Ti Kanis', they had exchanged few words until she began to attend his classes. If he were honest, George too was slightly in awe of her beauty, a rose amongst the thorns. Sofia turned the heads of many a man on the island whose blood remained hot.

"What's wrong with you Alexander?" George asked one morning as Sofia entered the classroom and Alexander, who had been laughing and joking only seconds before now sat down, his head buried in his book. "Cat got your tongue? I'm sure Sofia would appreciate your attention". Alexander looked sheepish.

"I'm afraid to speak to her", he whispered. "She seems so perfect and look at me, becoming a bent and disgusting cripple". Alexander's response surprised George. He had never before acknowledged the increasingly visible signs of leprosy, but he was clearly self conscious in front of this woman. George made a mental note and decided to try to play cupid at the earliest opportunity. In fact, that day came the same week. Many of the villagers were gathered at the taverna when George was talking amongst a crowd of people of whom Sofia was one. They found themselves talking about theatre and George happened to mention that Alexander, short of a courtroom in which to playact, had become involved in setting up a theatre group on the island and that he would be delighted if she were to go along and join them. Alexander arrived later that night and so George formally introduced them to his great delight.

There was now no shortage of entertainment on Spinalonga with the islanders pooling some of their money to rent projectors for film shows, the Karagiosi puppet shows, staged with intricately home made wooden puppets and now, thanks to Alexander and his friends, the island amateur dramatics group. Some weeks after George had introduced Sofia to Alexander, the island was treated to Aeschulus' Agamemnon with Sofia giving a very respectable performance of the doomed Cassandra, cursed by the God Apollo to have true visions of the future which no-one would believe. Ironically, George knew exactly how that felt! Quite aside from the cultural exploits on the island, love blossomed between Sofia and George's dear friend Alexander who beamed from ear to ear whenever her name was mentioned. A few short months later, Sofia and Alexander approached George with some wonderful news.

"We want you to be the first to know that we are to be married", Alexander was bursting with joy.

"And we'd like you to be our 'Koumbaro', Sofia added, taking George's hand in hers.

"Well, if I knew what it was, I'm sure I should be delighted to be your kom... what? asked George.

Sofia grinned, delighted to educate him in some more of the Greek customs.

"Koumbaro. Georgio, there are many traditions in Greece and this is one of the nicest ones. The relationship of Koumbari to the wedding couple is to be their closest and most honoured friend".

Sofia continued to explain the office of Koumbaro which it turned out, had some similarities with the office of best man or maid of honour in Britain, but has much more significance. The

Koumbaro, she told George is actively involved in the wedding ceremony and has the very important task of holding and exchanging wreaths over the heads of the couple as they take their vows. George laughed and hugged his dear friends whose happiness overjoyed him. At least one of the couples here were making a success of things, he thought. Taking both of Sofia's hands in his own, George assured her that he would be the proudest man on earth to act as Koumbaro for them.

This was a golden period on the island. Confidence was growing on the mainland that leprosy could not be as easily transmitted as had once been believed. As long as the disinfectant procedures were closely observed and no healthy person's open wound came into contact with a wound on a leper, it was acknowledged that there was little danger to visitors. Friends and family now began to visit the island more and more, to the extent that the island plays were performed monthly for mainland visitors which even included the Mayor of Crete. For Alexander and Sofia however, this development meant so much more. Their families were able to attend the wedding and it was one of the happiest days George experienced on the island with everyone invited to the celebrations.

Never a religious man, George was nevertheless imbued with the spirituality of the occasion, awed by the simple majesty of the beautiful little Church, its flickering candles and the Greek Orthodox ceremony with its haunting music and dignified ritual. He felt honoured and an important member of the congregation, playing his part in sealing the union of the couple. The Koumbari, Sofia had told him, symbolises mankind and the priest symbolised heaven. Each of them join together to consecrate the union of the marriage.

Later, everyone made their way to the town centre which had been decorated with flowers and bunting where a feast of smells and colours caressed the senses. Spit roast meat, souvlaki covered in oregano; stifado, kleftiko, massive bowls of juicy salads, feta cheese, stuffed minted vine leaves, tzatziki, bread, baklava, Greek Yogurt, fruit and honey all awaited. Long tables were set out and the whole village celebrated long into the night.

After the finest meal in George's memory, the tables were cleared and the dancing began. Many wore traditional Cretan dress, the men in their pantaloons, 'vrakes', long leather boots, white shirts, embroidered waistcoats and the black beaded Cretan scarves wrapped around their heads. The women wore their brightly coloured skirts, intricately embroidered aprons and white headscarves. Many of the old people, particularly the women, dressed in black. Even those whose limbs had been eaten away or amputated bravely joined in as best they could, enjoying the atmosphere and the music. In usual form, Nikos and Yiannis led the dancing as the bouzouki started up, displaying their talent in the Pendodzali dance, their intricate footwork creating a fast, exciting, evocative and flowing movement of grace and style. Soon, everyone had formed a circle and the more able bodied were leaping and twirling to the beat of the music. George saw Alexander mouth the words, 'S'agapo', 'I love you', to Sofia and felt momentarily envious, though not in any way resentful of their completeness. He was however concerned for Alexander. He looked tired and drawn throughout the day and not by any means his usual self. As for Sofia, the last weeks had taken their toll on her and George noticed her eyes were looking tired and sore by the end of the day, their usual sparkle dimmed somewhat.

Sadly, this was a love story doomed to be short lived. Shortly following their marriage and during a blissful period for them both, Sofia became pregnant. Whilst George was overjoyed for the couple, he was fearful of what afflictions the child may be born with. He needn't have worried though.

When the time for the birth arrived, Manolis was called out to attend Sofia and anxiously, George paced the floor outside with

Alexander, whose own strength was deteriorating markedly, his facial skin beginning to crack and weep, his hair becoming patchy. Looking at him that day, George's sorrow was profound as he realised that Alexander would probably not live to see his child grow to adulthood. Sorrow, for the moment however, turned to joy as they heard the cry of the newly born child and Manolis emerged from the house into the bright heat of the day, a bundle of such perfection enveloped in his strong arms. As he brought the child to them, Alexander's face lit up with his characteristic grin as his gaze fell longingly into the face of the cherubic little boy held by Manolis.

"He is perfect, Alexander. There is nothing wrong with him at all. He does not have leprosy. With the instruction that Alexander should touch with his own skin only the swaddling wrapped around the child, Manolis carefully handed the bundle over to his overjoyed father whose tears of joy and wonder fell so copiously that George was moved to tears himself. Alexander could not speak and merely gazed at his newborn son, longing to kiss him, but knowing that he must maintain his distance, for his, was the kiss of death.

Sofia was severely weakened by the birth of her child and she was unable to care for him in those early days as she might have hoped. Nothing however could have prepared the couple for what came next. Manolis was compelled to register the birth of the child on Crete and the Medical Governor had to be informed. Few children had been born on the island, but of those who had, none of them had leprosy. However, it was the rule on the island that children must be removed to the mainland and placed in the care of an Athens hospital.

Manolis had done his best to persuade the medical commission that the child would be in no danger by staying with his parents and assured them that he would be actively involved in his care. Despite begging and pleading with the Commission to allow the child to stay, the Medical Governor decreed that the child must leave the island.

It was a bleak and terrible day when Manolis asked George to accompany him to Alexander and Sofia's house to carry out the evil deed. The Governor had wanted to send officials in to make sure the job was done, however, Manolis had felt it would be less cruel if he and George were to break the news to the couple and ensure the removal of the child in the most sensitive way possible. He had told them nothing of the negotiations he had undertaken to try to keep the child with his parents, wishing to spare them worry and unhappiness at a time that should have been joyous. It was going to come as a terrible shock to them therefore when the two men arrived to take the child. The Commission's boat remained in the bay as Manolis and George made their way sadly and solemnly to the little house. Neither of them spoke. A stone was in George's heart and the tears were never far from his eyes, dreading the betrayal he was about to commit. Wasn't he, after all, the Koumbaro? Closest and most trusted friend, not only to the wedding couple, but traditionally to any child born to them as well. George was torn between his conflicting obligations to the child to whom he was now bound, unsure of what course of action was truly in his best interests. Manolis knocked on the door and Alexander, thin and tired answered, his weight now held by a single crutch. Despite his pain, a smile of pleasure passed across his face as he invited his friends to enter. His smile soon dissolved however as they explained why they were there.

"No, please", he begged, "There must be some other way. Sofia won't survive this cruelty Georgiou. I won't survive this". His eyes pleaded with George who found it difficult to maintain his gaze. Manolis explained that he had tried to persuade the authorities to allow the child to stay, that he would take it upon himself to care for the welfare of the child but that his pleas had gone unheard. George shook his head helplessly as Manolis rose to go into the little parlour where Sofia sat serenely cradling her child. He held Alexander back, the tears coursing down the cheeks of both men.

"How can you do this to me?" he pleaded. "How can you do this to her?" George shook his head helplessly, hopelessly. He could see Manolis in the other room kneeling before Sofia, trying to explain what he had to do when suddenly the most heart rending cry filled the room. Sofia refused to hand over the child and Manolis was forced to enter into a struggle with her, both mother and child becoming hysterical. George ran to help him followed at his heels by Alexander.

"Let him go Sofia" he said resignedly. "There is nothing we can do. It is best for him".

"Sofia, he will eventually go to your families to be brought up. Think about it. This is no place for a child. There will be no-one else for him to play with and there would always be a danger he would hurt himself and come into contact with the disease. You must think of him", George pleaded desperately trying to reason with her despite his own misgivings about the situation.

Sofia prostrated herself on the ground, grabbing Manolis' ankles, pleading desperately with him to relinquish her child, sobbing wildly, tearing at her hair, dignity forgotten in the struggle to save her child. Alexander went to her side and knelt down, gently releasing Manolis from her grip. Manolis retreated with the child, screaming in his arms, his distress manifest. George who had been looking on in the last few minutes, unable to convince himself that their actions were in anyone's best interests, now approached the couple. They were sobbing in each others arms, oblivious to George's presence. He knew there was nothing he could say or do to comfort these poor people. Alexander looked at him, his icy stare warning George to come no closer. His pain had blinded him to the fact that this was neither the fault of Manolis, nor George. With a wave of his hand he dismissed

George and he knew he must leave them alone in their grief.

Only a short time later, George saw Sofia standing alone and grief stricken on the shore, watching the little boat carrying her precious child to the mainland as she sank once again to her knees, her cries echoing across the island and haunting George forever more. Joy had turned so quickly on this island to despair.

To compound the grief and horror of that day, George was the one to find Sofia and Alexander dead in their home when he went to check on them a few hours later. Approaching the silent house with trepidation, fearing at worst their hatred he entered, but was immediately struck by the stillness of the place. To his horror, George found them moments later, lying together on their bed, their wrists cut in a suicide pact, entwined in each other's arms. They knew they would never be able to come to terms with the loss of their beloved child.

Manolis and George blamed themselves. Could they have done anything to prevent this? At the time, they doubted it, but all the same, their guilt was more than they could bear. George would never forget the look of utter betrayal which Alexander gave him on that day; the last look that would ever pass between them. Grief threatening to choke him, George went to the little theatre and remembered the joy and the friendship he had found there. Never before, had George experienced such self loathing and he knew that Manolis felt the same.

Everyone had been astounded by the birth of that beautiful, healthy child and it was looked on as something of a miracle. If anything positive had come out of that episode, it was the miraculous nature of the birth which Papas Evanggenelis used to exemplify and promote the benefits of love and marriage which even on the Isle of the Damned could create a tolerable existence. At the funeral of Alexander and Sofia, he said that the couple had emulated the Miracle of the Ten Lepers on the day Jesus had made his way to the cross when 20 completely healthy babies were born to leprous couples. For his part, George could not reconcile this benevolent god with the cruelty he had bestowed on such innocent people and for a time after that George turned his back once again on all suggestion of a God.

DECISIONS

From the moment he heard of Alexander and Sofia's deaths a change came over Manolis, an unshakeable guilt seared upon his soul, unable to accept that there was nothing more he could have done. Whilst he had heard of similar situations in the past, it was not something which had happened during his time on the island and he had hoped that the gradual enlightenment of the people of Crete in relation to leprosy might have worked in favour of the child being allowed to remain on Spinalonga with his parents.

Now, months later, he still awoke at night, sweat pouring from his brow as he relived Sofia's terrible cries of anguish as her child was snatched from her arms forever, her milk flowing as the child cried for her miles across the sea. Manolis had come here to help and heal, not to bring suicide and despair to the people he loved.

Over the past few months, Manolis' friendship with George had strengthened, and their shared grief over Alexander and Sofia cemented their bond. George though had also caused him many sleepless nights with his strange conversations which unnerved him deeply. Though Manolis was fond of the young man, he was, in equal measure afraid of him. It was as though the man were a wraith of some future time or a prophet. If so, why was he here? Was it to bring hope, mystery or fear? Was he a messenger of good or evil? Manolis could not tell. He was a rational man however and it was difficult for him to accept that there was anything other than a physical or mental cause of George's strange ramblings. Aside from these matters, Manolis liked the young man who had surprisingly become reliable in offering his help and support, although much of that, he knew was down to Irini's persuasion and George's fondness for her.

After much soul searching and, in the shadow of the latest

tragedy, Manolis had begun to feel his ability to deal with island life gradually ebbing away and after much soul searching, made the decision finally, to find himself pastures new. He felt that he had failed in his well-meaning attempt to improve the lot of the lepers but the continual pressures of the outside world and the fact that society would never relinquish its prejudices meant improvement of the islanders' lives would continue to be impeded, probably throughout his lifetime. Manolis felt he wasn't a strong enough leader or negotiator to lead them through the darkness and he decided it was time to make way for someone else. He was tired now and defeated. As such, he was no good for the people he cared for.

His decision made, Manolis sought out Irini and confided in her his plans to leave the island. She listened, quietly, stunned into silence at the unexpected turn of events. As he spoke, her entire world seemed to collapse around her. How could she live without Manolis here? There was no-one else she could turn to or share her deepest thoughts with. There was no-one else who knew her so intimately that words were superfluous. Her eyes told the entire story as Manolis explained his reasons for leaving the island, tears glistening and brimming like tiny waterfalls cascaded over her soft lashes, yet still, the unspoken acknowledgement of the deep and unshakeable love which neither was able to confess to the other.

Seeing her distress, Manolis grasped Irini's hands.

"Irini, you know that I love you more than life itself. I wish I could say to you come with me. Truly, I believe that you do not have leprosy. If I were to convince the authorities to re-test you, would you then consider leaving the island? We could begin again. It doesn't have to be in Crete. We could go somewhere where no-one knows us".

Irini spoke quietly, uncertainly.

"My dearest Manoli. You know I cannot leave here. I feel safe now amongst these people. I could not help my poor husband, but I can help those who are like him. I would not be welcomed back on Crete and if the family were to hear about my return, I fear they might do something terrible to me and possibly to you. They are very powerful and my freedom would create a terrible threat to their estate. Believe me Manoli, you are better off without me. I will only bring heartache and trouble for you"'

Manolis, though he expected this response, nevertheless was devastated. He had hoped that he might persuade her to leave the island behind if he could have proved she was clear of leprosy. Perhaps, after all, she did not love him as he had hoped. Perhaps, it was only because of him, her fear of hurting him, that she had avoided any deeper relationship with Georgio after all.

Dejectedly, Manolis removed his hands from hers and straightened. Not wishing to make her feel guilty about her decision, he gathered himself and spoke without emotion.

"I am sorry Irini. It was forward of me to make such a suggestion. It was preposterous. The authorities have made their diagnosis and it was wrong of me to suggest there might be hope that you are clear of leprosy. I should never forgive myself if I had turned out to be wrong. I fear also I may have misinterpreted the depth of our friendship, Irini. I have been harbouring false hopes myself, you see. I know that Georgio will take good care of you when I am gone".

"No!", Irini cried. "Don't be so cold with me Manoli! You misunderstand. I don't love Georgio. I love you with all of my heart and soul. I wish with all my heart I could be brave enough to find out the truth about my disease and to face whatever future is out there but I am afraid Manoli! Don't you understand? As long as I don't know whether I am a leper, I still have my dreams that one day I will be cleared or they will find a miracle cure. But if I take the test now and I find I am infected, what is left for me? All of my hopes are shattered, I have only the certainty of a life of pain and misery to look forward to. At least this way I can survive; or at least, I could until you announced that you were leaving". Irini slumped to the ground, her head in her hands and trembled violently as she sobbed in despair, alone and abandoned by the one man she had loved so well. As her tears subsided a little she spoke almost to herself, "Either way now, what difference? My life can only be one of misery and pain when you go Manoli".

"I am so sorry Irini, but what can we do? If you do not want to find out the truth, we can never find an answer to this dilemma".

There was no consoling Irini as Manolis slipped away, now more confused than ever. Irini loved him. He knew that now. Try as he might though, he could not convince her that they should try harder to get a new test for her. For his part, he could no longer contemplate a life on the island, simply watching helplessly as those he cared for died, one after the other. In truth, he would have married Irini whether she had leprosy or not. He didn't care. As far as he was concerned, a short period of happiness was enough for him in a world of suffering and misery, but he knew Irini would never have agreed. He had reached a stalemate in his life and no longer knew which way to turn. How long must a man be expected to live amongst the sorrow and guilt of death? How long could a man do so? He felt that he had come to the end of his ability to witness daily suffering and to withstand the torture of loving someone with whom he could never share a normal life. His mind was made up. He had to go.

Irini sat slumped against the wall of her little house, stultified by shock and devastation at Manolis' unexpected announcement. As he had walked away from her, she wished that she had the courage to run after him, agree to the test and, if all was well, to leave the island with him and start a new life. Even as she thought it however, she knew she could not go through with it. She persuaded herself she was needed here, especially if Manolis went, but deep down, she didn't want to know that despite her hopes, she was probably just a leper, unclean and unworthy of happiness. Curling up in the corner, Irini cried herself to sleep in blissful ignorance of the new trials she was about to face.

"Gateway to a Fortress,
More gateway to distress
Less gateway to a fortress
For a leper more or less"
ISLAND OF TEARS
William Ronald Hawkins

ACT OF WAR

George had his own troubles to deal with shortly after the deaths of Alexander and Sofia. He awoke one morning to discover a lack of sensation in his hand. He had arisen that day and, as was his habit, he went to throw open the shutters to bask in the golden morning sunlight. For the first time however, he encountered some difficulty in grasping and turning the wooden catch. There was a weakness in his grasp which he put down at first to having slept awkwardly, perhaps trapping a nerve or muscle. It was only when he went to boil some water for his coffee that his concern grew. As he tried to remove the pan from the stove, he was unable to bear its weight in the affected hand and he dropped it clumsily, spilling hot water and burning his hand. The weakness was one thing, but the fact that he barely felt the boiling water as it had cascaded on to him was quite another.

George inspected the painless injury and observed in horror as it reddened and blistered. He felt nauseous as the certainty of his fate crept over him, his heart racing, adrenalin kicking in.

There was no doubt in his mind. He had seen it often enough now. He had developed the first symptoms of tubercular leprosy. Fear gripped George as the grim reality of his future (or was it his past?) set in. He slumped in a chair, not knowing what to do next. His mind raced and once again, the unreality of his existence here troubled him. Had he been brought here by strange forces as a punishment? To be stricken with probably one of the worst diseases known to man? George now knew from the stories of the Greek Gods that they could be vengeful and their punishments terrible. Perhaps leprosy really was the punishment for his terrible sins, an apt end for someone who had shamelessly exploited the weak without giving it a second thought.

Dressing quickly, George set off to the hospital, hoping that Manolis might be able to give him some comfort. As he approached the building, Manolis was just leaving to make his morning calls, or so he thought. George shouted to him but when Manolis looked up, he could see his face was worried, distracted.

"Kalimera Georgio. You have just caught me. I am just leaving for the mainland. A boat is waiting for me". Manolis fumbled with the lock. "Some news... the Medical Commissioner wishes to speak with me. I'm sorry Georgio, I don't have time to stop. I will see you later".

With a friendly slap on the shoulder, Manolis brushed hurriedly past George whose mouth was opening and closing like a goldfish as he tried to find the words to stop him from leaving right now. He needed some peace of mind and Manolis was the only one who could help. At first, his words wouldn't come out, but, in his anxiety to speak to Manolis, George blurted out to his retreating figure,"I think I have leprosy, Manoli". Manolis turned to look at George, his expression softening, and spoke gently, but firmly as though explaining to a recalcitrant child.

"But you have always had leprosy Georgio. It is why you are here. What is so different today than it was yesterday?"

"No, you don't understand", George began helplessly. "Look, I've burned my hand". He held out the injured limb, the skin reddened and blistering.

Manolis inspected the hand. "Indeed, this looks nasty. Are you in pain, Georgio?"

"No! That's just the point! I can't feel it at all!" George found it hard to keep his tears at bay.

Manolis nodded. "It is as I had feared Georgio. You are now entering the next stage of leprosy. There is nothing I can do right now for that particular development which will not wait until later my friend. Irini will be along in a minute. Wait for her here. She has the key to the dispensary and will tend to your wound. I will look at it again on my return". Manolis gave George an apologetic smile, but he was anxious to get on his way.

"I will see you later, friend", he said as he turned away towards the bay and was quickly gone from George's view.

George felt deflated and in a state of agitation. What could be so pressing that Manolis could not tend to his friend's injury? George sat down to wait for Irini. Perhaps she would know what was going on. When she arrived however, Irini, looking drained and washed out, as though she had been crying all night could not, or would not, George suspected, shed any light on Manolis' sudden departure for the mainland. Instead, she beckoned him into the dispensary and dressed the raw, swollen hand that George held out. He wished, for once, he could feel the pain that such an injury should cause.

George spent the rest of the day alone. Irini had been in no mood for talking that morning and so he had taken his leave from her immediately after she had finished dressing his hand. He was unable to help out with anything in the village today anyway so he retreated to his home, closed the shutters and contemplated this latest turn of events. He wondered how the people here lived with the knowledge of what they would become. He hardly dared to think about it. Climbing the stairs, George stood out on his balcony which overlooked the village. Everywhere were signs that the people of this island strove for normality, for a sense of continuity in their upside down, devastated lives. Their industriousness had ranged from the simplest of activities, such as the laying out of the small gardens, filled with an abundance of colour in the borders and brightly coloured urns, to the complexity of any one of the businesses now opened in the town. Signs of the island's and the people's evolution were now everywhere. This was most certainly a 'renaissance' period when emancipation of the Spinalonga lepers had at last begun to give them a glimmer of hope for the future. George had never managed to come up with an explanation for his presence on this island of the 1940s.

He still tended towards the possibility of a lucid dream and yet, if that were the case, how could it last for such a long time? When, if ever, would he wake up? Something told him that was not the explanation but he resolved that the time was coming when he must make some effort to find the answer. Time was becoming short now as the leprosy had become manifest.

Having spent the rest of the day mulling things over in his mind, George decided his best course of action would be to return to Crete where he could retrace his steps. Maybe he would find that the whole episode had merely been an illusion. If that were the case, then it followed, didn't it that the leprosy was illusory? He knew that to make a successful escape, he would have to speak with Nikos and Yiannis. Recalling their conversation months previously, hadn't they spoken of escaping from the island again? George thought that although they had spoken with enthusiasm that night, in truth, they had little stomach for it and the futility of previous attempts had probably deterred them from repeating it. He suspected that talking about escape and planning the detail of it was sufficient to keep their dreams alive, but that the reality was probably something quite different.

George cast his mind back to earlier that day and wondered why Manolis had looked so agitated that morning and why the Medical Commission had unusually summoned him. As dusk began to fall, George decided to face the world once more and strolled down to the harbour to wait for the boat to return. To his great dismay however, Manolis did not return that night and it was the next morning with an urgent hammering on his door that George became aware of his return. Sleepily, he called out.

"Alright, alright, give me a minute". George staggered down the stairs, barely awake and threw open the door.

"Get dressed quickly", Manolis instructed him. "Meet me down at the harbour. I need to speak with you away from other ears. I will see you in a few minutes".

George struggled to throw on some clothes but responded as quickly as he could to the urgency of Manolis' command. A cursory wash and he was ready to face the day. He walked briskly through the Lion Gate and found Manolis perched upon a rock, staring absently out to sea. As George approached, Manolis turned, his dark eyes penetrating and intense.

"Georgio, I don't know how to say this, so I will come to the point quickly. I now know for sure that you are not the same as us". George's heart began to beat rapidly. Had he heard something on the mainland? Had Manolis discovered something about his lurid past? Was that why the Medical Commission had wanted to see him? A sudden thought came into George's mind. He was going to be arrested! That must be it! He was convinced, as he stared into Manolis solemn face that he had been found out. Nothing however was further from the truth.

"Some of the things you have said in our conversations have been very strange Georgio, but they have been things which made me think. Please forgive me for this, but at first, I thought you were simply deranged. I now have cause to think otherwise however. Tell me, Georgio, whilst I myself struggle to believe in such things, do you think that you have some kind of supernatural power? Prophetic powers perhaps? Are you a clairvoyant or something of that nature?"

George was surprised at this development of the conversation and he was momentarily unsure how to respond. He decided however, to be as candid as possible. After all, if Manolis had become aware that things were not as they should be, then perhaps his friend might be able to help him.

"Manoli, I don't know the answer to your question. I wish I did, but I am a confused and bewildered as you are. Why do you ask?"

"You told me once that Crete would be invaded by the Germans. I now have reason to believe that this may indeed come to pass. Things are not looking so good for us just now. If you have the gift of prophecy you may be able to help us my friend. For my own peace of mind, I would like to clear up the mystery that has been troubling me about you, but, for the people of this island, you might be able to help me decide what actions I must take".

George was disconcerted by Manolis' open acknowledgement that there was some 'other worldliness' about him. Now that he had been confronted about it however, George had no idea where to start or what to say. He ran through the various answers he could give in his head and imagined what Manolis' reaction might be if he just said; 'Well Manoli, I am actually a former drug dealer who was on the run for killing a girl in London in 2005 when I had this accident and met Charon. You know? The mythical ferryman of the dead who brought me here, back to a 1940 leper colony where I've now contracted leprosy'. It sounded crazy even to George, and he was living it! Manolis waited for a response, all the while scrutinising George as he struggled to find the right words.

"Please Georgio, this could be important. You may be able to help me". Finally, when George spoke, it was to give Manolis a sanitised version of his story. He couldn't face going into the whole nightmare and besides, such a confession might have worked against him in more ways than one, he thought. George explained therefore to Manolis that he believed he had been born in London and had been visiting Crete on a holiday in 2005. Whilst touring on a motor scooter, he had the accident, knocking him out cold. On regaining consciousness, he had stumbled along the coast, heading towards Elounda where he met the old man, Charon. The rest, Manolis already knew.

"So, there you have it Manoli. Am I a time traveller, am I in a dream or am I just insane? I don't know. I have no idea what is reality any more.

Even as he spoke, George knew the whole thing sounded ridiculous. He was embarrassed. Manolis remained silent and deeply pensive for a few moments but when he spoke again, George was astonished by his implicit acceptance of the few facts he had given him.

"What do you know of the war Georgio?" he asked quietly, almost in a whisper.

"Not much", George confessed. Beyond the general details, he could only tell him of the atrocities discovered later about Hitler's tenacious and single minded pursuit of the perfect Aryan Race, the horrors of the holocaust and fate of the Jews which would not be fully known for many years hence. George was able to tell him that Germany was vanquished in 1945 but that there were many long years ahead. Manolis looked haunted. Perhaps he was: by a spectre from the future.

"Yesterday, Georgio, October 28th, Mussolini invaded Greece with his Italian army. Our troops are now engaged in battle, along with the allied forces to protect our country and its people". He thought carefully, as though fearing his next question, or perhaps, more accurately, the answer.

"Georgio, do you know if the Greeks shall keep Hitler out?

George shook his head. The bookshops in Crete had been full of books chronicling the fall of the island to the Germans and he had read a little about it in the guide books.

"I don't know much about the history of the war as it affected Greece Manoli. I read a little about Crete's involvement in the war when I arrived on the island and I know only this. Crete will be central to Hitler's plans because of the British airfields on the island which are apparently crucial to the Germans. They are planning an assault on Russia and the airfields here are central to the striking of Rumanian oil fields which the Germans need to carry out their plans. Aside from that, by securing Crete, the British will be driven out of the Eastern Mediterranean giving Hitler unimpeded access to Cyprus, Egypt and Malta.

"And will Hitler succeed?" George looked at Manolis' strained, frightened face and responded as gently as he could.

"Yes. As I understand it Manoli, Crete will fall to the Germans. I don't know precisely when but the fight will go on and the British and the allied forces will all work together with the Cretan resistance movement to undermine the German presence here and finally, they will be defeated. Crete will go on to become a very prosperous island in years to come. That is all I can really tell you Manoli". His hands clasped tightly in front of him, so tight in fact the knuckles showed white, Manolis merely stared out to sea, lost in his thoughts. His distress was clear.

"I was going to leave the island Georgio. I had made up my mind that I would go, but now, well, how can I abandon these people to who knows what fate?"

George had to admit he had no idea how the war would affect Spinalonga and its inhabitants. He had never even heard of the island before arriving here.

"But why were you planning to leave Manoli?" George now asked. "You love your work and the people here and they adore you." What brought you to this decision? This really puzzled him. George could not imagine Spinalonga without Manolis. He was the engine that kept it running and it was his home.

"Because I have done as much here as I can. I think maybe it is time to move aside and let someone else come in. Perhaps it will be someone with new ideas, greater knowledge who can really make a difference. Maybe someone will come who will be able to fight more effectively for the people. I have failed them. It needs someone strong, who can convince the authorities that these people are not to be feared and reviled, that they can live useful lives and be integrated into communities and that there is no need to take healthy babies from their mothers in such a cruel fashion. Other arrangements could be made". With his last words, the true reason for his decision became apparent.

"That's what all this is about, isn't it? Alexander and Sofia. You're blaming yourself. You couldn't have done anything about it Manoli. Nor could I. We tried to ease the pain for them that's all. It was out of our hands. The alternative was to let the Medical Commissioners' men go and carry out their deed and that would have been brutal". Manolis shook his head.

"The people here need a voice. Someone who can help them fight for proper and fair treatment. Look at poor Nikos. He has neither heard of nor seen his children for years. I have tried to find out what became of them for him but no-one cares enough or listens to me. What use am I?"

"Look how much has changed for the better since you and the President have been here. The people are healthier; they've got autonomy, their independence. They can tend to themselves to a greater extent and they have you to turn to when they can't. They've even gained more acceptance amongst Cretan society. Who would have guessed in the early days of the colony that friends and relatives would actually come and visit on the island, or that the people here would have cinemas, a theatre or businesses? Most important of all, is that everyone here now has a purpose. Something to live for. You've been a huge part of this metamorphosis Manoli. Of course you're going to lose some people and of course you won't be able to solve everyone's problems. The important thing is that you are here. Everyone knows you do your best. You can't leave Manoli. Especially not now. You are going to be needed more than ever now".

As George spoke his final words, he raised his bandaged arm to show Manolis. Saying nothing, he looked up at him. The unspoken message needed no elaboration. George had begun to rot, just as everyone else on this island. Manoli drew in a deep breath and his expression became more focused, resigned, even. He had reached a decision and George knew that Manolis was going nowhere. He stood up from the rock on which he had been sitting.

"You are right Georgio. What was I thinking of? How selfish I have been. Come, let's get back and take a look at this arm of yours. I fear we have some bleak times ahead of us".

And of course, Manolis was right. George's worst fears were realised when Manolis examined his arm. Much of the feeling had gone and it was clear that the nerves had been attacked by the disease, the familiar whitening of the areas around them clearly visible. This was just another horror in his catalogue of what? Time travel? Dreaming? No matter how hard George tried, he couldn't work out what all of this meant for him. On many a clear evening he would sit at the harbour, staring out sea, hoping to catch a glimpse of the strange old boatman who had brought him here. So far however, he had been disappointed and the silent, lapping waters had remained undisturbed by any passing traveller.

That evening, after his discussion with Manolis, George went to the taverna where Nikos and Yiannis sat, their usual jovial, devil may care attitudes replaced by a more troubled and perplexed distraction. News had spread throughout the island of Mussolini's invasion of Greece and the talk that night was of the now highly uncertain future. Anxiety spread as the realisation that many of the men of Crete would have to go to mainland Greece to fight the Italians. Everyone was fearful therefore for the family and friends who would now be caught up in this struggle and whose lives were in imminent danger. An atmosphere of agitation was present in the taverna that night. There was no laughter or merriment as the grim realisation of the consequences of Mussolini's actions sank in and once again, the powerlessness of the people on the island to go back to their homes in order to say goodbye or say a few words to those who would be going to war. Everyone here had so much unfinished business and the frustration of that now threatened to erupt as the tension grew.

George's own mind drifted back to his conversation with Manolis when he had told him more about the holocaust. His response brought a chilling possibility to mind. If the Germans could so easily exterminate so many simply because of Hitler's idea of an imperfect race, what then could they do to an island full of helpless and much feared cripples? The answer was too terrible to contemplate.

Manolis had given no indication of his thoughts after George had confessed his belief that he was 21st century man, transported back in time, but he must have appeared to be an incongruous prophet of doom whatever Manolis' impression. He did however seem to implicitly accept George's tale. George, for his part, could not understand Manolis' reticence over something which was so bizarre. He had asked him whether he thought he had a madman on his hands. Manolis had merely shrugged his shoulders, and with his usual pragmatism responded,

"What is madness anyway? Aren't we all possessed of madness from time to time? No Kyrie, you are different, but not mad. I have experienced many things as a doctor which I could not explain Kyrie. A wife, moments before death, speaking to her long dead husband, grasping an invisible hand; a man, snatched back from the jaws of death, only to describe following a brilliant light which led to his dead family and friends in a place he described as the Elysian Fields. That same man relating things he could not have known about from a vantage point outside his body as his spirit hovered precariously between life and death. As for you Georgio, perhaps you are a clairvoyant or a visionary or perhaps the powers of our ancient Greek Gods have indeed been invoked to bring you here. Who can tell? But for the moment, you are flesh and blood and you have brought us no harm so I embrace and welcome you as all of the other outcasts on this island. Perhaps one day, we shall solve your mystery, but for now, we have more urgent matters to deal with". George was comforted and grateful for Manolis' continued acceptance of him and he hoped he was right, that one of these days, he would find the answers he sought.

For a time after Greece entered the war, there appeared to be no discernible difference in the lives of the islanders. George continued to teach his English classes, though his health progressively deteriorated. He dreaded the day when his skin would swell and crack like that of so many here when all he would be able to do was nurse his wounds and suffer the pain and humiliation of watching his body gradually rot away. So often, the only treatment which Manolis could offer was amputation of a limb. There was now many a sufferer on the island whose limbs had, one by one been removed to prevent further spread of infection and to prolong life. It was all but over for those sorry creatures who had only one limb remaining. Once the infection ravaged the last remaining limb, it seemed there was no hope of survival. The shock to the body from the amputation or the spread of infection ended the suffering shortly afterwards. The idea of becoming an amputee filled George with dread and he was determined that should he reach that sorry state, he would refuse that option. George could not envisage himself atop a trolley, pushing his legless torso along with weakening arms. Better, he reasoned, to be dead. And yet, how did so many of the islanders opt for multi-amputations in less than ideal surgical conditions? Ultimately, does the fear of death overcome the horrific alternative? Certainly, most of those who were in that category faced life full-on with as much fortitude, industry and cheeriness as they could muster. George's admiration for them knew no bounds though he could not help but feel sickened by the sight of those whose stumps oozed and twitched and whose decaying remains reeked in the unforgiving heat.

Alone in his house, George cried out in horror at the thought of what he would surely become. What strange world had he been abandoned into by Charon on that fateful day? And who, or what was Charon? According to Manolis, he was a messenger of the ancient gods, charged with ferrying the dead over the Styx to Hades. Was George really dead then, caught up in some strange underworld?

One night, when the moon was full and it shone so brightly, illuminating the surface of the twinkling sea, George threw his head back and called out the name of Charon, falling to his knees in despair and begging him to come back for him. He knew that normal life did not lie beyond these waters. His only hope of return was if Charon took him back. George no longer cared that if he went back to his own time and place he would be returning to prison. Nothing, he reasoned could be worse than this living interment on a strange island fortress where the residents were literally the walking dead. A spell in prison would be luxury compared to the condemnation of death in such a slow and painful manner. Looking desperately out to sea, George hoped that by some means, he may invoke Charon's return but he saw nothing and heard nothing more than the gentle lapping of the sea against the rocks and the chirping of the cicadas breaking the silence.

Throughout the weeks and months that followed, the islanders would receive snippets of information from Crete about the progress of the war which made for depressing news. Many young Cretan men were lost in the battle with Mussolini in the Albanian mountains and, on more than one occasion, either when visiting relatives or a supply boat came to the island, a howl or a wailing would rip the air as someone, somewhere on the island, received news of the death, loss or injury of a loved one. As if life were not cruel enough, here, misery now heaped upon misery. The Greek spirit however, could not be extinguished and somehow, life continued more or less as normal on Spinalonga.

George called in to Yiannis' shop one afternoon however to find him agitated.

"Georgio" he greeted him. "I am worried. Nikos has had a fever and since coming out of his delirium, he is insistent on escape. He says he cannot wait any longer to find his girls. He says he heard them calling to him and he must go. Kyrie, he is gripped by a madness. He is in no state to think of escape".

George knew from Manolis that Nikos was deteriorating rapidly. He had developed a ravenous infection in one of his legs and Manolis was close to amputating. Nikos however was having none of it - he would fall over when he danced, he said, and if he stopped dancing, he would surely die. For now, Manolis had acquiesced, but George feared Nikos would die anyway without treatment and he would need to be persuaded if his life were to continue. He was deeply saddened by this. Nikos was indeed the life and soul of the island. If his dancing stopped, George reckoned all dancing would stop on the island. It was his joie de vivre which had been infectious He decided to visit him and set off for the old Venetian house he lived in. Nikos took pride in his little home, tumbledown as it was. His garden was a blaze of colour and he kept a couple of chickens which clucked lazily around the yard. He had grown attached to the birds and rejected any notion of killing them for the pot. They were the only things in the world which gave him any affection he said. They did, however, lay wonderful eggs and whenever Nikos had called in to see George, he had always brought a handful of fresh eggs in offering.

The gate was becoming slightly overgrown as George pushed it open with some difficulty. The front door was ajar, but Nikos unusually, was nowhere in sight as he knocked and called out to him. Stepping inside the gloomy room which was shuttered against the sunlight, George was immediately struck by the bittersweet, cloying smell of decaying flesh, which was now so familiar to him. It was made worse by the stifling heat of the house. Raising his arm to cover his nostrils, George fought back the urge to vomit. Flies circled the room as food on the table became mouldy and putrid, some uneaten meat a heaving, and pulsating white mass as maggots clung and fed from it. Further into the house, a doorway led to Nikos' bedroom. George knocked and entered. There on the stone based Cretan bed, Nikos lay, his injured leg laid stiffly and painfully out in front of him, the infection weeping through the bandages. George feared what would happen if the flies moved in on him and shuddered at the thought.

"Nikos?" he said quietly, so as not to startle him.

"That you Georgio?" his voice was weak.

"Yes, it's me Niko, how are you feeling today?" George asked gently. He sat down on the stool next to the bed. Nikos' voice was weak as he struggled to reply.

"Not so good today, Georgio, not so good. They want to butcher me like an animal. Take off my leg! I say no - how can I dance the Pendodzali with only one leg?" He turned his head away from George, his voice now almost a whisper.

"I might as well be dead anyway. What is left for me? I will never have a life again. My dear wife is gone, my children taken from me. I will never feel the loving caress of any woman or the little hand of a child in mine. Why go on?"

George had never heard Nikos sound so defeated before and it was deeply troubling to do so now. It had been Nikos and Yiannis who had kept him going through the bad times and he didn't now want to let Nikos down. What George said to him next troubled him, but he knew only a shock would rouse him from his self-pity.

"Nikos, there is a war on, and mark my words, it is soon going to get worse. You have two children on the mainland where there is heavy fighting. Niko, they will be frightened, alone and bewildered. They will be wondering about you as much as you do about them. You can't, for their sake, give up now Niko. Friends and relatives have been able to visit the island for months now. There is no reason why they could not come here to see you if you could only trace them. You must push harder for information and see if you can't get in touch with them." For long moments Nikos was silent, but miraculously, he turned back towards George, his filmy, rheumy eyes, sad, but with a just discernible determination firing back into them. Slowly, he sat up.

"You are right Georgio. Thank you. I must not forget the most important things in my life. I must live long enough to tell my children I love them and to make sure they are safe. Now, help me up, I must talk to you about something". George obliged and grasped Nikos behind his back as he painfully swung his legs over the side of the bed where he sat, gathering himself for a few moments. No words passed between them until finally, he revealed his thoughts.

"I am afraid, Georgio. I am afraid of the operation. I have heard the screams of many who have suffered amputation. They do not have the anaesthetic or proper tools. I do not know if I can go through with it".

"Niko, things are different now. Manolis would not let you suffer. You know that. We have morphine here now and a new hospital with equipment thanks to the President. We even have a new laboratory which will soon be completed. When was the last time you heard screams coming from the hospital?"

"Not for a long time", he conceded, "but these things haunt you Georgio".

George could well understand his terror and did not confess to his own regular nightmares about it. He was certain however that whilst the ordeal remained a horrific prospect, Nikos would not suffer the tortures of his predecessors.

"Niko, I give you my word that I will go with you and make sure that you are properly anaesthetised before I will let anyone touch you and I will help you all I can to get back up once it is over". Nikos nodded his approval.

"For my children, I must do this" he said.

And so it was that George persuaded Nikos to undergo the

operation which would prolong his life. His satisfaction however was to be short lived and had he known what was to come, George doubted he would have intervened in his decision, allowing him to die quietly and with some dignity.

MAY 1941

George fulfilled his promise to Nikos, having first satisfied himself by speaking to Manolis that he would not know anything about the operation. Nikos was already weakened by infection and George was concerned that the trauma of the operation would kill him anyway. Either way, he was between a rock and a hard place and his chances of survival were definitely better with the operation.

True to his word, George went into the little operating theatre with Nikos and spoke soothingly to him as Manolis administered the anaesthetic. Within a short time, he was out cold and George took his leave. He could not though, as Yiannis had done all those years ago, sit with his friend and watch the proceedings.

Once it was all over and Nikos was able to recuperate, his strength returned in some measure and the old spark of mischief returned. Despite his almost comically grotesque appearance, he resumed his visits to the dances and chased the women as though he were an Adonis, flirting and leading them to the dance floor as he hobbled on a wooden peg leg, still maintaining, it has to be said, some of the old rhythm, though none of the fancy footwork. After a few raki however, his co-ordination deteriorated and he would end up sprawled on the floor, laughing as his companions hoisted him back upright. George was delighted to see he had regained some of his old zest for life. Poor Manolis though, was now haunted by the man, putting more and more pressure on him to make enquiries of his children. Manolis, to his credit, took up the challenge and began a concerted campaign with the Cretan Government for answers. Unfortunately however, the Government was soon to be pre-occupied with much more pressing issues than tracing the children of a leper.

On 20th May 1941, George awoke early as usual, the heat beginning to build in his house, where the gaps in the shutters failed to provide a shield. He washed and got ready to go into the town square where he used the room at the back of Yiannis' shop for his English class. He made some strong Greek coffee to start the day off with a kick and went out to sit on the little patio he had fashioned at the front of the house. This was his latest habit and one which was far healthier and more pleasurable than those he had previously indulged in. George's arm continued to trouble him, though fortunately, Irini and Manolis had tended the burn wounds quickly enough to avoid the complications of infection. The prognosis however, seemed far from optimistic. His peaceful early morning start was shattered during the next few seconds when he thought the world was drawing to an end.

Suddenly, and without warning, George heard a roaring far above him in the sky and he experienced the surge of adrenalin often experience by a dreamer falling off an imaginary cliff half way between sleep and waking. Almost as soon as he heard the engines, George knew exactly what they were. He had watched enough war films in his time to identify the aircraft above as German Luftwaffe. At the same moment, the islanders came out of their houses, many slowly and painfully, those who could barely walk, shuffling out into the street to see what was happening. Everyone who stood there that morning was witnessing the terrible onslaught by the enemy on Crete. From that moment, the community could not imagine what life would hold for them on the island but the collective fear as they watched events unfold way above their heads was almost palpable. For what felt like a long time, there was silence amongst the people on the island, the only sound coming from those evil, metal birds flocking overhead in the cobalt sky. News of the war's progress had come from the mainland over the preceding months via the visiting merchants, family and friends. There had been little unease, partly due to the laid back, laisser-faire nature of the Cretans but possibly more due to the protection of the allied forces who now occupied Crete.

'The Satire', the island newspaper had reported, courtesy of their resident newshound, Stavros, details of the war since October. Everyone knew therefore that the Cretan defence consisted of about 9,000 Greeks, made up from three battalions of the 5th 'Crete' division of the Hellenic Army, the remainder having been posted in Greece to defend the German onslaught. In addition, a battalion of men, made up of both fully trained soldiers and cadets from the Cretan Gendarmes together with an assortment of transport and logistics personnel, and remaining members of the 12th and 20th Hellenic Army division who had escaped back over to Crete, were under the command of the British forces.

Many of Crete's trained men were fighting on the Greek mainland and a number of recruits from the training centres in the Peloponnesus had also been deployed to the island. An original British garrison was supplemented by a further 25,000 Commonwealth troops evacuated from the mainland. In truth, there was something of a rag-tag feel to the mix of troops on the island, many of the Australians and New Zealand contingents working with autonomous command, some without any effective leaders and most without heavy equipment. The islanders heard that on April 30th, a new Commander, Major General Bernard Freyberg had been appointed. Whilst Crete had not been invincible, it was fair to say it did feel well protected. As they saw the Luftwaffe fly across to the island however, in swathes, the vulnerability of its fortifications was apparent. The fact that these airborne menaces were here for the sole purpose of causing destruction and curtailing freedom struck fear into the most confident. Here were probably the most vulnerable of Greek society, from the most infirm to the perfectly healthy; all of them stood craning to see the airborne invasion of this beautiful land which was, irrespective of its size such a central focus of the military operations on all sides. Thankfully, none of those standing here, but George and to some extent, Manolis, knew of the atrocities which the Germans so fastidiously carried out. Had they known, they would perhaps have been less calm.

It was just after 8 a.m. and Manolis, standing near the hospital watched in horror with the rest of the community. He looked over at George who in that moment felt the reality of current events strike him with overwhelming ferocity. He realised that he was now enduring what his grandparents must have experienced. A shiver went through him as he also realised that for Manolis, his uncanny prophecies were coming true before his very eyes. He knew then, that he was dealing with an extraordinary situation which neither he, nor Manolis was equipped to understand.

Everyone watched in awe as gliders, dive bombers and low flying fighter planes flew west in the direction of Chania and Rethymno. Moments later, they heard the distant rumbling of what could only be explosions as bombs were dropped, disabling allied airfields, telephone communications and antiaircraft guns. In astonishment, the islanders watched as thousands of tiny black dots excreted from the planes which within moments sailed gently to the ground, waves of silk fanning out above them as their parachutes opened. All during this time the distant sounds of gunfire and explosions could be heard but they could not discern from which side they emanated. There was an eerie silence amongst those now gathered upon Spinalonga, each person no doubt wondering how this latest travesty would affect their families and friends, and of course, they themselves, people who had already been engaged in their own personal battles for life and freedom for many years. George caught Manolis' eye and he beckoned to him.

"We must maintain some order here or people will begin to panic", he said. "I think we shall gather everyone to the Church to talk about what is happening here".

George agreed that for now, they should all try to keep together until news of what had happened could filter through to them on the island. Manolis hoped that someone would come from the mainland to tell them. As they gathered in the little church, the priest, Papas Evanggenelis, led some prayers and a short Orthodox service. Many of those gathered were sobbing and wringing their hands in grief, fearing the worst for their loved ones back on Crete. After the impromptu service, Manolis stood up and suggested everyone should try to keep calm. He himself would try to get to the mainland to find out what information he could if no-one else came in the meantime. No-one worked that day. The terrified residents remained together in the centre of town, drinking coffee (some resorted to the raki and the ouzo), periodically staring at the skies wondering when the onslaught would end. No-one played backgammon or cards that day, an air of solemnity pervading the island, a sense of doom slowly wrapping its tentacles around it, holding the people in its grip like an octopus draining the life from its prey. There was little talk amongst the islanders, the nervous clicking of the komboloi and baglieri worry beads providing the most outward displays of anxiety amongst the men.

The islanders waited, but no-one came to Spinalonga that day so Manolis decided he would try to get across to Crete to discover what he could. That night, as dusk began to fall, Manolis launched the little rowing boat which was locked away for emergencies. There had been activity over Crete all day and there were two further waves of German aircraft and paratroopers which arrived in the afternoon. It became apparent later that the morning envoys had landed near Maleme and Chania, the second and third attacking Rethymno and Heraklion respectively. Fear and despair filled the island as the true extent of the invasion became clear. As George said his farewell to Manolis, he feared for him, knowing that the Cretan waters must also be fraught with danger.

The very survival of the colony however may depend on any intelligence he could gain and Manolis was bravely determined to travel across.

Following Manolis' departure, no-one wanted to be alone that night, each person fearing what may happen next, most of the islanders fearing for the safety of their loved ones. Everyone huddled to gather in groups in the town centre, seeking mutual comfort, speaking in quiet, muted tones, as though they feared being overheard by the unseen enemy. A few, particularly those with children back on Crete became hysterical and had to be physically restrained from trying to leave Spinalonga by any means possible, the torture of not knowing their fate driving them to temporary insanity. They made determined efforts to get to the shore intending to swim across. It took great strength to persuade them of the folly of this course of action, but with much persuasion, others managed to convince them at least to wait until Manolis' return. If anyone could make it across, it would be him. Spirits sank however when, after three days, Manolis had not returned. There had been aircraft seen flying overhead and the occasional explosion heard but the furious activity of the first day had not been repeated. No-one came from Crete and everyone's fears increased, not only now for their love ones, but also for their own survival as it became apparent that without the regular visitors from family and merchants, the islanders were completely isolated and without the means to survive. With Manolis gone, there was no medical care on the island as everyone else had commuted daily. There were sufficient stocks to last for a number of weeks, but after that, who could tell what the future would hold?

Each morning and each evening at sunrise and sundown, George would make his way to the shore, hoping to catch a glimpse of Manolis' boat returning with news. The communication breakdown was the worst aspect and the collective imagination of the islanders was perhaps worse than the potential reality. At the end of the third day and still no word from Manolis, George began to fear the worst. He spoke to Yiannis that night.

"Yiannis, we must come up with a contingency plan in case Manolis doesn't return or ...", George looked meaningfully at him, not really wishing to voice the unthinkable, "in case he never made it back to Crete". Yiannis lowered his eyes, clearly fighting back his emotions as he too contemplated Manolis's possible fate. To George's surprise however, he refused to engage in future planning, preferring to remain steadfast in his optimism.

"Manolis will return," he said defiantly. "God will not allow such a good man to come to any harm".

"But Yianni", George argued, "We must look at the reality here. Anything may have happened to Manolis, he may have been taken prisoner, he could have come under fire on the water. He may be dead. And if he is, what will become of us and everyone here? We must think about it for their sakes". To his complete shock, Yiannis rounded on him, his bulk towering above him.

"God will take care of Manolis", his eyes burned with a fiery determination. "He will return and all will be well. Now let that be an end to it!" He turned from George and limped off, his big shoulders hunched as though carrying a heavy burden upon him. He had never seen Yiannis so angry. He was also angry and hurt at the ferocity of his attack though and George shouted after him, his face burning in retaliation and humiliation,

"Do you think God has looked after any of the good people here Yianni? Because I don't think he has and I don't think he will single Manolis out for any special treatment either! You can't bury your head in the sand Yianni, we must consider this! It is naivety not to!" Yiannis stopped in his tracks and turned back to face George.

"If God has forsaken Manolis, I accept he has truly forsaken us all. We are finished if that is so and no amount of planning will help us. So go and make your plans Georgio, but do not delude yourself that they will do any good. We have always been dead men walking, perhaps we are now to lie down and get some peace sooner than we thought". He shook his head sadly. "But I, Kyrie, I prefer to believe that God will protect Manolis and we will find a way to survive. If I stop believing that, then there is no hope and I cannot go on anyway. Please do not take away my faith and my hope. Manolis will be back, so go, Georgio, do what you feel is necessary, but I am putting my faith in God and in Manolis". Yiannis moved away once more, his shoulders hunched, the pain he suffered more evident today than ever before. For the first time in a long while, tears burned George's eyes and threatened to spill over. He wiped them with the back of his hand. If he allowed himself the luxury of tears, now, he would never stop crying. He would cry for his old life, for his dear friends, Alexander and Sofia, for Manolis, who was surely dead and for the people of Spinalonga who now, more than ever looked close to death.

At first, George was indignant over Yiannis' stinging rebuke but of course, he could not blame him for clinging on to hope. He was right. What could any of them do if Manolis had been unable to reach the mainland? They were all cripples now and it would be suicide to make the attempt. And yet, if push came to shove, Yiannis and George were probably the most physically able to make the attempt. Everyone else was too weakened or completely disabled by the disease to stand a chance. If Manolis, whom George had come to regard as his friend and mentor failed to return, how would any of them manage without his guiding and reassuring hand? They would be like a rudderless ship drifting towards certain destruction.

George knew that Yiannis had not borne any ill will by his outburst which was merely a manifestation of his defence mechanisms, but equally, he was frustrated by his unwillingness to face up to reality. In need of some solitude, he returned to the shore where he sat on Manolis' favourite rock to think, his head buried in his hands. He must have fallen asleep as when next he looked up, the sun was just disappearing below the horizon. Rubbing his gritty eyes, George hoped that the sensation was just the effects of sleep and not a sign that they were now being attacked by leprosy. Focusing on the horizon, he could just make out a tiny black dot silhouetted against the fiery orange sphere of the setting sun. He stood up and watched for a few moments and, as the figure grew closer, George could just make out the shape of a person in a boat floating gently towards the shore.

"Manolis?" he whispered, not daring to hope. He shielded his eyes from the sun's glare and continued to watch the approaching figure. Finally, as it became apparent that it was indeed Manolis he saw in the distance he called out his name, louder and more confident this time. Now jumping up and down, partly in joy, partly with the intention of attracting Manolis' attention George waved both his arms above his head and shouted. Seeing him, Manolis waved back. He was still a few minutes from the shore so George ran towards the village, making his way directly to Yiannis' house. He hammered on the door and as Yiannis opened it , George's beaming face must have told him the whole story. Yiannis' old familiar grin spread across his face, lighting up his ravaged features. Grabbing his hat, he stepped out and shut the door behind him.

"What did I tell you?" he scoffed, slapping George on the shoulders. "God would not let us down". George shook his head in mock despair and laughed.

"You can't be so bad after all, Yiannis", he joked as they made their way quickly back to the shore. Hurrying down through the Lion Gate, the two men stood poised to help Manolis disembark from the little boat which was bobbing inland. Yiannis and George waded out to pull him in the final few yards, as his arms, weak with rowing grew visibly slower and heavier.

As they approached the boat, the water lapping at their knees, one look at Manolis' face told them everything about the situation on Crete. He looked as though he had not slept in days, his appearance unkempt, his expression haunted and a pallor to his skin George had never seen on him before. Yiannis and George each took an arm and hoisted him from the boat. None of the men spoke, neither Yiannis nor George wishing to hear too quickly the bad news which now seemed inevitable. The trio was observed anxiously by some others who had gathered at the shore, waiting to hear what had befallen their beloved homeland and people. Reaching the town, everyone gathered around Manolis as he took a seat in the taverna. At first he seemed unable to speak, trying to find the words he needed to articulate all that he had seen and learned over the last days. Some of those present grew impatient and fired questions at him.

"Did you see the Germans Manolis?"

"What has become of our people?"

"What damage has been done to the island?"

At last, after downing a glass of the all purpose, medicinal raki, Manolis was able to speak, his thoughts now gathered.

"The situation in Crete is very grave". Looking up, he met the eyes of each person individually, leaving each and every one of them in no doubt that they must prepare for the worst.

"The island is in chaos and devastation. It is every man, woman and child for themselves, but a brave fight is being waged by our people and the allied forces. When I arrived at Elounda, I made my way straight to Heraklion to see what I could find out. There, I heard terrible stories of violence and bloodshed. One man described Hitler's planes as coming at them like winged devils, landing and taking off again in swarms like bees. The people, afraid and angry, attacked grounded enemy planes with their bare hands until nothing but wreckage remained. One thing is for sure. Our people will not go down without a spirited fight. They are furious and their fury gives them strength. All over the island, armed forces have been joined by Cretan civilians and a battle of the bloodiest savagery is now being fought". Taking a moment to gather his thoughts, Manolis paused to pour himself a glass of water.

"Upon the first wave of the invasion, there were stories of many Germans being killed by our brave people who fight in the olive groves and villages using knives and crudely fashioned clubs. An old man was said to have beaten a German paratrooper to death using only his walking stick. Our people prepared themselves for further invasion and, as the second wave of enemy paratroopers reached our land at Rethymno and Heraklion, many brave souls inflicted heavy casualties upon them, determined to defend with every last breath, our Cretan shores. So successful in fact were the allies and civilians that the Germans were initially thwarted and they failed to secure any stronghold over the island. The Germans had attempted to take us by surprise by attacking the island over a prolonged period, but, their tactics were flawed. We did not however, keep the upper hand for long. Within hours, the Germans had regrouped themselves and, realising that the Cretan defence was going to be brutal, their renewed attacks were ferocious".

Cries of anguish filled the room as Manolis continued relating his news. Manolis himself was, George thought, deadened, his voice without emotion, a flat monotone, shock and fatigue mingling to create an air of detachment.

"Even now, an acrid smell and a thick black cloak of smoke hangs over Crete where the Germans, now recovered from their initial shock have begun their reprisals. My friends", Manolis looked up, sorrow now etched in his expression, "they are burning down entire villages and embarking upon the wholesale slaughter of families with no regard or mercy even for women and children. Anyone who is discovered to be actively helping the allies is tortured and put to death". A gasp of horror emanated from within the group and murmurs of "Animals!", and "May God preserve us from these devils" could be heard. Manolis nodded and continued.

"I heard of one young man just outside Heraklion who was found to be running messages for the allies. When the Germans caught him, he was tied, face down to one of their armoured vehicles and dragged across rough terrain until his face was scraped away and his only relief was death". Finally, the dead expression which Manolis had carried fell away as his face crumpled and he began to sob. Burying his head in his hands, his shoulders trembling, the tears came and it was a long time before Manolis recovered himself sufficiently to continue. Although the war had been going on for some time, nevertheless, until now, it had been waged remotely from Crete. When it did finally come to the island, the Cretans had been strangely shocked. The reason for this became clear as Yiannis now spoke up, filling the uncomfortable silence, broken only by Manolis' barely stifled sobs.

"Crete has been attacked by oppressors throughout the centuries, all of whom, without exception have been defeated. I think this time, we took it for granted it would be the same. Our people though, did not bargain for the power of the Germans. I fear my friends that death is now circling above us like a black vulture waiting to swoop". Yiannis, perhaps all hope now extinguished and his heart heavy, sat thoughtfully and silently for a few moments, trying to gather courage to ask the question to which no-one wished to hear the answer. Eventually, closing his eyes, he took a deep breath and framed his question.

"Manolis, have you any news of the Acrotiri Peninsula? Did you hear of Elos?

"I am sorry Yianni, I have no specific news of your home village, but I know for a fact that nearby Kandamos was razed to the ground by the Germans and most of the people there, though they fought like Trojans were either butchered or burned to death.

A few survived with injuries". Yiannis visibly recoiled, his poor deformed hands laid out helplessly in front of him.

"I should be there to protect them!" He stood now, the force of his anger causing him to push the chair he'd been sitting on backwards so that it fell over. "What use am I as a man, sitting here on an island while my family, women and children fight the German dogs?" Yiannis could barely contain his frustration and, feeling the need for solitude, he left the taverna, leaving the rest of those present subdued and pensive. Presently, Nikos took his crutch and hobbled out to find Yiannis, the strain of all he was now enduring shrivelling his pathetically wizened features even more. What more would these people and indeed George, be forced to endure, he wondered. Manolis spoke quietly, his thoughts gathered.

"Things are looking very bad, Georgio. Although the Germans failed with their initial attack, the allied forces are being forced back. The Germans are determined to take Maleme and the news is that they are succeeding. The paratroopers have set up a strong defence and they have troops in the mountains. I think we are about to fall to Germany and God only knows what that might mean for any of us".

In fact, they knew no more for several days. No-one came to the island, as they were either trying to pick up the pieces of their shattered lives, or detained, actively fighting the enemy which, as Manolis had described was not an activity merely confined to the military, but by a fearsome Cretan resistance movement, *the andartes* and ordinary men, women and children. The Germans had initially been shocked by the civilian reaction and ferocity with which the Cretan people fought to protect themselves.

Finally however, on 2nd June, one brave soul waited until darkness fell and rowed over to the island. The man, Vasilis, had been a faithful visitor since Spinalonga had permitted families access and he was able to visit his beloved son, Mitsos. With care and stealth, Vasilis had managed to negotiate the short crossing without being seen and had arrived, drawn and tired looking, shortly after midnight. He had gone straight to Manolis before seeking out Mitsos. George later learned the bleak truth from Manolis. Crete had now fallen to the Germans. Things had moved on quickly from 29th May when German forces had established contact with reconnaissance elements who had successfully advanced through enemy held territories. They joined with German forces in Rethymno and reached Heraklion the next day. All over the island, Italians and Germans had advanced and the British forces were evacuated, sustaining huge losses and constant attack over the four days it took the Navy to evacuate 15,000 British men to Egypt. Crete was now alone in its fight against the enemy and those on Spinalonga were just alone.

THE ESCAPE

News quickly spread throughout Spinalonga of the fall of Crete and an air of desolation and fear crept through the little community. Visits from families and friends had long since ended and no-one on the island knew what might have become of their loved ones. Anxiety, fear and a sense of restlessness pervaded the town. The people knew they were now totally at the mercy of unknown forces and the whim of those who now controlled Crete. From a period of optimism and social improvement, the people of Spinalonga were plunged once more into the darkness. The better future they had all worked for and dreamt of was drifting away like footprints in the sand. Worse still, the emotional and mental pressures on the community were profound, the enforced isolation, breakdown of family connections and communication all contributing to the general air of depression. Illness during those first weeks ran at a high level with deterioration in the general condition of many islanders rapid and grave.

Only Vasilis continued to risk his life to bring snippets of news and small quantities of food to the island. The information he brought however was grim. The Cretan death toll was massive, but so far, Spinalonga had been spared attention from the Germans. One afternoon, sitting on a log near the jetty, Vasilis confirmed to the people of Spinalonga what they had already concluded. The Germans, only too aware of who resided on the island were too fearful to approach. Spinalonga was simply left alone therefore, as the lepers presented no danger to the Germans as long as they were contained, isolated and, neglected. Vasilis had heard through his Cretan resistance connections that the German army units had been forbidden to visit the island. This of course, would not have worried the community one iota, however, Vasilis delivered his most devastating piece of news. The Cretan population had also been forbidden to visit Spinalonga. No more traders would be permitted to come over with supplies. The Germans were deeply fearful of contamination and the spread of leprosy in Crete. The islanders had been quarantined but without the benefit of aid. With the arrival of the Germans, all of the old ignorance and prejudices had returned and the lepers were once more people to be shunned, a forgotten and forsaken people.

"Not only have they forbidden us to come here", Vasilis went on, sadly, but the Germans have set up posts around Plaka, Elounda and Kolokitha to ensure that no-one on Spinalonga can contact the mainland or any of the occupying forces."

"Pah!" exclaimed Yiannis, "Do they really think they can keep us here?" Nothing has stopped us from leaving the island in the past if we had a mind to - and nothing will stop us now! The Cretan people, have never succumbed to an enemy and they will never do so now! And that includes us, Vasilis!"

Vasilis looked on sadly, shaking his head slowly, as Yiannis reached the end of his proud and determined outburst.

"No, Yianni, you do not understand. The Germans are so determined to keep you isolated that they are prepared to shoot anyone trying to leave the island. If they see me leaving the island, God forbid, they will shoot me too". Vasilis now turned to his beloved son, Mitsos. With tears in his eyes, longing to reach out to his boy and gather him in his arms, he bade farewell to the son he had worshipped enough to risk his life for. Each of the men knew that they may never see one another again. Mitsos had begged Vasilis not, under any circumstances to attempt to breach the German security posts again. He could not bear the agony of wondering each time his father came to Spinalonga whether he had made it back to the mainland safely. Vasilis for his part had at first vehemently opposed his son's wishes, refusing to bow down to the will of the Germans. He, of all people knew that if no-one tried to make the journey, the people of Spinalonga, including his beloved Mitsos were condemned to perish through starvation or infection and a terrible unknown future. In reality though, he knew that if he tried to reach the island, he would, without doubt, be shot. He had seen the devastation wreaked upon Crete by the Germans, the brutality of their actions when disobeyed. What use would he be to his son dead? At least if he were alive, he might lobby support on the mainland to get help to the Spinalonga community. For these reasons and, because he did not wish to cause his son further distress, he promised only to return if and when he could be certain of doing so safely.

With one last glance back at his son, a nod of understanding passed between them and moments later, Mitsos stood at the water's edge watching his father's little boat sail out of the bay as he prayed against the odds, that he would reach his home safely, avoiding the German guns.

The heart had been ripped from the once thriving little community. As Manolis graphically put it, the people of Spinalonga were cursed, much as Prometheus had been condemned to eternal agony, nothing ever breaking the cycle of misery to which he was exposed. So it was with the islanders. Just as Prometheus had been chained to a rock by Zeus, with vultures poised to rip out his liver which re-grew daily, the citizens of Spinalonga faced new pain and indignity with each new day. It seemed that like Prometheus, their suffering would go on for eternity.

Conditions on the island worsened. Food was in short supply and there was no Government in Crete upon whom the people could rely to ensure their welfare. As summer turned to winter, food became a scarcity and, as, the islanders later discovered, thousands died from starvation on Crete. The death toll on Spinalonga too, was rising. Each night the men of Spinalonga gathered, holding counsel and debating what could be done to help the situation. Anger, resentment and frustration were creating a tinderbox of discontent and at any moment the tension threatened to spill over into irrationality and hasty actions.

Eventually, unable to bear the isolation, starvation, lack of communication and above all the helplessness of their situation, Yiannis and Nikos called at George's home one fateful afternoon.

"It is time, Georgio. Niko and I are leaving the island. I must have news of my family for I cannot endure not knowing their fate. The agony will kill me as surely as the Germans. I will reach the shores of Crete, or die in the attempt. I no longer care. As for Nikos, he is going to Athens by whatever means possible". Yiannis' eyes scrutinised George for his reaction but nothing was forthcoming, so stunned was the other man by the announcement from his friends.

"You asked us to tell you if we decided to go. You are welcome to join us if you wish. There is no moon tonight. All we can do is hope that the Gods are with us to protect us from harm".

George maintained his stunned silence. He didn't know what to say. Torn between his desire to leave the certainty of a slow lingering death on Spinalonga and his fear of a painful, though probably instant death at the hands of the Germans, he could not in such a short time weigh up the options. Of anyone on the island, George believed in the power of the pagan Gods and, he feared them. Hadn't Charon torn him from his own time and abandoned him here to live the life of a leper? What other eternal horrors might be arranged for him next? Yiannis and Nikos said nothing, but, the tension in the air was palpable as they waited. George knew without doubt that the two men wanted him to go with them - needed him to go with them. In their physical condition, what they proposed would be nigh on impossible without the assistance of someone stronger and more able bodied. George also knew however that neither of his friends would pressurise him into making such a decision. In his last life, back in good old London,

George would have laughed in their faces, "What, risk my life to help you two? Not a chance!" But now, George had learned a few things about compassion, about loyalty and about friendship. He paced the room, torn between his desire to help his friends and the high probability of death they all faced whatever the decision. Hysteria built in him giving way to a sudden and unnerving burst of laughter. Yiannis and Nikos looked at each other as though George had taken leave of his senses. In those moments, he probably had. Thinking back over his time on Spinalonga, it seemed he had spent a lifetime here. So far, though he had tried to convince himself otherwise, it seemed that this was no dream and George could gain no comfort from the idea that all of this was just a nocturnal (if seemingly eternal) dream. This was a nightmare from which he now felt he would never be awoken. His back to the two men whose friendship he treasured, George now looked out of his window, gazing with deep affection at the familiar street and the familiar faces who passed by. What are my options? George mused silently. Stay on Spinalonga and rot, or starve to death? Or do I take my chances with the others and maybe even get help for those left behind here? Maybe I could at least get some food and aid back to them somehow. Maybe by leaving the island, the spell which is holding me here may be broken. George's mind raced with the seemingly endless possibilities and consequences of the decision he must now make. He turned back to the men who had supported him through the worst of times and knew what he must do. They had been so strong for him in the last months but now, he saw in their faces uncertainty, dejection and defeat, where previously he had seen strength, pride and the refusal to be beaten by circumstances. It was George's turn to be strong for them now and whatever the outcome of their journey, he could be at peace with himself, knowing he had done his best for the people he now loved so well.

"I'm with you Yianni", George stated simply and decisively, his assuredness belying the uncertainty and fear which he felt. The faces of the two men opposite him lit up, relief and gratitude washing over them. George had given them hope.

"You are sure about this Georgio?" asked Nikos. We do not want you to feel that you must come with us. This is momentous decision and you know the risks as well as we do".

"Niko, there is no decision to make. We have been friends for a long time and I could not have survived here had it not been for you two. In any case, if we do not go, what is left for us here? At least we may be able to persuade the authorities to get help for the people of Spinalonga if we do nothing else".

Buoyed up by George's decision, Yianni stood up and slapped the table in satisfaction, his determination fired with confidence that with the young man's help, they at least stood a fighting chance of getting across the water. Moving across the room to George, he gripped him warmly by the shoulders.

"Good, good", he grinned. "Thank you Georgio from the bottom of our hearts for this. We shall leave in the early hours. We will meet at the harbour at 1.00 a.m."

"But how shall we get across? Only Manolis has the key for the boathouse", George now asked. Yiannis shook his head.

"We cannot take the boat. Manolis may need it for an emergency. In any case, a boat floating upon the water would make us a sitting target for the Germans. No. We shall have to drift across. Nikos and I have collected some wood which we shall put together as a raft to keep us afloat. If we grip onto that, hopefully we shall not attract the attention of the Germans so easily. They will perhaps think it is driftwood if they see anything at all".

Despite his resolve, George was horrified. He was not a strong swimmer and had always hated the unpredictability of the sea. The prospect of grasping on to a piece of wood for the duration of the crossing in pitch darkness filled him with terror. Panic rose in his throat just thinking about it. Nevertheless, he nodded his agreement, knowing that he had no choice other than to go along with the plan the men had already worked out.

"Now Georgio, we have much to do so we shall take our leave. We shall see you at the harbour".

After Yiannis and Nikos had left, George sat alone in the little house which had in so many ways become his home. Holding his head in hands, he agonised over the decision he had made and pondered his fate. If the Germans didn't blow his head off, the sea would probably get him. And if neither of those finished him off, starvation or leprosy surely would, George thought wryly. What a choice of options I have!

These were not the only things which troubled George about the plans however. How on earth would Nikos manage the crossing? He was far from strong and it would be difficult enough for Yiannis and him, even with the benefit of all their limbs. The more George thought about it, the more agitated he became and finally, he resolved to speak to Yiannis and strode from his house in the direction of the shop. Yiannis was working as usual, though now he was only repairing shoes and boots, leather by now a scarcity. He could only rely on remnants to keep his trade going. As George entered his shop, he looked up, his usually cheerful disposition now replaced by solemnity and an air of distraction.

"Georgio!", he exclaimed, as the young man walked in. His surprise was momentarily displaced by uncertainty. "I hope you have not changed your mind about our plan? I do not wish to pressure you, of course, but, I will need your help to ensure that Nikos gets across safely".

"No, Yianni, of course I haven't changed my mind. I would never let you down. Besides, we have to do something".

"Then - what brings you now? I think that something is troubling you."

"It's Nikos who is troubling me Yianni", George replied, somewhat sheepishly. "You surely don't think he can manage this crossing do you? He will almost certainly drown in his condition. With one leg missing, his mobility and buoyancy will be greatly impeded. Even if we do succeed in getting across the water, what then? Don't you think we will be the most obvious men in town when we surface? Yianni, think about this, I beg you. Nikos cannot go. Not for his sake, nor ours. We will be so preoccupied with his safety that we'll be unable to look out for ourselves. We'll be sitting ducks for the Germans"

Yianni said nothing and a momentary silence followed. George knew, even as he spoke, that his words were not being well received by Yiannis who now squared up in defence of Nikos, his features, even in their state of near obliteration by disease became thunderous. George knew he had touched a raw nerve and almost immediately as he spoke the words, he regretted them. To George's immense shock, Yiannis lunged at him so fast that he had no opportunity of defending himself. He grabbed his shirt in his huge fist and slammed him against the wall. George knew that the man was holding back and the thought of what he would be capable of, even in his weakened state was terrifying. He brought his face up close to George's, a grotesque mask of rage and spoke with slow deliberation emphasising his words to ensure there could be no misunderstanding.

"Georgio, it hurts me to speak this way to you, but, do not, ever suggest to me that Nikos should be left behind. I love you as a dear friend, but Nikos has been my closest companion now for many years. He is my brother. We have shared our sorrows and have leaned on each other since the day we met. He, more than any of us, needs to leave this island now. He knows the risk he is taking as we both do. Neither you, nor I, are going to deny him the opportunity of finding his children. Besides, what else is there for him now? No. He will go with us and we will take care of him. We may all die in the attempt, but at least we will go down fighting". Yiannis released his grip on George. "Now, do we understand each other Georgio?"

George was so shocked by Yiannis' response that he could, at that moment, do little more than give a feeble nod of understanding. Calmer now, Yiannis released him, and, returning to his old self, he joked whilst dusting George down and straightening his clothes.

"Eh, forgive me Georgio. I am a little emotional today. I did not intend to be aggressive. Please, sit down. Have a little raki". Yiannis plucked a bottle of Raki from the shelf behind him and filled two small glasses with the liquid. George meantime slumped, slightly shocked by Yiannis' outburst into the chair as the surge of adrenalin which had coursed through him receded. As his breathing returned to normal, he watched Yiannis continue with his work, unperturbed and as though nothing had happened between them. George understood however the power of Yiannis' loyalty to Nikos and felt ashamed and cowardly that he had, once again, been more concerned for himself than for those who now depended upon him.

"I'm sorry Yiannis", he began. "I know how much Nikos means to you. I care for him too. It's just that I'm afraid for him", George paused for a moment, "I'm afraid for us too. Things are going to be risky enough for us without increasing the chances of harm to any of us".

"I know you mean no harm to Nikos, Georgio. Believe me, I have thought the same things as you, but this must be his choice. If he wishes to put his life in danger and take a chance of finding all that is dear to him, then who are we to try to stop him? Nikos, like the rest of us, has been denied his freedom to choose for so long. I, for one, will not endorse the exercise of power over him to prevent him from carrying out his wishes. I will be there, side by side with him, ready to help him all that I can". Yiannis continued with his work, methodically, mechanically, as he spoke. "I am all too aware, Georgio, that by taking Nikos with us, we could be bringing our own deaths closer". He moved away from the block on which he was working.

"Georgio, if it comes to saving yourself, or staying with us, I will not hold it against you if you choose life. Nikos and I, well, we have so little to lose. But you, you are not so sick. Maybe even a cure will be found before you become like us. If you see your chance to get across, you must go. Do not feel guilty about leaving us". Yiannis hesitated. "Just promise me one thing?"

"Of course Yianni, anything. What is it?"

"If you make it across and we do not, make it your business to find Nikos' children and let them know he never forgot them. For me, go to my village and find whoever is left of my family. Tell them that I loved them with all my heart and that until the end, they were in my thoughts". He nodded sadly. "That is all I ask. You are stronger and younger than us Georgio. Tell whoever will listen of the plight of our people on Spinalonga and get help for those who are left here".

George once more felt ashamed, chastened by his own desire for self preservation. He thought that he had been humbled over the preceding months into losing his selfishness, so overcome had he been by the kindness of the people he lived amongst. Now, he realised, he had not reached the level of altruism which Yiannis now displayed. 'These people took me under their wing, made a horrific experience tolerable and all I could do to repay them was to deny their right of freedom', thought George miserably. In his own estimation, he was a traitor to his people. Humbled and ashamed, he now spoke.

"I don't know what I was thinking about Yianni. I was just being selfish. Of course Nikos must go. No question about it. You have my word Yianni, that I shall be by his side all the way". His words sounder braver than he felt, but Yiannis was absolutely right. Their options were limited and George was not in a position to dictate or influence anyone's decision, nor, he knew, did he have any right to do so. These two men in particular, needed him now. A thought struck him and he grinned, voicing the phrase which now ran through his head.

"All for one and one for all!", George exclaimed as he stood, raising his glass of Raki in toast. He quoted 'The Three Musketeers' more confidently than he actually felt. Yiannis, for his part, returned the grin and repeated, "All for one and one for all!" enjoying the new catchphrase as George took his leave from the little workshop.

The mission itself was not for public knowledge. The men did not want anyone either trying to follow them or to prevent them from their chosen course of action. All the same, George felt bad when he dropped by to see Manolis who was busy carrying out a stock take of the ever dwindling medical supplies when he arrived.

"Kalimera Manoli", George greeted him as normally as he could. Looking up from where he knelt in front of the cupboard, though he smiled warmly, George could tell he was clearly troubled.

"Georgio", he said cheerily. "How are you?", he asked, continuing methodically with his work.

"I'm not so bad Manoli. Busy, I see?"

"Ah, things are not looking so good here Georgio. My stocks of antibiotics are so depleted, I think they will probably only last another week, if that". Shaking his head despairingly, he continued, "More worrying still, I have only one bottle of morphine left and at least two people in need of surgery". He glanced at George, sadly. "We are returning to the dark days Georgio and I fear all that is yet to come. I do not think I shall have the courage to operate without sufficient quantities of anaesthesia. I do not know what will become of these people now". He shook his head miserably, remembering George's prediction about the length of the war to come. "If it is true what you say, that we have another four years of this terrible war to go, then what does the future hold for us?". George looked on helplessly, unable to provide him with any comfort. "We cannot survive another four weeks like this, let alone four years", he sighed resignedly. "I might as well hang up my lab coat, shut up shop and wait for death like everyone else. There is no hope for any of us now". George had never known Manolis to be so defeated, so ready to throw in the towel. "While we still live and breathe Manoli, there is always hope. If there is one thing I have learned from my time here, it is that simple truth. And while there is still breath in our lungs, the desire and the will to survive will always remain". Manolis rose from his crouched position, rubbing his knees in pain, as he stretched them out.

"As you say Georgio, but how long will we all continue to breathe, I wonder? Still, my friend, I am glad you are here to keep talking some sense into this miserable pessimist! What would I do without you?" George could not tell his friend that soon, he would find out the answer to his rhetorical question. All the same, he would have liked to say a proper farewell to Manolis and assure him that he would do everything in his power to help the plight of the islanders if he were fortunate enough to reach the mainland. He could say nothing however and, choked with emotion, he was unable to respond. Instead, he wrapped an arm around Manolis' shoulder in a companionable 'man-hug' and slapped his back warmly and reassuringly hoping in some way, without words, he could communicate 'Don't worry, I'm here, all will be fine'. Manolis understood and was grateful for the gesture.

"You are a good friend Georgio. It has been good to have you here on the island". At that moment, Manolis looked George in the face and, as their eyes locked, his sincere features seemed to scrutinise George, reading his thoughts, for something in that moment seemed to transmit between the men. Perhaps, George thought, nerves or the duplicity of which he was a part, was written there on his face, for all to see. He didn't know exactly what it was, but at that instant, Manolis' smile evaporated momentarily and George felt that the other man knew this was their last meeting. Maybe, he thought, it was just his imagination, the product of a guilty conscience, but, as Manolis spoke, George felt he was saying goodbye to him.

Taking George's right hand in his, Manolis gripped his elbow firmly with the other and spoke firmly yet sincerely.

"You must take good care of yourself Georgio. Don't take unnecessary risks in your condition". That said, he turned away, but not before George saw the glint of a tear in his eye. George wanted to say something but emotion overcame him and nodding wordlessly, he turned on his heels and left quickly.

George knew he would need all of his strength for the night ahead, so he called in at the taverna and ordered a salad and souvlaki, a slow creeping dread reducing his appetite like a death row inmate partaking of his last meal. Sitting alone at his table, George pondered the irony of this practice. Who in their right mind wanted to eat when death was a certainty, waiting just behind a closed door? It was difficult enough for him, just knowing that his annihilation was merely a high risk. All the same, he knew that without sustenance, he would never make it. After forcing some of the food down, gagging as it clung to the dryness in his throat, George returned home, the heaviness in his chest threatening to suffocate him. He needed to rest before facing his terror. Sleep however, proved to be as elusive as his appetite had been and, as dusk began to fall, he felt more exhausted than usual, the emotionally draining day finally taking its toll.

George looked around the room surveying for the last time, the few belongings accumulated during his life on the island, each of the objects holding treasured memories. The beautifully crafted boots from Yiannis, the delicately sewn shirts from Athena, the gifts brought from each of the villagers here to make him welcome and which signified his unconditional acceptance within the community. He could take nothing with him on this journey, but he did collect up the little money he now had left and which he had been unable to spend during the last weeks due to the absence of merchandise arriving on the island. Sadly, he tore the sleeves from one of his precious shirts and legs from his trousers, converting them into shorts which would allow him to move more freely and unimpeded in the water. That done, he settled down for the final hours trying to calm himself and make ready to embark on probably the most dangerous escapade of his life. Never having been the athletic type, he was not, quite aside from his illness, the fittest of people.

Time passed very slowly for the remainder of the evening, George part willing it to go faster and get things underway, part wanting the clock to stay still and delay the inevitable. He was barely able to sit still, adrenalin coursing through his veins, occasional palpitations fluttering in his chest. He paced up and down, his mind going into overdrive until finally, it was time for him to leave the house and make his way to the harbour.

With a final look behind him into the little house, George closed the door and heard the familiar click of the latch as it fell shut for the final time. Walking along to the harbour, George could hear the comforting chatter of the cicadas in the warm night air as he negotiated the 'Green Mile' to whatever destiny now lay ahead of him. Approaching the harbour, he could see the outlines of Nikos and Yiannis who were gathering several large pieces of wood in varying shapes and sizes on the sand next to them. Nikos already looked tired and, as George approached, the other man sat down and remained there quietly for a few moments, conserving the little strength he had for the journey. Yiannis stood next to him, tying the last of the section of wood to the raft he had crafted. George knelt down beside Nikos, placing a hand on his shoulder.

"Are you alright Niko?" he asked, concerned at his stillness.

"We can do this another night if you aren't well enough", he suggested gently. It was with some effort that Nikos replied.

"No, I am fine. We must go tonight", he said with finality. There is no moon and the darkness will hide our approach to the mainland. Besides", he laughed mirthlessly, "when shall I ever be well enough? I, Georgio, can only get worse and this might be my one and only chance to find my girls". He looked determined, his jaw set firmly and defiantly against anyone or anything that might threaten to prevent him from his chosen course. He had removed the crude wooden limb which now lay next to him on the sand.

"We will all get on the raft Georgio", Yiannis explained. "The sea is calm tonight so it should be a smooth voyage. We shall use these pieces of wood as oars to steer us to shore". He took a knife, tightening the last knot and severed the end of the rope he had used to secure the wooden sections together.

"What happens when we reach the other side?" George asked, somewhat anxiously.

"You must go your own way Georgio. You do not have the mark of the leper visible on you and you will be able to disappear more easily than us. It is important that you try to alert people in Crete of the plight of Spinalonga and try to get help to the people here. I shall stay with Nikos. When we reach land, we shall make our way quickly into the hills. Travelling by night, I hope we shall reach Elos in a few days. From there, God willing, my family, if they have been spared, will help us with Nikos' quest.

George listened to Yiannis' plans with growing amazement. Clearly he had not thought any of this through. He took him aside out of Nikos' earshot.

"Yianni, you must know this is suicide for both of you. How are you going to get Nikos into the hills? He can barely walk now, let alone climb".

"Once we arrive, I'll make sure he is at least hidden from view before the dawn breaks. I will go out after dark tomorrow and see if I can steal a donkey from somewhere. They are used to trekking up and down the mountains. Nikos can ride while I lead the way".

It was an ambitious plan, but George couldn't help feeling that Yiannis was denying the near impossibility of his proposal. Or perhaps, he did him a disservice. Perhaps he knew deep down that the risks were overwhelming, but he was determined to see it through, even just for the sake of his old friend. Dawn would be breaking within a short time of the men reaching Crete and George could not envisage any possibility, even had they been able bodied, of them being able to travel the distance required to hide themselves from view before the island came to life.

As for himself, George knew Yiannis was right; that he could pass himself off as healthy and therefore blend into the surroundings. But, he wondered, where will he go? What could he do to get the help that was so badly needed on Spinalonga? As soon as people realised he had come from the island, he would be regarded with suspicion, shunned, possibly even turned over to the Germans. After all, weren't the lepers hated almost as much as the enemy? No matter how hard he tried, George could not begin to imagine what awaited him once he left Spinalonga. He wasn't even returning to his own place and time. Everything would be foreign and strange in wartime Crete and he could no longer rely on the sheltered little community he had known in Spinalonga. There was a bloody war being waged on the island, and George knew he was about to step into its midst.

George was desperately afraid that night as the little trio waded into the water, he and Yiannis each gripping Nikos by an arm, steadying him between them and finally lowering him and themselves onto the raft. Yiannis and George perched themselves on opposite ends for balance, with Nikos in the centre as they pushed the water away with oars which had been carved neatly into shape by Yiannis' still skilled hands.

Soon, they were moving far out from Spinalonga into the

deepest seas and, as George took one last lingering look behind him at the island which had sheltered and reshaped him, he saw, once again, the majestic form of the Venetian fortress looming far above, its circular walls enveloping the island, protecting it from outside peril. He shivered, not only from the sea chill, but with fear as the little raft drifted further and further away from the comparative safety of their former home.

Within fifteen minutes, they could no longer see Spinalonga. In fact, they could no longer see anything. The darkness had closed in around the men and it was so dense that George began to imagine that perhaps he had gone blind. Terror gripped him. There they were, atop a hastily built wooden raft in the middle of the ocean, with nothing to guide them and no way of telling if they were even going in the right direction. Panic washed over him and George found it difficult to breathe or swallow. He wanted to get off the raft, as rationality deserted him. It was Yiannis' voice which brought him back to his senses, beads of sweat now having broken out on his forehead and top lip.

"You OK there Georgio?" he asked.

"Y-yes, I think so", he replied uncertainly.

"Take a rest for a moment then. Let the current take us for a while. I am tired of rowing Georgio and I must stop to gather strength".

Reluctantly, for he feared the current could take them in any direction, George stopped rowing and just sat still, knowing all that lay between him and the abyss of a watery grave was this unsteady makeshift wooden raft. Incongruously, he either dozed off or fell into some catatonic state for a few moments and it was Nikos' voice which startled him into wakefulness, the sudden interjection in the otherwise silent night, almost causing him to fall from the raft. He jumped almost into the air.

"Look!" Did you see that?" Nikos yelled. George meanwhile squinted into the darkness, trying to focus and see what it was that had disturbed Nikos so badly. Hard as he tried though, he could see nothing.

"What Niko?" he asked. "What was it you saw?"

"A strange light in the distance. It seemed to beam out onto the water and then disappear. We must be close to shore now!" he exclaimed excitedly. Indeed, George could just make out some tiny dots of light on the coastline and relief flooded him as his senses of sight and spatial awareness gradually returned and the disorientation he had experienced began to recede. For a while, he had felt locked into a solitary world in which he had lost all sense of self. A world where one false move could have meant drowning alone in the middle of a dark sea of nothingness. His relief however was short lived and, as they drew nearer to the mainland, he saw with horror what had attracted Nikos' attention. Turning in 360° arc, he saw the bright beam of light, too late to avoid it washing over them as it reached far out into the sea. To his absolute horror, he realised it wasn't a lighthouse, but a search light. Seconds later, the light was back on them, picking them out against the night and blinding them, so accustomed were their eyes to the darkness. Yiannis dropped his oar and fell backwards, altering the balance of the raft, which, to George's terror, flipped over, throwing all three of them into the freezing water. Nikos gave a cry of shock and, in that harsh light, he saw his head disappear under the water, his buoyancy impeded by the fact of his amputated leg. George was terrified, distraught, but powerless to do anything to help Nikos, so consumed with fear of the water was he that he gripped onto the raft for dear life. He was frozen with terror. It was Yiannis who took control of the situation, submerging himself in the water to go in search of his old friend. Moments later, he came up once more, with Nikos, barely conscious now, in his grasp.

"Hold the raft steady Georgio, while I try to get Nikos back on". George did as he asked, all the while wondering what would happen now, as the searchlight, static over them, now clearly indicated that the Germans were aware of their presence. Perhaps they would send a boat out to pick them up and take them back to the island? George wondered naively. Within seconds however, he was rewarded with an answer as he heard the rat-tat-tatting of machine gun fire. His stomach sank. So, was this it? Are we to be filled with holes and left to die, injured and frozen out here? Such were the thoughts which passed through George's mind now. The inhumanity of it all was shattering. As the bullets showered down upon them, the raft disintegrated before their eyes and George was detached from the one thing giving him the confidence to remain afloat. Next to him, Yiannis still clung to Nikos who now jerked wildly under the shower of bullets. George tried, and succeeded momentarily to move out of the line of fire, but seconds later, he heard Yiannis howling like an injured animal and saw, to his horror, that in place of Nikos, he now gripped nothing but a bloody pulp, an oozing mess of blood and bone where Nikos' face had once been, glistening grotesquely in the harsh light. He struggled not to black out as his stomach leapt in disgust and sorrow at the grizzly sight which now confronted him.

"Let him go Yianni", George cried. Let him go and swim out of the light. You are a sitting target now". But Yiannis continued to wail, refusing to let go of Nikos' poor ruined body. George tried to swim over to him, keeping his head low in the water, but suddenly, awareness of the fact that there was nothing below his feet and that he was suspended only by his own limited power to float washed over him. Losing confidence, he started to flail about in the water, his panic causing him to sink, taking huge mouthfuls of the foul salty water.

"Resurfacing momentarily, he called, "Yianni, help me, help me please! I don't swim well". Realising there was nothing more he could do for Nikos and that George needed him, Yiannis gently let go of the corpse which now sunk below the water's surface. "Go in peace my dearest friend", he uttered. Moments later, he was at George's side.

"Thank you, my dear Yianni, thank you", George cried as he felt strong arms grip him, keeping his head firmly above the water, his breaths coming in short gasps as he tried to steady himself and regain his equilibrium. Yiannis too, was exhausted.

"Remember your promise to me Georgio", his breath came in short gasps, "if you survive this, find our families and tell them that we tried to reach them. Let them know how we fought to be with them and how they were always foremost in our thoughts".

Tears now coursing down his cheeks, the sheer hopelessness of their situation evident, George looked into Yiannis' big, earnest face and despite his feeling of impending doom, promised him he would do all he could.

"But we will survive this Yianni, both of us", George cried. "You'll see". Yiannis grinned, despite their circumstances and yelled in defiance,

"All for one and one for all!" as another storm of bullets rained down upon them. At that moment, George felt a blow to his chest, the force of it ripping him from Yiannis' grasp. A flash of light burst in his head like a flashbulb and his eyes lost focus. Warmth, and a sense of relief seemed to fill his body and he felt himself floating almost contentedly as the water enveloped him and he gave up the will to fight. Ready now to succumb to his fate, his head slipped under the water and George began his descent into the inky blackness below him, air slowly releasing from his lungs as the water filled them. He felt no panic. Just a sense of overwhelming peace as he resigned himself to death.

His peace however was short lived. Just as George was about to take his final breath, an arm plunged into the water from above and, as it did so, a hand grabbed his arm which he held aloft as he made his descent. George felt himself being pulled from the sea and extraordinarily, back from the brink of death. Moments later, he was being pulled into a boat and, as he looked up at his saviour, he recognised the baleful gaze of that surly old man who had heralded this whole nightmare. For there, gazing down upon him, was Charon. George's last thought before losing consciousness was what a good thing it was that he had remembered to bring his money with them. Who, otherwise, would have paid the ferryman?

REFLECTIONS

As the little raft had set sail from Spinalonga, one lonely figure stood in the harbour watching the motley crew of mariners as they disappeared into the darkness and the distance. Manolis had felt a deep loneliness suddenly, his feeling of isolation and powerlessness exacerbated by the departure of his closest friends. He could have felt hurt at his exclusion, that not one of them had allowed him into their confidence to share their plans, but he knew, deep down, that their failure to do so was more from concern for him and to protect him from carrying a burden of responsibility than a snub. They knew, as did Manolis, that he would have pleaded and cajoled and begged them to reconsider their decision, all of which would have only made the situation much worse. They knew also that he could not have accompanied them. He was needed on this island and, for better or worse, they and he knew he must remain here.

Manolis' sorrow however, was profound. Deep in his heart, he knew that tragedy was lurking ahead in those waters and that he was unlikely to see any of the three men for whom he had such deep respect and liking ever again. Manolis' own visit to Crete had shown him that the Germans meant business and that they were merciless in their treatment of civilians. They would think nothing of murdering the little trio of cripples for their tenacity of spirit and the perceived danger they would present if successful in reaching the mainland. From the account given by Vasilis, the Germans were taking no risks that anyone could leave or visit the island and they would literally take no prisoners in dealing with anyone found to be breaching their fortifications. They held little value in the preservation of life so Manolis was under no illusion that his friends would be shown any mercy because of their infirmity. Quite the contrary if Georgio's account of Hitler's pursuit of the perfect race was true.

Manolis knew also that if, by some miracle the men did reach the other side, they would try to bring help to the island. If they were caught however, well, the possible consequences to those left here on Spinalonga could be dire. It was this fact alone which caused him anger. How thoughtless could they be? Had they not heard anything of what he had told them on his return from Crete? But then, how could he really blame them? Nikos and Yiannis had been proud and respected men before disease struck them down. They had been the protectors of their families until their autonomy had been stolen from them and they had been shipped away, broken and emasculated to this once gloomy island. How fear must have gripped their hearts as they had approached the looming fortress, knowing that this would be their prison until death. How could anyone sit back whilst their families were being butchered and their villages torched? In their position, wouldn't he have done the same? What right did he have to condemn them for taking back control of their lives? Weren't those left on the island doomed anyway?

So lost in his thoughts was he that Manolis failed to hear the gentle footsteps approaching him through the sand. He started a little as he felt a hand slip into his.

"So, they have gone." Irini whispered.

"Yes, they have left us Irini", he responded with a sigh. "But, how did you know about it when I did not?"

"George came to see me this afternoon. He wanted to say his goodbyes to me personally. He begged me not to tell you as he feared you may try to stop them. I agreed to keep his secret for both of your sakes as I was afraid you might want to go with them when you heard of their scheme and I could not have borne that Manoli".

Irini had been shocked when George turned up at her door that afternoon. He was flustered and nervous as he spoke. He made her promise, before he told her anything that she must stay silent; that the safety of everyone on the island might depend on the success of their mission.

"But you must not go, Georgio", she had begged. "This is suicide. They will shoot you if you do not drown first".

"Irini, I have many reasons for going along with Yiannis and Nikos tonight. One of them is to try to get help for the island but one of them is to try and find the answers to questions I have never dared tell you about. This voyage is probably the most important one of my life Irini". George had tears in his eyes as he pulled Irini close and held her for a few moments. She knew that George's mind was made up and there was nothing she could do to dissuade him so she held him tighter, her own tears spilling out. As they pulled apart, their eyes met and their lips locked in their first and last kiss which was the sweetest George had ever known.

"I meant it when I said that I loved you Irini. I still do, but I know that Manolis is the one for you. I know why you won't be with him Irini, but when all this is over, promise me you will have the test. Don't waste your life, and his, needlessly. Please".

"I will try to do as you ask Georgio. I love you very dearly, you know that. God be with you tonight and I shall pray that we meet again. Thank you for doing this. You will not be forgotten on Spinalonga, I know. I shall miss you with all my heart Georgio".

George, unable to bear it longer had swept Irini up in one last hug and turned to the door. Without looking back, he hurried back home to make his final preparations.

As Manolis turned away from the harbour, his hands disconsolately thrown in his pockets, his shoulders hunched and tense, he said a prayer under his breath knowing that he would only have to wait a short time before the repercussions of his friends' actions would be apparent. Throwing his arm across Irini's shoulder, the two of them walked back to the village, their sorrow palpable.

RETURN OF THE PRODIGAL

Coming to, the first thing George became aware of was the starkness of the white clinical walls and the rhythmic beep, beep, the only sound he could hear. He lay flat on his back and, trying now to move his head and arms, he was restricted by the wires and tubes which were attached, it seemed, to every part of his body. His mind was foggy and random thoughts came and went. When he started to experience joined up thinking, his recollection happened with a suddenness that hit him like a forceful blow. The next moment, he was bolt upright, tubes ripping from his body screaming, "Yianni, where are you? Yianni?"

Seconds later there was a flurry of activity as people rushed into the room, three women in blue tops and trousers and a man in a lab coat who tended quickly and efficiently to the discarded tubes and the injuries caused as a result of their sudden, rough removal. The women spoke soothingly, in English, telling George he was safe and to be calm now, that everything was fine. He felt the prick of a needle as something was administered to his arm, calming him within moments. He was completely disorientated and, as he later discovered, making no sense to staff as apparently he was speaking Greek. Although he understood what was being said to him, his mind was still assimilating his new circumstances and it took him a while to be able to communicate again in his own native English.

It took the medical staff some time to tend to him but after they were satisfied that he was comfortable, they all left and it was suddenly quiet again. George, throughout this time had been unable to speak, partly due to whatever drug had been administered to him and partly due to his language confusion. Calmer now, his mind slowly recovering clarity, George recalled the last moments before he lost consciousness. He remembered being separated in the water from Yiannis, trying to avoid the bullets and now reliving the terror he had felt as Yiannis' grip had loosened on him as he sank, exhausted and unable to remain afloat into the freezing sea. Just as the relief of relinquishing life had washed over him, he remembered the disembodied arm which had reached down into the depths and gripped him. How this had been possible, George would never know as in his estimation he had at that moment been several metres below the surface. He recalled how he had been pulled, gasping and coughing into the boat with such apparent ease and how, lying there, half drowned he had looked into the face of none other than Charon. He now dimly recalled the gist of the words he spoke as George lay there like a bloated wet fish in the little boat.

"You have done well my friend. You have achieved your purpose and more. You shall be rewarded. You have learned that life is bestowed upon you as a precious gift and above else, it should be valued. I hope we shall not meet again for a very long time". His words were delivered as a warning.

"Now, give me your coin for the journey and we shall be off." Shivering uncontrollably, too traumatised for anything other than silent acquiescence, George had dug into the pockets of the cut off trousers he wore and thankfully, found the one coin which had survived the waters. There were no searchlights now, nor any bullets..

"Yiannis", George implored him. "We must find him and bring him aboard". He clambered to his knees and looked helplessly into the darkness. "Quick, help me look!" But Charon did not respond and merely flexing his oars, rowed the little boat on his intended course.

"Yiannis has his own destiny to fulfil" Charon had responded matter of factly. "Now, close your eyes and sleep. We have a long journey ahead". Too tired to protest and sensing that Charon would brook no argument, George obeyed, wondering what terrors the old man had in store for him now.

George's mind was so addled on waking that it did not immediately occur to him, or strike him in any way strange that everyone was speaking English or that there were computers, a television and other instruments of 21st century technology in his room. It was some hours later when his mind finally got round to processing this information. When one of the nurses (as he now recognised them to be) came in, he asked her where he was

"You're in hospital in London", she smiled. "You're quite a miracle. We'd almost given up hope on you. Your Mum and Dad were so thrilled when we called them. They've barely left your side for the last three months".

"Three months!" George exclaimed. Then, "Tell me, what year is it?"

"It's 23rd October 2005", she replied matter of factly. 'My God!', he exclaimed, as he realised he was back in his own time. He almost leapt out of bed to dance and hug the woman.

George's initial euphoria lasted only moments as his memory came back in floods and a feeling of dread suffocated his initial exuberance. What does life hold for me now? Shame and prison, surely? And what of Mum and Dad? The last time he had seen them was on a television screen as the news of his conduct had been revealed in its full unexpurgated glory. George's spirits sank to an all time low as he realised he now had a whole lot of new horrors to face. Crazy as it might seem, he longed for the safety once more of Spinalonga.

George was overcome with emotion when, later that morning, his parents walked in to greet him. His father was the first to open his arms wide and gather him in his tight embrace. He held George close, his beaming face filled with tears of joy. His mother followed on to hug him, stroke his hair and his face, the strain of the past months now evident in the greyness of her hair which was uncharacteristically untended. After a few emotional moments, his father spoke.

"George, I am sorry. Forgive me? This was all my fault. I should never have pushed you so hard and made you do things which were unsuited to you. None of this would have happened I am sure if I had only let you find your own way". He broke down and sobbed, as he held his son's hand and buried his face in the sheet. George, who had never seen such a display of emotion from his father was confused and it took him some time to find the courage to speak.

"Mum, Dad, this wasn't anything to do with you. I was a directionless, lazy, good for nothing bastard and I am so sorry for the shame I have brought you". George's parents both looked at him quizzically as he went on, "Tell me, what will happen to me now? Am I to be tried and go to prison?"

His parents merely looked blankly at him, his father shaking his head in confusion.

"Prison?" he laughed. "You don't go to prison for messing up your job! OK so you left a bit of a balls up at the stock exchange and yes, I had a bit of a red face for having got you the job, but, it is all forgotten now."

It was George's turn to be confused. "But, what about Jenna Hawkins and the others? I saw the reporters asking you questions when she died and I disappeared. I was so ashamed and afraid."

George's father shrugged helplessly, looking at him as though he were mad.

"Who is this Jenna Hawkins? What others? What are you talking about?" he asked.

"You mean, no-one is dead because of me?"

"Dead!" George's mother now exclaimed. "Of course no-one is dead, why should they be?" Oh George, you must have been hallucinating in the coma, or perhaps you are delirious?"

And so it was that George learned his parents' account of the foregoing months. According to them, on the day George had walked out of the Stock Exchange, he had begun to show the signs of some sort of breakdown due to the stress he had been under and his excessive drug abuse, which had not become apparent to them until some time later. George, they told him, had been unable to kick his habit alone and a period of rehab also failed to get him entirely clean. One dreadful binge later however and it was clear to both his parents that they had to do something to help him.

During this time, George's father realised how much pressure he had put upon him in recent months and suggested that after another period of rehab, he would pay for him to go to Crete where he felt George would find some peace to recover and recuperate. It would, he had said, work its magic in restoring him to physical and spiritual health and give him time to consider his future. Desperately, George had agreed. Whilst touring on a hired scooter, he had indeed been thrown from the mountainside. Fortunately for him, it seemed, a tour bus had been behind him and those on board had witnessed his demise. An ambulance had immediately been called and apparently, he had to be resuscitated several times as his heart had stopped beating, due to extensive internal injuries and blood loss.

Despite dying several times however, somehow George had survived and had undergone surgery for the internal injuries and haemorrhaging in his head. George however had not come round after the operations and the Doctors had broken the news that he was in a persistent vegetative state and that it was unlikely he would regain consciousness. The doctors had tried to persuade his parents to let them switch off the machine which kept him alive but they had steadfastly refused until just days ago when they had finally accepted that perhaps it would be kinder to let him go. The night he had awakened was going to be his last as the machines were due to be switched off the following morning. George had been lying here motionless for three months, only, in his own experience, he had been living another existence in a long distant past.

As his parents finished their story, Geroge looked on in wide eyed amazement. It was all so hard to take in. So, he hadn't killed anyone? He hadn't been a drug dealer! That part of his life had somehow been erased and he had returned to a clean slate. Still though, hardly daring to believe what he was now hearing, he couldn't help but ask what now seemed like a very odd question to his parents.

"I haven't got leprosy have I?" He looked from one to the other of his parents, waiting for a response. His mother just looked on worriedly. She was convinced George had taken leave of his senses. Perhaps he had. Oddly however, his father looked more perplexed by the apparent non-sequitur.

"Leprosy, George? Why would you ask such a thing?"

"Because while I was.... well, wherever I was, I believed I was on a little island, called Spinalonga. It's a leper col...

"I know what it is, George" his father interjected, somewhat abruptly, he thought. His parents exchanged glances and, recovering himself, his father asked him what he knew of the place.

Leaving out any reference to Charon, he related the details of his 'lost' months, or was it years? George's father was clearly agitated as he told his story, punctuating it with the odd, 'How could you know this?' or, 'Impossible! This is preposterous!' As he continued however, his father would pace the room or look out onto the hospital grounds, lost in thought. As he neared the end of his tale where he had been separated from Yiannis by the bullets, his father's expression was one of sheer incredulity. Although by now, George was feeling drained and exhausted, he had to know why his father was so obviously full of consternation.

"Dad? What is it? What's wrong?" It was only a dream. I've been lying here for months, not in Spinalonga. So, why the strange looks?" Dmitri Fitrakis regarded his son, scrutinising him as though searching for something in his face.

"George, what you have told me, it is quite incredible. I do not know how you could have got such detailed information. How could you have known these things? We have never told anyone about it! He spoke almost as though to himself.

"What things? I must have read some of it and just made up the rest I guess. Does this island really exist?"

"Oh yes, George, the island exists alright and yes, there is some information readily available about it but, you could not have obtained that depth of information from any book and there are few now living to whom you could have spoken for such an account. You see George, you have just told me, in precise detail, the events of my own father's, your grandfather's life".

George was shocked. His Cretan grandparents were long dead before he was born and although his father had never spoken much of them, he hadn't really found it strange, never having known either of them.

"But you've never told me anything about my grandfather. How could I know anything about his life?" Dmitri shook his head, mystified.

"I do not know George. You see, I was very proud of my father, but, it was better for us in those days not to speak of him and the habit died hard. He was, as you have said, a leper. He was taken from us in 1940 to live on the island of Spinalonga. Our family was ostracised for many months after he was diagnosed and banished. No-one would visit us, people would stop speaking as we approached them. By association with my father we had become untouchables. In my village, we were unwelcome, everyone believing that we were infected and therefore to be feared. Some were even determined to drive our little family away and resorted to cruelty and violence. Stones were thrown at us, our olive grove was attacked. My poor mother lost not only her husband, but also the comfort and security of the home they had built together. She suffered from a deep melancholy, a depression I suppose they would call it today. Finally, she could take no more and she decided to move us back to Chania where her family still lived. From that day onwards, she cautioned us never to speak of my father to anyone outside the immediate family. If asked, we would merely say that he had died in an accident. That way, no-one could know the truth and our persecution would end".

"But by that time, family were able to visit the colony. Are you saying that you never went to see him?" There were tears in his father's eyes now.

"No, I am ashamed to say George, we did not. Whilst we lived near Aghios Nikolaos, we did not dare go to the island for fear of reprisals. Matters were bad enough. Then, when we moved to Chania, well, we were anxious not to draw attention to ourselves. You have to remember also, that travel was laborious then. We did not have ready access to buses or cars back then. Less than a year later, came the German invasion and it was impossible to visit Spinalonga. Shortly after the German occupation, my mother died of a heart attack. Her sister however would say that she died of a broken heart and you know, I think she was right. My mother carried a deep burden of guilt having forsaken my father but she did what she thought was best for us. I, of course, was only a child at the time, as were my brother and sister. We were only dimly aware of all that went on around us, our childish preoccupations often taking precedence over the complexities of the adult world. In time, we came to believe that our father was indeed dead, just like our mother. We thought of ourselves as orphans. During that period, people just wanted to survive the occupation. It wasn't until ten years later that I finally developed a curiosity about my father, who may, I thought then, still actually be alive. I made enquiries of the Medical Commission about him as there were still many lepers left on Spinalonga. It was then, to my deep distress,

I was told that he had been involved in a escape attempt after the invasion with two others. They had all been killed, my father, Georgio and his friends, Yiannis and Nikos".

George gasped in amazement as his father confirmed that final detail for him. The whole thing was inexplicable. How could he have lived in his grandfather's shoes and known so much about him as he lay motionless on this hospital bed? He had heard that there was something called a genetic memory but that in itself didn't explain everything. How, for example had part of his own personal history been erased? No drug dealing, no Jenna Hawkins. Everything George remembered had been so real and yet... here he was in a London hospital where he had apparently been for months. He had never gone near Spinalonga. It was truly baffling. Right now though, George had little energy to figure anything out. Nevertheless, he felt a kind of elation. He hadn't, it seemed, killed Jenna Hawkins. Maybe that was all part of the same madness. Had he simply been shown some alternative possible destiny? He tried hard to remember. Dad had said he had flipped after the Stock Exchange debacle. So, had he ever dealt in drugs at all, he wondered? Or maybe, maybe he had just taken drugs and had been so off his face he had simply hallucinated it all? Sighing, he lay back on his pillows. It was all too much for him. He couldn't think any more. His father smiled and took his hand.

"Welcome back my son. I cannot begin to tell you the joy in my heart that you've returned to us. Now, get yourself fit my boy and you have my word I will not pressure you to do anything again". George smiled contentedly.

"Dad, I don't think you'll have to pressurise me. I've got lots of plans for my life now and I swear, I'll make you proud of me yet."

"I'm sure you will son. I'm sure you will".

A last hug from his father and a shower of delighted kisses and tears of happiness from his mother and they left him to rest.

George noticed how they seemed to stoop more and the lines on his mother's face were more deeply etched than he had remembered. They had, it seemed, all learned something, George thought, about what they valued most in life and where their priorities should lie. He had been given a new start and he swore he wouldn't make the same mistakes again. But first, he had some loose ends to tie up.

"Each time for one more day we pray
Our timeless life in disarray
That man would ever pray to die
On such a beautiful day." ISLAND OF TEARS William Ronald Hawkins

REVELATIONS

It was many weeks from the moment of his first re-awakening in that hospital room before George was able to resume any 'normal' activity. Normality however had become a relative concept as he no longer really knew what that was. His muscles had wasted and weakened through immobility and he suffered excruciating headaches residual from the accident in Crete. He had constant flashbacks from his life on Spinalonga (or was it his grandfather's life?) and often, he would wake in the night, sweat beading his face, wondering what particular 'reality' he might be entering now. It was terrifying, the knowledge that just by going to sleep it seemed, he might very well go into some other world, that he could never be entirely sure what was reality. Perhaps this modern life was really the dream and he would wake up back on Spinalonga or on Charon's boat, or maybe in that cold, dark and terrifying sea with a shower of bullets threatening to reduce him to the same glistening pulp as Nikos. Somehow though, he didn't really think that he would be returning to the Spinalonga of 1940. He felt that in some strange way, he had been shown this life for a very particular purpose.

Nevertheless, George's dreams were vivid and he could still hear the bombs, see the searchlights, feel the vibration as the bullets hit the raft, disintegrating it, and the water lapping around him. Most terrifying was when he awoke, holding his breath, the sensation of suffocation as, in his mind, the water entered his lungs. On his good nights though, he remembered with fondness the wonderful souls on Spinalonga who had been so influential in reshaping his life and values. He was grateful to them and indeed, to his grandfather who had reached out across time to show him that compassion and respect will bring greater reward than cruelty and exploitation.

Over those weeks, George and his father spoke much more about his Grandpa Georgio. In fact, he had been English and had married George's Grandmother, a Cretan woman. Taking her name, Fitrakis, he was accepted over the years as a true Cretan. He learned to speak Greek fluently, but in times of stress reverted to his native English language.

George's father, quite naturally, found it hard to come to terms with these strangest of experiences he related, however, he did tell him that his father was said to have been a clairvoyant and that people had travelled from miles around seeking his help before he had been banished to Spinalonga. Perhaps therefore, he had indeed reached out to George across worlds to save him from his own path of destruction or maybe George had himself inherited his grandfather's sixth sense which had been awoken by his visit to Greece and the near death experiences he had endured. From Dmitri's knowledge, the trail on Grandpa Georgio's life had gone cold following the escape. After the war, Dmitri's family had left Crete, taking him and his siblings to Athens. After attending university in Athens, Dmitri explained how he had embarked on his career in international banking and subsequently moved to England and how it was many years later he discovered that his father had died in the Cretan waters that night.

To George's great delight, his old friend Charlie came to visit him one sunny afternoon, just as he was getting his legs back in working order. They went for a stroll in the hospital grounds. From what he told George, he was able to piece together some of his last known movements.

George, it seemed, had indeed succumbed to taking cocaine and the addiction had taken hold of him. Shortly after his dismissal from the Stock Exchange, Charlie had found him doing cold turkey at the flat. He had begged Charlie to give him the details of his dealer, Gaz and eventually he had introduced them. That much then was true. George however, was too preoccupied with his own consumption of the drugs and he had, according to Charlie, never started dealing. George had begun to show the side effects of heavy drug use though and paranoia had set in. On the night he left for Crete he had apparently called at Charlie's, convinced the police were after him because he had killed someone. George had emptied his bank account and, the arrangements having been made by his father, he had fled the country. In fact, the only person who was after George was Gaz because he had taken a supply of cocaine on the slate from him on the pretext that he would start dealing in order to pay him back. Instead, he'd apparently binged on the lot. Somehow, George confused everything and his drug induced paranoia had created the Jenna Hawkins scenario. The next thing Charlie heard of George was after the accident when he was brought home. He himself had cleared George's debt with Gaz and, having seen the state of him, no longer indulged his own moderate cocaine habit.

George's relief was immense. He really hadn't killed anyone. Nevertheless, curiosity led him to investigate things just a little further. Finally, he was strong enough to leave hospital and after a couple of weeks staying at his parent's home, finding his feet back in the real world, he returned to his flat.

One afternoon, George happened to pick up the telephone directory to seek out a plumber for his washing machine which had packed in, when he turned for some reason to the residential numbers. He found himself flicking through the 'H' category examining the entries for Hawkins. He was shocked to discover that these people did in fact exist and, in the part of town he had expected to find them. Dropping the directory, George had picked up his car keys and driven to the council estate which was so familiar in his memory. He parked outside and waited for a while, until finally the door opened. He recognised immediately the woman with blonde ponytail, her face, probably once pretty but which now belied her comparative youth, the ageing effects of weight loss and enslavement to cocaine etched in her pinched features. Alarm now gripped George. Was our fate mapped out for us? Could we change our destiny? Had his been changed by Charon's intervention? And if so, had that meant a change of destiny for Jenna? Or was she going to die anyway, without his help? He didn't know, but on impulse, he leapt from the car and ran up to her.

"Excuse me? Are you Jenna Hawkins?" She eyed him suspiciously.

"Who wants to know?" she asked.

"Forgive me, I know this sounds rather strange, but, do you recognise me?"

"Ain't never seen you before in me life! Now, what d'ya want?" she asked, patience clearly wearing thin.

"Jenna", he began helplessly, "you have to stop the drugs before it's too late!" George found himself blurting out, sounding even to himself like some evangelical preacher. She must have thought he was a crazy man, he thought.

"Whacha talkin' about? What's it got to do wiv you anyway? Who the fuck do you think you are coming up to a complete stranger an' lecturin' them? Fuck off and mind your own business". She took her leave, looking back only once as she muttered, "Fuckin' do gooder social workers. Get a fuckin' life of yer own and never mind meddlin' in others."

As she bustled off, George could only watch, wondering whether their destinies were so closely entwined that his new direction would have the butterfly effect upon her life and save her from an early death. He hoped so, but of course, he would probably never know.

****

Finally then, some months later, when he was fit enough, George had just one more place to go to fit together the final pieces of this jigsaw puzzle. As the 737 touched down at the airport in Heraklion, he felt the flutter of nerves, his apprehension and indeed anticipation building as he headed off to the place where all of this had started. Hiring a car this time, he set off once again in the direction of Aghios Nikolaos where he booked into the large modern Hotel in town, the Hermes. It was late now, too late to go on one of the many tourist departures to Spinalonga. He would have to wait until morning, so he headed off to the town once more, this time to explore with an easy conscience and without his previous drug induced delusions. He enjoyed the familiarity of the place and looked forward to the day he would perhaps come here for good.

He awoke next morning, refreshed and ready for his first real excursion to Spinalonga. There were various operators in the town offering a variety of options from guided tours of the island to a whole day spent first on Spinalonga and followed by a barbeque in a nearby cove. What would the people he had known in the leper colony have made of the frivolous amusement their island home now offered? He, for one, found it difficult to reconcile his own experience with the island as a tourist attraction but then, wasn't it also a memorial of a kind? At least the people were remembered in this way and the plight of the lepers would never be forgotten.

In the end, George chose one of the simple guided tours (no barbeque) and paid over his 12 euros. Stepping onto the boat, he decided to shelter from the morning heat on the lower deck. The tour was busy and tourists filled both decks. Eventually, the motor revved into life and it gathered speed into the familiar open waters. The guide, a woman, took up a microphone to give the passengers the health and safety routine and to advise everyone on arrival at the island to ensure they stayed together due to the many other groups who would also be there. George's apprehension was growing, but he also felt a strange resentment that the island, his island, was being desecrated by a crowd of thrill seeking ghouls, as he perceived them at that moment. How could they ever in their wildest imaginings know how life had really been on Spinalonga?

Within a short time, the guide announced their approach to Spinalonga but for George, it needed no introduction. Stepping out onto the outside deck he saw once more, the majesty and forbidding austerity of those circular sentinel walls of the Venetian Fortress. Again, he was awestruck and, as the boat neared the shore, he was seeing the island he had visited only in his darkest dreams. A place of despair, tragedy yes, but also a place of quiet dignity, courage, hope and a testament to the human spirit. In his life, he had never been here and yet everything was as he had known it so intimately. The familiarity of his surroundings was overwhelming and all the feelings the place had invoked in him returned. He even looked down at his hand, expecting to see the marks of the disease he had carried signalling the onset and advancement of leprosy.

He was stirred from his reverie by the guide's voice over the loudspeaker asking passengers to form an orderly queue to disembark via the ramp which had been fixed to the boat. She advised everyone to go to the Museum kiosk, taking their tickets with them for admission. That done, George climbed the all too familiar steps and entered the tunnel, now referred to as Dante's Tunnel, to the village. He felt nauseous, the impossibility of his experiences all the more striking now he was on the island. This was far more than the mere *deja vu* he had expected. An entire history was unfolding before his eyes in a series of flashbacks which simultaneously traumatised and intrigued him.

The visitors were huddled in a crowd around the tour guide who told her practised and sanitised version of the island's story. Against the rules, George decided to break away and carry out a solitary tour of the island which inexplicably he knew so well.

There were indeed crowds of tourists in different groups and the old quiet ambience and the spell of the island was broken by these armies of intruders. Somehow though, as he passed through the familiar streets he managed to tune out of the noise and the hubbub of different languages and the odd Japanese tourist darting here and there clicking cameras.

The island had clearly been deserted for a long time, with many of the buildings now in complete dereliction. However, a process of renovation and restoration was in progress. Whilst a part of him was pleased to see the historical preservation, acknowledging the memorial to those who had lived and died here, it was ironic that the island was now being better cared for than it had been when attention was most desperately needed.

Passing the little parade of shops, George noted the brightly coloured and newly painted doors and shutters which gave the street a cheerful aspect. He stopped for a moment, outside Yiannis' leather shop where he had spent many an hour chatting or teaching English through in the back. The doors were firmly locked now however, and he could not view the inside. One of the crumbling Venetian houses was being restored to its former stone glory and inside one of the four tavernas, the one George had most often frequented and which was now exposed to the elements, he noticed the little carvings of ships in the wall, which he recognised instantly. Looking more closely, there on the wall were the carved numbers '1940' which, he recalled, had been etched by one of the younger islanders commemorating his birthday. Overall, the island was much as it had been when Charon had first left him here. Many of the doors to the houses were half open and weather beaten, the interiors of the houses overgrown with weeds and snaking branches, as before, the remains of domestic touches, blue and yellow plaster, empty cupboards and discarded baskets the only evidence of former life on the island. George was happy to see that there were signs of further improvement to the island facilities after his departure. People must have survived for sometime after 1941 because he saw that the laboratory building had been completed and that a modern block of flats which had not existed during his time here had been erected. He quickly inspected the new block, venturing further than he knew would have been permitted by the tour guide. From his cursory inspection, George could see there were spiral staircases, light brackets and tiled areas which looked like cooking areas. The building was slightly incongruous, so different and out of keeping was it from the rest of the antiquated architecture of the town.

George longed to be alone on the island to see if he could once more pick up on the atmospherics, which although still palpable, were disturbed by the presence and mood of the invading crowds, oblivious to the subtler undertones of the human stories which haunted this, his former island home.

Sadly, he wandered past the disinfection room once more, recalling the many visitors and goods which had passed through its walls before returning to the mainland. Looking down into the room below the road where he now stood, George shivered despite the rising heat of the day. It was a spooky experience returning to a familiar place in which, by all accounts, he had never set foot before. He had hoped to find some answers to the mystery by returning but, at the same time, he had feared the forces which could, he supposed at any time, snatch him back into that terrifying parallel world.

One more place to go, he thought, and then back to the tour guide to join the happy throng of voyeurs.

Turning to his left, past the Disinfection Room, he descended the familiar steps, passing through the archway with its white Venetian lion. George halted in his tracks however, as he saw, sitting on the very same rock as he remembered, the solitary figure of a man, the size and shape of whom even from behind, he instantly recognised as Manolis. The hair was no longer the ebony mass of curls it once was, now whitened with age. The shoulders, no longer as broad and muscular, but bent, stooping slightly and frail. In contrast, George was exactly as he had looked in his 1940 incarnation. He hesitated. He was unsure how to approach him. How could he offer him any explanation for this uncanny re-union, which, nevertheless, George suspected was probably less co-incidental that it might seem. He need not have worried. Sensing George's presence, the man glanced back over his shoulder and seeing him, he slowly rose, grasping a walking stick which lay next to him. George looked into the familiar face, older now and more careworn, but still the gentle, handsome features he recognised from his youth. A grin spread across the man's face as he recognised George and with the aid of his stick, he began walking towards him, his free arm outstretched in readiness to welcome him with his embrace. He was clearly overjoyed to see him as they held each other.

Eventually, Manolis pulled away and held George at arms length scrutinising him.

"I have been expecting you Georgio", he began. "Ah, it is uncanny", he said shaking his head in wonderment. "You are so like him. Like two peas in a pod! It is as though the years between us have fallen away and I am standing here with my old friend."

Unsure how he should respond, George said nothing but smiled warmly as Manolis seemed eager to continue.

"Your grandfather Georgio, he said you would come one day and that I would know you. And indeed, here you are. I would have recognised you anywhere". He chuckled and taking George by the arm, he led him down to the shore where they perched once more as they had done back in 1941.

"A strange man, your grandfather. He had the gift of clairvoyance you know. He astonished and terrified me with the things he knew. He told us exactly what would befall Crete in the War and he spoke of many things which have come to pass. Space travel!

Can you believe it - he even knew about these things. Before he died, he told me you would come to the island seeking answers and he asked me to ensure you got them".

"But, how did you know I would come here today?"

"I did not know Georgio. That is your name isn't it? Your father named you after his own father didn't he?" George nodded and he continued.

"You see, I come here all the time these days. It was only a matter of time before we would meet. He told me you would find me, so, I have just waited and here you are. Now, you have questions for me, I think?"

George's mind was blank for a few moments as he noted the island seemed to have become silent and empty despite the number of tourists whom he knew to be there. Strangely, he could neither hear nor feel their presence. It was as if Manolis and he were alone here once more.

"My grandfather escaped during the war?" George began, deciding to go with the flow. "Do you know what happened to him?"

Manolis nodded sadly.

"Alas, Georgio, your grandfather died along with his brave friends, Nikos and Yiannis. They were cruelly gunned down and murdered in cold blood by the Germans who feared the lepers more, I think than the war itself, judging by the security they placed on the island. Your grandfather, he knew he was going to his death, but I think he refused to believe it. He hoped to reach the mainland to get help for the islanders and to find his own family. We were about to starve to death here and the medical supplies were low. Either way, stay or go, we were all going to die. Nikos and Yiannis, they were near death due to the leprosy and they wanted to find their families for whom they feared now that the Germans were in occupation. They were tortured, day and night, wondering what had become of their people. They could not have rested any longer and they also knew the risks they took."

"What happened to Spinalonga after the men were killed?"

"I was afraid, Georgio, that the Germans would simply bomb the island, exterminate all of us in cold blood. It seemed the most likely outcome as they would not want more escapees leaving Spinalonga. Ironically however, quite the opposite happened. After Yiannis, Nikos and your grandfather were murdered; all hope was now extinguished of getting help from the mainland.

It was the morning after they left that I knew they hadn't made it. None of them had actually told me of their plans, but on the night they left, I had been unable to sleep. Perhaps it was a sixth sense of my own, but I felt something in the air that day. I had given up trying to sleep and decided, as was my habit, to walk down to the harbour and listen to the sound of the sea which always had a calming and soporific effect on me.

It was then that I saw them. They were on a raft, drifting out into the sea. How vulnerable they looked that night. Three sick and weak men trying to take back some control of their lives. I was distraught, but I understood their decision. I knew if they made it across, they would try to bring help, at least get some medical supplies and food over here. But, it was not to be. I was alerted to their fate next morning by the cries and shouting of some of the villagers. I ran out of my house to find out what was going on, but my heart was already heavy. I knew what I was about to hear.

It was Athena, the tears coursing down her cheeks who broke the news to me. Yiannis' body had been washed up on the shore, mangled and bullet ridden. If one was dead, I surely knew that all three must be gone. Athena was distraught. She and Yiannis had been close. I immediately went down to the harbour and I too broke down and wept as I saw this once vital and courageous man's body, torn apart so cruelly. I remembered my dear friends, brave, kind, good men, who had so determinedly overcome their disabilities only to end their lives, mutilated at the hands of the enemy.

The island was in deep mourning that day. I think many had lost the will to go on. The people were becoming sicker by the day. Many were in constant pain for lack of drugs to ease them and starvation was making us all weak. Our spirits had been broken by this final act of cruelty". Manolis paused for a moment and, as George looked into his face, he could still see how much pain he felt as he recounted his story. Then, a smile broke out on his face as he continued.

"But then, a miracle happened! We were all gathered at the Church the following day, joined together in mourning for those whom we so badly missed when the sound of aeroplane engines roared above us. I stood, listening intently for a few moments, fearing the worst. I was certain this was the reprisal I had expected in response to the men's escape. After all, the Germans would not wish to allow a repeat of this. The atmosphere inside the Church was tense as we waited to hear an explosion, or the outbreak of gunfire. Perhaps this would just be a warning. Why waste ammunition on us when we would soon be dead anyway? Minutes passed however and nothing happened. The engines began to recede. Finally, unable to contain myself any longer, I told everyone crammed into the little Church that day to remain where they were. Carefully, I opened the church door, just a touch. I must have gasped out loud at what I saw, because at that moment, people were clamouring behind me.

"What is it Manoli?"

"What have you seen? Is it so terrible?"

I opened both doors then, allowing all to see the miracle descending from the skies. Hundreds of little parachutes were floating to the island, each carrying a box with a red cross on it. I turned to look at everyone, my face now beaming from ear to ear, barely able to contain my laughter as I explained these were

Red Cross parcels which would contain food and hopefully, medical supplies. Leaflets also littered the ground and I dashed out to pick one up. As I did so, the first parcel reached the ground. I read the leaflet out loud so all could hear. It said that the parcels contained food and medicines and that they were being dropped in response to the three men leaving the island. It confirmed that all had been shot to prevent contamination on Crete. It stated that providing no-one made any further attempts to reach the mainland, regular drops would be made and our welfare would be assured. I could not believe it! I was overjoyed as we tore open those parcels. For the first time in many months, I could breathe easy.

I asked everyone to return to the Church where I led a very special eulogy to the memories of our dear friends whose deaths had not, after all, been in vain. They might not have succeeded in reaching the mainland, but their actions had guaranteed the future for those left on Spinalonga. They had unselfishly given their lives for us. How Yiannis would have laughed that the Germans were so afraid that the lepers may try to leave the island that they were prepared to bribe us to stay here! The lepers had single handedly vanquished all recent invaders, from the Turks who fled when the colony was established to the Germans who now sought to subjugate our people! Who could have guessed our friends would become the unlikeliest of heroes? They would all have appreciated the joke.

So Georgio, we survived the war. That was our greatest achievement, I think. And it was all thanks to your grandfather and his two friends. Sadly however, they did not manage to fulfil their own hopes of finding the families they loved so dearly." Manolis stared wistfully out to sea and smiled in remembrance of those days gone by.

"Of course, the story of Spinalonga does not end here. The war years were difficult, but less so, because of the escape. Food and supplies, though not plentiful, were adequate. Much of the good work done during the pre-war years to bring about all the social improvements was halted, but, I am happy to say, after the liberation of Greece and when the war ended, the work was resumed. Social security payments resumed, only now, instead of 30 drachmas a month, each person received 20 drachmas a day. It was a massive boost to those left on Spinalonga. Ours was the first Cretan village to receive an electric generator donated by General Papagos, the Prime Minister, which you see remains here in the harbour. The older houses were fitted with wiring to receive electricity which was paid for by Crown Prince Georgios, Governor of Crete, and the new buildings which you see near the hospital were built to provide new accommodation.

Finally, Spinalonga became a normal village and although we remained isolated, the community thrived. The Governor also made sure there were improvements in the treatment of leprosy. He sent two other doctors here and together, working as a team, we provided the best care possible. Of course, sometimes the people here developed other illnesses which were more difficult for us to treat on the island. The governor recognised this and to our joy, he put two army ambulances at our disposal which transported more complicated cases to the hospital in Heraklion. Finally, the people here were being treated as human beings and there was a growing recognition that the disease was not so easily transmitted. In 1953, a cure was discovered which led to greater freedom and more social integration for the lepers.

Sadly, the people here during this period were still ripe for exploitation. It seemed that those who lived on the island would always been seen as a goldmine, ripe for the picking by those with few scruples. Can you believe, it? Some healthy people even tried to be banished to Spinalonga because the social security payments here were so good!"

Some things never change, George thought to himself as

Manolis once more lapsed into silence, clearly angry as he still remembered the injustices dealt to his people. He thought of Britain and the abused Social Security system which operated back there. Human nature would always produce those who thought they could get a better deal for themselves without effort. Manolis looked tired and drawn now, but he continued with his story.

"With better treatment and better understanding of the disease, the lepers were eventually permitted legally to leave the island for short periods providing their papers were in order and approved. Guards were employed by the Governor of Spinalonga to ensure the system was properly policed. However, even that had its pitfalls as it gave power to unscrupulous characters who would refuse to approve paperwork without bribes. Other officials in charge of the island set themselves up as middle men in the sale of goods on the island. They would buy the merchandise from the traders and then add their own huge profits on for personal gain. Happily, the governor was a sharp man who kept a close eye on things in Spinalonga. He knew that there would be a burning resentment from many Cretans at the wealth of the lepers and that exploitation and extortion would, left unchecked, be rife. He was fastidious in his measures to protect the islanders and his vigilance paid off.

Some things did not change altogether however. One of the most painful practices on the island was the removal of healthy children born to leper families. The governor was unable to stop this, the welfare of the children always being regarded as paramount. He knew that it was cruel for both the parents and the children who were sent to hospital in Athens and kept in isolation for years of observation. When the children were removed, it was under the pretext it would only be for a short time, but of course, it soon became apparent that this was a lie. The governor was a good man, someone whose philanthropy towards the lepers knew no bounds. He agonised over the problem and finally, he arranged for the mothers to visit the children accompanied by one of the Guards. The Children born here from that time onwards all grew up knowing their parents and lived healthy lives, proud legacies of the wonderful people of Spinalonga. So you see Georgio, Spinalonga, once known as the 'Island of Tears' or 'Island of the Damned' was in fact in many ways, an 'Island of Miracles'."

George remembered with deep sadness the fate of Alexander and Sofia after their beloved child had been torn from them. If only things had been different for them, he thought.

"When did the last of the lepers leave Spinalonga?" George asked.

"Ah, it was 1957 when I left with the last remaining 10 survivors. When the cure was discovered in 1953, gradually the isolation of the island was eroded as leprosy was decreed as neither infectious nor incurable. It was decided that many of the lepers could be treated in the hospital in Athens whilst others were able to resume their lives as free citizens returning to their families. Of course, I was so happy for them, but nevertheless, as I stepped into the boat for the last time, it was with immeasurable sadness. My useful life, I felt, was over. I had devoted my youth to the lepers and consequently, I had no family of my own but them. I now faced loneliness and years stretching ahead of me without purpose. It was then it struck me that I owed it to Nikos, Yiannis and your grandfather to see if I could trace their precious families and to tell them of their heroism and what it had meant to those of us left on the island.

Records were not good from those days and it took me a full eighteen months of detective work, travelling all over Crete, following leads from village to village, often reaching dead ends in my search. Nikos' children in fact were the easiest to trace. They had been adopted by an Athenian family and were now grown up of course. I was heartened that they had never forgotten their father and they were deeply saddened to hear of his brutal death at the hands of the Germans. I could tell though that there was a sense of closure for them in the knowledge that he had yearned for them and tirelessly sought for information about them. They were so proud of all he had achieved and loved the stories of his dancing and his escapades. It was, they said, as they remembered him and how they would wish to remember him.

Alas, Yiannis' family proved impossible to trace. In a way, I thank God he did not make it to the mainland for I discovered that all of his family were butchered by the Germans during the early part of the invasion. To have survived and gone on to discover such a thing would have been too much for anyone to bear. By the time I found your grandfather's family, your own father had moved to England to continue his career. I wrote to him and his sister telling them of their father's heroism.

My quest had occupied my mind for some while, but eventually, I had to face the fact that I must now settle down somewhere and find myself a place in life again. In truth, I was somewhat institutionalised by my years on Spinalonga and I was restless and a little afraid of the outside world. I chose Kritsa to settle down in and set myself up as a doctor in the town. It was small enough to make me feel secure, but close enough to the town of Aghios that I could slowly begin to re-integrate myself into normal life. Of course many of the old Spinalonga inhabitants kept in contact with me and we visited each other once I had a base, so in fact, life was not so different. Finally, Irini, a perfectly healthy woman who had been banished to Spinalonga for evil reasons, to prevent her from inheriting her poor husband's money, came back into my life after many years apart." Manolis laughed a little. "Your grandfather and I both loved Irini you know, Georgio but she refused to entertain either of us in those days. She had her reasons of course but it was many years after we departed the island that she came back to me and declared her love. I had never dreamed it would be possible for me to find such happiness and companionship. We married shortly afterwards and lived together a few short, but very happy years when death came to claim her too. Looking back, I was fortunate. I had much to be thankful for during my life for which I shall always be grateful."

Although Manolis had aged, the man George had known still shone through. His compassion, love and humour were still very much in evidence. It was so strange for George to stand here on the island, with a man who had been such a close companion and yet could only see and know him as the grandson of the man he had known. The two men sat now, in companionable silence, lost in their own thoughts. George knew now that he would never actually make sense of the strange and fantastical adventure which had ultimately led to his salvation. It was Manolis who broke the silence again.

"Your grandfather, hah, he was a strange one Georgio. And you, you are so like him it is uncanny"'

With growing astonishment, George listened intently to Manolis as he described his grandfather's arrival on the island, the way he had run off into the night and how at first he could not accept that he was infected with leprosy. Such was his denial that he convinced himself that he was healthy.

"Ah yes", Manolis continued, "I remember the first night he arrived on Spinalonga. He tried to escape but..."

"But he didn't succeed and fell asleep over on the grassy knoll near the Church and was found next morning by Nikos..." George finished. Manolis held him firmly in his gaze for a moment.

"I see you also have the gift young man. I have never made this information known to anyone. It was while he was on the island that your grandfather's ability to see things in the future became stronger. He told of things that I now know were absolutely true. He was convinced you know, that he had been brought here by Charon, ferryman to the underworld. He scared me, but intrigued me at the same time. He was an intelligent man who used his skills wisely and gave back to our little community far more than he took out.

Before leaving the island, he sat here with me one day and told me that his son would have a son of his own and that you would return to Spinalonga seeking answers to help you in your own life. He asked me to help you find them Georgio. I hope that our talk today has helped and that Spinalonga has worked some of its magic upon you too."

"Thank you Manoli, for everything. I think that in spite of its history, Spinalonga is a place which brings out the good in life and in people. It has a positive energy radiating from it which I shall use to dispel any remaining notion that it is the 'Island of the Damned'. I plan to come here now and set the record straight for all to read", George explained.

During the past few moments, a breeze had kicked up in the harbour. As George now looked overhead, black clouds were gathering in the previously clear sky. He shivered a little as a strange atmosphere seemed to descend. Turning to look back in the direction of the Lion Gate, just for a moment, it seemed to bustle into the familiar life he had once known, the buildings back to their original state of the 1940s, signs of life everywhere and, just out of the corner of his eye, in peripheral vision he saw the odd figure in Cretan dress moving around. When he shifted his gaze to look in the direction of the movement however, all was still again. Confused, George turned back to speak to Manolis but, he was nowhere to be seen. He had simply vanished. There was nowhere for him to go except out to the sea. George had been looking towards the Lion Gate, which was the only route which led up to the island. Frowning deeply, he scanned the horizon and called out his name, "Manoli, Manoli, where are you?" then, he caught sight of something bobbing up and down on the increasingly choppy water. It was a boat, inside of which, sat two men.

The man facing him was Manolis. George gasped as the familiar figure of the other turned, regarded him for a long moment and waved his farewell, his brooding features and unkempt beard confirming his identity. Manolis was being carried away by Charon. Manolis smiled at George as he raised his hand.

"Farewell Georgio. We shall meet again in some distant time. Yiannis, Nikos and your Grandfather send their regards to you. You have been offered the gift of life by them. Remember it always and use it wisely." The clouds seemed to dissipate as George watched the horizon and, as the sun blazed once more into view, he shielded his eyes from its rays, blinded by its radiance forcing him to squint in search of the little boat. Hard as he tried though, he could no longer see the little vessel. George waited there on the shore for what seemed like an eternity, finally accepting that he would see no more of Manolis. Making his way through the Lion Gate and back up to the island, the tourists re-appeared, their tour guides once more animated as they recounted their well rehearsed story.

EPILOGUE

After returning to Crete from Spinalonga that day, George made his way to Kritsa, intent on finding out more about Manolis. He was too late however. He discovered that Manolis had died just a few days previously and that his funeral had been only that day. George knew then that he had made his final journey with the ferryman and that he would be with Irini and the others, safe in the Elysian Fields.

George felt he had indeed been given a rare and strange gift by the mystical powers of the gods and the intervention of his grandfather. Somehow, mirroring the steps of his grandfather, his own near death experience had entwined their souls allowing Charon to fetch him and deposit him in a place where he would learn through the experience of suffering, the true value of life and health. It had not however been George's moment to die and having experienced life through his grandfather up until the moment of his death, Charon had once more ferried him back through the Portal which separates time, life and death, endowed with the knowledge he needed to put his life back in order.

George's father spoke often about his son's experience and he showed him the letter he had received from Manolis. He now understood that because of his own fatherless childhood, he had not developed his parental skills well and that this had affected their own relationship. From the day that George had awoken from his coma, he and his father worked determinedly to rebuild those bridges and George now knew that he had his father's support to exercise freedom in his future choices.

Shortly after his last visit to Spinalonga, George returned to study as a teacher and, after a couple of years polishing up his Greek, he returned to Crete to live. There, he became an English teacher and a writer. From that day on however, whenever he needed a wake - up call, or a reminder of just how great it is to have freedom, health and vitality, he would climb aboard the little ferry and find a quiet spot on his own to remember his life as one of Charon's Children.

CHARON'S CHILDREN
BY Jacqueline Dempster

ABOUT THE AUTHOR

Jacqueline Dempster lives in Fife, Scotland with her son, Graham. She is qualified as a solicitor and is a partner in her own Employment Law and Theatre School businesses.

Jacqueline has been a frequent traveller to Crete over the last few years and hopes one day to have a home there. A visit to Spinalonga triggered her interest in the fascinating history of the island which intrigued her so much she was compelled to write "Charon's Children", her first novel.

February 2007

BIBLIOGRAPHY

"Spinalonga - the Leper Island" Beryl Darby - Efstathiadis Group
"Spinalonga - The Isle of the Damned" - Victor Zorbas - VZ Publishing
"Don't Fence Me In" - Leprosy in Modern Times - Tony Gould
"Island of Tears" - William Ronald Hawkins - Efstathiadis